*Mrs Dorothy Davison*
*2845*

SARAH ...
rich in adventure, evoking all the
nostalgia, the pleasure and pain of a
bygone era – an era covering the
General Strike, the London of
tramcars and picture palaces and fights
in the East End, of India and the
twilight of the British Raj . . .

And through the stormy, perilous
years between the two world wars
moves Sarah – gay, proud,
courageous, avidly seizing whatever
life has to offer and emerging
triumphant . . .

'What do you do with a novel when
you have finished reading it, and have
passed it around to family and friends
so they may be bewitched by the
magic of excellent escape reading?
Our Sarah will have a place of
honour on the fiction shelf between
Scarlett and Rebecca.' – *Los Angeles
Times*

'Authentic and sympathetic' – *Homes and
Gardens*

'Fast-moving, well documented . . .
well populated' – *New Statesman*

SARAH WHITMAN – a sequel to
THE MARIGOLD FIELD

Also by Diane Pearson

THE BRIDE OF TANCRED
THE MARIGOLD FIELD
CSARDAS

and published by Corgi Books

Diane Pearson

# Sarah Whitman

**CORGI BOOKS**
A DIVISION OF TRANSWORLD PUBLISHERS LTD

SARAH WHITMAN
A CORGI BOOK 0 552 10414 0

Originally published in Great Britain
by Macmillan London Ltd.

PRINTING HISTORY
Macmillan edition published 1971
Corgi edition published 1973
Corgi edition reprinted 1975
Corgi edition reissued 1977
Corgi edition reprinted 1977

Copyright © Diane Pearson 1971

*Conditions of sale*
1: This book is sold subject to the condition that it
shall not, by way of trade *or otherwise*, be lent, re-sold,
hired out or otherwise *circulated* without the publisher's
prior consent in any form of binding or cover other than
that in which it is published *and without a similar
condition including this condition being imposed on
the subsequent purchaser*.
2: This book is sold subject to the Standard Conditions
of Sale of Net Books and may not be re-sold in the U.K.
below the net price fixed by the publishers for the book.

This book is set in 10pt Times.

Corgi Books are published by Transworld Publishers Ltd.,
Century House, 61–63 Uxbridge Road,
Ealing, London, W.5.
Made and printed in Great Britain by
Hunt Barnard Printing Ltd., Aylesbury, Bucks.

*For Arthur A. J. Lloyd*
*Who knows the meaning of hard work . . .*

## *Acknowledgements*

My thanks and acknowledgements to: Mr Pat Bacon of the Inner London Education Authority, Mr Frank Bailey for his information on the General Strike, Miss D. Erb and Miss F. Erb for their memories of the Borough, Mr Zygmunt Frankel, who advised on the background of David Baron, The Church Missionary Society.

# One

THERE was to be another public thrashing in the Hall.

Throughout the morning an air of taut, overstrung hysteria had been growing steadily in the classroom beginning—when Sammy Alexander had been sent for by the headmistress at playtime, and had failed to return—with a stillness compounded of sheer terror and progressing rapidly—as Sammy's desk remained oppressively empty—to nervous fidgeting and occasional bouts of laughter.

Sarah, who had been miserable enough when Sammy had first disappeared into the gloom of Miss Bennett's room, found the atmosphere in the classroom contagious. She began to catch from the children a feeling of mob fear and unruliness. To be thrashed by Miss Bennett was terrible enough, but a public thrashing meant that one's crime transcended the normal sins. Public thrashings were reserved for such depravities as stealing, bad language, misuse of the lavatories, or other crimes which generally came under the heading "filth." The thrashings took on some of the sanctity of capital punishment, and the boys who had suffered it were treated with a kind of awed reverence by their classmates for several days after the ordeal. It was felt that the victims had looked into the nether regions, and had survived.

Sarah, in company with every other teacher in the school, would do anything to prevent a public thrashing. The children became unbalanced and hysterical and the teacher miserably aware of his or her own incompetence—for Miss Bennett had a genius for conveying that the sins of the pupil were only a reflection of the sins of the teacher. On this occasion Sarah had been unable to prevent the punishment. Sammy's sin had been too heinous and too public to be suppressed.

The last lesson before the dinner-bell sounded should have been arithmetic, but she found it increasingly difficult either to concentrate herself, or to control the mounting panic in the classroom. Finally she gave up trying to teach the ambiguities of nine apples cut in halves and quarters to be distributed amongst three boys and three girls. She decided that the most she could strive for was to maintain some kind of discipline and prevent them from disintegrating into total disorder. She made the cupboard monitor pass round sheets of grey paper and coloured chalks, and she drew a map of the world upon the blackboard for them to copy. She could hear the concentrated breathing of thirty-seven children and the occasional snap of a chalk-stick as someone pressed too hard. She could also hear scuffling and the sound of stifled whispering.

"Stop whispering, Gertie," she said, without turning round from the blackboard. "Have you finished crayoning your map of the world?"

Gertie Alexander, sister of the missing and condemned Samuel, unaccountably began to cry. In class they fought so much with one another they had to be seated at opposite ends of the room, but, in an emergency, family unity brought them together.

"Bring your map to me."

Sobbing miserably, Gertie came to the front of the class and Sarah caught the smell of her, which was the smell of the whole class. She was so used to it that most of the time she ceased to be consciously aware of the combined aroma of malnutrition, chalk, and dung from the harrier's yard that ran alongside the playground. It was the harrier's yard that was the cause of the present trouble. Most of the school, but in particular Class Three which was Sarah's class, liked to play "running up the dung-hill." This involved a long, gathering-speed flight up the length of the harrier's yard, and a final leap to the top of the dung-hill. Sammy Alexander excelled at the sport. Indeed he was so good at it that he had become bored. A mixture of bravado and goading from the other boys had compelled him to heights hitherto unsurpassed. On discovering the head-mistress's bicycle leaning against the adjoining wall of the playground and the harrier's yard, he had plastered dung over every portion of the bike to which it would adhere. He had finished by writing SHIT in chalk across the saddle. Every time Sarah thought about the SHIT she had to suppress a nervous giggle. The thought of anyone writing, or saying, SHIT to Miss Bennett filled her with a combination of terror and laughter and at various times throughout the morning she found herself forgetting that she was Miss Whitman, teacher of Class Three, and was imagining herself to be Sammy Alexander, locked in the staff-room cupboard awaiting the wrath of Miss Bennett.

She stared down at the snivelling Gertie and hoped, desperately, that her gloomy tears would not spread to the rest of the class.

"Show me your map, Gertie." She held out her hand, wishing that Gertie's mother wouldn't dress the child's hair with a large butterfly bow. It didn't match Gertie's dingy blue-grey smock dress and the boots with the splitting seams. Gertie continued to cry.

"That's very good, dear," Sarah said gently. "But you've crayoned all of Africa red. It should be *nearly* all red, but not quite."

"Yes, Miss." Gertie's nose was beginning to run.

"You're getting mixed up with India. That's *all* red."

Gertie sniffed and wiped the sleeve of her smock along her upper lip. The sleeve was permanently stiff and soiled with having to serve as handkerchief be-cause Gertie regularly lost her handkerchief—only it was really a piece of rag—on her way to school every morning.

"What's going to happen to Sammy, Miss?"

"Miss Bennett will have to punish him. He was very, very, naughty. You were all naughty for letting him do it."

Secretly, she had a great admiration for Sammy's courage. At eight he had dared to do what she, at twenty-one, dared not do. He had, with ribald vulgarity, challenged the terrifying authority of Miss Bennett. She just wished Sammy had been in another class. It was the fourth time this term that someone in Class Three had precipitated a public thrashing.

"Sammy never wanted to come to this school, anyway," sobbed Gertie. "He wanted to go to the Jewish Foundation with Billy Silver."

"Marie Cominetti next door to me goes to the Catholic school," remarked someone conversationally from the front row.

Sarah felt control slipping rapidly away. She had a quick vision of leading her class into the hall with each child in the throes of hysterics.

"All sit down and be quiet! Gertie, go back to your seat and re-do the British Empire in red! Copy it exactly as I've done it on the board."

Tense silence settled again. Sarah sat down at her desk and wondered—gloomily—if the morning and the thrashing would ever be over.

On the window-sill stood Class Three's attempts at gardening—three flaccid runner-beans growing out of wet blotting-paper in a jam-jar, and a flannel full of mustard and cress. Of the two, the runner-beans smelled the worst—like the junior boys' lavatories in the playground.

Sometimes, when she looked at the runner-beans, she had an overwhelming compulsion to run away from the school—run over to the other side of the river to Victoria Station and get a train back home to the village—to the big trees and fields, and ditches and hedgerows growing an abundance of thorns and weeds and wild flowers. She thought of the runner-beans in her pa's garden—rows and rows of them, green and lush with red flowers and too many beans hanging from each stem.

She thought of the clean sky and the cleaner wind, and her father and younger brothers cutting logs, breaking soil, and planting young cabbages in the clay. She hated the runner-beans in the jam-jar.

There were times when she looked out of the classroom window, which was so high that one could only see a bit of the sky and the roof of the building opposite, and watched the clouds being blown to the south. She imagined them drifting over the village, over Tyler's woods and Sandy Bottom, and the square Norman church, and then on over her pa's cottage and away over the Downs to the sea, to the Channel and the Bay of Biscay and then to Spain. And she would forget about the clouds and look, instead, at the faded map hanging at the back of the classroom, and she would travel from Spain across to Egypt—to the unexplained horrors of Tutankhamen's Tomb—and then down through Africa—treading in the steps of Livingstone—until she came to the Cape and visited the places where her pa had fought the Boers a quarter of a century ago. And still south, south to icebergs and brilliance and stars in the Pole sky, and a stone cross on the snow-covered grave of poor Shackleton. The classroom would become smaller and stuffier and she would be filled with impatience for all the things she was going to do—all the places she was going to see—all the strange, different people she was going to meet and the exciting, splendid things that were going to happen to her. She leaned forward on her desk and she stared hard at the crayoning children without really seeing them. Sammy Alexander was for the moment forgotten and she moved forward into a private dream of countries and colour and huge, wild horizons—mountains, deserts, seas—all the things she had read about but had never seen. All the things she wanted to see—must see.

Vaguely, her elbows still resting on the desk, she heard someone knocking on the classroom door. Before she could call "Come in" the door opened and Miss Enderby scurried across in front of the blackboard, plucking nervously at the jacket edge of her rust jumper-suit and trying to smile without letting her top denture slip too noticeably.

"Miss Whitman," she whispered. "You are to report to the Head's room. At once. I will look after Class Three for you while you are gone." She plucked at the

suit again and blinked quickly at Sarah. "I should go
as soon as possible, Miss Whitman. As soon as possible."

Sarah felt the blood drain straight down to her feet.
Class Three was incredibly silent as dread removed
their hysteria from them. For a moment, pupils and
teacher were united in terror.

"Is something wrong, Miss Enderby?"

Miss Enderby tried to smile and failed. "I should go
now," she faltered.

Sarah smoothed the coils of hair—worn low, one
over each ear—said loudly, "Thank you, Miss Enderby," and left the classroom. Outside in the passage
she tried to walk briskly and with purpose, ignoring the
sick turning of her stomach and the growing certainty
that she, and Class Three, were once more in trouble,
a trouble she could ill afford because she was still only
in the second term of her first year's probation and—
she thought grimly—the way things were going she
would almost certainly be out of work at the end of
the year. She did not see how Miss Bennett could fail
to give a bad report on her to the committee.

The post had been incredibly difficult to find, partly
because work—any work—was hard to find, and partly
because her training had been slightly—unorthodox.
She had left her village school at fourteen and had
passed a year in domestic service (not the best social
background for a schoolmistress, as Miss Bennett had
pointed out at her interview). At fifteen, thanks to the
efforts of an eccentric village schoolmaster who de-
plored the waste of a talent, she had gone to work in
an East London Church school. The post had been
that of a nursery teacher—unofficial, unpaid, and in-
volving work that was truthfully more nursing than
teaching. In return for caring for a class of thirty six-
year-old infants she had been given her keep and intensive evening tuition that had enabled her to pass the
first of the exams which eventually qualified her for a
place at a teachers' training college. The remainder of
her progress had been equally stringent—two years at
secondary school during which time she had continued
to live at the Church school, earning her keep by be-

coming a general factotum of menial and secretarial work—and finally the college, a time of strained economy when she lived on small grants and whatever money her father was able to spare from his narrow income—already strained to capacity by four younger children, and an elder daughter who had to be kept in a home for the mentally sick.

Sarah, when finally qualified, flushed with the triumphant success of a six-year fight against penury, had met with the humiliating reality of the unemployment problem.

She had passed several weeks waiting in the office of the local education committee—along with many other unemployed teachers—for a vacancy to occur, for a teacher to fall sick or be dismissed so that she could be sent along "on supply" and thus have a chance perhaps to fill a more permanent post. She had been fortunate. The teacher at her old Church school had recommended Sarah to Miss Bennett as a good, Christian girl, who came from a poor, but good Christian home. Sarah had been sent "on supply" when a vacancy occurred and had subsequently been called in, interviewed, and given a year's probation at Miss Bennett's school—for that was the way Miss Bennett thought of the foundation—as *her* school. The two terms of Sarah's employment had not been happy ones for she had a double responsibility to perform well—as justification for her father's years of unselfish economy, and because Miss Bennett had taken her as a favour to the friend at the Church school. Sometimes she had the feeling that Miss Bennett deliberately made things harder for her, gave her more unwelcome tasks than other members of the staff. Every time she was rebuked or humiliated by Miss Bennett, her fear of unemployment and a bad report to the committee grew worse. There were some nights when she found it impossible to sleep for worrying about it.

The door of the headmistress's room had a top cross panel of pale grey glass and the glass was the same colour as Miss Bennett's eyes—and as transparent and cold. Sarah knocked timidly on the door.

"Who is it?"

"Miss Whitman."

"Enter."

Miss Bennett was seated but her sitting, like her walking and her talking, was barely controlled, tense energy. She was in her late forties and was agile, hard and vigorous. She wore her hair in two thin coils bound round her head and when she caned a child the coils sometimes came unwound as she swung and thrashed. As Sarah came diffidently into the room she saw that Miss Bennett's face was whiter than usual, her mouth more rigid.

"I am sick of the conduct of your class, Miss Whitman! Sick, ashamed, and extremely angry! I am beginning to wonder if you have any idea at all of how to discipline children!"

She suddenly sprang from her chair and took two quick strides round the desk so that she was standing right in front of Sarah.

"Have you any idea what that child has done? That miserable, filthy child who is a disgrace to the school!"

"Sammy Alexander, Miss Bennett?" Sarah could feel her knees shaking. She knew that if Miss Bennett became too aroused, too incensed by her own anger, she was quite capable of slapping her, Sarah, as though she were a pupil.

"I do mean Sammy Alexander, Miss Whitman." There were two spots of glaring colour high on Miss Bennett's cheekbones. "Sammy Alexander was locked in the staff-room cupboard until his punishment this afternoon. Do you know what he has done, Miss Whitman! Do you know what he has done!"

The horrifying word, SHIT, sprang before Sarah's eyes and she suddenly wanted either to giggle or be sick. She closed her eyes and said, "No, Miss Bennett. What has he done?"

"He has run away, Miss Whitman. That is what he has done. He has climbed out of the cupboard window and has run away. He has deliberately flouted my authority and I am angry! Very, very angry indeed!"

Sarah swallowed. "Yes, Miss Bennett."

Miss Bennett lifted one of the registers from her desk

and crashed it down hard. The pen-tray and the ink-well jumped and rattled on the desk top.

"Are your pupils given so little discipline that they think they can disobey me when I am going to punish them?"

"No, Miss Bennett ... that is ... well, I mean ..."

"What do you mean, Miss Whitman? Just what do you mean?"

Sarah swallowed hard again and then said as quickly as she could, "I think he was probably afraid, Miss Bennett."

"And so he should have been," said Miss Bennett menacingly. "I intend to make that child so afraid he will never think, speak, or write filth again."

"Yes, Miss Bennett." Sarah stared hard at the floor. The boards were stained and varnished and in the centre lay a worn blue and grey carpet square.

"That child will be brought back to school. He will either be brought back in a few weeks' time by the school inspector, or he will be brought back by you. I need hardly tell you, Miss Whitman, that if the inspector has to bring him back it will read very badly in your report to the committee."

Miss Bennett sat down again and Sarah allowed the muscular guard of her body to relax slightly. She didn't think Miss Bennett would try to hit her from a sitting position.

"I don't know if he'll come back just because I say so, Miss Bennett. I don't know what I could say to make him come back."

"That is something you must work out for yourself, Miss Whitman. The boy is your pupil, therefore you must bring him back to school." Miss Bennett was suddenly calm. Sarah had not had sufficient experience of her swift changes from rage to rigid control and the calm alarmed her more than the threatened violence.

"Should I ... I mean ... Are you still going to give a public thrashing, Miss Bennett?"

Miss Bennett picked up a pen and dipped it in the inkwell. She removed a hair from the nib and began to mark something in the register.

"Bring Samuel Alexander back to school, Miss Whitman. That will be all."

Sarah stood waiting for a moment, trying to think of something she could say or do to clear the situation, both for herself and for the cowardly but homeward-bound Sammy. Miss Bennett raised her eyes and stared at Sarah, a look so compounded of contempt and derision that Sarah slowly flushed and turned towards the door.

"There is one other thing, Miss Whitman, before you go."

"Yes?"

Miss Bennett dipped and wrote again. "It has been observed that a man waits for you occasionally towards the end of school, at the staff entrance. I would be obliged if your . . . followers . . . could wait elsewhere. It gives the school a bad name."

Sarah felt the flush darken and spread. She felt humiliated and ashamed and she began to hate Miss Bennett with a personal antagonism that had nothing to do with Sammy Alexander or the fear of losing her job.

"He's a friend!" she said angrily. "He's a friend of my family. My mother and father have known him for years and he just comes to see me sometimes . . ." She realised how feeble the excuse sounded, how very feeble and . . . untrue. Miss Bennett put the pen down and stared at her again. "You may go, Miss Whitman."

The stare said everything. That Sarah was twenty-one and here as a personal favour, that her blue woollen dress was old-fashioned in spite of the efforts to shorten it to the new just-below-the-knee length, that her stockings were black instead of fashionable beige, and wool instead of art-silk. The look said that she was the daughter of a village postman and that she had no right to be a school-mistress and did not know how to behave as one. She left the room.

Outside in the passage she walked with trembling legs to the school notice-board just inside the entrance. She re-read the notices, repeating them slowly to herself without absorbing their sense. She felt sick and she had a pain in her chest that she felt sure would be better if only she could cry, only she mustn't. "How am I going to get him back to school?" she murmured, and then she straightened her back, smoothed the lace collar on her frock, and tried to walk briskly back to her class-room.

Well, she thought, attempting a jauntiness she did not feel, that's fixed poor old Charlie Dance. If he wants to meet me after school from now on he'll have to wait round the back of the harrier's yard.

She was twenty-one. She was tall, and she was well built, too well built for the styles of the twenties so that even if she could have afforded the flat-bosomed, narrow-hipped frocks that were fashionable, she would not have looked right in them. Her face was beautiful and would have been more so had she worn her hair in any style other than ear-phones, which were her attempt at being "in the mode" without it costing money. Eyes, large, hazel and expressive; face, high-boned and with the rich cream and pink complexion of a girl whose formative years have been spent growing up in the country. She walked badly because she thought she was big and unattractive. Her mother had spent several years telling her so. On the rare occasions when she forgot she was big and ugly, she walked with an eager swinging stride that betrayed enthusiasm and a zest for life. She had a face that appealed, especially to older people, because it was young enough to register hope but humble enough to register compassion. Old people stopped her in the street, on the omnibus, in shops and in friends' houses. They liked talking to her because she listened and they didn't feel ashamed of their ailments—the slipping dentures, the palsied hands, the tendencies to forget in the middle of a sentence—because they sensed that Sarah knew how to look after someone who was old and sick—sensed that she had been taught it was her duty to look after old people if necessary. Not like so many young girls these days who only thought about earning money and going into picture-houses.

To young people, the people of her own generation,

she was an anomaly. She looked old-fashioned and her clothes were all so wrong that the girls she met at the training college would feel sorry for her but amused as well. And then she would suddenly wear a flower or a scarf in a certain way, and she would still look old-fashioned but at the same time vivid and . . . different. She had a quick wit and could, when in a certain mood, make everyone laugh and feel tremendously happy, but when the chatter turned to Charlie Chaplin, or Clara Bow, or Mary Pickford, she just looked stupid and mumbled incoherencies that no one could understand. And she went to some queer old religious meeting or other on Sundays. Not every Sunday, and had they but known it the Sundays when Sarah went to worship grew less and less as she freed herself from the influence of her home village. For desperately, so desperately, Sarah wanted to belong to the gay, bright things that were happening about her. She wanted to laugh and flirt and queue up outside the galleries to see *St Joan,* and *No, No, Nanette,* and *Hay Fever* and be able to join—like everyone else—in singing the whole of "Ain't We Got Fun," to know what people were laughing at when someone shouted, "And Felix kept on walking." She wanted to belong, but there was something wrong with her because whenever she tried all these things she didn't really enjoy them. For the first fifteen years of her life she had lived in a small village where religious standards taught that all worldly pleasures were sinful, and the orthodox habit was difficult to break. And the strange thing was that sometimes, as well as feeling guilty, as well as feeling lonely, she was bored with all the exciting, gay things that were happening about her.

And although she knew she was not clever or pretty, although she didn't fit in anywhere, there were the other things, the moods of sheer, delighted elation, the moments of pure happiness and a sense of anticipation. They happened for the slightest of reasons, lights going on in a November street, the first spring wind from the country disturbing the city air, the vital, vulgar faces of men selling fruit in the street markets, all these things could make her unbelievably happy and then she knew she could do anything, write a book, paint a picture, reach up and swing on the moon. And when this happened she didn't care about her clothes, or not belonging, or being ugly. She was content to have the moments for herself. At these times she felt sorry for everyone else because they had nothing. Once, when she tried to explain the way she felt to Charlie Dance, she had seen how her words distressed him. They were embarrassing and out of the ordinary and he didn't understand what she was talking about. She'd never mentioned it to him again, but she had felt sorry for Charlie Dance because he never experienced ecstasy the way she did. And she was very, very fond of Charlie. There were times— when she was worried about things—when she needed Charlie. She worried a lot—about exams, and about her brother who was a sailor, and her sister Harriet who lived in a home for backward girls. She worried about letting her pa down after all he had done for her, but even while she worried a grim perseverance made her plod on, miserable and sometimes afraid, yet determined to go through with her next ordeal—whatever it was.

As soon as school was over for the day she copied down Sammy Alexander's address from the register and set her feet grimly in the direction of the Old Kent Road. The Alexanders lived six floors up in a large prison-like block of flats, each of which consisted of three rooms and a sink outside on the landing which was shared between two families for washing and kitchen purposes. Flights of filthy stone steps led up to each flat and washing—most of it surprisingly clean— blew from lines strung across the balustrades. The well-areas between the sections of the buildings were narrow and dark and the light that filtered down into the flat windows was dim, even on a bright day. The Alexanders were lucky because they lived near the top and got more light than anyone else.

Sarah paused at the bottom of the steps and wished— heartily—that she had never heard of Sammy Alexander. She tried to reflect on what type of people the

Alexanders were. Poor, naturally, but did the bow in Gertie's hair indicate a family pride that made them chauvinistic and defensive when one of their number—albeit a young one—was in trouble? She tried to recall how many Alexanders there were. Gertie and Sammy, and in the class below hers there was Maud, and in the one below that, George. And there was sure to be a baby. There always was. But it didn't matter how many there were, what mattered was how she got Sammy back to school and his public thrashing.

She hesitated, trying to gather up courage before mounting the steps. A man with a fish barrow walked past her shouting, "Shrimp-o! Shrimp-o!" and when he saw her waiting on the bottom step he said, "Wanna buy some shrimps, luv? You get a live crab with every pint."

Sarah looked into the enamel tray on the barrow and saw the small, greenish brown crabs lying in half an inch of water. Several were dead and the remaining ones moved feebly against their lifeless companions.

"No thanks," she said, shuddering slightly.

"Shrimp-o! Shrimp-o!" called the man cheerfully, pushing past her. She took a deep breath and began to climb the stairs. On the fifth flight she passed Gertie Alexander who was sitting on a step eating a slice of bread and dripping. Gertie's eyes grew round and huge and she forgot to chew when she saw Sarah.

"Good afternoon, Gertie," said Sarah briskly, pretending a confidence she did not feel. "Is your mother in?"

Gertie gulped and nodded. She twisted her body round and watched Sarah continuing up the steps.

On the sixth landing were two doors and the sink. A man in a sleeved vest was washing at the sink and when he saw Sarah he shook the drops of water from his hair and stared at her in the same way Gertie had stared. Sarah studied the numbers on the two doors and knocked on the left-hand one. When no one answered she knocked again, louder.

"It's no use knocking," said the man in the sleeved vest. "They'll think it's the tally man come for 'is money and they won't answer. You'd best shout who you are."

Sarah smiled weakly, then bent down and put her mouth to the keyhole.

"Mrs Alexander," she called. "Mrs Alexander, are you in? It's Miss Whitman. The schoolteacher."

She put her ear to the keyhole and she could hear the noisy hum of several voices—men's voices—some of them shouting. She hammered again on the door and called once more. "Mrs Alexander, can I come in and see you for a few moments?"

The shouting inside grew louder and still the door didn't open. The man in the sleeved vest suddenly pushed her out of the way.

" 'Ere, let me 'ave a go," he said, crashing into the door with both fists. "George! George! Shut up talking and open the door! The schoolmarm's 'ere."

The hubbub inside ceased abruptly. And then the door opened and a thin, tired-looking man with curly hair gave her the stare again, the stare to which she was rapidly becoming accustomed since entering the flats.

"Yes?" he said quietly. Sarah cleared her throat.

"I'm the schoolteacher. I wonder if I could come in and have a word with you, Mr Alexander?"

"The wife takes care of all that kind of thing."

"Yes . . . well . . . if I could talk to her then."

"What about?"

Sarah gulped and tried to smile in a smooth, efficient way. "As a matter of fact it's about Samuel . . . Sammy. A little spot of bother at school . . . perhaps if I could discuss it quietly with you, or your wife . . ."

"Been a little bugger again, 'as 'e?" asked Mr Alexander unruffled. "All right then. You'd better come in."

He stepped back into the room and she had a swift impression of a tiny room crowded with men and cigarette smoke. They were sitting round a table and in front of one of the men, a young one, was a pile of papers and letters. As soon as she came into the room they all stopped talking.

"This 'ere's the schoolteacher," explained Mr Alexander to the men.

There was a scraping of chairs, a fumbling with caps

(which in most cases were still being worn on their owners' heads) and they stood up mumbling, "Evenin', Miss . . . Pleased to meet yer, Miss . . ."

She was acutely embarrassed. She knew that if one of their own womenfolk had come into the room they would not have stood up. They would have ignored her, or shouted " 'ullo," and then continued with their conversation.

"How do you do," she said nervously. "I'm sorry to disturb you."

On their faces was the abashed deferential look she had seen on the faces of her ma, and her Aunt Betsy, and occasionally even on her father's when they were talking to people of importance or "gentry" in the village. She didn't like it when her own family wore this expression of servile humility, and she didn't like it now when these men behaved as though her position of schoolmistress made them inferior in her presence. She felt she was a fraud and she was ashamed for them. She wished they would sit down and get on with their meeting.

"The wife's in the other room," said Mr Alexander, jerking his thumb over his shoulder. "You go in there if you want to see 'er."

She nodded, smiled diffidently, and walked towards the door, aware that they were all watching her. Then she noticed that one of the men, the young one at the head of the table, had not stood up. Illogically she was annoyed.

"Good evening," he said as she passed him. He had very hot brown eyes that contrasted with a pale serious face. He was not abashed, nor deferential, and after greeting her he returned to the study of his papers.

"You go and talk to the wife," said Mr Alexander reasonably. "She'll sort out whatever's wrong."

"Thank you," replied Sarah, not looking at Mr Alexander, but at the young man who had remained seated in a room where everyone else was standing. "I'm sorry to have disturbed your meeting."

She opened the door into the kitchen and before she had closed it she heard the young man saying, "Let's waste no more time. We still have a lot to decide . . ."

Mrs Alexander was surprisingly tall and, like her husband, thin. She had soft, dark hair that was cut short. On anyone else it would have been a bob, but with her sad, white face it only looked like a cheap, time-saving way of doing her hair. Her well-shaped face could have been beautiful if it hadn't been so patient and resigned. She looked up when Sarah came in and she gave a small half-twitch of her mouth, a tired courtesy of a smile. She gave the impression of a woman who expected the worst and usually got it.

"Mrs Alexander?"

The woman nodded. "You'll be the schoolteacher, I suppose. I thought someone would probably come along ever since Sammy told me. Sit down then."

Sarah sat, feeling faintly surprised. She was quite sure that if she had run away from a public thrashing at school, she would not have told her mother. Mrs Alexander obviously knew about the misdemeanour and accepted it with composure.

"He's a handful, my Sammy. I'll give him that. He's a handful sure enough. Said he put horse dung on Miss Bennett's bike. Is that right?"

"And wrote sh. . . a dirty word on the saddle," said Sarah.

Mrs Alexander nodded. She put a slice of bread onto a plate and placed a jar of red jam beside it.

"Then he nipped off before Miss Bennett could cane him," she said affably.

Sarah began to feel a little better. Mrs Alexander was taking it all so calmly, was so unruffled about the whole thing that it seemed likely there would be no difficulty about getting Sammy back to school.

"I'm afraid the headmistress is rather angry," she said, almost apologetically. "She feels her authority has been flouted and she has sent me along to persuade you to send Sammy back to school."

Mrs Alexander nodded again and began to set plates and knives round the table. "Thought that's what you'd come for," she said kindly.

For the first time in a long and depressing day Sarah's spirits began to lift. The misery of the interview with Miss Bennett, the general fractiousness of

Class Three, and—strangely enough—the annoyance
she felt for the young man in the other room, all these
things receded a little and she began to feel more like
Miss Whitman, schoolteacher, coping with a difficult but
not insurmountable class problem. She thought what a
very nice woman Mrs Alexander was.

"So you'll send him back tomorrow, will you?" she
asked.

"No."

She smiled at Sarah and turned away to take down
cups from a dresser.

"He's terrified. He's a little horror, I grant you that.
And his father'll wallop him for his dirty ways. But I
can't send him back to school. He's terrified you see."

Somehow the calmness had turned to stolid passivity.
She wasn't arguing or pleading. Just stating simple
facts—that Sammy was not going to return to school.

"The problem is," said Sarah breathlessly, "that if
he won't come back on his own the school inspector
will make him come back, and that will be bad for
everyone. And really, Mrs Alexander, you can hardly
expect Miss Bennett to let him go unpunished. That's
hardly reasonable, is it?"

Mrs Alexander paused for a moment, staring down
at the table and letting her thin hands rest on the oil-
cloth.

"No," she said slowly. "No, I don't expect him to go
unpunished. That's not reasonable. He's done wrong
and now he must take what's coming to 'im. But it's
those public beatings . . ." She turned away from the
table and walked back to the dresser. It was made of
wood and contained a teapot, some odd cups and a pot
with a rent-book and various papers sticking out of the
top. She reached up for the teapot but remained with
her face turned away from Sarah.

"You know . . . she enjoys those beatings. That Miss
Bennett, there's something wrong with her. It's not just
punishing children for her. It's more than that. I've
watched her, and watched how she enjoys it, thrashing
the children in front of the whole school . . . She never
did it to me. I was too afraid of her and I made sure I

never did anything wrong. But I've watched her beating the others . . ."

Shocked, Sarah realised that Mrs Alexander was only a few years older than she herself was, that probably only about twelve or fifteen years had elapsed since she had been at the same school and under the discipline of Miss Bennett. She stared at Mrs Alexander's face—white, drawn, thin—and the hacked-off hair and the resigned eyes, at the defeated slump of the shoulders and the old woman's hands. Mrs Alexander smiled.

"Didn't think I'd remember my school days, did you?" she asked wistfully. "Well, I remember. I remember her and her thrashings. And I'm not letting Sammy go back to that, whatever he's done." She carefully measured three spoons of tea into the pot. "I'm sorry if it means you're going to get into trouble," she said. "I expect that's what it will mean, won't it?"

She was a tired, young-old woman who had nearly given up, but not quite. She still had a little strength left, and she was saving it for her children. She reminded Sarah of her father. Mrs Alexander was worn out, beaten down by work and poverty, but she still had a sense of personal identity.

"I expect you think I'm just a silly mother who believes her boy should be treated different from everyone else's boy."

"No. No, I don't think that."

"And I suppose you're wondering why I won't let him go back, when all the time I know the school inspector can make him."

Sarah knew she had no right to make terms with Mrs Alexander. She was there to enforce the ruling of Miss Bennett, to uphold the authority of the school. She ought to try and get Sammy back to school before the inspector had a report on the matter. But she knew Mrs Alexander was right. And she knew it wasn't authority or school rules Mrs Alexander was flouting. It was the unrecognisable something in Miss Bennett, the something that made her hair come down when she thrashed children, that made her hands shake with rage when either pupil or teacher defied her.

"Mrs Alexander. If I promise to try and persuade Miss Bennett to thrash Sammy privately, will you let him come back tomorrow?"

Mrs Alexander stared with anxiety into Sarah's eyes.

"Oh, it's not going to be easy," continued Sarah quickly. "I'm as terrified of her as you are. And I'm new to the school and I'm on probation and she doesn't like me very much. I shouldn't be saying all this to you, but I know what's wrong. And I'll promise to do my best. He will be beaten in her room, but not in front of the school. Will you let him come back?"

All the composure left Mrs Alexander's face. She looked nervous and uncertain and she began to twist her apron between her hands.

"I'm not sure . . ." she murmured.

"I know what you're going to say." Sarah put her hands on the table and leant forward. "I can't promise, but I'll try. I'll do my very best to convince her it's the only way. You see, if we leave it to the inspector, we'll all be in trouble, and he'll get the thrashing anyway."

Mrs Alexander didn't answer. She stood twisting the apron and staring hard into Sarah's face as though trying to take energy and purpose from someone who still had fight left in them.

"All right. . ." she faltered at last. "If you think you can persuade her to punish him privately . . . yes . . . yes, I'll send him back. Not in the morning. In the afternoon. In the morning you talk to Miss Bennett. He'll come back in the afternoon."

She stared again at Sarah, seeking reassurance, and Sarah forgot everything but the need to comfort and sustain Mrs Alexander, to show her that not everyone was crushed, to prove that someone could still hit back, even at Miss Bennett.

"I'll go to see her in the morning," she said briskly. "I'll do what I can—everything I can." She rose from her chair and pulled her hat firmly down over her ear-loops. "I'd better leave you now. I'm sorry if I've held up the tea."

Mrs Alexander flushed, reminded suddenly of her social duties. "I'm sorry," she mumbled. "I should have offered you something, a cup of tea or something. . ."

Sarah shook her head and walked towards the door, and then she remembered the men in the other room. "Oh . . ." She paused and turned her head back to Mrs Alexander. "Shall I go through? I mean . . . when I came in they were having some kind of meeting . . . your husband and his friends. Shall I wait . . . until they've finished?"

"They'll 'ave to finish now," said Mrs Alexander bluntly. "I've got to give the children their tea and I'm not asking all that lot to stay." She pushed past Sarah and opened the door. The men were standing up now, buttoning coats and winding scarves round necks. The young man was stuffing papers into a carrier bag.

"Tea's ready," said Mrs Alexander. "And the school-teacher's going."

Mr Alexander smiled. He had a nice smile and it made him look a little younger. "Bye then," he said kindly. "Hope it's all sorted out, whatever it is."

Sarah nodded, said "Good-bye, Mr Alexander" and hurried towards the door. On her way she glanced again at the young man. He was really rather interesting to look at with his intense brown eyes and his neat crop of short-cut curls. She hoped he would look at her but he didn't. He was talking animatedly to one of his colleagues, waving handfuls of papers in the air to express a point of argument and then shoving them untidily into his carrier bag. He's really very rude, she thought irritably. At least he could acknowledge my presence in the room.

"Night then," said Mr Alexander and closed the door behind her.

When she passed Gertie on the stairs she said automatically, "Your tea's ready Gertie. You'd better go up," and then she heard the pounding of several pairs of feet coming down the stairs after her and she drew over to one side.

As they passed her, caps came off again and she was treated to a series of "Night, Miss . . . Scuse me,

Miss . . . Ta, Miss" that went on indefinitely and was accompanied by the noise of studded boots on the stone steps.

Finally he—the young one—came, still engrossed in conversation with his companion . . . "It will work, I tell you! This time it's going to work because this time *everyone* believes in it." Something about the way he pronounced "work" wasn't quite right and she wondered if he were foreign. "And if we organise properly, if it isn't left to chance as it has been before, nothing can go wrong!"

There wasn't room for both of them to pass her on the stairs and she had to press right back against the wall to let them get by.

"Good evening," she said.

His companion fell at once into the pattern of humility. Cap came off and he mumbled, "Night, Miss. Thank you, Miss," as he pushed past her. The young one stared at her without even seeing her. It was obvious from his preoccupied expression, by the way he continued talking, that he did not even notice she was there.

"I tell you, if every group does exactly what it's supposed to do, we shall win. I've worked it out exactly—using everyone we've got. . ."

What made it worse was that to get past her he had to twist slightly to one side and change his carrier bag from one arm to the other. And still she didn't penetrate his consciousness. He pushed past and clattered down the stairs ahead of her.

And suddenly his indifference proved the final depressant in a day that had been disastrous right from the beginning. She hadn't been able to cope with Class Three. She had had a miserable and humiliating interview with Miss Bennett and she would almost certainly lose her job at the end of the year. She had been treated as an outsider by a group of men who, in other circumstances, would have accepted her as one of themselves. And she had been ignored by a young man with an interesting face—no, not ignored, that was the wrong term for his detached withdrawal. It was just that she was apparently so utterly nondescript, so completely lacking in personality, that he hadn't even noticed her.

And tomorrow she had to face Miss Bennett and tell her that Sammy was coming back to school, but on certain conditions. She felt tired and a complete failure. When she reached the bottom of the steps she had to fight an overwhelming desire to sit on the bottom one and rest her head against the dirty wall.

I want to see Charlie, she thought suddenly. I want to see Charlie Dance. I'll go round after tea and see how Ma Dance is this evening. Charlie might be there.

She turned onto the pavement and her foot knocked against something on the kerb. When she looked down she saw it was one of the shrimp-man's crabs. It was dead. A piece of dirty newspaper blew up against it and it was already stained with filth from the pavement. "I want to see Charlie," she said aloud, and her eyes unaccountably filled with tears.

She ate her tea quickly that night and then she went upstairs to her room, took down her hair and rewound it into exactly the same shaped loops. She rummaged at the back of her underclothes drawer and brought out a small box of neutral-coloured face-powder. She dipped a corner of her handkerchief in and rubbed it carefully across her nose. Then she hid the box back in the drawer and blew the tell-tale dust of powder from the dressing-table top. She knew Aunt Florrie wouldn't care if she used face-powder—but she was bothered that the next time Aunt Florrie saw her ma she might mention it. And she didn't even want to think about her ma's comments on "painted hussies."

She put her hat and coat on, quietly shut the door of her room, and sped down the stairs.

"Just going out for a while, Aunt Florrie," she called, hoping she could get out of the house before Florrie could catch and question her. She had her hand on the latch when the kitchen door opened and Florrie's anxious, coarse face stuck out into the passage.

"Where you goin', dear?" she asked chidingly.

"Round to see how Ma Dance is." Sarah felt the familiar surge of irritation. She knew it was good of Aunt Florrie and Uncle Max to have her as a boarder. She knew that if Aunt Florrie hadn't offered to have her, then her ma and pa would probably have made her stay with one of the London Meeting families. She was very grateful, but she wished that Florrie and Maxie wouldn't take their temporary chargeship so heavily. Every time she went in or out of the house, Florrie would ask her where she had been, or where she was going, for how long, and who with.

She opened the door to get away and Aunt Florrie followed her to the doorstep. "I meant to go round meself this morning," she said guiltily. "Tell her I'll be round tomorrow and I'll bring her a nice pot of marmalade, some o' that I made meself."

"All right."

"And what time do you think you'll be in?"

"I don't know," said Sarah irritably. Florrie reddened and made a disapproving noise with her tongue.

"I know you don't like me keeping an eye on you, me girl," she said righteously. "But I've known you since you were a tot and I promised your ma and pa I'd see you were all right. I aim to treat you the same as I treat me own girls. And I like to know what they're up to. So don't you tut at me, young lady."

Sarah growled beneath her breath and opened the iron gate. "I don't know when I'll be back," she said again. Florrie came out of the door and leaned on the gate. "I wonder if I ought to come with you," she said, looking harassed. "I suppose I should really. I haven't been to see ma since day before yesterday."

Sarah moved quickly away, quickly so that Auntie Florrie couldn't rush back and get her coat. "I'll tell them you'll be round tomorrow," she called back, and then she started to run until she was at the corner of the street. She stopped and looked back. Auntie Florrie was hanging over the gate talking to the woman next door. Her arms were folded comfortably over her stomach and she had obviously settled down for a good chat in spite of the cold evening. Sarah was continually amazed at Aunt Florrie's ability to bear discomfort in the cause of a good gossip. She was able to hang out of an upstairs window, spine bent forward and shoulders bearing the weight of a broken sashcord, for two or three hours at a time shouting down to a neighbour several gardens down. She would lean, with the dustbin lid in one hand and a package of rubbish in the other, discussing pregnancies, drunken husbands, who was drawing ·dole and for how long, whose children had fleas, impetigo and rickets, and whose children were likely to get fleas, impetigo and rickets. Frequently she would talk for so long that she only had a few minutes to get Maxie's tea ready and then she would have to rush round the kitchen, throwing things onto the table, screeching instructions at anyone in earshot— "Maudie, get the kettle on; Cecil, find where I put those kippers; Sarah, be a love do and get the bread cut"—because Uncle Maxie, like the rest of the Dance family, was a man who liked his food put before him the minute he stepped into the house. Sarah often wondered how it was that her ma, who was spiteful, energetic and bad tempered, had maintained a friendship all these years with Auntie Florrie who was easygoing, slovenly and cheerful. They had been friends since they were girls in service together and, although they hadn't met very often since marriage and children had made the distance between London and the village an insurmountable one, the friendship had persisted. Perhaps, thought Sarah wryly, that was the reason the friendship had lasted—because they didn't see each other very often.

It was cold, but it wasn't the dreary cold of winter. Walking briskly along the street she began to feel warm and cheerful at the thought of seeing Charlie. She dodged round two small girls playing "higher and higher" and when she came to the main road she glanced quickly round to make sure no one was looking at her, and then she stepped smartly into the new red telephone box that had recently been installed. She read the directions and looked at the slots in which to put the money. Then she lifted the sound piece and held it to her ear, but put it back quickly before an operator at the exchange could notice anything odd. I'd like to make a telephone call one day, she thought. Perhaps I'll know someone to telephone one day. Or I could call a fire engine, or the council offices, or someone like that. She blew softly into the mouthpiece and then she thought she'd better come out of the box before someone saw her and wondered what she was doing.

There were buds on the trees in Trinity Square, tight, green buds and it was the first time she'd noticed them. And the sky was suddenly rosy and the street lights were coming on, and then the wind dropped and at last she could smell spring. "Hello, Alfred!" she shouted to the old stone statue in front of the church. "You won't have long now. Spring's coming and the swallows will soon be back. They'll sit on your head and cover you in bird lime and you won't look at bit like King Alfred, that's if you are Alfred in the first place."

She swung out of the square, across the street, past the pub on the corner—the piano was thrumming already and someone was singing "Always" in a rich, porty voice. I wonder if I can afford a new dress this spring, she thought, cream, with a sailor collar and a sash round the hips. I think that would look nice. Or maybe I should cut my hair? No. I daren't. What would ma say if I cut my hair! But I must do *something*. I must do something different now that spring is coming. She was breathless with walking quickly, and with excitement because spring was coming and something was going to happen to her. Something must be going to happen to her. It was spring.

Charlie opened the door himself and when he saw her his round, good-natured face beamed into a surprised wide smile. "Luvly!" he said warmly. "I didn't know you was coming round, Sary. Luvly!"

She had forgotten why she had wanted to see him so badly, but now she remembered. Everyone had disliked her today, Miss Bennett, the children, the young man at the Alexanders'. But Charlie didn't dislike her. Charlie thought she was wonderful. She had only to walk into a room and Charlie was happy, just because she was there.

"You're going to stay for a bit, aren't you?" he asked, afraid that now she was here he was going to lose her already. "I mean, why don't you stay and 'ave a bit of supper?" His face broke into a grin again, unashamedly delighted. "Ever so pleased you've come round, Sary! Really, ever so pleased!"

Sarah smiled. "I thought I'd better see how ma was."

"She'll be lots better when she's seen you. Always better when you come round, Sary. Wish you boarded with us instead of Maxie and Flo. Love to 'ave you we would, only there's such a lot of us."

There were a lot of the Dances, so many that Sarah had never really worked out the final total of ribald, red-faced, generous extroverts who teemed in and out of the three-storey Dance house. Ma and Pa Dance had gustily produced fifteen children. Three of them, Charlie and two sisters, still lived at home. Another daughter, Maisie, widowed by the Battle of the Somme, had brought her four children and had settled happily back with ma and pa. Next door lived Clarence Dance, with wife, five children, and two more whose Dance father had been killed at Verdun. In the same street lived more Dances, daughters, sons, grandchildren, nephews, nieces. In the adjoining streets they spread further, stretching away to the furthest Dance house in the neighbourhood which was Unce Max and Auntie Florrie. No one, not even the Dances themselves, could give the sum total of their tribe. Some of them had died, some had been killed in the war, but for every Dance who left a grieving gap in the family, several more came along to fill the space. The children didn't seem to belong particularly to any one set of parents. At one time Maisie would be looking after six small Dances who all had measles; "Well, love, as my four 'ave got 'em, you might just as well bring Joycie and Cyril round 'ere, then you can 'ave Bertha's kids while she gets over 'avin' the baby."

The Dances who had died were wept and agonised over, then their photographs were prominently displayed on mantelpieces and shelves, and charabancs were hired on the anniversaries of their deaths to take the family, smothered in large floral tributes, to the cemetery. Those who died in the war were mourned on Armistice Day with tears and black arm bands and a full family muster at the Cenotaph. Then they all went back to ma and pa's for a slap-up tea. The Dances found it impossible to grieve quietly. They grieved, and loved, and fought, with noise, with ostentation, with the need for being together, for embracing each other, for living in and out of each other's houses. They hugged and kissed each other when they were happy, sad, drunk, and in pain. Dance girls liked to have their bedrooms full of other Dance girls when they were ill, or getting married, or in labour, or dying.

Everyone lived at exactly the same standard of financial comfort as everyone else, because when someone fell out of work, or a husband died, the rest of the family just moved in and everyone cut back on their expenditure. If a Dance had a win on the horses, there was a party, a big, noisy rollicking affair at which someone was usually sick and, invariably, at least two Dance wives got pregnant again.

And over the teeming, thriving, multiplying warren of the Dance tribe, presided Ma Dance, seventy years old, unable to leave her bedroom, huge and bronchial with dropsical legs and feet, beloved by husband, children, grandchildren; still able to tell a daughter-in-law exactly what she thought of her, directing the way the children should be reared, the husbands managed, the right way to do a belly of pork or a pig's head. She knew, before the girls themselves knew, who was pregnant, and she still mourned for her dead sons, but not too often because there just wasn't the time. Her grandchildren adored her although she couldn't remember all their names. They crawled and bounced all over her bed and she slapped and kissed them and told their parents what they were doing wrong. She had an inexhaustible supply, for the whole world if it had so needed, of interfering, noisy, insensitive love.

She knew, by some weird kind of Dance osmosis, exactly what was happening in the house, in the street, in the family. When she was having one of her "turns" and the family were creeping in through the front door and talking in whispers so as not to disturb her, she would suddenly wheeze from her pillow, "That's Gladys just come in. Send 'er up. I want to talk to 'er. I bin 'earing things about that 'usband of 'ers and it's time she took 'im in 'and."

Sarah had only just stepped inside the door when the thick, gravelly voice of Ma Dance rasped down the stairs. "That's Sarah! That's our Sarah then. Come on up, love. Nobody else 'ere at the moment. Come up and see old Ma Dance, darlin'."

Sarah grinned at Charlie and climbed the narrow stairs. The walls on either side of her were tall and papered in brown fruit-and flower-patterned wallpaper. She didn't knock on the bedroom door because it was wide open.

"Come in, darlin'! Come in! Come and give old ma a kiss then!"

There was a chair by the head of the bed but no one ever sat on it because ma liked her visitors to sit beside her on the bed where she could touch them. Sarah bent over ma and two mammoth arms locked round her shoulders and brought her face down to ma's. "How you bin, Sary love? How you bin?"

Ma lay smothered in two feather mattresses on a brass bedstead. (She enjoyed the days the bedstead was polished as she could lie back and shout instructions to the unfortunate granddaughter whose lot it was to "do out" ma's bedroom.) A large mahogany wardrobe stood in one corner, a large tallboy in another, and a dressing-table stood blocking out the light from the window.

Ma, wearing a pink flannel nightgown, held Sarah away from her, looked into her face, then hugged her again.

"Always cheerful you are, Sary. Always cheerful. I got to say that for you. You ain't a looker like your ma was, but you're always cheerful!"

Sarah was used to being told that she wasn't pretty like her ma had been—indeed her mother had been the first to tell her so—and she tried not to let it bother her any more.

"We can't all be beauties," she said stoically.

"Indeed we can't, me gel, indeed we' can't." Ma heaved herself up on the pillows and Sarah stood and plumped them up behind ma's tremendous shoulders.

"Remember your ma, I do," said ma nostalgically. "Little tiny thing she was, with the neatest figure you ever saw. And 'er 'air that black! And always full of life! Always makin' us laugh she was ... a great one for a party she was. Used to do impersonations of Marie Lloyd ... 'My Old Man' and them songs, you know ..."

"What? My mother?" Sarah was astounded. That her mother had been pert and pretty she could believe. But that Anne-Louise, who was a narrow-minded scold to all her children, had ever sung and danced at a party was incomprehensible to Sarah.

"That's right! Used to do Marie Lloyd, and Kate Carney, and all o' them. Tiny she was. Guess you take after your pa, eh, Sary?"

"That's right." She was unusually abrupt and it must have registered with Ma Dance for she suddenly put her swollen hand over Sarah's and clumsily patted her fingers.

"Don't you worry, gel. You're a good gel, and you're sensible. You wouldn't do what your ma did. You wouldn't go off and leave poor Maxie like she did, without a word. Practically engaged they was! And suddenly off she goes to her village without a word. Left 'im broken 'earted she did. And the next thing she's married your pa."

Sarah had heard it many times before. The story of Uncle Maxie and her mother, and how her mother had jilted Uncle Maxie and gone home and married Jonathan. She had heard the story from the Dances on innumerable occasions, because the Dances loved to repeat family history whenever they had an opportunity. She knew the story, but she didn't believe it. The thought of Uncle Maxie, stout, one-armed from the war, and married to even stouter Auntie Florrie, ever being in love with Anne-Louise, was completely unbelievable.

"I expect it was for the best," she said lamely to Ma Dance, and ma nodded vehemently.

"It was that, gel, it was that. And Florrie's made my Maxie a good wife, a good wife . . . in spite of she can't do a bacon pudding proper." She patted Sarah's hand again. "No gel, you may not be a looker like your ma, but you're the gel for my Charlie. My Charlie thinks the world of you, and you're a good gel. You wouldn't go off and leave 'im the way your ma left his brother."

Sarah wriggled uncomfortably on the edge of the bed. She knew that all the Dances took it for granted that one day she and Charlie would be married, but every time ma made direct reference to it she felt an uneasy sense of depression—not because of Charlie or because she did or didn't want to marry him—but because the family all took it for granted that she would.

In the beginning, when she had first come to London to start her training, she hadn't seen much of Charlie. But whenever she had a day off, or was feeling miserable and lonely away from home, she had come over to visit Maxie and Florrie, and somehow Charlie had always been there, protective, admiring, and flatteringly older than she was.

No word of marriage had ever been spoken between them. She was too busy qualifying and Charlie always seemed absorbed in family and settling into some kind of post-war employment. She loved the Dances, and Charlie was one of them, the one of whom she was most fond. When she was tired or disheartened—like she had been this evening—Charlie's devotion was balm to her hurt. She had never been so transparently worshipped before and it was a new and sustaining experience.

But whenever she thought of marriage to Charlie it depressed her. Charlie would be kind and he would adore her. He was nice to look at, fair-haired and blue-eyed, and he was taller than she was which was agreeable. Whenever she walked along the road with Charlie she felt small and feminine instead of a great lump. But the thought of marrying Charlie, of becoming a Dance and losing her identity in the gregarious battle of the family, profoundly depressed her. I've too much to do, she thought with some urgency. Too many things are going to happen to me. I can't become a Dance yet, not just yet. Perhaps I will one day in the future, years from now! But I can't marry Charlie now. However much I need him, I can't marry him yet.

Every time Ma Dance or one of the family made a reference to her and Charlie getting married she felt trapped and uncertain—wondering if perhaps they were right and knew better than she did. And every time Ma Dance reminded her of her mother's disloyalty—jilting a Dance boy and marrying someone else!—Sarah shared the guilt with her mother.

Now Ma Dance beamed at her—a young girl's face staring out from the centre of multitudinous moons of fat. "No, me gel," she said smugly. "You're not like your ma. You're the faithful sort, you are. You wouldn't hurt my Charlie, I know that."

Sarah smiled weakly. "He may not want to marry me, ma."

Ma tutted. "Course 'e will, love. Course 'e will! Soon as 'e finds a job and gets settled. That why 'e's not said anything to you. Can't marry you till 'e finds 'imself a job, can 'e?"

The Dances were still comparatively affluent. Their menfolk, including old Pa Dance, gained their living largely from Billingsgate. But there were too many Dances now for the fishmarket to provide employment for all of them and, by mutual family agreement, the portering had gone to the Dances with large families, whilst the side jobs, the tallying and so forth, to men like Uncle Maxie who only had one arm and would find it difficult to get work anywhere else. Charlie, single and living at home, had to find work when and how he could, the odd bit of portering at Covent Garden, temporary coalman, brewer's drayman, road sweeper. His situation was demoralising but he was in a far more fortunate position than over one million of his fellow countrymen. He was unemployed, but he was assured of a home and sufficient food.

"Yes," said ma with assurance. "Don't worry, Sary gel. Soon as my Charlie gets a regular job, 'e'll be thinking about poppin' the question."

From downstairs came the noise of the front door slamming, of many voices, of feet tramping in rooms and on the staircase. Ma Dance's face was once more suffused with energy as a new wave of life transformed her sick and ageing body.

"Bertha, darlin'! Give us a kiss then. 'Ow's Bertie? And you've got Rube's kids 'ere too. Where's Ruby then? Mind the baby! 'E's pulled that dressing-table runner off..."

The children swarmed over the bed, in and out of the wardrobe, swung on the door-handle and fell up and down the stairs. There were suddenly too many of them and Sarah felt suffocated and smothered in children . . . in ma . . . in Dances.

"I've got to go," she said rising quickly. "I mustn't be late. Auntie Florrie said I wasn't to be back late."

"Charlie will walk you home," said ma confidently, simultaneously kissing one of the children and slapping another. "Bye bye, dear. And ask Florrie why she 'asn't been near me for two days." She sounded plaintive but it only lasted a minute. "I'll expect to see 'er tomorrow," she finished on a more threatening note.

Sarah smiled and escaped from the room, from the communal noise that was beginning to drain her of energy. She turned at the door and waved generally to the room at large. Then she breathed deeply and walked down the stairs. Charlie was waiting. He had his overcoat on and his cap was set jauntily on one side of his head.

"Let's go for a walk, Sarah."

"I'm going home," she snapped, and immediately felt ashamed when she saw the hurt on his face. "Oh come on then, you can walk home with me if you want to. I'm sorry, I didn't mean to be rude."

She wished she could go home on her own. She was tired and overwhelmed with the family and she thought how nice it would be to walk back through Trinity Square alone. To make sure the trees were budding and to smell the spring again. Charlie fell into step beside her.

"You all right, Sarah?" he asked anxiously.

"Why?"

He grinned. "I don't know. I thought you seemed tired. Like I said, there's so many of us. Sometimes I think we make you tired."

"Oh, Charlie!" She felt ashamed all over again—ashamed and cheered because Charlie had realised what she was feeling. He didn't follow her moods very often. When he did she was filled with delighted surprise.

"What would I do without you? I'm so mean sometimes, and you're always so nice to me."

Charlie grinned again. "Ma's a bit much at times, ain't she?"

Sarah seized his arm and hugged it. "She's lovely, Charlie. It's me that's bad-tempered. I had a dreadful day at school, and I had to go and see one of the parents and . . . oh it's just been a dreadful day, Charlie!"

"That old Miss Bennett again?" asked Charlie sympathetically.

Sarah nodded. "You're not to wait outside school for me any more, Charlie. She spoke to me about it. Said it gave the school a bad name. And then I had to go and see these parents and there was a man there who was rude to me."

When she was talking to Charlie she often forgot that his mind worked at a slower pace than hers. She would jump from one subject to another without pause or explanation and then would feel irritated because Charlie couldn't follow her. Now he looked bewildered. He stopped walking and turned to stare at her, a small frown settling between his eyes.

"What man?" he asked.

"At the Alexanders'—the parents I had to go and see. They were having some kind of meeting and all these men were sitting talking and looking at papers. And this young man was there—he seemed to be some kind of a leader—plotting something they were. And I could tell he didn't like me."

"Oh, Sarah," said Charlie, amused. "You're always imagining things about people. Always pretending they're burglars, or royalty in disguise, or explorers or something." He chuckled and began walking again.

"You've got such an imagination, Sarah. I never knew anyone with an imagination like you've got. Saying he didn't like you! Why shouldn't he like you?"

"He didn't," she said stubbornly. "He had brown eyes and I didn't imagine it because when I left and said good-bye he just ignored me. Pushed past me on the stairs and didn't answer."

"Did he," said Charlie frowning. "Well I wish I'd been there. I'd have taught him his manners. There's no call for that kind of thing."

"And he had a carrier bag full of papers," said Sarah without really hearing. "He was foreign I think. He looked foreign."

"Ah," Charlie's frown cleared swiftly from his face. "Well that explains it, doesn't it. If he was a foreigner of course he'd behave like that. You forget it then, Sarah. Don't worry about it if he was only a foreigner."

She felt the surge of irritation again, the frustration that often occurred when she was talking to Charlie. He completely missed the point and now that he had solved the incident to his own satisfaction, he did not see what else she needed to worry about.

"Let's not talk about it any more," she said abruptly, and Charlie smiled and patted her shoulder. They were nearly home and when they reached the gate Charlie bent and kissed her cheek. "Don't you worry, Sarah. Don't you worry about that foreigner."

He watched her pull the string with the key on through the letter-box and when she went in he waited for a moment, feeling pride because Sarah was his girl and he had just walked her home. He didn't walk her home very often because he wasn't earning enough to take her anywhere. He didn't like that. A bloke should be able to spend a lot of money on his girl, especially a girl like Sarah. He ought to be able to take her to Hampstead, and the pictures, and the Variety. He ought to be able to treat her to teas at Lyons, and buy her flowers and coloured glass bangles and those gewgaws that girls liked so much. Sarah deserved everything he could give her, and so far he had given her very little.

He had first met her when she was fifteen, and he was prepared to wait because Sarah was the most beautiful exciting creature he had ever known. He didn't understand her, but he understood himself and knew that Sarah was something he must capture and pin down with a wedding-ring and a home and a brood of children. He was afraid of that elusive "something" in Sarah, the something that made him worry he might lose her, and the something that, at the same time, gave Sarah that mysterious quality that he wanted to capture for himself, to explore, to discover, to understand. He had never known another woman, or anyone, who had the magic, the gaiety, the sadness that was Sarah. He loved his ma, his sisters, his sisters-in-law, his nieces, he loved them all because they were as he was. They were noisy and they quarrelled and laughed and they all understood each other and nothing would ever split them up. But Sarah was a dream, Sarah was a secret for a man to fathom out. He would never know Sarah the way he knew his sisters, but he would always adore Sarah, would always want to find out about her, and watch her, and listen to her.

He waited until the light came on in her room and then he turned and began to walk slowly home. Must try and think of a way of getting into a safe job, he said to himself. It's no use until I'm earning a regular wage. I must get a proper job, somehow I must.

Sarah saw him standing there, saw him looking up at her window and tinkering with the latch on the gate. Dear Charlie, she thought affectionately, and then she turned away from the window and forgot him.

He *was* rude to me, she said to herself later as she climbed into bed.

Yes, he definitely was.

## *Two*

WHEN Sarah arrived at school on the following morning she remembered it was her day for handing out the hot milk and malt to the children who had been classified by the school doctor as suffering from malnutrition.

She hated milk duty because it meant that every sick, thin, undernourished child in the school was gathered together in one classroom, all staring at her with eyes that were too large in their pale faces, all waiting with a kind of mute apathy for the spoonful of malt, for the mug of hot milk. These children were present all the time, but when they were seated in the classroom, dispersed amongst the other children who were only normally poor, the effect of them wasn't so overwhelming, so morbidly depressing.

Most of them were clean, but not all. They wore clothes that were handed down from elder brothers and sisters or by charity visitors. The clothes were either too big, sleeves hanging down over matchstick wrists, or too small, cutting tightly into armpits and groin. Sometimes the boots were so large that they were tied round the legs with laces in order to keep them on but no one, as yet, had come to school with bare feet. There were days when Sarah felt strong and courageous and handed out the milk with cheerful patience, encouraging the children, trying to imbue them not only with vitamins, but with hope and determination to get better, get older and move into a life where malt and hot milk were not needed. There were other days when she just felt depressed. The whole thing was hopeless.

The weak, quiet children would grow up into weak, quiet men and women who had no fight left in them. On these days there didn't seem any point in trying.

Today, with the knowledge that she must face Miss Bennett and tell her about Sammy Alexander, the children seemed unbearably slow, unbearably irritating. Standing in a long shuffling line they moved—it appeared to Sarah—with deliberate hesitation, each one taking an unconsciously long time to lick the malt from the spoon—with a secret smile of pleasure or a grimace of dislike, according to their individual taste—and even longer to sip the warm milk from the enamel beakers. When Miss Enderby came into the room bearing Sarah's cup of tea from the staff-room the break was nearly at an end.

"Miss Enderby," snapped Sarah. "Could you finish milk duty for me? I must see Miss Bennett before this afternoon. I will take your duty for you on Friday."

Miss Enderby's face blanched as it always did when the Head's name was mentioned. She teetered nervously back on her heels.

"Can it not wait until the dinner-break?"

Sarah irritably poured some milk into another mug and slopped most of it on the floor.

"It can, if it must," she said. "But I would really like to get it over with now."

"Well ... I don't know ... Miss Bennett might not approve ... you remember when Miss Larkin and I exchanged duties, the Head noticed, oh yes, she noticed that we had exchanged ..."

"Oh for goodness sake!" shouted Sarah, pushing the milk jug into Miss Enderby's hand. "Just pour the milk out and I'll tell Miss Bennett it was all my idea." She flung out of the milk room, wondering with furious frustration how on earth Miss Enderby could be terrified over such a small thing as exchanging milk duties when she, Sarah, had to face an ordeal with Miss Bennett that made her stomach turn cold.

Along the passage, and up the stone stairs, worn into a gentle curve on the centre of each tread by hundreds of children in studded boots; along the upper corridor, buzzing with the soft sounds of break-time that were still kept under control by the invisible authority of Miss Bennett. Sarah swallowed, smoothed her hair, and knocked.

"Who is it?"

"Miss Whitman."

"Enter."

Miss Bennett was sitting graciously back in her chair sipping tea from a bone china cup. A tray laid with teapot, milk jug, sugar basin, and a plate of garibaldis rested on the desk. Miss Bennett set her cup back on the saucer.

"Miss Whitman?"

Sarah swallowed again. "Excuse me interrupting your break, Headmistress. But I wished to speak to you about Sammy Alexander."

Miss Bennett poured a little milk into her cup and lifted the teapot. "I looked at your register this morning, Miss Whitman. I see that the boy has not returned to school."

"But he will, Miss Bennett. He will be returning this afternoon. I went to see his parents last evening and Mrs Alexander promised me the boy would come back to school this afternoon."

Miss Bennett finished pouring her tea, dropped two cubes of sugar into the cup and stirred very slowly. "I am delighted to hear it, Miss Whitman. I would have preferred that the child had returned this morning, but nonetheless I am gratified to hear he will be in class after the dinner-break."

Sarah's legs began to feel extraordinary and she wondered if she would be able to see the interview out without having to lean on Miss Bennett's desk.

"I'm afraid that getting him back to school was not as simple as I had hoped, Miss Bennett," she said nervously. "His mother at first refused. Then she agreed that she would let him come back if the public thrashing was waived." She dared not look at Miss Bennett's face but she was aware that the spoon had ceased to revolve in the cup. Miss Bennett was sitting unnaturally still.

"So I promised Mrs Alexander that there would be no public thrashing," she finally blurted.

The room was so quiet she could hear her own heart thumping. Then there was a violent crash and the sound of breaking china as Miss Bennett pushed her cup off the end of her desk.

"You did what!"

Sarah dared to look at Miss Bennett. She was standing, leaning slightly forward over her desk with hands—fingers spread wide apart—flat on the top. Her face was white and the eyes were concentrated into small brilliant points of fury.

"I had to, Miss Bennett," she gabbled in terror. "I had to promise otherwise Mrs Alexander would never have let him come back to school. She agreed that he must be punished, but privately, not in front of the whole school. If I hadn't promised she wouldn't have let him come back."

Miss Bennett's face didn't change but her hands and body relaxed slightly.

"This afternoon, Miss Whitman, immediately after the dinner-break, you will assemble Class Three in the Hall. I shall send Mr Janning along to collect Samuel Alexander as soon as he arrives at school. On your way back to the classroom, please tell the rest of the staff that I want full assembly after the dinner-break."

She was terrified—of the breaking cup, of Miss Bennett's eyes, of the violence which she always sensed in the woman. Under the terror was the slower but more prevailing fear of the loss of her job. But even with the terror and fear she was still shocked at the significance of Miss Bennett's words.

"You're still going to thrash him?" she asked with disbelief. "After I gave my word to Mrs Alexander, you're still going to thrash him?"

"I have given you my instructions, Miss Whitman. See they are carried out."

"I gave my word to the boy's mother," Sarah said slowly. "I know I had no right to give it. I was presuming upon my duties. But that means I should be punished, not the boy. You cannot punish the boy. You can punish me, but not Sammy Alexander."

"Miss Whitman," hissed the Headmistress. "You are

impertinent, undisciplined, and emotionally disgusting. Your entire conduct in this matter is thoroughly offensive." Sarah didn't take her eyes from Miss Bennett's face. She stared carefully at the rigid features and the nerve that trembled in Miss Bennett's neck. Her contemplative stare infuriated the older woman even more.

"Moreover, Miss Whitman, I shall expect you to sit on the platform and, if necessary, hold the boy when I punish him."

"I'm afraid I can't do that," said Sarah coldly. Suddenly she wasn't afraid any more. She was sick, and angry, and deeply ashamed, but she wasn't afraid. She almost hoped that Miss Bennett would stride round the desk and hit her because then she could strike Miss Bennett back and release some of the anger in her heart.

She stared with loathing directly into Miss Bennett's face.

"I shall stay in the body of the hall with my class."

She did not wait for anything else. She just turned and walked out of the room. She heard Miss Bennett scream, "Come here! At once!" and she took no notice. She didn't slam the door or look back to say any of the things that were simmering in her mind. She shut the door quietly and then walked slowly back to the empty room of Class Three. Her brain was working quickly, making calculations, mentally checking on how much money she had saved to see her through unemployment.

She'll have to report me to the committee before I'm properly sacked. And I'll sit it out until then, she thought methodically. I won't leave until I'm actually dismissed. I'll have a breathing space that way and at least another week's salary, if I'm lucky.

She picked up a pencil and began to make calculations on the back of a text book.

Of course she can demand my instant dismissal. But I don't think she will. If she does that the committee will want to know why and I don't think she'll welcome them asking questions. No, I've a week, perhaps even more.

4

And then the sinking misery of wondering, What am I going to tell pa?

The thunder of returning feet into the classroom broke her introspection. She had two lessons to get through before the dinner-break.

When she led her class into the hall Miss Bennett was already standing on the platform. Mr Jannings was holding Sammy and one of the teachers from Junior Boys was present to help Miss Bennett if needed. The boy's teacher was a young trainee student and he looked trapped and miserable.

Gertie Alexander was crying again and Sarah, deliberately flouting the unwritten law of the school, took the child's hand and held it all the time throughout the assembly.

She was aware that Miss Bennett was looking at her, and she stared coldly back, daring Miss Bennett to call her up onto the platform in front of the school. The headmistress glared, the ice-eyes again pinpointed into fury, and then recognising something implacable in the stance of her youngest teacher, she looked away.

"Sammy Alexander, of Class Three, is going to be punished for *filth*," she stated to the school. "And anyone else who uses *filth* in my school will be punished in the same way." She picked up the cane and turned to Sammy. "Come here."

Inside Sarah something screamed, No! You can't hit him! Just look at him. How can you hit him?

Sammy was small, pathetic, weedy. His hair was too long and his clothes didn't fit. One sock was wrinkled down over his ankle and his face was thin and frightened although he was trying hard not to cry.

"Hold up your right hand."

Timidly he extended his fingers towards Miss Bennett and Sarah saw the woman suddenly swing her whole body back with the cane. Sarah closed her eyes.

She heard the thwack of punishment, the sound of one or two children quietly crying. She sensed the distress of the rest of the staff and knew that if she looked at Miss Enderby the old lady would be shaking and staring at the floor. She felt waves of humiliation, of shame, of hysteria amongst the children.

"The other hand."

She opened her eyes. The coil of hair had come unwound from Miss Bennett's head and swung every time she threw her body violently back with the cane. On Miss Bennett's face was an expression of fanatical delight. Sammy Alexander was white and his teeth were chattering but he was determined not to cry.

Miss Bennett finished. She turned her back to the school and placed the cane on the table beside the staff hymn books and the Bible. She lifted her hands to her head and recoiled the piece of hair. Then she breathed deeply and turned to face the school.

"Let nothing of this kind occur again. School dismissed."

Feeling tired and old, Sarah led her class from the hall.

To Jonathan Whitman, a village postman who had been a gardener, a soldier, a shepherd and a dreamer, only three of his children had won a part in his heart, the two children of his first marriage, and Sarah who was the firstborn of his second wife.

Harriet, his eldest child, he had come to love too late. A difficult birth, a tormented childhood and an impatient stepmother had resulted in her inability to lead a natural life. She was not insane, but she had taken refuge from all the nightmares of her childhood in a small protected world of her own making. She was in a home for mentally backward girls, visited by her family once a month, a permanent reminder of early neglect, and the careless cruelty of his second wife.

Peter, his sailor son, he loved. But somehow he could not find expression for that love. The stepmother who had intensified his elder daughter's abnormaily had also driven a chasm between him and his son. Peter had run away to sea, and his home loyalties were given to an aunt who had offered the affection his stepmother could not give. He loved his father, his father loved him, but it was too late for their affection to be conveyed.

But Sarah—beautiful Sarah—she was the child of his heart, and the gulf that Sarah's mother had jealously tried to drive between them had not succeeded in destroying their delight in one another.

He had watched his wife deliberately tear down the girl's defences, convince her she was ugly, stupid, lazy and incompetent. He had watched and had dared do nothing because intervention on his part would provoke the unleashed hatred of a woman who was jealous of her own daughter.

He had seen the girl's spirit broken and her talent nearly destroyed, and had despised his own weakness for letting it happen.

But nothing, no cruelty or weakness or misfortune, could ever annihilate the bond between him and his daughter. He knew that Sarah felt the way he felt, that she had a tiny core of self which would always sustain her, give her sudden joy when she had no reason to be joyful, give her strength when she most needed it. She had grown on—past him—her mind was now bigger and less trammelled than his but the bond was still there. Whatever she did, he could understand because— if his life had been different—he would have done those same things. He felt pride in her achievements, but the pride was only secondary to the fact that he had found someone in the world who thought as he did, who felt as he did, who was searching as he himself searched.

He knew all these things of his daughter, but there was one thing he did not know. He thought that Sarah was as he himself was. He never recognised the restlessness in her that she had inherited from her mother, Anne-Louise, the restlessness that was sometimes vivacity, sometimes discontent. He did not see this in his daughter because it was not in himself.

She usually came back to the village once every two months or so, but after the thrashing of Sammy Alexander and the almost certain dismissal that was about to follow, she felt a sudden need to see her pa, and her brothers and cousins, and her Aunt Betsy whom she, as well as her sailor brother, loved more than Anne-Louise, her mother. She always felt depressed at the thought of meeting her ma and especially on an un-expected visit because one never knew in what mood Anne-Louise would be indulging. But she had to take a chance on her mother this time because of the need to see her pa.

It was April; and as soon as she stepped from the train out into the quiet of a country station she felt better. The train disappeared down the track and the silence was broken by first one bird, then another. A lapwing lifted slowly into the air and drifted over the station fields and she saw a yellowhammer on the hedgerow that separated the platform from the fields. All about her was the smell of the village, the cold, damp, open smell of rain and green moss.

She hurried over the wooden steps and handed her ticket to Mr Watkins.

"Ha!" said Mr Watkins inquisitively. "Didn't think this was your Saturday for visiting, young Sarah?"

"T'isn't," said Sarah cheerfully. "I just wanted to see my pa ... and my ma They don't know I'm coming."

She flung out of the station and climbed over the stile into the fields. She heard Mr Watkins shout, "You'd best go round by the road, Sarah Whitman. You'll get mud all over your fine city clothes if you go that way." But she only waved without turning round and began to swing up the fields towards the wood.

"Lala la la," she called, imitating the yellowhammer who had followed her from the station. "Lala la la." The fronds of new ferns were growing in the woods, and coltsfoot and celandine, and she was suddenly strong again. She could bear Miss Bennett and the coming dismissal. She could bear the hot milk and malt and the faces of the sick children in the city. She could bear the young man who had ignored her on the stairs and she could bear being an apology of a person who was utterly inferior to everyone else in every possible way.

"Beech, birch, ho-rnbeam and oak!" she sang. "Oak and hornbeam, beech and birch."

She stopped by a patch of muddy earth. The five-toed print of a badger led across the soil to a small rise fifty feet away and she stopped singing and walked quickly across to see if the mouth of the set was near the hummock. A great heap of rubbish—twigs, leaves, grass and tree bark—was piled around the set where the badger was turning out his old winter bedding. She knelt by the mound and crumbled a clod of earth in her fingers. "Old cat," she said to herself, not of the badger, but of Miss Bennett. Then she wrinkled her nose slightly at the scent of the badger's rubbish, stood up and tried to brush the mud from her skirt.

She didn't go to the front of her pa's cottage. She skirted round the fields until she came to the big meadow at the top of the garden and then she jumped across the ditch.

"Hullo, pa," she said to Jonathan who was splitting strawberry roots.

The tired, high-boned face, an older replica of her own, lit into a swift smile.

"Sarah, girl! My Sarah!" When they hugged each other she was only a little shorter than he was. She loved him so much she wondered how she was able to manage with seeing him so rarely. But then, seeing him so rarely, meant moments like this, the surprise and the delight and the sense of something strong to support her.

"Suddenly had to come and see you, pa. I wanted to talk to you and I couldn't wait until next month."

Jonathan wiped his hands on the sides of his trousers and smiled. "Did you come through the wood?" he asked. "Did you see the old badger's set? He's turning out for spring."

She nodded, and they began to walk slowly towards the hives. "And the bees are coming out early this year," he went on. "Have to be careful. I don't want them caught in a cold spell."

"Pa," she said quickly before her nerve failed and she decided she didn't want to worry him with her troubles, "I may have to leave the school. I've had a bit of trouble with Miss Bennett."

He didn't look at her. He picked up a trowel and began to scrape mud from his boots. "Better tell me now, love. Before we go in to your ma."

"Well, pa. It's about this boy, about this Sammy Alexander . . ." Slowly, because she was trying to remember everything exactly as it happened, she told him about the thrashing and the Alexanders. When she had finished Jonathan nodded and put the trowel in his pocket.

"I think you did everything, Sarah. Yes. You did everything you possibly could at the time. Now there's one thing more you've got to do."

Sarah swallowed. "You mean go and see that poor woman, pa. Go and see Mrs Alexander."

He smiled. "We'll go and have tea now. Your Aunt Betsy's here, and your cousin May. They'll be pleased to see you."

He put his arm round her shoulder and hugged her again. Then he moved away from her a little and they went down the garden towards the cottage.

Every time she came home the cottage seemed a little smaller, and her mother a little sharper. It was funny because nothing else seemed to change—the woods and the fields didn't change, or her father, or Aunt Betsy. Just the cottage and her mother. When she walked in, Anne-Louise was making the tea.

"Oh," she snapped. "It's you." She looked put out, but then she shrugged and came round the table, lifting her face towards Sarah's. "You've mud all down the front of your coat," she remarked.

Sarah dutifully kissed her. "Hullo, ma," she said quietly. "I thought I'd give you all a surprise. Where're the boys?"

"Out and about," said her mother, turning away to the stove. Sarah went to her Aunt Betsy who hugged her and then held her back at arm's length. "My!" she said. "Ain't that smart, Annie? Just look what the city folk are wearing now. All loose and baggy and . . . elegant!"

Anne-Louise carefully studied the made-over coat and dress that Sarah was wearing. She had a good dress sense and in spite of bearing several children and rearing them on an infinitesimal income, she still looked smart and had a certain style about her. Sarah, who could feel no natural affection for Anne-Louise and was often afraid of her, nonetheless had a kind of detached respect for her mother's views on fashion.

"It's too short," she said bluntly. "And I don't like the baggy look. What's the point of having a neat waist if you've got to hide it with a sloppy bodice like that. You look much nicer in something fitted."

Sarah grew very earnest. "I know that, ma. But it's the *fashion*. One's got to wear everything loose and droopy." She hesitated and said, "It *can* look quite nice, you know."

"But not on you," said Anne-Louise disparagingly. "You're too big to look stylish in that kind of thing." She turned away and immediately lost interest in the subject of city fashions. "Has your father told you our news?" she asked brightly. "About the gas? It's coming to the village. We're having two gaslights, one here and one in the parlour, and a gas cooker for when we don't want to light the range. Eight shillings down and twopence a week rental. What do you think of that?"

"I'm having it too," said Aunt Betsy from the sofa.

Sarah grinned at her favourite aunt. Betsy was plain, round, well scrubbed and courageous. She had survived the war grief of a lost husband, had reared five children, and still had enthusiasm for the small delights of life.

"It's marvellous, Aunt Betsy! You won't have so many lamps to clean, and you won't have to light the range on hot days." She turned and nodded to her cousin. "Hullo, May," she said diffidently. She always felt sorry for May, Aunt Betsy's second daughter. Mary, the elder, had been apprenticed to the village dressmaker because Aunt Betsy was determined that at least one of her daughters should be taught a trade. When May came to leave school there was no money and not much choice of employment. May had been forced to go into service, and had moreover filled the post just vacated by Sarah who was on her way to better things. She always felt mean about her cousin having to fill her old job—as though it were somehow her fault.

May smiled and stared enviously at Sarah's dress. How strange, thought Sarah. At the school and in London I'm the old-fashioned, dowdy one, but here it's different. May is looking at me as though I were really stylish and smart.

May was wearing an old cut-down dress of Betsy's. It had been well made-over—no point in having an apprentice dressmaker sister if she couldn't alter the family wardrobe—but it was unmistakably 1916 vintage. It had a waist, and the skirt was too full. It was red silk and it had been Betsy's best dress before her husband had died. Betsy didn't wear red any more, and so it had become May's best dress to wear on her afternoon off when she went out to tea with her ma.

"I think your dress is *most* elegant," she said slowly to Sarah. "You look really different in it. You don't look like the same Sarah I went to school with."

"Well I am," said Sarah stoutly. "And this is only my old blue dress that I've altered. I shortened it, and put a belt round the hips and sewed a lace collar on. It's like me, the same old thing underneath with a bit of fancy trimming on the top."

Aunt Betsy giggled, got up from the sofa, and followed Anne-Louise out into the scullery to fetch the cake. May quickly pushed the door shut and hurried round to Sarah.

"Sarah," she whispered. "Do you think you could get me a post in London? If it was someone you knew, ma would let me leave the village. I do *hate* working at Fawcett's . . ." She blushed and looked miserable. "He's such a *dirty* old man."

Sarah remembered that Mr Fawcett was a dirty old man, and indeed he had made her life humiliating and miserable while she had worked there. Her sympathy for May turned into a responsibility—she felt it was incumbent upon her to try and find some kind of job for her cousin in London.

"I thought of asking old Mr Masters at school," May

hurried on. "You know, he was so good at helping you to get away from the village—going to college and everything. I wondered if he would help me to find something—only domestic of course." She paused and added wistfully, "I would love to come to London."

She was pretty, but she had a dowdy, crushed look that came from a well-disciplined life devoid of any exictement whatsoever. Her blue eyes lacked animation and her hair—dark brown and very curly—was drawn back into a severe and unenterprising bun.

"I'll try," said Sarah. "You ask Mr Masters and I'll see what I can do in London. Maybe the Dances know someone who wants a domestic. There isn't much work at the moment but—yes—you ask Mr Masters—and I'll see what I can do."

Aunt Betsy stumped back into the kitchen with two plates, one had half a fruit cake and the other an untouched treacle tart. "You'll see what you can do about what?" she asked sharply.

The girls looked at one another, then glanced away.

"About her hair," said Sarah, suddenly inspired. "I promised I'd try and do her hair like mine. Ear-phones are more fashionable than a bun."

"Tea," said Anne-Louise coming back into the kitchen and banging the teapot down on the table. Jonathan came in and sat in his chair and then the back door slammed and three of her younger brothers hurried in, said " 'Lo Sarah," sat in their places and bowed their heads.

"Oh God, our Father . . ."

She closed her eyes with the rest of them, but she realised how much she had changed. She understood—so well—her cousin's desire to venture out and try her fortune in London. She understood, and she knew that the Dances, the Alexanders and all the families like the Alexanders, Miss Bennett, and the young man who ignored her, had made it impossible for her ever to live in the village again.

# Three

ALL the way to the Alexanders' she prayed they would be out—and knew that if they were it wouldn't solve her problem. It would just mean she would have to delay facing Mrs Alexander until another evening. Walking through Trinity Square she remembered what she was going to say. "I didn't actually promise Sammy wouldn't be thrashed in public. I just said I would do my best to see he wasn't. And I did do my best."

She knew it wasn't any good. A woman like Mrs Alexander wouldn't be interested in finer definitions of words and their meanings. She had trusted Sarah, and Sarah had betrayed that trust. The interview was going to be an unpleasant one.

Oh dear! she thought, her steps growing slower as she mounted the stone stairway. I do seem to be having a lot of disagreeable meetings with people at the moment.

Since her last trial of strength with Miss Bennett, nothing had happened. Miss Bennett ignored her and it was just a case of waiting until the report to the committee filtered through and her employment was terminated. She tried not to think what would happen after that. Once blacklisted, it would be almost impossible to find another post.

She knocked on the door, wondering if there would be a delay like the last time and hoping that there would be. But the door was opened immediately and Mr Alexander, once her identity had registered, stared coldly at her and said, "Yes?"

Sarah cleared her throat. "Could I speak to your wife, Mr Alexander?"

He didn't answer for a moment. His face was quite expressionless and he leant with one hand on the door handle and the other on the frame.

"I think you said quite enough to her last time you come, didn't you?"

She could feel colour mounting over her neck and face but a stubborn persistence kept her standing at the door when all she really wanted to do was run down the stairs and never see the Alexanders again.

"That's why I've come," she said doggedly. "To try and explain what happened . . . and . . . and to apologise."

"It's a bit late for explaining things, ain't it?" he asked aggressively.

She heard Mrs Alexander call, "Who's that? Who are you talking to, George?" and then the door opened a bit wider and Mrs Alexander stood there. When she saw Sarah she flushed and wiped her hands nervously down the sides of her overall. Mr Alexander put his arm round his wife's shoulder and Sarah began to feel she was heavily outnumbered.

"It's the schoolteacher, come to interfere and make a bit more trouble," he said unpleasantly. Mrs Alexander hurriedly opened the door a little wider.

"Well, there's no need for all the neighbors to know about it," she said, looking flustered and uncomfortable. "I don't want to talk about it on the doorstep. Come in if you must."

Miserably Sarah stepped inside. She felt just the way her ma always described her, huge and clumsy and ungainly. Her feet seemed to be twice their normal size and she tripped over the door mat and mumbled "Sorry" to the cold faces of the watching Alexanders.

She had thought, when waiting at the front door, that nothing could possibly make her feel more wretched. But when she saw the young man, the foreign young man, sitting at the table she realised she was to be spared nothing.

"I'm sorry," she said reaching for the door handle.

"I didn't know you had company. I'll come back another time."

Mr Alexander walked over to the table and sat down. "You can say what you've come to say. I'm not ashamed of letting my friends know the kind of treatment my son gets from his schoolteacher."

"Yes . . . but . . . as it's private family business, I thought . . ."

Mr Alexander suddenly stood up. "It's a bit more private than my boy had when he was walloped, ain't it?" he shouted. "You've only got one witness. My son had the whole school watching him, didn't he? And the janitor and a master to stop him from running away. In a fine old state he was when he came home . . . crying . . . all the evening he was crying . . . wouldn't eat his tea or nothing. And a right old time the missus has had getting him to go to school since then. Frightened of going to school he is. So you get on and say what you've got to say, and then get out!"

Mrs Alexander was bitting her lower lip and she kept trying to interrupt her husband. She put her hand on his arm in order to quieten him, "You'll only make it worse, George," she said tremulously. "You'll make it bad for Sammy."

With a deep sense of hurt Sarah realised the woman was afraid of her . . . afraid of the power she wielded at school. In Mrs Alexander's eyes Sarah was a monster who must be classified alongside Miss Bennett.

"I don't want to hurt Sammy," she said softly. "I never wanted him thrashed. I tried to stop it. I did my best to persuade Miss Bennett to punish him privately. I wouldn't hurt him."

"Looks like it, don't it?" said Mr Alexander nastily.

Her temper flared. She had come expecting anger, an icy rejection, or even a pathetic lack of defence of any kind. She had not expected to be bullied and she was stung into fighting back.

"I didn't have to come, Mr Alexander!" she snapped. "I did my best to stop the public punishment, and I failed. I should not have presuaded your wife to let the boy come back to school. I should not have made promises I could not keep. So I have come here to say I'm sorry. I can't do anything to put it right. All I can do is say I'm sorry. And if it will make you feel any better I can tell you that I am quite likely to lose my job over the whole business!"

She was nearly crying, partly because of being bullied but also with rage. "I'll go now," she choked. "But before I do I'd like to point out that Sammy isn't the only one who is terrified of Miss Bennett. And Sammy can only be thrashed, not put back on the unemployment list." She strode towards the door and opened it. "Good day to you. And I hope you . . . and your friend there . . . have enjoyed being unpleasant."

She darted one brief glance at the young man. He was sitting staring down at the table and his face bore no expression at all. Then he was blotted out by the figure of Mrs Alexander who had followed her to the door. "Don't mind George," she whispered anxiously. "He didn't mean to be so rude. It's just he's got a lot on his mind at the moment . . . you know . . . with the railways and the strike coming and all. He was upset when Sammy came home that time. He don't mean to be rude."

Sarah tried to smile but she was struggling not to cry and the smile turned into a grimace. "I'm sorry, Mrs Alexander. I tried. I really did try."

Mrs Alexander nodded. "That's all right, dear. I know what that woman . . . I mean Miss Bennett, is like," she hesitated and asked, "Are you really going to lose your job?"

"I expect so," said Sarah wearily. "But I'd have lost it anyway. I keep doing things wrong. She doesn't like me very much."

"Well I'm sorry about that," answered Mrs Alexander softly. There was a moment of indecisive silence and then she added, "Would you like to come back for a cup of tea?"

Sarah shook her head. "I'll go now."

"All right then. Good-bye. And don't mind Mr Alexander. He didn't mean it."

Sarah walked down the stairs. She hoped, fervently, she would never have to come up them again.

She was putting her books together in the staff room two days later when Miss Enderby twittered nervously into the room. "Miss Whitman . . . a man . . . waiting at the staff entrance. He asked for you. And really . . . Miss Bennett . . . you know she doesn't like it. She spoke to me some time ago about men waiting for you outside the school."

Sarah frantically stuffed the last of her books into the second-hand music case she used as teacher's bag. "Drat Charlie," she muttered. "I told him not to wait there! He'll get me into even more trouble, not that it matters now I suppose." She forced her arm into one sleeve of her coat, jammed her hat down hard and ran for the door, trying to put the other arm in her coat as she ran.

Why can't he do as he's asked! she thought irritably. She hurried out and looked quickly in either direction. There was no sign of Miss Bennett in the passage and she slammed the outer door of the staff entrance behind her. Then—when she saw the figure waiting for her— she stopped.

It wasn't Charlie. It was the young man. He was leaning up against the school railings with his hands in his pockets. He was wearing a belted navy-blue velour coat and no hat. His hair was dark and very curly. When he saw her he took his hands out of his pockets. "Hello," he said.

She was disconcerted, and she was trying to get her arm into her coat sleeve, but she still had wit enough to look along towards the window of Miss Bennett's room.

"I've something to say to you," said the young man.

She saw movement—a shadow—behind the window. Desperation finally got her arm into her coat and she said very quickly, "Well can you say it somewhere else, please. Not in front of the school railings. I'm not sup- posed to have men . . . people waiting for me outside the school. I've been told about it."

She began walking away from the school and as soon as they came to the side road she turned into it. The young man had studs in his boots and they made a loud ringing noise on the cobbles.

Once the immediate threat of Miss Bennett was removed she was able to dart a quick glance at him. He was very serious, but this time he was looking at her—noticing her. His eyes were a lightish brown and although he wasn't smiling—did he ever smile?—he didn't look as absorbed in his own thoughts as he had the first time she saw him. Automatically she began to follow her normal route home to Auntie Florrie and Uncle Max.

"I decided I had to say something to you," said the young man very earnestly. "You see, I know you're a bourgeois do-gooder who is grinding down the faces of the poor, but I still think it was very brave of you—morally brave—to go and see the Alexanders after what had happened. I thought a lot of you for doing that."

She was astonished.

"What do you mean?" she asked angrily. "A bourgeois do-gooder? What are you talking about?"

He began to walk faster, explaining and waving his hands excitedly in the air. "Of course you're bourgeois," he said vehemently. "Middle-class bourgeois education, and coming into poor people's homes to interfere with their children. You don't really know anything about poor people at all. You go round teaching their children, handing out things to the poor and thinking you're being kind and helping them when of course you're not. You're treating them like pets, like you would a dog or a horse—give them enough to eat and lots of discipline and they'll be all right."

She was so astounded that she couldn't even answer. Rage and indignation bubbled inside her but the young man didn't even notice. He was too busy talking.

"But after I saw you the other evening, I decided you weren't deliberately grinding down the faces of the poor. I decided you were just ignorant of what's going on around you. I think you *mean* well, but you've had too easy a life to understand about things." He pushed his hand into his pocket and pulled out his cap. "I wondered where my cap was," he said without pause or change of voice.

Sarah took a deep breath and gathered her rage for one outburst of indignation.

"I think you're the most rude, objectionable young man I have ever met," she said furiously. "You were rude to me the first time you saw me—pushing past on the stairs and ignoring me. You don't know anything about me, nothing at all. You've no manners, no manners at all. You're . . . you're rude!" She was so incensed she couldn't even think of a new word to use. Later she would be able to plan an intelligent and cutting reply in which she would coolly and decisively tear his righteousness to shreds. But at the moment she could think of nothing but "rude."

He stopped walking and faced her, looking bothered and surprised. "*Was* I rude?" he asked. "I mean, was I really rude?"

"Yes," said Sarah curtly.

"How was I rude?" he asked disarmingly. Sarah fought for words. She was angry, astonished, and roused as she could never remember being roused before. She tried to tell the young man why and how he was rude.

"You don't tell people that they're —what d'you call it—bourgeois and face-grinders when you don't even know them. You don't know anything about me. Nothing at all. You've no right to say things like that to me when you don't know anything. Why, you don't even know my name!"

"Yes I do," he said imperturbably. "It's Sarah Whitman. I found out from the young Alexanders. And I know lots about you. You don't spend as much time on arithmetic as you should and you're always talking about Egypt and India and places where there are mountains and deserts. You're good at reading and you put lots of expression into the books and no one in the class really listens because they like watching your face when you read. It makes them laugh."

Sarah's face was instantly transfused with hot colour. "They like you though," said the young man hastily. "Even though you're bourgeois. But then those children are too young to know that you're one of the enemy."

"Good-bye!" said Sarah.

She quickened her stride and so did the young man. And her gesture was wasted because almost at once they came to Aunt Florrie's and instead of sweeping away from him she had to stop and fumble with the gate.

"Do you live here?" he asked, stunned, gazing up at the narrow terraced house with the three feet of concrete that separated the front door from the iron gate.

"Yes," she answered savagely. "I sit in my little upstairs room by the window that is always getting broken because the boys are playing rounders in the street. And when my Auntie Florrie gives me long enough on my own I brood over new ways of grinding down the faces of the poor."

He suddenly looked very uncomfortable. He took his cap from his head and stuffed it back in his pocket. "Well I still think you're bourgeois," he muttered. "But just the same, I wanted to tell you that I thought you were brave—going to see them. Lots of people wouldn't have done that."

He spoke English just like any other Londoner, but there was something different about it—the odd phrase that was out of place—an occasional intonation on the wrong syllable. And the way he used his hands when he was talking, that was foreign too.

"You're not English, are you?" asked Sarah. She hadn't meant it to sound cutting or patronising but he flushed and said aggressively, "Yes, I am. I'm as English as you. I was born two days after my family landed here and that makes me just as English as anyone else in this country."

He seemed to be sensitive about it and she was human enough to feel pleased that she had stung him into a defence of some kind. She made a note to remember that the next time he called her bourgeois she must call him a foreigner. And then she realised that already she was planning what to say when they met again, and that was ridiculous. Why should she ever see such a rude young man again? She looked at him, and was startled to see how his face had changed, had become vulnerable and unhappy with all the fire and animation drained away from him.

"What's the matter?" she asked.

"Nothing. Nothing the matter." His misplaced speech was more pronounced.

"Oh, no! Surely you're not upset because I asked if you were foreign?"

"Not upset." But he was. She could see that he was unhappy because of her remark and she could see, too, that for him, being called a foreigner was far, far worse than it was for her being called bourgeois—whatever that was.

Impulsively she put her hand up and touched his arm. "Oh, please! Don't be hurt because I asked if you were foreign. It isn't important—only it *is* important if you're upset. I didn't mean anything. I was just interested because—like the children said—I love talking about places far away— countries over the sea. Please don't be hurt!"

It became very important to her because she knew that people—everyone—had inside them a special deep place of hurt, or it could be shame, or guilt. And you could fight someone and quarrel with them, and it was still all right providing you didn't cut into that private pain and use it as a weapon. She knew her father's personal agony was her sister Harriet, living out her life in a home for the abnormal. And her ma couldn't bear to speak, or even to think, about pa's first wife.

"Please," she said fiercely. "Please, you mustn't be upset. I couldn't bear it if I'd made you unhappy."

And then he smiled—a warm, bright, exciting smile that completely changed his face and made his eyes turn lighter in colour.

There was a gaiety, a style about him that made him seem young and relaxed and full of fun.

"You've a lovely face, Sarah Whitman," he grinned. He gazed down at her for a moment and then she became aware that the lace curtains in Aunt Florrie's parlour were stirring against the windowpane.

"I'm going in now." She didn't really know what to

say to him, but because his smile was so wide and infectious she had to smile back.

"Good-bye," he said.

He put the cap back on his head, stuffed his hands back into his pockets and walked jauntily down the road. When he came to the end he looked back, then vanished round the corner.

"And I quite forgot to ask his name," she said dreamily to a curious Aunt Florrie who was opening the door in her face. "I completely forgot to ask his name."

# Four

SHE made up her mind that, if she saw him again, the first thing she would ask would be his name. But when the time came she was so agitated she forgot everything but the need to get him away from the school gates as quickly as possible.

She came out of the staff room in time to coincide with Miss Bennett. The headmistress inclined her head and, in silence, they walked together to the staff entrance. Sarah quickly leapt ahead, opened the door, and stood respectfully aside for Miss Bennett to leave first. When she followed Miss Bennett out into the yard she took one look towards the railings, and with sinking heart recognised the figure waiting for her. Miss Bennett turned a stony face towards her.

"I believe I have told you about this before, Miss Whitman."

"Yes, Miss Bennett. I am very sorry. I will see it does not happen again. I will get rid of him at once." She was gabbling and her last words were flung back over her shoulder as she hurried for the gate, anxious to get him away quickly before Miss Bennett could see him properly.

"I told you," she whispered fiercely. "I told you not to wait for me here. That's the headmistress and I'm really in trouble now."

She took hold of his arm and pushed him rapidly along the road in the opposite direction to the one Miss Bennett would be taking. Stubbornly, he refused to be hurried.

"A typical example of upper-class autocracy," he

said airily, staring back at the disappearing figure of Miss Bennett. "You have allowed yourself to be victimised by her birth and authority. You should stand against her. Fight for your rights as an individual."

"Oh, don't talk rubbish!" She hadn't been in his company a minute and already she was annoyed. "There's too many schoolteachers and not enough vacancies. I've probably already lost this place—over the Alexander affair—but I don't want to make things any worse than they are."

She had begun to hope that perhaps her dismissal wasn't as imminent as she had feared. Five weeks had elapsed since the thrashing, and still no letter of dismissal or an order to appear before the committee had been presented to her. Perhaps—she hardly dared think about it—perhaps Miss Bennett had not sent up a special report about her. Perhaps she was going to wait until the end of the probationary year and then send in a generally unsatisfactory account of Sarah's behaviour during the year, but without making a special point of the Alexander incident. Whatever was happening, Sarah was trying as hard as she could not to antagonise Miss Bennett any further.

"You are a typical sequence in the order of a present-day capitalist society," he answered. "You are a bourgeois oppressor of the poor who is, in turn, oppressed by your tyrannical headmistress."

"You're the most stupid young man I've ever met!" she retorted. "You just go around with your head in the clouds, talking nonsense that has nothing to do with the way people live, or work, or eat and drink or anything. And what do *you* do for a living? That's what I'd like to know. You're so clever at criticising me ... what do *you* do for a living?"

"I work on the railway," he said loftily. "I'm a railway clerk. But that is not my real work. I'm not always going to be a railway clerk. One day I'm going to lead the people into a perfect society!"

"Stuff!" said Sarah rudely. "You're just an impolite, aggressive young man who goes around annoying people. You're a rude, young, railway clerk, and one day you'll be a rude, old, railway clerk. What do you ever do about trying to lead the people into a perfect society?"

His brown eyes studied her seriously for a moment. "I do a lot," he answered. "I'm the delegate for my branch of the union—I'm the youngest there. And I'm making them all believe in it. We've got to believe in it because there isn't anything else. And I'm organising our part in the big strike for the whole of this area. That's what I was doing at the Alexanders'. When the strike comes this district is going to be the best organised in the whole of the country!"

"You're doing what!"

"Organising the strike. It's coming you know. A national strike. The whole of the country. Any time now."

"But . . . but that's wicked!" Living and working in a district where nearly everyone was poor, where several were unemployed, she still had never had a personal encounter with a revolutionary. One continually read about the terrifying Bolsheviks—evil, sacrilegious, bloodthirsty—but this was the first time she had come face to face with one.

His face suddenly flamed and he began waving his arms about, like he had the last time she had seen him. "What's wicked about trying to stop a miner's pay from being cut? What's wicked about that, tell me, eh? Some of them have to take a quarter less wages than they had before? So what's wicked about that?"

She hadn't expected him to say that. She'd expected him to shout something silly about oppressors and grinding down the faces of the poor, and the fact that he had come out with a reality that a lot of people were feeling bad about—nobody really thought the miner's pay *should* be cut—made her a little uncertain of how to argue.

"It's the *way* you're trying to stop it," she said earnestly. "Using force and starting revolutions. Making everyone stop work—not that you will because everyone says it will all be settled before that happens. But it's wicked and wrong to try . . . and it won't solve anything."

"So you tell me a better way!" he shouted.

She began to feel nervous. To be truthful she didn't

know too much about the miners and the way things were happening at the moment. She knew there had been something called a Sankey Commission, and now there was something called a Samuel Commission, and everyone felt very relieved because Commissions had a kind of omnipotent sound about them, and they would be able to sort everything out so that everyone was pleased. She knew that there had nearly been a strike last summer but that Baldwin had settled it all at the last moment. And this time it would probably be settled in just the same way.

"Go on. Tell me!" he shouted again.

"They can settle it by discussion," she said feebly. "If everyone behaved sensibly and talked about things, there's no reason why it couldn't be settled by discussion."

"They've been discussing for five years! Five years! And what has happened?"

"I don't know what's happened," she flared back at him, tired of being bullied and tired of being made to feel she was stupid. "I don't know what's happened, but I do know that sensible God-fearing people wouldn't start strikes and revolutions just because of a lot of Bolshevik talk."

"That's the kind of stupid bourgeois thing you would say!" he stung back. "Only ignorant, middle-class people like you and the families you come from talk about God, and duty to one's betters and all that rubbish!"

She was really angry then, because when he sneered so disparagingly at God-fearing people she immediately thought of her pa, and her Aunt Betsy, and all the people in the village who worked hard, and went to Meeting on Sundays, and were honest and had very little money but were too ashamed to let anyone know about their poverty.

"I'm just sick and tired of hearing you talk about my middle-class background," she raged. "My pa's a country postman and I managed to become a teacher because of getting government grants and because my pa gave me a bit of money from time to time. He's worked hard all his life, and he's never oppressed anyone, and what's more he's polite and doesn't bully people . . ." She suddenly became aware that he was laughing at her and it made her even more angry.

"And I think what you're doing is wicked! You're going to someone like that poor Mr Alexander who isn't clever enough to understand things for himself, and you're talking him into doing all kinds of things that will only make trouble for him and his family."

"You're lovely, Sarah! You're lovely," he said excitedly. "When you lose your temper and you get upset you're really beautiful . . . you're strong and warm and . . . I nver saw anyone so beautiful when they were talking about the miners before."

She was confused. She had never met anyone like him and she didn't understand him. He was quick and volatile—at one point talking silly nonsense that made him ridiculous, and then somehow turning it into something personal. He was bad-tempered and good-humoured all in the space of a few seconds and she didn't know how to talk to him. And she felt tired from arguing. Charlie never argued with her like this. Charlie was most restful to be with.

"You don't listen to anything I say," she said irritably. "You've closed your mind to everything but your own ideas."

"But you don't say anything worth listening to," he replied amiably. "You see, you're blinded with the things you've been taught all your life. For a start you still believe in God. And everyone knows that there's no such thing . . . believing in God is ignorant superstition."

He had gone too far. For Sarah—with a strict nonconformist background—it was more than blasphemy—it was a negation of everything in her life . . . of her father, grieving over Harriet, of her Aunt Betsy who still cried in private over the death of her sailor husband, of her own achievements which had been brought about by people who believed in God and therefore wanted to help her. If there was no God to comfort and sustain, then how could they all bear their grief and poverty?

"I'm sorry," she said quietly to him. "I have to go now. Good-bye."

The animation left him and his face became shuttered, expressing nothing at all because he sensed her rejection. A barrier had risen and now she wasn't prepared to agree or disagree with him. She had closed herself away behind English politeness.

"Could I see you . . . I mean I would like to talk to you again if . . ."

"I'm sorry," she cried. "But we don't really believe in the same things, do we?" To see him again would be a betrayal of her father and her family, of her brother Peter who had no one close to him except herself, and even a betrayal of the generous, lovable Dances who hardly ever went to Church, never said grace at mealtimes, who drank, bet on horses and generally behaved in a worldly way but who nonetheless, believed in God. How could they survive the sorrow of their war-dead if they didn't believe in God?

"Good-bye" she said again, and she walked away and left him.

She still didn't know his name but now it didn't matter because she wouldn't be seeing him any more.

His name was David Baron. In the old country it would have been Baranowicz, but then in the old country a great many things, other than his name, would have been different. In the old country he wouldn't be working on the railway, or belong to a trade union, or speak to strange young women in the street the way he had spoken to Sarah. In the old country he would have been, like his father and his grandfather, a shoemaker, a worker of fine leather, making the high, soft boots that were worn by the merchants of the nearby towns and the local kulaks, making harnesses and saddles for minor government officials. He would live, as his father had lived, in a three-roomed house along with his parents and numerous brothers and sisters, and when the time came for him to marry he would wed a girl selected for him by his parents and the local marriage-broker.

His parents had come, as so many had come at the turn of the century as an escape from the pogroms of the Tsarist régime. They had originally intended to go to America, but his mother, with two small children and another about to be born, had stated from her berth in the overcrowded ship that she had to have her baby on dry land. They had a cousin who lived in Whitechapel and they had left the ship—after a heated argument with the captain about a refund of fares—and had arrived on the cousin's doorstep at eleven o'clock one January evening in 1900. Two days later, David had been born, the first of their "British" children, the one most dear to their hearts, and the one they most expected to bring them credit.

They hadn't intended to change their name. They were proud of being Baranowicz because, in the old country, it was a family much respected in the community. When Jacob Baranowicz had gone along to register with the authorities, the official behind the desk had asked, "Name?" and when the heavily accented reply had come "Jacob Avrom Baranowicz" the registrar had not bothered to ask about the spelling but had merely entered "Baron" on the form because that was the nearest English sound. Indeed, he was surprised that Jacob Baranowicz could speak English at all.

But Jacob Baranowicz, or Baron as he was now to be called, was an unusual young man, quite unlike most of his fellow *émigrés* escaping from the east. For he could not only speak English, he was also slightly conversant with English and American history, and knew a little of the social conditions of those two great democracies.

In his youth he had been a rebel, sullenly resenting the old way of life, the narrowness of a religious community turned inward upon itself. He was bright, and had studied well under the tuition of the village rabbi, although his allocated role in the community life was to be, as his father and grandfather had been, the village shoemaker and leather worker. As he grew older his rebellion increased, fretting against the confines of life where the pattern was strictly laid out, where he knew what he would do, the kind of girl he would marry, where he would live for the rest of his life. There was no challenge, no adventure. The only unexpected things that could occur would be the savage descents of Cossack youths, drunken raidings where a few women were assaulted, a few houses set on fire, and a sabre thrust through anyone who tried to defend their property.

He yearned for adventure, for the chance to break-away from the village and see the world beyond, but for Jacob and the young men like him, there was ho chance to explore. The laws of Imperial Russia made it difficult for them to test their abilities against the rest of the population. He must remain a shoemaker until he died.

And then, to the village, had come one of the most curious anomalies of the nineteenth century, a Quaker, the last member of a small group of Anglo-American Friends who were making quiet little forays into various countries, teaching a little, farming a little, but above all gathering information about the world about them.

John Watt had broken his leg in an experiment with some farm machinery. He had been left behind because the funds of the group were nearly exhausted, and on his recovery he had travelled as cheaply, but as widely as he could on his route home.

When he came to the village he had at first been shunned. The community had suffered too much from outsiders, and they had a combined fear and contempt for anyone who was not of their own society. And then he had encountered Jacob, a young boy avid for news of the outside world, for a chance to see new—strange—people who lived and worked in a life that was not bounded by the word of the old men and by the teachings of the *Torah*.

In all probability any other stranger to the village would have shocked and distressed the boy because, rebellious though he was, the traditions of his people were too deeply ingrained for him to accept ideas that were alien to his inherent faith. But—widely different as the two men were—there was still a strong similarity in their background. The Quaker community was an in-

drawn, interwoven society too. They did not even have
to explain to each other the meaning of a community
where every member was dependent on every other
member, where there were certain forms and rituals of
family and custom that must be carefully observed.
They did not have to explain to each other the value of
learning. Their teachings were different, but both knew
that learning was the most important thing in a man's
life. And there was the timidity—for Jacob the timidity
of a people continually at the wrong end of violence—
a people who were forbidden to défend themselves.
And for John Watt the timidity of a people who had
deliberately renounced violence, no matter what that
renunciation might bring upon them.

The middle-aged Quaker and the young boy had met
and almost immediately had been consumed by the
mental horizons of each other.

Somehow, in Russian that was nearly unintelligible
on both sides (for John Watt spoke it with the stiff
inflexibility of an Englishman, and the boy's first
language was Yiddish) they managed to converse. In
spite of the resentment and disapproval of the elders
and teachers in the village, John Watt had taught Jacob
something of the west, of the new democracies and of
political systems that seemed incredible to a boy whose
hereditary knowledge was of persecution and confine-
ment. With a speed that was the result of long frustrated need he had learned a comprehensive but ap-
pallingly pronounced English. And then the Quaker
had gone home, leaving a young man who had wit-
nessed his first taste of freedom.

Ten years later, when the pogroms had started again,
he realised the dream for which he had been secretly
saving ever since John Watt had left. With his reluctant
wife and two children he had set out for the great
countries of the west—arriving by accident in England
instead of America (later to be joined by three of his
brothers), but not too bothered because they were both
countries where a man could achieve an ambition—
could grow to a stature that was impossible in the old
country.

He could so easily have been disillusioned—by poverty, by prejudice, by the fact that he was a foreigner living in a country where foreigners were considered interesting but peculiar. That he was not disillusioned was due to his own temperament. He was still a shoemaker, he was still poor, and he still lived in a strict and closed community. But he believed that he could do all the other things if only he wished to. Sometimes he would get on an omnibus and travel to Richmond or to Windsor, just to prove to himself that there was no limitation on his travel. He would go to meetings—any kind of meeting—where he could hardly understand what was being said but could delight in the knowledge that the chance to be there was his.

To his beloved son, David, he had imparted his sense of freedom, his belief that in this country anything could be done if one desired it strongly enough. He could have trained the boy to be a shoemaker like himself—there was a good living to be made at the trade, but again he wanted to prove to himself that he, and his family, could if they wished work at any kind of trade in this country.

"My son," he would say fondly to his friends. "My son, he has a post on the railway! An important, responsible position! On the railway—like an Englishman! Can you see that in the old country?"

He could no longer follow the learning of his son. The boy had studied at evening classes and absorbed all kinds of ideas that were beyond him and the teachings of his generation. But he was proud of David because he believed his son was using the chances that life in this country offered.

And then, one day, he found that his son had absorbed the idea of freedom to the exclusion of everything else. The idea of freedom had replaced God, and the Jewish Law, and the belief of his people. His son, for whom he wished so much had become—like himself so many years ago—a rebel.

David, nurtured on freedom and the faith of personal achievement, had discarded God. He believed in Karl Marx, in the strength of peoples, in the dream of a Utopian society where, once poverty and ignorance were abolished, man would become a complete and perfect being.

He was more like his father than he knew. His rebellion was akin to his father's in the old country, and Sarah Whitman had captured his imagination just as John Watt had fired his father so many years ago.

Sarah, unwittingly, had the qualities to which both he and his father were drawn—a serenity, a strength that came from the soil, and a mysterious, unfathomable "something" that was a dream, a secret knowledge, a source of joy. He despised her for her ignorance and for her self-possessed assumption that what she believed in was right. But her face, her personality, her secret smile excited him emotionally and intellectually. She was so . . . English!

He had denounced God to her almost as a mark of defiance, knowing it would shock and offend her (and secretly he was a little shocked at himself). Her rejection had wounded him deeply. He had never thought that she would retire so swiftly behind her secret self—would cut him off from the exciting strength of her personality with just a very brief, "I have to go. Goodbye."

He was hurt and miserable and his hurt turned to disparaging hate.

"She's nothing," he said to himself as he stumped unhappily along the pavement. "She's typically English—arrogant and a snob with no time for anyone who isn't as English as she is. They're all the same, these people, and she's one of the worst. She's nothing, just an ignorant, bourgeois nothing."

But even while he tried to convince himself of her worthlessness, of her shallow ideas and beliefs, he knew in his heart that it wasn't true.

# *Five*

ON the evening of the first day of the strike, he saw
Sarah. He was on his way to do picket duty at the
station when he saw her riding on the back of a bright
red motorcyle. She was holding on to the young man
in front with one hand, and gripping tightly to her hat
with the other. The young man had his cap turned
back to front with the peak pulled well down over the
nape of his neck and Sarah was laughing. Her face was
flushed and her eyes bright and excited and David
Baron experienced a sudden jolt of pain because she
looked so happy. He hadn't really felt happy himself
since the last time he'd seen her, but then he had
realised that in the present scheme of things he had no
*right* to be happy. He was busy organising a social
revolution and there was too much to do for serious-
minded people to have time to be happy.

He was finding this particular revolution more difficult to organise than he had thought—he hadn't realised
just how much could go wrong if things weren't planned
down to the last detail. *His* strike was running beautifully, but reports were trickling in that in other parts
of the country, things weren't stopping as efficiently
as they should have been. And the reports from
Union Headquarters were confusing and sometimes
contradictory. He burned with frustrated energy because he felt that if only they had let him arrange
everything in the whole of the country, he could have
done it so much better.

His own band of strikers were imbued with the

overflow of his own energetic faith. He had inspired the
half-hearted, whipped the lazy into action, and in-
flamed the nervous with the heat of his own passion.
At one point, when the reminder from the railway com-
panies had been issued—"The Company desires to im-
press upon the staff that if they leave work in the manner indicated, they will be breaking their contract of
service"—one or two of the men with families had become afraid. The reminder was too obviously a veiled
threat of dismissal and consequent unemployment.
Again David had bolstered, encouraged, almost carried
the men along with his fiery strength. Sometimes he forgot that he was only twenty-six, he felt so old, so responsible for everyone, for the railway strikers, for the
miners, for everyone. And now that things were turning out to be a little muddled, a little badly arranged,
he felt it was all his fault. And he felt frustrated because he didn't have the power to set everything right.

The motorcycle pulled into the kerb a little way
ahead of him and Sarah climbed carefully down onto
the pavement. She straightened her hat and he saw her
laugh again at the grinning young man, and then wave
when the cycle roared away in a mixture of bangs and
fumes. He hurried up behind her and without any pre-
liminary greeting burst out with, "What were you doing
on that bike? This isn't your way home from school.
This is going in the opposite direction!"

Sarah looked sheepish. "I know. But I don't suppose
I'll ever get a chance to ride on a motor bicycle again.
And today, without any buses or trams, everyone is
giving everyone else rides. It's quite respectable, because of the strike."

He suddenly wished he wasn't responsible for running a revolution or leading the people into a perfect
society. He wished he had a job with lots of money so
that he could buy a B.M.C. motor bicycle and go roaring off down the road with Sarah on the back. Because
he wished it so very much he said stuffily, "This strike
is a very serious business you know. Too many people
are treating it as fun."

"I know." She was a little ashamed. She remembered

telling him that the strike wouldn't happen. And now here he was, wearing an arm band and looking very responsible and tired while she was accepting rides from young men on motor bicycles. Then she remembered the other thing—the way he had spoken about God and her family.

"Good-bye," she said swiftly, and began to walk back in the direction from which she had just come.

"Sarah!"

She stopped, but didn't look at him.

"Please. Can't I see you again? Perhaps we don't believe in the same things, but that's what is interesting about people, isn't it? The way we're all different?" He had struck the right note. Sarah could not resist anything that was "different."

"You're very different," she said reluctantly. "I never met anyone like you before."

"Will you see me again then?"

She considered. He looked older and more responsible and he was obviously trying to be polite. She smiled, warily.

"Yes. All right. I'll see you again. But not outside school. I'll meet you . . . here . . . no, at the Elephant. I'll meet you there."

"When?"

"Next week. This time next week." She was about to walk away when she remembered something. "I don't even know your name," she said.

"David. David Baron."

"David Baron." It sounded nice the way she said it. She had a slight soft burr of the country when she spoke slowly.

"Good-bye then." She turned and began to walk away. He watched her—tall, well-built, and walking awkwardly because she knew he was looking at her. She seemed to carry a bright warmth with her and everyone around her looked dull and ordinary.

When she had disappeared he began to run down the Old Kent Road, dodging in and out of the masses of people walking and just standing about. Suddenly the strike was wonderful again. He would be able to manage everything on his own. If necessary he would even go up to Wales and run their affair for them as well.

He got to Willow Walk Station and saw that the other pickets were already on duty and that some rather nervous students were in the shunting yard messing ineffectually about with the engines.

"Come on, lads!" he said excitedly to his followers. "Up on the bridge over the line!" He felt so happy he had to stop himself from laughing out loud. He grabbed several lumps of coal from the siding and raced up over the bridge.

"Scabs! Blacklegs!" he shouted joyfully to the students below, and threw the coal down on their heads.

She had been called round to a family meeting at the Dances' and, because of the bicycle ride, she was late. When she got there they were all up in ma's bedroom and she had to squeeze past Maisie to get inside. Charlie beckoned her over to stand beside him but there were too many oversized Dances to push round and so she shook her head and stayed where she was, sandwiched between a large Maisie and an even larger Aunt Florrie.

"And so," wheezed ma from the bed, "me and Dad have talked things over and we've decided that the family must stand by the country—like we did in the war! Ain't that right, pa?"

Pa, in collarless shirt that sported a brass stud at the front, nodded heartily. "T'ain't that we don't feel sorry for the miners," he breathed noisily. "We do. I've said to yer ma many times, 'Ma,' I've said, 'those poor little kids in Wales ought to come down 'ere and 'ave one of your good feeds. That's what they need.' 'Aven't I said that to you, ma, lots of times?"

"You 'ave, pa. You 'ave. But what I say is, feeding the poor little devils is one thing. Threatening to murder the King and Queen is another."

This was too much, even for the Dances. Charlie looked a bit bothered and said protestingly, "Who said anything about murdering the King and Queen?"

Ma turned her mighty body in the bed and the pink

satin cover heaved and writhed over the convolutions
beneath. "That's what they did in Russia. Murdered
their poor King and Queen. And when things like
strikes start happening 'ere, then it's time the family
put a stop to it."

There was mumbled assent in the room. The menfolk cleared their throats and grumbled their accord
with ma's basic political reasoning. Maisie turned to
Sarah and said, "Well, of course, ma's right you
know."

"And so," ma pontificated, "all you boys what are
not working at the moment, you get up to Whitehall
tomorrow, and sign on for doing your bit for the country. That's what we think is right, don't we, pa?"

Pa rubbed his hands over his stomach. "Got to do
your bit," he growled. "I'm too old, and besides they
need me down in the market. But, Charlie, you can go.
And Bert and Sid. And you girls over there. Tell your
'usbands to get on and do their bit. We can spare two
of them from the market."

There was an affable silence in the room. It was
compounded of family unity and a complacent sense of
everyone knowing they were right. It irritated Sarah
and she felt a sudden urge to annoy them all.

"What about the miners?" She was horrified as soon
as she had spoken and she couldn't think what had
made her throw such an explosive comment into the
room. They all turned, stared at her, then looked at ma
for an answer. Ma breathed heavily.

"Like pa said, we're sorry for them. Goodness knows
with Charlie and Bert and Ivy's Sid, all out of work,
we know it ain't easy when the money stops coming
in. But striking ain't the way to settle things. They
ought to sit down and 'ave a good talk with Mr Baldwin."

"But they've been talking for five years! And nothing's happened!" And then she remembered where she
had heard it before—remembered whose words she
was quoting, whose opinions she was expressing, because they weren't really her own. She didn't believe in
the strike any more than the Dances did. She thought

it was wrong too, and now that wretched David Baron had made her say something stupid in front of the family.

Ma stared hard at Sarah. "You trying to say you think it's *right*, Sarah?"

"No, of course not," Sarah mumbled.

"Where'd you get all these Russian ideas then?"

"No one . . . nowhere . . . I was just talking to someone and . . ."

Charlie was staring at her now with an expression of hurt reproach on his face and, remembering her promise to meet David Baron next week, she was aware of a double disloyalty, to the family ideals, and to Charlie.

"You want to go against the family?" solemnised ma.

"No. Of course not."

"Right. Then let's 'ear no more nonsense like that. It's all decided then. Down to offer yourselves to the country." The serious business over, ma relaxed and shouted to Maisie, "Let those kids come up. I got some 'umbugs for them."

There was a changing shift of Dances—large old ones replaced by large young ones. Charlie, in the general jostle, managed to get alongside Sarah as she was going down the stairs.

"What d'you say all those things for, Sarah?" he asked troubled. "I know ma goes off, and half the time she don't know what she's talking about. But why did you say those things? She don't understand all that business with the miners' talks and so on. You shouldn't upset her like that with things she don't understand."

"But you agree with her?"

"Not with what she said. But I agree with what the family's decided. I think we've all got to go to Whitehall tomorrow."

She felt mean again. Here she was upsetting poor Charlie and Ma Dance, and it was all those silly ideas she had culled from David Baron.

She began to look forward to seeing him next week.

It was a strange week, a warm week of long, soft, early summer evenings. The streets were packed. No one had ever realised that quite so many people lived in London and now they were all out, strikers, walkers, strollers who wanted to see the fun. Sometimes the streets were pleasant and amiable to walk in. At other times, not.

Buses were stoned, the windows broken, the drivers pelted with eggs and decaying refuse. A bunch of "gay young things" who were having the time of their lives acting as special constables, found themselves directed into a Whitechapel cul-de-sac where they received the contents of the local chamber-pots on their heads.

It was equally rousing in other parts of the country. In Hull a determined effort to get a train service working met with bitter opposition. Trains were turned over and burned until finally the Navy threatened to move in and restore civil order. In Leeds an angry crowd gathered around buses that had been organised to take wool workers to their factories. In desperation a Union leader pulled a revolver on the inspector of the depot, claiming he would use it if the buses ran. The stucco-ornamented fun piers of Brighton, Margate, Scarborough and the holiday coast were used to unload coal, petrol and food. Revolution was rife and it was only the British sense of the ridiculous that prevented it from becoming a reality.

The day before she was due to meet David, rumours began to circulate that the strike would soon be over. No one, least of all the Union leaders or the government, seemed to know what was happening, but somehow things had become a little half-hearted. Men were drifting back to work, one or two, here and there. Discussions were reinstated and there was a feeling that everything was about to crumble, that the country had won and that soon everyone would be back at work.

There were so many people at the Elephant that she had to push and fight her way to the place where she was meeting him. And the crowd began to frighten her a little. They were in an ugly mood and the majority of them were obviously strikers who were confused by the conflicting reports—on the one hand the strike was to be continued—on the other that it had already been called off. When she met David she was shocked to see how ill he looked—completely drained of colour and with his eyes sunk right back into his skull.

"Are you all right?" she asked curiously, and was embarrassed when his eyes filled with tears.

"It's off," he choked. "They've let us down. Thomas, Smith, Cook—they've given in. Given in and we've lost. All for nothing—all that work and planning—convincing everyone it was right—the first time it had ever happened, and all for nothing."

He was jostled by a surge from the crowd behind and his apathy was such that he made no attempt to push back or even hold his place on the kerb. She felt terribly sorry for him, he was so obviously distressed and broken, that her natural sympathy asserted itself. She didn't understand how anyone could be so upset over such an . . . impersonal thing as the strike, but his sincerity was obviously real.

"It's the first time anything like this has ever happened," he said, unashamedly brushing his hands across his eyes. "The first time people did something for someone else, without thinking what they were going to get out of it. That's why it was worthwhile. We were doing it for the miners—and it's all been for nothing."

She pushed her hand beneath his arm, trying to comfort him with physical contact. "Come on," she said gently. "Walk down with me. Let's try to get away from the crowd."

It had thickened and it surged again behind them, past him, and out into the road. They pushed a little way down the Old Kent Road but instead of fewer people there were more, and finally they found they were packed round—unable to move except in the way that everyone else was moving. In the distance, to the east, could be heard a low growling noise.

A lorry, guarded by policemen, appeared from the direction of the docks. It was moving carefully, right in the middle of the road between the tramlines, as though anxious to keep the crowds at equal distances on either side. She didn't see what happened but the noise that she had heard in the distance suddenly broke round her and she was caught into a violent movement of people thrusting towards the lorry. A brick flew over her head and smashed into the side of the lorry, just missing the policeman who was riding on the front. Whistles began to blow and the noise from the crowd ceased to be the shouting of individual men and became the roar of a mighty uncontrollable animal.

David Baron grasped her arm and tried to pull her away from the road and the police-guarded lorry.

"We'd better try and get out of here," he said urgently, forgetting his distress for a moment as they were drawn violently forward, then back, with the surging of the crowd.

She tried to move, but couldn't. She was hemmed in, trapped, and she was frightened because all the faces round her were wild and inhuman. The man behind her who looked as though he was ordinarily just a plain, agreeable kind of person, pushed her violently to one side and she fell on another man who swore at her and struck her hard in the chest. Her hat was knocked from her head and when she tried to pick it up the crowd surged again and it was lost under hundreds of milling feet. She felt David's arm suddenly wrenched away from hers and she turned to see him scrambling to his feet after being thrown on the ground.

"David!" she shouted. They were separated. She tried to keep control of the panic mounting in her stomach and then a stone, meant for the lorry, now too far away for anyone to hit, struck the side of her cheek and she gave way to hysteria.

"David!" she screamed, and began to claw and thrust her way through the crowd, trying to reach the shop doorways at the back of the pavement. An incredibly loud cracking noise broke through the shouting of the crowd—as though some gigantic beast were dancing on a tin-plate roof—and she saw the front window of a shoe shop spring into a myriad of silver lines and then fall in a shower of glass. The crowd around her began to mill faster, most people trying to disperse in any direction they could, anxious to run before the police moved in.

She panicked again and started to run with them, and then David appeared in front of her, put both his arms restrainingly round her waist and held her tightly against him.

"Stand still," he said quietly. "Just move to one side, look innocent, and keep still. If you run, the police will be after you in seconds."

They came almost immediately, pounding through the crowd which, incredibly, had thinned within a few seconds. They ran, as David had warned, straight past those who were standing still, following the paths of the people who had been panicked into flight. Whistles were blowing and every time there was a lull in the noise the irregular pattering of mounted police could be heard.

She remained still as he had instructed, but even when he could feel that she was once more in control of her hysteria he made no attempt to remove his arms from her waist.

Into her body, bruised and frightened from the crowd, welled a sensation of warm excitement. The face of David Baron was a few inches from her own and although he was only slightly taller than she was, he seemed to overwhelm her with his body. His arms were pulling her closer, they were strong and warm and . . . alive. A shiver ran over her, an excited, breathless trembling that grew worse at every point where her body touched his. When she looked into his face she noticed what a beautiful mouth he had, very full and red and firm.

"Sarah!" he gasped, and then he added a muttered phrase in a language she did not understand.

She looked up at him again and saw, reflected, the image of her own desires. Their faces were nearly touching and she could sense how it would be if he kissed her, how it would be to feel his mouth on hers, his hands touching her face and hair. He spoke again, hoarsely and incoherently in the language she did not understand and then, suddenly, she was pushed from behind and abruptly he let her go—so abruptly her body felt as though a piece had been severed from it. She remembered, in a distant sort of way, that she was standing on a crowded pavement beside a broken shop window with mounted policemen moving in on the mob.

Two men dashed up to the window and began to snatch shoes from the display. Police whistles blew again, the crowd surged and thickened once more. There was the sound of running feet, horses whinnying, hooves striking sharply on cobbled stones.

She was surprised when he pushed her—pushed her hard and violently into the doorway of the cobbler's that adjoined the shoe shop. She had just regained her balance when she saw the two mounted police bearing down on them. They were trying to get to the broken window and were using horses and batons to push through the crowd.

"Stay where you are!" shouted David. He tried to get through to her, and then the policeman's baton caught him on the side of the head.

It happened before she even understood why the policeman had hit him—later she thought that the blow wasn't even meant for him, he had just intercepted a clearing thrust of the baton.

He lurched to one side, and then she saw his face change, saw temper and disappointment and angry frustration well up into his eyes. All the futility of his work, his broken dream of a united fight, all the loss of his ideals and the integrity of the men he had trusted, were centred on the policeman who had hit him with the baton. And because her body had so recently been held warm against his, she was able to think with his mind, to know the despair and unhappiness that was boiling in his heart.

"You bloody rozzer!" he shouted. He flung himself forward, ignoring the horse and the descending baton, and threw all his weight upwards, clutching the bottom of the policeman's tunic and pulling with all his strength. When he had the man over far enough he jumped up—baton blows descending on him all the time—and clutched the policeman round the neck.

"I'll get you down!" he cried. There were tears raining down his cheeks—tears from the pain of the blows and tears from the pain of his wasted work.

"I'll get you down, you bloody rozzer!"

He hauled and clung at the man on the horse. The policeman's helmet fell to the ground and he tried to turn his horse so that the balance of his attacker would be disturbed. It was no use. Agonised fury had given David the strength of battle against both man and beast.

It took three constables to get him away from the mounted policeman and the last she saw of him was being dragged away through the crowd. He was fighting every inch of the way.

She waited for twenty minutes—twenty minutes in which she became slowly and burningly aware of shame—embarrassment at the dreadful public spectacle she had just been part of. Supposing Miss Bennett had seen her—seen him holding her close on the pavement and then fighting a policeman on a horse. She wanted to cry with shame and humiliation. It was horrible and degrading, losing her hat and having to stand still by a broken window in case the police arrested her for breaking it.

He was dangerous. She had only known him a few weeks and already he had brought confusion and trouble into her life. He had waited outside school and provoked another rebuke from Miss Bennett. He had made her upset Charlie and the Dances over the strike, and now she had only narrowly escaped arrest in a public riot. A shudder ran over her when she thought of Miss Bennett, and her ma and pa, and the Dances, learning of her arrest in the street. She had an immediate and urgent need to go home, back to Aunt Florrie's, to sit in Florrie's kitchen drinking tea, nice and safe and away from dangerous thoughts and ideas.

As soon as the crowd had thinned she left the doorway and hurried along the street. At the first side alley she turned off in case the whole thing started again. One of the men who had taken the shoes from the broken window was kneeling on the ground rummaging among the stolen footwear.

"All bloody left shoes!" she heard him say. "Not a pair in the whole bloody window."

It was as futile as everything else had been on this miserable day.

The strike was over—but everything had to go on just the same—school, and the Dances, and Miss Bennett, and trying a find a job for her cousin May. Empire Day was just over a week away. The flag-pole must be erected in the playground, the Union Jack unfolded and the creases shaken out, the children selected for representation of the different countries.

It was difficult choosing the children because of the costumes. The Britannia costume belonged to the school, but the others, the Scottish kilt, the Indian sari, the green and red skirt and shawl of Ireland, had to be provided by the parents. It meant the same children dressed up every year, those whose parents could afford to convert an old plaid dress, or to invest in some crêpe paper, or lend a sheet for a sari.

Sarah, still trying to atone to the Alexanders for the Sammy incident called Gertie out and told her she would be Britannia on Empire Day. She was cheered and felt a little of her strike depression lift when she saw Gertie's face brighten. None of the Alexanders had ever been chosen for the Empire Day parade, nor the Nativity Play.

On 23 May she saw Gertie out of the classroom with all the others. She could hear the child chattering all the way along the passage.

"My mum's goin' to wash my 'air, and I've got a white 'air ribbon—it will do for Sundays, see—and I'm gonna wear my white socks only I got to take them off as soon as it's over . . ."

Her voice disappeared along the passage and Sarah packed her bag and followed the children out. She was gloomy and miserable. Every time she closed her eyes she could see the face of David Baron, agonised with fury and frustration. Every evening when she left school she hoped she would see him leaning against the school railing waiting for her. She no longer cared if Miss Bennett complained. She just wanted to see him, to know what had happened to him. For she had no

way of discovering his whereabouts other than asking
the Alexanders, and she could not bring herself to return there, not yet.

At night she remembered the other thing—standing
close to him in the middle of a surging mob but being
oblivious of everyone else for just a moment. At night
she turned restlessly on her bed, unable to forget the
moment. During the day she was just miserable, about
everything.

She watched Gertie Alexander skipping along the
road and thought apathetically, at least Gertie's happy.
That's nice, that Gertie is happy.

So when Gertie arrived next morning with swollen
eyes and—as usual—no handkerchief, she was surprised.

"Are you crying because you don't want to be
Britannia?" she asked kindly. Gertie began to cry
afresh and said "No."

"Well, we can't have Britannia crying on Empire
Day. You've got to lead the procession, dear. It won't
look right if Britannia is crying."

Gertie tried to stop and succeeded slightly. When
the time came for her to put on the robe and helmet,
Sarah pulled her quietly to a corner of the classroom.
"Now what's the trouble, Gertie?" she asked quietly.
"Why have you been crying?"

At the unexpected sign of sympathy Gertie broke
down again. Sarah hurriedly produced a piece of paper
for Gertie's nose in case the Britannia costume should
suffer.

"It's me dad," sobbed Gertie. "He's got the sack. He
was one of the leaders in the strike and he's out of
work. My mum was crying all night and she says she
don't know what we're going to do. No one will take
him on now."

She felt a heavy, leaden weight descend on her heart.
She had thought it was some childish tragedy but it
was the same old nightmare that hung over all of them.
Prophetically, her words to David Baron—about leading poor Mr Alexander into trouble—had come true.

"What about your father's friend?" she asked slowly. "Mr Baron. What's happened to him?"

Gertie was crying so hard she could only just hear her through sobs and sniffs.

" 'E's got the sack too. Only 'e's in prison for three months so 'e won't 'ave the sack till 'e comes out."

From the playground came the sound of Class Four leading the school out into the procession. Gertie picked up her trident and, sobbing bitterly, led her class in the wake of the previous procession. Wales, Scotland and Ireland who walked immediately behind Gertie, were gloomily subdued by her weeping.

When they had all gone Sarah still didn't move. She remained kneeling on the floor and suddenly she put her head down on the nearest desk and let tears soak into the sleeve of her blue dress.

She could hear them all outside, the chanting voices of children wearing drab costumes of madeover clothes and crêpe paper.

> "Today's the Empire's birthday,
> The 24th of May,
> Salute the Flag, salute the King,
> On glorious Empire Day!"

# Six

COUSIN MAY, whose full name was May Elizabeth James, had all the disadvantages of younger daughters. Born only a year after her elder sister she had come second best in most things. Mary, the elder, was the favourite of her mother. Good, honest Betsy tried very hard to have no favourites, but Mary was her firstborn and she was pretty and healthy and bright, and she had been conceived after a long period of anxiety and worry which had somehow ended when Mary was born. Betsy could not help associating Mary with the good times, the happy times.

May had come too soon after the first child. She was very much like her sister to look at, but smaller, not quite so healthy, not quite so pretty. It was as though an old engraving stone had been used too much and the final print had produced a very faded replica of the original. There was never the time to give her, as Betsy had given to her eldest child. She had every material care that a good mother could give—food, warm vests in winter, careful nursing through sickness (she seemed to be ill more often than Mary). But somehow, when it came to playing, or talking, or sharing little secrets, Betsy never had the patience to go through it all again.

It didn't matter at first because May—again like many second daughters—became the favourite of her father. She was slight in build as he was, and her eyes were dark blue like his instead of the bright, clear blue of Mary and her mother. And there was another thing

they had in common, they were both "givers"—
generous sometimes to the point of foolhardiness.

Matthew gave to the people he loved, to his wife, his
children, his friends. But May gave to anyone and
everyone. Partly it was wanting to be loved, but mostly
it was just the pleasure of being able to offer things
and make people happy. She liked making people
happy. As a child she had once given her boots away
to a small boy in the village who had no footwear. The
thrashing she received had ensured that nothing of that
nature ever occurred again, but still she continued to
give everything that was hers.

Her tragedy was the death of her father—"My girl,
aren't you, love? My special girl"—killed at sea when
she was twelve. Her mother, bereft and grieving, had
drawn even closer to Mary, and May, between a united
mother and sister, and the little ones who were too
young to be really involved, had found she was the
odd one out, very lonely, and no longer anyone's girl.

She bore her unhappiness with the silent stoicism that
had been her father's. She was human enough to feel
envious when Mary was aprenticed to the village dressmaker, but she was sensible enough to know that there
was not sufficient money for two daughters to be given
a trade, and she accepted her inevitable employment
in service with fatalistic fortitude.

Two things gave her comfort whenever loneliness
and depression threatened to close in upon her. One
was the condition of her cousin Sarah, the other was
the presence of Peter, Sarah's half-brother. Watching
Sarah cheered her because she saw that Sarah was in a
far worse position than she herself was. Sarah had a
mother who actively hated her. Sarah's life was just
one long gloom of scoldings and slaps and very often
Sarah would come round into her Aunt Betsy's garden
with her eyes all red from crying. When she was like
that May felt almost happy because she could give
Sarah something to cheer her up, a handkerchief, or a
box of crayons, and Sarah would talk to her for a while
and May would realise how lucky she was in having
Betsy for her ma.

And of course there was Peter. He wasn't really her cousin, only by marriage, but Peter was dearer to her than her own brothers, sometimes almost dearer than her ma. He was a sailor like her pa had been, and he was quiet. Her pa had been quiet. But the best thing of all about Peter was that he had loved her pa as much as she did. Peter had thought his Uncle Math the most wonderful man in the world, and she loved Peter for that.

The first time she had seen Peter in uniform she thought he *was* her pa. It was eighteen months after the telegram—missing at sea—had arrived and Peter walked into the kitchen with the seaman's rolling gait and the assured maleness that had been her father's. She had burst into tears and run from the room, but since that first time she had waited eagerly for his shore leaves, growing more and more excited when she knew he was coming, and falling under a pall of misery when the leave came to an end.

Her life was not exciting, but it was safe and surrounded by people she knew and a pattern of work, worship and small village social events with which she was comfortably familiar. She was content, until she saw her cousin Sarah, changed by city life into a smart, elegant young woman, talking differently, walking differently, wearing beautiful clothes and—May had noticed it though neither of their mothers had—facepowder. And for the first time in her life May wanted something for herself. She wanted to be as stylish as Sarah so that the next time Peter came on leave she would have something even nicer to give him—herself, madeover and renovated.

When the winter of 1926 turned to the spring of '27, and still Sarah had not been able to find her a city job, she decided that she *would* ask Mr Masters, their old schoolteacher, if he could help her. Mr Masters had set Sarah on the road to London, so perhaps he could also help her. She didn't expect miracles—like being turned into a teacher the way Sarah had—but surely he could write to his friend in Stepney, the way he had for Sarah.

Mr Masters did not fail her. He wrote, and the progress of May's job followed exactly the same route as Sarah's post at the school. From Mr Masters to the friend in Stepney, and from the friend in Stepney to Miss Bennett at the school.

She couldn't believe how lucky she was! To get a job not just near Sarah, but actually working for Sarah's headmistress. She sat down at once and wrote to Sarah.

When the letter arrived, Sarah felt quite ill. She stared at her cousin's round, childlilke handwriting and thought of loving, not very strong, generous May under the terrifying, unbalanced rule of Miss Bennett. And May would be living-in, no chance of escaping from Miss Bennett. She was horrified and she hurriedly wrote back to May telling her not to come, to stick it out in the village a little longer, to wait until Sarah had managed to find a more congenial mistress.

She had reckoned without May's quiet determination. May had, at last, been given a chance. Nothing, no one, was going to make her throw it away. She arranged the day for the interview. She put on her best dress, the red one (which didn't really suit her) and she travelled up to Victoria, her heart fluttering with anticipation, her hands spread on the seat on either side of her so that the nervous perspiration on her palms would not stain her cheap cotton gloves.

Sarah was waiting for her at the barrier: She looked anxious and was thinner than when May had last seen her.

"Do I look all right?" asked May nervously. "Do you think I'll suit?"

Sarah linked her arm through her cousin's and steered her through the station crowds. "I wish you'd think about this, May. She's a terrible woman. I don't know what her brother is like. No one has ever seen him. But she's terrible. We're all afraid of her."

May's face set into a stubborn mask, "I don't care what she's like. If she thinks I'll suit, then I'm taking the job. I want to work in London. And it can't be worse than working at Fawcett's. Just one lady and a bachelor gentleman to look after—it can't be worse than Fawcett's."

They began walking up Victoria Street towards the river. It was a nice afternoon and May was early for her interview.

"Will you promise me that . . . if she's too . . . horrible, you'll leave. Will you promise that?" Sarah urged.

"Of course I'll promise—but it won't be," said May confidently. "I'm sure it won't be." She stopped and clutched Sarah's arm. "Oh look, Sarah! Isn't it exciting! Big Ben and everything. Oh Sarah! It's going to be wonderful working in London!"

"I hope so," said Sarah glumly. She was wondering what refinements of cruelty Miss Bennett would be able to inflict on Cousin May. She could not understand Miss Bennett, and indeed she had given up trying. Fully expecting a termination of her employment at the school, she had waited nervously for the end of her probationary year. Nothing had happened. The term had drawn to a close and the expected letter, the summons to the committee or to see Miss Bennett still had not arrived. She had finally reached a point of nervous suspense where she could no longer wait for fate to evolve at its own speed. She had begged an interview with Miss Bennett and had raised the matter herself. Miss Bennett had smiled and said coolly, "So far as I know, Miss Whitman, the committee has no intention of terminating your employment. What made you think you would not receive a permanent appointment?"

"My . . . you said . . . I was under the impression you were not satisfied with me, Headmistress."

Miss Bennett's ice-eyes bored into Sarah. "I am not satisfied, Miss Whitman. Not satisfied at all." She leaned across the desk and with one of her swift changes of mood she banged her fist down. "I deplore failures, Miss Whitman! I deplore and detest failures in either teacher or pupil—and I consider you a failure, Miss Whitman. I consider you one of my greatest failures. But I do not intend to give up! No indeed, I do not intend to give up!"

Sarah was incapable of speech, but a dismal sense of foreboding began to settle on her. Miss Bennett smiled.

"We are going to have another try with you, Miss Whitman," she threatened.

"I see, Headmistress," Sarah faltered.

"Tell me, Miss Whitman," she continued. "How do you spend your salary? You receive fifteen pounds a month. Obviously you do not spend very much of it on your dress. I should be interested to hear what you do with your money."

Sarah's temper flared. The question was impertinent and outside of Miss Bennett's duties. But, on the point of rebelling, Sarah remembered she was being given a second chance and would be unlikely to receive a third.

"I have a younger brother," she said stiffly. "He has been fortunate enough to win a scholarship and I am assisting with his education."

"Ha!" enthused Miss Bennett "Another embryonic country schoolteacher!"

She would have loved to have reached over the desk and slapped Miss Bennett across the face. She felt murderously, wilfully hateful toward the older woman and nothing but physical violence would relieve that hatred. She clenched her teeth hard together and thought, I must keep my job. Whatever she says, I must keep my job.

"May I go now, Headmistress?" she demanded with as much passivity as she could muster.

"By all means, Miss Whitman. By all means. But do remember. We shall be watching your progress with interest . . . great interest."

She hated Miss Bennett, she was afraid of her, and the motivations of Miss Bennett's existence were beyond her comprehension.

If she had understood, she would have realised that she need never worry about being unemployed again. For Sarah was as necessary to Miss Bennett as the public thrashings. On one occasion, the Education Committee had sent Miss Bennett a young, very clever and competent teacher who was possessed of a small private income. It had been the unhappiest period of Miss Bennett's career. She could not fault the young woman on teaching or behaviour, and the private income gave the

teacher an independence that enabled her to treat Miss
Bennett with cool and only just sufficient respect.
When she had left the school—for a better post—Miss
Bennett had vowed never to accept a teacher like her
again. She favoured tutors like Miss Enderby, who was
too old and frightened to disobey her, or Sarah who
had received her post as a personal favour and was too
poor and unsure of herself to rebel. Only—and this was
the delightful part—sometimes she did rebel, and then
Miss Bennett was able to hold the rebellion as a threat
against her.

When the chance came of taking Sarah's cousin as a
domestic in her own house, she had seized upon it.
Sarah was now doubly indebted to her and, moreover,
would be constantly reminded of her social and eco-
nomic background. Neither Sarah nor May need ever
have worried about their respective posts. Miss Bennett would have relinquished neither of them.

When they arrived at the Bennett house—a large,
early Victorian three-storey building in the Kennington
Road—Sarah watched her cousin disappear inside with
a feeling of extreme anxiety. The anxiety had not lifted
when, half an hour later, May came clattering down
the steps from the front door.

"I've got it!" she burbled excitedly. "Thirty-six
pounds a year, half a day, and two evenings a week off.
Starting next month."

"Won't it be too much for you?" asked Sarah pessi-
mistically. "It looks a big house from outside."

May was so happy she said nothing, not even Sarah's
gloom, could detract from the brightness of the day.
"It's beautiful inside, Sarah! It's electric! And there's a
telephone in Mr Bennett's study."

"Did you see him?" asked Sarah curiously. She had
often tried to imagine what Mr Bennett was like and
had failed. Miss Bennett seemed above normal relation-
ships—like having parents and brothers and sisters.

"No, just his study," prattled May happily. She
bounced along the road towards the Oval, Sarah stump-
ing grimly behind. "He's awaiting the Call," May
added.

Sarah stopped walking and turned to stare at her cousin. "He's going to die?" she asked astonished. May giggled.

"To foreign parts," she said. "Teaching the heathen. He's been out in Ceylon but had to come back because of ill health. Now he's waiting for another Call."

Ceylon! Beautiful women in saris picking tea in exotic fields . . . white elephants trampling disobedient slaves to death . . . gods with hundreds of arms and legs, and eyes made of rubies!

"I'd like to have a ride on a tram," said May prosaically.

"Fancy living in Ceylon," answered Sarah dreamily. "It's off the south-east corner of India, you know. Latitude 8°. Capital, Colombo. Chief export, tea. Highest mountain, Adam's Peak, 7,360 feet. That's the geography. But there's all the other things that geography doesn't tell you. The sun, and snakes as thick as a man's thigh, and weeping women casting themselves onto their husband's funeral pyres."

"I've never ridden on a tram," said May wistfully.

Sarah's mood of gloom had magically dispersed. She turned and grinned at her cousin, then gave her a quick hug that made May flush with suppressed pleasure and happiness. Sarah grabbed her arm and began to run her along the road. "Come on," she bellowed. "Which way do you want to go? Back up to the river, or down to Brixton market?"

They began to run, holding onto their hats and whooping with laughter as they arrived at the tram stop and leapt on just in time.

"Perhaps it's a good thing you're coming to London," huffed Sarah as they collapsed onto a seat. "You won't like working for Miss Bennett, but we can have some fun on your evenings off. And you can come out with Charlie and me whenever you like."

Since the strike—since the terrible shaming evening when David Baron had been carried struggling to the police station—she had been virtuously spending most of her spare time with Charlie and the Dances. David Baron had never tried to see her again and she was

glad. He was disruptive and he made her uneasy—
broke into her dreams and made her disagree with her
friends. She had succeeded—almost—in pushing the
memory of him away into the part of her head which
she labelled, "embarrassing and uncomfortable things."
David Baron with his dangerous ideas and lack of self-
control, his warm body and violent temper, was best
forgotten. He wasn't reliable, not like Charlie.

May suddenly realised that the back of the tram seat
swung right over to the other side and she flushed
again, gratified and childishly pleased at yet another of
London's sophisticated delights.

"Well, we're going to Brixton," announced Sarah.
"What would you like to do when we get there?"

May clutched her bag tightly between her hands.
"You said there was a market," she reminded Sarah.
"Could we buy some things . . . presents to take home?
I'd like to buy something for ma."

"Oh, May! You're *always* spending your money on
things for other people. Why don't you get something
for yourself?" She loved May, who could not love
May? But at the same time her cousin annoyed her.
She was too readily a doormat for others, too eager to
take second place in everything. "Get yourself something pretty to wear, a hat, or some special material
for a dress. Yes, that's what we'll do!" She twisted
round in her seat and faced May, firing her with enthusiasm. "We'll get some material for a dress, and
when we get back to Aunt Florrie's I'll measure you
and cut it out. Then when you come up to London
you'll have a really stylish frock ready to wear!"

May's face went red and white by turn. "What
colour?" she asked, and Sarah stared at her cousin
through screwed up eyes. "Blue," she said after a
moment's consideration. "Blue marocain with a lace
inset down to the hips and a sash cut on the cross."

"Wonderful!" breathed May. "I've enough money.
I've got all my month's money from Fawcett's."

The tram ground and swayed along the road, forcing
bicycles, motor-cars, and horses and carts into the
side. When they reached Brixton the Saturday crowds

were so thick the people had overflowed into the gutter. The girls jumped off the tram and joined the crowds pushing their way into the market. May stopped at a sweet stall and bought a bag of locust beans and an everlasting stick. Underfoot was orange peel, tram tickets, and an occasional cigarette card that was pounced on by a small boy buffeting a path through the legs. Sarah paused long enough by each stall selling material to feel the quality of the fabric.

She was idly flicking through a rack of blouses—8d each—when she heard her cousin say, "There's a man selling purses over there, Sarah. Out of a case. I think perhaps I'll get one for ma." Sarah went on moving the blouses along the rack—Miss Muffet prints and really very good value for 8d—dimly aware of the shouting voices—"Purses! Purses made from genuine leather offcuts! A bargin, ladies, a quality bargain at 6d each! Real leather purses at 6d!"

The voice was familiar. She had heard it before, and then she looked up and saw him. Saw him standing on the other side of the covered lane, an upturned box in front of him with a case resting on it. She felt so sick and shocked she wanted to run away before he saw her. She felt sick because he looked broken, undignified and rough. He was thin and his nose seemed bigger than she remembered. His jacket was frayed at the cuffs and he didn't look like a young man any more. He looked small, and bent, and very strained. She hated him because no one had any right to look like that. No one should be that beaten and defeated, not when they had led a strike and fought three policemen and held her tightly in the middle of a public street. She hated him so much that her eyes filled with tears and she couldn't move.

"What's the matter, Sarah?" she heard May ask, but she couldn't answer. She wanted to move away but it was too late. He looked across to the blouse stall and, before he had time to be ashamed, he smiled, a smile that showed the way he felt, warm and relieved and delighted to see her. Then he remembered, and the smile faded and his face shrank into anonymity. He

banged the lid of the case down and didn't even stop
to snap it shut, just lodged it under his arm and rushed
away through the crowd.

"David!" she called, but it was too late. He had
vanished and if he heard her he pretended not to.

She knew May was staring at her and she knew tears
were running slowly down her cheeks but she couldn't
do anything about them.

"He didn't want to speak to you," May said gently.
"Was he a friend?"

Sarah didn't answer. She swallowed hard and pulled
her shoulders back.

"I think he was embarrassed," continued May. "He
looked as though he was out of work. You know how
dreadful it is—remember how ashamed Charlie is
when he can't get work. I expect he didn't want you to
see him like that."

"Well it's over now," said Sarah briskly. "Let's get
on and buy your marocain."

They bought the marocain, and the lace, and a
brooch for Betsy. And May—very daring—bought a
long string of blue glass beads which she would never
dare to wear at home because beads were "worldly."
Brooches were all right because they pinned collars and
lapels together, but beads were purely ornamental and
somehow not nice.

When they were going home on the tram May said,
"You're not still upset are you, Sarah? About your
friend? That David, you're not still upset are you?"

"No," said Sarah shortly.

"Oh, good." May sighed and stared out of the window at the darkening streets. The two girls fell silent,
each occupied with private dreams, moving singly in
worlds they believed were occupied by other people.

"Sarah," said May timidly. "Will it take you long to
make the dress? I mean . . . do you think you'll have it
finished in time for . . . the next time your brother
comes home on leave?"

Sarah looked into May's childlike, anxious face. "I'll
try," she answered dispiritedly.

How simple it was—to be May—in love with Peter.

It was the best summer May had ever known. It was the summer of the blue marocain dress, the summer of London for the very first time, of "Keep the Home Fires Burning" played on a barrel organ in twilight streets that smelled of lime trees and hot pavements. The music should have made her sad because it was about the war and it was played by an ex-soldier with the Mons Star on his coat. But nothing, nothing in the whole world could make her sad that summer.

It was the wonderful summer when Peter's ship was berthed at Gravesend for refitting prior to a far-eastern tour, and Peter seemed to be on leave all the time—coming up to London, and down to the village, handsome, smiling, joking in his quiet droll way and encouraging them to do all kinds of terrible things, like go to the pictures, and smoke a cigarette.

Whenever she looked back on that summer she could never remember being so happy before. She tried to remember things, like working for Miss Bennett—which wasn't nearly so bad as Sarah had made out—but all she could remember was the four of them, Sarah, Charlie, Peter, and herself, strolling through evening streets, going to the zoo, crying over Ronald Colman in *Beau Geste,* and then running furiously for the tram so that they could get her indoors before 9.30 when Miss Bennett put the bolt on.

It was the summer when, miraculously, she managed to catch something of Sarah's personality, Sarah's excitement, Sarah's verve and dash. It was as though the two girls, who had both been lonely until now, fused together and became one sparkling, vivacious entity. They could do nothing wrong. On May's afternoon off she would go up to the school and wait for Sarah and then they would walk over the river to the Strand, their arms round each other's waists, chattering excitedly about what was in the shops, what everyone was wearing, what was on at the theatre. And then they would saunter into Lyons and have baked beans on toast and cream cakes at the beginning of the month, and a buttered bun and a cup of tea at the end of the month when funds were running low.

And because they were excited, because for the first time they had discovered in each other a friend, their confidence and assured manner of walking, talking, looking at people, made them instantly attractive to all the men they passed in the streets.

It was nice to be admired. May couldn't ever remember being admired so much before and Sarah forgot she was big and ugly. Once, walking past Southwark Cathedral, two wags in boaters and Oxford bags tried to pick them up and they felt worldly and brazen as they rejected—with dignity—the offers of an evening at the Variety and a fish and chip supper.

When they went back to the village they knew, without telling each other, what things not to talk about. They left off the face-powder and behaved quietly and modestly. But on the train going back to London they smiled at one another, spirits lifting, eager and in a hurry to get back to the city.

Sometimes Sarah was moody and said she didn't want to go out. Once May caught her crying and Sarah wouldn't say what it was that made her sad. But it was always easy to divert Sarah's gloom with a new idea, a suggestion for an outing they hadn't been on before, and if all else failed May would tell her about Mr Bennett's study that was filled with curios from Ceylon—carvings and a brass gong and an umbrella stand made out of an elephant's foot.

One tiny thing marred her pleasure that summer. The first time Peter came on leave he had leapt up the stairs at Aunt Florrie's and banged on Sarah's door. When they'd opened the door he had bounded into the room, put an arm round each of them and swung them out into the air saying, "My two favourite girls!"

It was like that all the time. He had bought them both a present, two shawls that came from Spain and the shawls were identical in colour and pattern—everything. If Sarah wasn't free to go out, then he would smile and say, "We'll wait. We'll wait until Thursday, or Saturday, when we can all go out together." In the old days it would have been enough. It would have been more than enough just to have Peter home so often and taking them out to all the new wonderful places. But now it wasn't enough because she didn't want Peter to think of her in the same way that he thought of Sarah. She wanted to be different from Sarah and she wanted Peter to look at her in the same way that Charlie looked at her cousin. She wanted to be special for Peter.

The best day of all that summer came in September. They took a bus to Richmond and Aunt Florrie had made them up a basket of sardine and tomato sandwiches and a bottle of cold tea. When they got to Richmond they walked down to the water's edge and Charlie and Peter moved away and went into a whispered consultation that involved the chinking of coins and mumbled additions and subtractions. Then Peter came back to the girls.

"Right," he said with precision. "We're going to take a punt for the afternoon."

"But Charlie can't affor . . ." Sarah began, and then she stopped as Peter frowned guardedly at her. Charlie led the way to the boathouse and jumped down onto the punt. His face was red and shiny and as soon as he got in the punt he took off his jacket and rolled it carefully against the back of the wooden seat.

"There you are, girls. There's a cushion for you," he said importantly. "Come on now. Peter will see you in and I'll be here to steady you."

Sarah could have stepped in quite easily without any help, but she was suddenly touched by the sight of Charlie's gratified face. Poor old Charlie, she thought. He loves giving things to people, just like May, and he can't afford to do it very often. She obligingly gave a little squeal as she left the bank, and convincingly clutched Charlie's arm, giving him such a warm, affectionate smile that he rocked violently and made the punt go up at one end.

"Cast off forrard, cast off stern!" shouted Peter, and the punt moved away from the bank.

It was hot, and hazy, and soundless. Water midges hung a few inches above the surface of the river and in a little while the girls could feel the sun burning their bare arms. Sarah trailed her hand languidly in the water, the way she had seen a lady do it in a magazine illustration. Every so often, especially when Charlie was punting, drops of water would spray off the pole onto the other three and they would shout at Charlie, not really meaning it but just enjoying being four friends together, being part of a set, a group, having fun, not worrying about school, or housework, or the Navy, or being unemployed. Four people together, safe for one afternoon and feeling sorry for everyone else who was on their own.

"Don't we look nice together?" said Sarah dreamily. It was the kind of daft thing that Sarah was always saying, but they looked at each other and saw themselves with her eyes, a hot summer's afternoon and the quiet reaches of the Thames, two young girls in cream sailor dresses and white stockings and canvas shoes. May had a bandeau tied round her hair. And Charlie and Peter were tall and strong. Charlie's hair was bleached nearly white by the summer sun and Peter was brown-skinned and smiling, the way he always was.

They pulled into the bank and lodged the punt against the root of a willow that hung over the water. Farther up the river someone had a gramophone and, through the heat, came the lazy nostalgic strain of the "Sweetheart Waltz." It was a green and golden afternoon—green river, green willows, green banks—and gold in the sky, in the colour of the girls' dresses, on Charlie's hair, and shining above the surface of the water.

"I wonder where we'll all be ten years from now," murmured Sarah. "Do you think we'll all get the things we want? Or just some of them, or none of them?"

May flicked a few spots of water onto Peter's face, hoping to rouse him and perhaps make him tease her, but Peter only smiled and lay back with his eyes closed.

"All I want is to get a job," said Charlie, but because they were all together and because of the afternoon, he was able to say it without fear or shame. "If I could get a good job I wouldn't want anything else..." He stared at Sarah, at her soft face and the

curve of her body pressed against the linen dress. "Not
for a little while, anyway," he added. "I wouldn't want
anything more for a little while."

The water lapped gently against the side of the punt.
May slapped at a water midge that was crawling up
her arm.

"What do you want, Peter?" Sarah was playing her
favourite game—dreaming, and making everyone else
join in with the dreams.

"I don't *want* anything," he grinned. "What I'm
*going* to do is leave the Navy when my time is up, and
with the money I've saved I'll be able to go home and
really start work on pa's meadow in a big way . . . do
it properly . . . not like pa's done it. Try to buy the
meadow instead of renting it, and go in for bees and
poultry as a real business. Pa's got no head for business . . . he knows the animals and the soil all right,
but it's got to be managed properly, made to expand."

Sarah stared at her brother in surprise. "I never
knew you wanted to go home again," she said. Peter
avoided her eyes. He pulled a leaf from the willow tree
hanging over the water and put it between his teeth.
"Uh-huh," he said non-committally. Then because
Sarah was still staring at him, he added, "I don't want
to spend the rest of my life at sea. I want to go back
to the village one day . . . settle there and make a
living."

"That's what I want too," agreed May eagerly. She
couldn't say in front of them all what she really
wanted, so she settled for enthusiastic support of Peter.
Sarah and Peter glanced towards each other over May's
head and their eyes exchanged a knowledge of May's
secret that was no secret. Poor May—said Peter's face,
and—Don't hurt her—answered Sarah silently.

"What about you, Sary?" demanded Charlie hope-
fully. "What do you want?"

"To go all the places that Peter has been to, and all
the places he hasn't been to," she answered longingly.
The music coming from upstream had changed, *"Ra-
mona, when day is done I hear you call . . ."*

"I want to see the pyramids, and Everest, and the

lost city of the Incas! And wander round the world learning new languages and talking to strange people and having . . . adventures!"

"But you can't do that for ever," said Charlie earnestly. "Why, even Peter is going to settle down one day. You can't go having adventures for the whole of your life."

Sarah waved a hand irritably in the air. "Oh, I suppose one day I'll have to settle down, but not for years and years. I want to *do* things first. That's what I want!"

"And I want my tea. Where are the sardine sandwiches?" asked Peter quickly, because Charlie was looking very red again and he could tell he was getting upset. "You know, the only one likely to get his wish is Charlie. I expect when the time comes I won't be able to leave the sea . . . any more than May here will be able to give up the delights of London." He tweaked the end of her bandeau, silencing her vehement protests. "And poor old Sarah! How are you ever going to travel round the world, Sarah? You'll have to save up for years!"

She grinned. "I expect you're right," she said happily. "So for now I'll settle for tea and another trip upstream to see who's playing a gramophone."

After tea they stepped out onto the bank and wandered along for a little way. Charlie held Sarah's hand and that left May to walk behind with Peter. And because it was summer, and the trees were green and the river made soft lapping noises against the bank, because May was so very pretty and her dark curly hair had come loose under the bandeau, because her eyes were so adoring and so hopeful, Peter leaned forward and kissed her.

That was the happiest day of May's entire life.

# *Seven*

THROUGHOUT the autumn and winter that followed, Sarah watched the condition of the Alexander children steadily deteriorate.

It was a dreary winter anyway. Peter had gone and probably wouldn't be back for a year. May was trying to be composedly gay about his absence and Sarah found her pathetic courage both irritating and reproachful. May had also provided another thorn in Sarah's side in her relationship with Miss Bennett. May was quite suited with her post. Miss Bennett was out at school for most of the time and Mr Bennett—while awaiting the Call—was comparatively little bother. And May couldn't see why Sarah had painted such a black picture of Miss Bennett who was really very friendly. Indeed, during the preparation of the evening meal she would often come down to the kitchen and talk to May, asking her questions about the village, and the family, and about what she and Sarah used to do when they were children. May, gullible and trusting, chattered on about her own mother, and Sarah's mother, and told Miss Bennett how they had just had gas fitted into the cottages, and about poor Harriet, Sarah's sister who was "funny" and lived in a home for backward girls. And about the terrible time Anne-Louise had slapped Sarah in full view of the assembled village because she had danced with Charlie. Miss Bennett was so interested that May was flattered. Sometimes, just occasionally, she caught a glimpse of Miss Bennett's violent temper and then appreciated that she might not

*always* be such a nice woman to work for, but fortunately May had never been the cause of an unbalanced
explosion. It was usually Mr Bennett who provoked the
rages. He seemed frightened of his sister and always
gave in hurriedly when they had a difference of opinion.
May thought it was very strange that Mr Bennett
should be afraid of his sister when one considered that
he had lived in foreign parts amongst the savages.

And every tiny piece of village gossip, all the shaming anecdotes of Sarah's childhood, were dropped
casually at staff meetings by an amused Miss Bennett.
"I hear your mother is doing away with her oil-lamps,
Miss Whitman? What a blessing for her. And how
pleasant she will find it not having to cook over a wood
fire." The staff would titter appreciatively, especially
Miss Enderby, not because they wished to be unkind or
humiliate Sarah, but because they felt safer laughing
when Miss Bennett obviously wanted them to laugh.

And again: "Miss Whitman comes from a very clever
family, ladies. Did you know her father passed his
postal exam when he could hardly read or write!"

She was sometimes foolish enough to flare back at
Miss Bennett but she always regretted it. The delight
in the older woman's face, the pretended coldness of
the voice—"I consider your remark impertinent, Miss
Whitman. I think some kind of apology is called for,"
that secretly masked a gloating pleasure at the loss of
control and the mumbled apology before a silent staff,
made Sarah conceal her fury whenever she could. She
tried to remonstrate with May, but May didn't—
couldn't—understand how such remarks could be
offensive.

"She meant it kindly, Sarah. I'm sure she did. She
takes an interest in you like she does in me and she
was praising you when she said you came from a clever
family. Your pa *was* clever to pass his postal exam. I
don't see how you could be upset about that."

And through the scourging of Miss Bennett, the
martyrdom of May over Peter's absence, the glumness
of Charlie who was unable to pick up much casual

work that winter, she had to watch the pathetic poverty of the Alexander children grow worse.

Gertie and Samuel had moved up into the next class, but Maud Alexander was now under Sarah's constant surveillance and she could observe, at first hand, the declining conditions of the family.

There were the material things—wearing plimsolls instead of boots when the weather was bad, clothes that were patched with different colours or not patched at all, the sores round Maud's mouth that were painted with gentian violet by the school doctor. And there were the things that showed that the spirit—the pride— of the family was breaking too. The girls no longer wore bows on their hair and their plaits had been hacked off because there wasn't the time or energy to keep them nice. Sammy didn't fight to stand at the front of the playground lines and lead his class into school. He didn't quite have the strength to fight. He wasn't ill, just apathetic and enervated.

Gertie Alexander was the one who suffered most. It always was the eldest girl who suffered most. She was the one who had to run down to the corner shop for a pennorth of tea and please put it on the slate. She was the one who had to look after the children while ma went out cleaning, and answer the door to the tally man and the rent man and tell them no one was in and she didn't know where the money was kept. It was the eldest girl, too, who was closest to ma. The times when ma wanted someone to talk to, someone to share in the agonising worry of how to care for the family, it was Gertie, or Doris, or Kath, or whoever was eldest, who bore some of the anxiety and dread.

That winter Sarah watched Gertie turn into a wizened facsimile of her mother—thin, white-faced and with tired shoulders. The sawn-off hair emphasized the resemblance. Gertie's nose still needed attention and she still constantly lost her handkerchief—another strain on the family resources—but in spite of this Gertie was no longer a child. She had turned into a little, worried old woman.

At the end of the Christmas term Sarah asked the

school doctor to authorise free hot milk and malt for the Alexanders, and halfway through the spring term— when the weather had turned to bitter, sleet-filled winds and the children came in every day with thin, pinched faces and red-rimmed eyes—she asked him to put them on the free meal ticket list as well. There were plenty of children in similar circumstances in the school, but because she knew the Alexanders, because she somehow associated herself closely with them, their plight affected her more than any of the others.

She had done the best she could, she assured herself. They had hot milk every day and three dinners a week. There wasn't anything more she could do. But the concern at the back of her mind didn't lessen, it grew worse. Everytime she looked at Gertie it grew worse.

Leaving school one afternoon at the end of March she caught sight of Gertie trudging along in front of her and, on impulse, called the child back.

"Do you have to go straight home this evening, Gertie?" she asked as they moved out into the playground and leaned forward into the wind.

"Yes, Miss," said Gertie apathetically.

"Only I wondered if you would like to come out with my cousin, Miss James, and myself and have some tea with us."

Gertie flushed. "I'll have my tea at home with my mum and dad," she said stiffly. Sarah pretended not to notice.

"Only I was telling my cousin, Miss James, about you the other day. About how you were Britannia the year before last and how you came top 'in arithmetic over all the others, and she said that you should come and have tea with us as a sort of prize."

Gertie walked stolidly on beside Sarah until they came to the gate and the shivering, waiting figure of May on her afternoon off.

"This is Gertie," said Sarah, hoping that May would not disclose the fact that she had never heard of Gertie before. "She's coming to have some tea with us."

Between May and Gertie there were no barriers of occupation or class authority. May said, "Hullo, Ger-

tie," hunched herself into the collar of her coat, and
began to talk about the mess the chimney-sweep had
made in the Bennett sitting-room that morning. Gertie
didn't say anything but when the time came for her to
turn off and go home on her own, she remained with
them, walking close to May and shuddering every time
the wind hit them.

When they came to the tea shop she hesitated, but
Sarah quickly opened the door and said in her best
classroom voice, "Hurry up, Gertie. We're making a
draught with this door open." Gertie obediently followed her in and, once in the atmosphere of warmth
that was pervaded with the smell of hot yeasty buns
and tomato soup, a small smile of anticipatory pleasure
lit her thin face for a second.

They sat at the table and studied the menu. The
sight of the child's pitiful face had succeeded in completely destroying Sarah's appetite but she said briskly,

"I think I'll have sausage and baked beans with
bread and butter, tea, and buttered bun. What about
you, May?"

May looked surprised. It was the end of the month
and neither of them had much money. May hadn't
planned on anything more than tea and toast.

"Well . . ." she said, and then felt Sarah kick her
under the table. Over Gertie's head—she was studying
every item on the menu with avid concentration—
Sarah mouthed, "I'll lend you the money out of the
rent," and nodded expressively towards Gertie.

"I'll have the same then," said May quickly, and to
the waitress, "Three sausage and baked beans, a plate
of bread and butter, a pot of tea for three, and three
buttered buns—if that's all right with you, Gertie?"

Gertie's face was suffused with a delicate glow of
warmth and happiness. She had been about to ask for
bread and butter because that was the cheapest. She
could see someone on another table eating sausage and
baked beans and the embarrassment of having tea with
Miss Whitman and her cousin evaporated in the knowledge that she would shortly have a portion of her own.

The sausage was beautifully cooked, crisp and brown

all the way round, like her mum did them. She took a
long time shaking salt and pepper over the beans and
arranging mustard—they never had mustard at home—
on the side of her plate the way Miss Whitman was
doing. It was the first time Gertie had even eaten in a
tea shop. She studied everything very carefully, the
china, and the waitresses, and the way people hold
their knives and forks. She waited until Miss Whitman
and her cousin had started to eat and still she didn't
pick up her knife or cut her piece of bread and butter.
She wanted to hold the moment a bit longer, the
moment with the plate of sausage and beans in front
of her, and the cup of tea, and a buttered bun when
the beans were all gone.

Sarah, cutting and eating with an enthusiastic busyness she did not feel, found it the most tasteless meal
she had ever eaten. The food clogged in her throat and
settled in a hard indigestible lump in the middle of her
chest. The child's face, undernourished and so pale it
looked dirty, was more than she could bear.

"Eat your tea, Gertie. It will get cold," she said
briskly.

Gertie cut off a piece of sausage and slowly carried
it to her mouth. Then she suddenly dropped her fork
onto her plate and began to cry.

"I can't eat it, Miss. I'm sorry . . . I can't eat it."
The knives and forks all fell back to their plates.
Sarah and May stared at the table, at the buns, at each
other's faces that reflected Gertie's unhappiness.

"It's my mum," dirty, putty-coloured tears fell onto
the baked beans. "My mum should be 'aving this tea.
My poor old mum doesn't 'ave anything. She should be
'aving this tea . . . I don't want it . . . thank you very
much, Miss . . . it's a lovely tea . . ." She put her hands
over her face and tried to cry quietly because she was
eleven and she was in a public place. She didn't make
any noise but her shoulders shook slightly. After a little
while she took her hands away. Grimy streaks of wet
lay across her cheeks. She took a deep shuddering
breath and made a conscious effort to control herself.

"I'll go home to my mum now," she said, getting up

from the table. "I'm very sorry about the tea, Miss. Thank you very much."

May quickly rummaged in her handbag and produced a paper bag. "You must take the buns home, dear," she said, hastily scooping them into the bag and handing them to Gertie. "Take the buns home for your mum."

"Good-bye, Miss. Thank you very much." She walked down the tea shop looking tiny and frail and ugly. When the door had closed behind her May and Sarah looked at the plates in front of them.

"I can't eat my tea," said May.

"No."

"I'll have something to drink though."

They sat glumly sipping tea, three plates of congealing beans cooling rapidly in front of them.

The following night she went round to see the Alexanders.


The woman who answered the door was almost unrecognisable. She stared at Sarah for a moment and then said tiredly, "Oh, it's you, Miss. Come in."

Sarah tried to prevent shocked consternation from registering on her face. She could not believe that in two years a woman—any woman—could have changed so much. She reminded herself that Mrs Alexander was still only in her early thirties but, when she looked at the terrible face in front of her, the reality of the woman's years ceased to have any meaning.

Mrs Alexander's skin was a waxen yellow, her eyes seemed to begin just above the chinline and end somewhere in the middle of her forehead, they were so shadowed in huge dark circles. She was thin to the point of emaciation and she walked as though she had a permanent period, bent protectively forward over the pit of her stomach.

The flat was extraordinarily quiet considering that the three younger children were at home. Maud and Georgie were sitting on the floor in a corner of the kitchen folding paper spills out of old newspapers. Teddy, the youngest, his legs distorted by rickets, sat on a chair by the window, staring listlessly down into the area well. It was the wrong kind of quietness, Sarah decided. It was the quietness that came because no one had the energy to do anything that required physical effort.

"Sit down," said Mrs Alexander. She didn't wait for Sarah to sit, she sagged into a chair by the table and leaned forward, taking the weight of her body on her arms. The entire flat was filled with the watery, stale smell of poverty.

"Gertie told me you took her out to tea last evening. That was kind of you."

Sarah shifted uneasily in her chair. "I don't want to be interfering or rude, Mrs Alexander," she said apologetically. "But I wondered if there was anything I could do . . . I was thinking about the Board of Guardians?"

Mrs Alexander shook her head. "We're no worse than many others," she said tiredly. "We've got the dole, and Sammy does a morning and evening paper round. And my Gertie's just got herself a Saturday job. Doing all the brasses down at the Seven Bells. We can manage."

"Would it help if Gertie took the Labour exam next year? I'd try and arrange it so that she could leave before the proper time if it would be any help." It was sometimes possible for children of poor families to leave before the statutory time providing they passed a test showing that their educational standards were at a reasonable level.

Mrs Alexander smiled, a thin, beaten-down smile. "I don't think the Education would let her take it," she said. "I know Mrs Appleby's Elsie took it. But that was because Mr Appleby died and there wasn't any money coming in at all. It's nice of you to bother. But we can manage."

"It's just . . . you look so ill, Mrs Alexander."

She nodded again, and slumped forward even further over the table. "I haven't been very well, dear. Not well at all."

The colour of Mrs Alexander's face, the huge dark

eyes, the dragging way she moved her body, suddenly
became explanatory to Sarah who had seen her own
mother almost permanently in the throes of pregnancies
and childbirth.

"Are you having another baby?"

Mrs Alexander jerked upright in her chair and said,
"No! No, I'm not having another baby! I can't have
another one. We won't be able to manage."

"I'm not prying," said Sarah earnestly. She had forgotten she was a schoolmistress. She was right back
on the other side of the fence, the side she had always
lived on, where people were poor and had too many
children and didn't know how not to have them. "I
know what it's like you see. My ma had too many
children, although we were lucky and my father was
never out of work. I had to help when she was ill . . . I
was the eldest you see . . . I know how bad it can be.
I'm younger than you, but I do know how it is . . . to
feel so ill and not to know how to manage and look
after the rest."

"I'm not having a baby," said Mrs Alexander defiantly, and then she began to cry.

Sarah looked again at her bent body and yellow
skin, and then she looked over to the sink—because
that's where these things were always kept—and saw,
standing beneath, a bucket of rags, soaking in cold
water that was faintly tinged with pink.

Mrs Alexander's huge expressive eyes stared at her,
entreating Sarah not to understand.

"How long have you been like this?" breathed Sarah.

They both looked across towards the children, and
then lowered their voices.

"Three months."

Sarah was too frightened to ask how it had happened. She wanted to pretend to herself that Mrs Alexander had just had an accidental miscarriage. She
didn't want to think about anything else that might
have happened.

"Have you been to the doctor?"

Mrs Alexander's eyes pleaded again. She shook her
head.

"I can't," she whispered. "I'll get into trouble. He'll find out what I've done and I'll get into trouble."

Sarah clenched her hands tightly together under the table. She wasn't shocked. She was frightened because it was the first time she had directly encountered the depths to which a desperate woman would go. She thought about her own family . . . her mother and her Aunt Betsy . . . and wondered if, in spite of being God-fearing people, they would have done the same thing if their circumstances had driven them to it. She didn't think they would . . . they were too strong. However desperate and bad things were, she somehow felt her family were strong enough to bear the bad things. But Mrs Alexander wasn't strong like Sarah's family were—and Mrs Alexander didn't have the family all about her—helping and chipping in when things were going through a bad period. And she didn't have the assurance that God was on her side if only she stuck it out.

And then Sarah had a quick perceptive flash about her own mother, about Anne-Louise who was so selfish and spoiled it was only the people and community around her who made her conform to the standards of village behaviour.

If my ma had been born in a city, she thought. And if she'd married someone other than pa, she'd have done it. In similar circumstances, she'd have done it.

"You'll have to go to the doctor's," she said quietly. "You can't go on for three months like it. You'll have to go to the doctor's."

"I'll be better in a while. I'm not only bad like this because I took too much stuff . . . the woman in the bottom flat . . . she gave me the stuff and said to take four spoonfuls. But I couldn't afford to take the . . . the risk it might not work . . . so I took double . . . I had to be sure . . ."

The pale haunted face, the dreadful eyes, the whispering over the kitchen table; bile rose suddenly in Sarah's throat, and with it a sullen, hating resentment of men, all of them, even the best. Mr Alexander couldn't help being out of work, couldn't help having five children to support on the dole, but it wasn't right

that Mrs Alexander should have the horror of making
the decision, of living with her own shame and guilt, of
whispering dirty tragic secrets over a kitchen table.

"What are you going to do?" asked Sarah.

"I'll get better," she answered with weary confidence.
"I've had five children, remember. I was like this after
the last one, but it got better. It just takes longer, that's
all."

She had to believe her because she didn't know what
else to do. And perhaps Mrs Alexander was right.
After five children she probably knew the way her own
body worked. Sarah undid her handbag and took ten
shillings out. It was part of the money she should have
sent back to the village that month. She pushed it over
the table toward Mrs Alexander.

"It's not charity," she entreated. "You can pay me
back one day."

Mrs Alexander clasped a terrible, clawlike hand
round the money and began to cry again, very quietly
and tiredly. "You're so kind," she said. "You're not
like one of them at all. I forget you're their teacher.
You're like us. You're just like us."

Sarah stood up to leave and Mrs Alexander dragged
after her.

"Don't let it happen to you, dear," she said tiredly.
"You've got a job. Keep it, no matter what happens.
Do whatever that old girl says . . . thrashings . . . anything so long as you keep your job. And be careful
about getting married. Don't let it happen to you if
you can help it."

She couldn't get out of the flat quickly enough. The
despair and hopeless lack of courage seemed to seep
from the walls. She had to get out quickly before she
caught the disease of apathetic defeat.

Outside in the street she was glad that the wind was
so cold and violent. It gave her something to fight back
against.

Two months later Mrs Alexander collapsed in the
street. She was returning from her cleaning job—three
shillings for a morning's scrubbing at the Seven Bells—

and had just spent a shilling of it in purchasing a large marrow bone, three pounds of potatoes and two pen-north of pot herbs with which she intended to make a dinner broth. When she collapsed the potatoes rolled all over the pavement and her first words on regaining consciousness in the public ward of Guy's Hospital were, "The vegetables . . . did someone pick up the vegetables?"

Gertie Alexander received temporary permission to stay away from school and look after the family. Occasionally Maud was away too, coerced by family pressures into giving extra help. The rest of the family grew even scruffier, more pallid, more apathetic.

Sarah was surprised to see Gertie waiting outside school one evening. Gertie now looked so like her mother that Sarah ceased to associate her with the child who had once been in her class.

"Hullo, Gertie," she said quietly. "How's your mother?"

Gertie's face, tense and grey, stared up at Sarah. "She wants to see you, Miss. She's come home from hospital, and she says will you come round and see 'er."

"I'll come now." She was glad that at last something was happening where she could help. She dreaded going to the Alexanders'—she always seemed to be dreading going to the Alexanders'—but now they were so much her family that she was relieved to be called on for positive action.

The flat was reasonably clean. The double bed from the only bedroom in the flat had been brought into the living-room and there were clean, patched sheets over the mattress. Mrs Alexander was lying propped up on several pillows. Her face resembled—exactly—a skull. Transparent, yellow skin was stretched tautly over jutting nose, cheekbones, and prominent jaw. A sickly, sweet smell came from her mouth. She smiled when she saw Sarah. Sarah smiled back but the sight of the grinning death's head made her shudder.

Gertie went straight up to her mother and put her arms round shoulders that were mercifully covered in a flannel nightdress. She lay her face close against her mother's and kissed it. She lifted one of the clawlike hands from the grey blanket and held it against her cheek. "She's getting better now," she said to Sarah. Sarah walked across to the window and stared hard at the flat on the other side of the well. She swallowed, then turned back into the room and crossed to the bed.

"How are you?"

Mrs Alexander nodded very gently. "It's nice to be home," she answered, and then the door from the kitchen opened and Mr Alexander came in with a plate of bread and butter and a cup of tea.

At the sight of him Sarah felt again a sudden surge of resentment and dislike, the same resentment she had felt when she had visited the sick woman before. It's his fault, she thought aggressively. It's his fault she's like this. It's his fault and she's the one that's going to die. And then she looked at his small, tired crumpled face under the curly hair and the lump came back into her chest.

"A nice cup of tea, love," he said gently. "And try to eat something, eh?"

Mrs Alexander shook her head, but took the cup from his outstretched hand. With Gertie and her husband watching she sipped slowly from the thick white china, then, exhausted, handed the cup back to him.

Neither of them, neither he nor Gertie, seemed to notice Sarah. Gertie sat on the bed with her arms round her mother's shoulders and he, after a meaningless smile and a "Hullo, Miss," sat stroking his wife's hand.

"She'll get better now we've got her home again," he said reassuringly. "We'll soon get her better now." He put both his hands over his wife's arm and suddenly tears began to stream down his cheeks. "Oh, Gawd!" he sobbed. "Oh Gawd! You'll get better now you're home again, won't you, old girl?"

Then he got up and stumbled across the room to the kitchen. Mrs Alexander whispered something to Gertie and the child followed him.

"I'm going to die," she said to Sarah when they were alone.

"No."

"They told me at the hospital. I've got a weak heart and pernicious anaemia, and . . . other things. It's all gone wrong inside me. I should have had it done when Teddy was born. I'm going to die."

She did what the others had done, put her arm round the thin shoulders. There wasn't anything she could say. She hoped the physical contact would speak for her.

"When I'm dead," said Mrs Alexander tiredly, "they'll probably try to split up the family. I expect the Board of Guardians will take over. Gertie's not old enough to manage on her own and there's no one to help out. I've got no sisters and George's people are still in Scotland. So they'll try to put the kids in homes." She grasped Sarah's hand in her own papery thin one. "George won't know how to fight them. He don't know what to say. You'll help, won't you? You'll tell him what to say so as the family can stay together. You're educated, see. You'll know how to put it. You go and see them with him and tell them how important it is . . . they've got to stay together . . . that's all that people like us have . . . just each other . . . nothing else . . ."

She fell back panting against her pillows. The sickly sweet smell was very noticeable. "You'll help, won't you? You know how to talk to people. My poor George . . ." The haunted eyes blotched over and tears began to run down the side of Mrs Alexander's jutting nose. Sarah couldn't speak. She nodded.

"It's got to be someone who knows how to make them understand. My Gertie . . . she's a good girl . . . she'll try and manage somehow . . . just so long as they don't put her in a home . . she'll look after her dad . . ." She raised a corner of the sheet and wiped her face. "Oh, God!" she murmured brokenly. "I don't want to die."

I mustn't cry, Sarah thought to herself. Whatever I do I mustn't cry. She's enough to bear without that.

She swallowed hard, and held her ribs taut, staring hard out of the window and trying to think about the flat opposite, about the washing hanging on the line, about all the people living in the flats below. The atmosphere in the room grew less heavy. There were the sounds of people living all around them—the murmur of Gertie and her father in the kitchen—the sounds of families screeching and shouting and bawling up the area well through the warmth of a July evening.

"There's someone at the door," said Mrs Alexander tiredly, all emotion now drained away from her.

Sarah stood up, and as she turned away from the bed her control broke and tears flooded suddenly into her eyes. When she opened the door David Baron was standing there.

He was even shabbier than the last time she had seen him and his shabbiness was emphasised by the magnificence of a large bunch of carnations held in one hand, and a bunch of black grapes in the other. He looked awkward and uncomfortable. When he saw Sarah he mumbled inaudibly and shuffled the grapes and the flowers into alternate hands.

"I won't stay," he said to Sarah. "I'll just leave these for her. Tell George I'll bring some more things on Friday."

Sarah held the door wide open. "You've to come in," she choked. "You've to come in and see her."

He walked over to the bed and stared at Mrs Alexander. He tried to walk gently but he was so uncomfortable he knocked against the foot of the bed and the woman winced. His face flamed and he quickly drew back.

"These are for you," he mumbled, putting the flowers and fruit on the bed. Mrs Alexander smiled.

"That's nice," she said gently.

"Are you all right for everything?" he asked. "Do you need anything? You just let me know what you need and I'll get it for you."

She smiled again. "All that lovely fruit you sent me in hospital. And the flowers . . ."

"You let me know," he blurted again. "You let me know and I'll get it for you."

Sarah felt sorry for him. He was shocked by the sight and smell of Mrs Alexander and he was awkward in a sick room. He didn't know what to say, or do. He wanted to show pity and compassion but he didn't know how. When Mr Alexander came back into the room he jumped to his feet and walked towards the door.

"I'll go now, George," he said, relieved. "Just brought a few things round. And I'll come again Friday." Mr Alexander nodded.

"You let me know, George. Anything you want . . . anything at all . . . for your wife or the children . . . let me know and I'll get it . . ."

He was out of the door and away . . . away from the dying woman and the sad, small man with the crumpled face. The carnations and the grapes looked lurid and bizarre lying so close to Mrs Alexander. She was leaning back on the pillow, her eyes closed and her lips colourless.

"Will you go now, Miss?" asked Mr Alexander politely. "The wife's tired, see, and she ought to 'ave a rest." His eyes were red-rimmed and agonised. "I've got to build 'er up again, see? Make her well like she was before. Never had anything wrong before, she hasn't."

"I'll go. If you need me specially send Gertie round."

She didn't look back before leaving the room. She knew what she would see—Mr Alexander sitting holding his wife's hand and staring at her terrible face.

David was waiting for her at the bottom of the stairs, hands stuffed into pockets, his face unsmiling and guarded. For a moment neither of them knew what to say but they were each aware that, whatever their personal feuds or memories, it was all unimportant compared with the dying woman upstairs.

"Where did you get the money for the fruit and flowers?" she asked abruptly, and equally abrupt he answered, "I stole them from the fruit market."

It was a warm evening. The thick glass windows of the pub on the corner—carefully opaqued out and showing the name of the brewery—were pushed up and showed a line of assorted caps that moved and tilted as glasses were raised, emptied, and lowered again. The smell of beer and sawdust wafted out. On the pave-

ment a row of cane chairs stood with their backs to the
wall. A couple of "old girls" were drinking port and
lemon and three small children squatted on the pavement playing dabs.

They began to move along the street. He annoyed
her because he walked apologetically just half a pace
behind. He annoyed her but she didn't want him to go.

"How are you?" she asked politely. "Have you got a
job?"

"No."

"You were selling purses in the market the last time
I saw you," she reminded him meanly—because she
couldn't forget how he had run away from her on that
occasion. His face flamed and he looked sullen and
resentful.

"I'm working with my father now," he said defen-
sively. "I'm learning shoes and leatherwork until I can
get something. We've been making purses from the offcuts and I'm trying to sell them. I'm living at home.
I've got to have a place to live, haven't I?"

She didn't know him well enough to understand his
sense of failure. He had thought himself above the
manacles of family and tradition and the old ways that
were, to him, the bad ways. He had gone back to his
family because he had nowhere else to go, because his
belief and trust in the Cause had been broken and he
had no faith in anyone any more. He had come out of
prison needing, more than anything, the reassurance
and strength of the family who scolded and railed and
wrung their hands in horror at his anarchistic manners
and atheistic beliefs, but who were there, ready to
absorb him back whenever he wanted to come.

"You look dreadful," she told him nastily. "Are you
ill?" She knew she was being mean but she wanted to
hurt him. He had held her against him and spoken en-
dearments to her in a foreign tongue. He had told her
she was beautiful and had made her feel warm and
excited. And then he had gone away and left her.
There was another reason she wanted to hurt him. It
was something to do with Mrs Alexander. If she could
fight and quarrel with David Baron about little things,

she might be able to forget about the sickly-sweet woman with the skull face.

"I'm not ill," he answered. "It's been a bad year, that's all."

And then she was ashamed of herself, and felt sick and miserable, about him and about the whole terrible evening.

"I'm sorry!" she burst out. "I'm so sorry! I'm being spiteful and I don't really mean it! I worried about you . . . when you went . . . when the police dragged you off that time . . . and now all this is happening with the Alexanders."

"Can I see you, Sarah? Can I see you again? Please!"

She began to cry. "Yes. Of course you can see me."

"Oh, Sasha! Sasha!" he choked. "That's what I call you in my head. That's my own name for you. It doesn't mean anything but that's how I think of you!"

"She's going to die," sobbed Sarah. "That poor woman is going to die."

"I haven't any money. But I must see you again!"

"If only I'd made her go to the hospital before, when I saw her before, she might not be dying!" She put her hands up to her cheeks and tried to stem her tears.

"I've no money. There's not enough in the business to give me any money. But you'll see me, Sarah? Sasha! Sasha! you'll see me?"

When she nodded he suddenly pulled her hands away from her face and brought them up to his mouth. Feverishly, his eyes closed, he kissed her palms and twisted them against his cheeks, murmuring, "Sasha, Sasha!" rubbing her fingers against his face, kissing them, twining them about his own fingers until she could hardly bear to be so close without enmbracing him.

"You mustn't do that," she cried.

"When shall I see you? I must see you soon!"

"I can't. Not often. I don't have time." Already she was afraid of him. Afraid of the violence in him, of the warmth and dark exictement in his eyes, of the way he was making her feel. She wanted to kiss him. She wanted to feel his face and mouth against her own, to

let the vigour and strength of his emotions sweep her
away from reason and common sense.

"You must see me!" he shouted. "I shan't let you
alone until you promise."

Nervously she stared round the street. A little way
up a bookie's runner, keeping a watchful eye open for
the police, was staring curiously at them. The people
sitting outside the pub, glasses in hand, all turned to
watch and listen.

"See me!" he shouted.

Humiliated and ashamed she snatched her hands
away. "Oh, stop!" she pleaded. "Stop shouting! Everyone's looking at us . . . I'll see you . . . I'll see you
again . . ." She paused, her emotion a confused tangle
of his warmth and violence, and beneath that the prevailing memory of Mrs Alexander.

"We'll go and see them together," she said inspired.
"We'll go every week to see that poor woman and
then you can walk home with me afterwards." She
was tremendously relieved. She had thought of a way
of not being alone with him for too long, and yèt of
seeing him, because she still wanted to see him. Somehow the fact of going to help the Alexanders set a seal
of respectability on their meetings.

He quietened, as though the Alexanders and their
troubles stilled his own passions.

"Yes, Sarah," he said humbly. "Yes. All right then.
If that's what you say, then that's what we'll do."

The hot brown eyes caressed and entreated, but she
remained firm.

"Friday, then?"

"Friday."

He tried to reach out and take her hands again but
she quickly thrust them behind her back, afraid to let
him even touch her. When they began, once more, to
pace along the road she wouldn't look at him, although
she was aware of his gaze on her.

She tried to be sensible and controlled but inside her
head raged the knowledge that she was going to see
him again—that they would meet and talk and play
the dangerous game of being together.

She felt no guilt at using the harrowing respectability of the Alexander family for their meetings. Everything about David was confused with the Alexanders. The misery, the grief, the poverty was all part of David and herself.

At the corner of the street she asked him to go. She didn't want Florric to see him. He touched her cheek with his hand and said once more, "Friday?" and she nodded, and the pattern of their future meetings was set—mirrored against the agony of watching Mrs Alexander growing steadily worse while her family tried to pretend she was recovering.

And when, in November, the tired sad woman finally died, the habit of seeing each other had become too strong to break.

Every Friday they continued to meet—outside the grim flats off the Old Kent Road.

# Eight

MAY got on quite well with the Dances. When she had
first come up to London she had been shocked but
fascinated by them—they were so *vulgar,* so *common,*
so fat and sweaty and so—*marvellous.* She had an immediate entrée into their family because of Sarah. Any
friend or relative of Sarah's was all right with the
Dances, all of them. It was quite plain that one day
Sarah was going to marry Charlie, and then they would
all be family, so to speak. May grew into the habit of
thinking of Charlie and Sarah together, in the same
way that she secretly thought of herself and Peter together. They were two couples, two pairs, who were
only waiting for the right things to happen, the right
time to come along, before they paired off properly.

Sometimes she became disheartened because Peter
didn't hang around her the way Charlie waited after
Sarah. He couldn't of course, he was away at sea for
much of the time, but on his first long leave after his
foreign tour, although he was pleased to see her, although he took her out several times, he seemed preoccupied with thoughts of his own. She wanted to share
things with him, to give him everything, all her thoughts
and wishes and ideas, she wanted to give them all to
Peter. But Peter, when she talked, just smiled, and listened, and nodded, but she felt he wasn't really there.
And he seemed to have lost his old exuberance, the
exuberance of that wonderful summer two years ago
when the four of them had laughed and swung their
way through London. He had grown thinner, had lost
weight that his six-foot frame could ill afford to lose,

and he looked tired—so tired that she really couldn't mind too much about him not seeming interested in anything.

She was envious of Sarah, having Charlie adoring her so much, but she didn't begrudge Sarah her good luck—she just wished Peter felt that way about her. She couldn't begrudge Sarah anything really. It was Sarah who had made London so wonderful. Sarah's room at Aunt Florrie's was hers to use whenever she wanted. She was invited to all the Dance parties and family festivals and although at first she was embarrassed—on one occasion Pa Dance, having drunk too much stout, got up and sang a song about having "Me little wiggle-waggle in me hand"—she realised that, without the Dances, life would indeed be dull.

One afternoon May opened the door of the Bennett basement kitchen in time so see Maisie descending the steps.

"Hullo," said May, surprised. None of the Dances had ever called to see her before.

" 'Lo, luv," panted Maisie, holding heavily to the railing down the side of the steps. "Cor, don't like these stairs much. Fancy coming down these after an evening at the Blue Eyed Maid." Her stout legs encased in ginger-coloured lisle stockings negotiated the bend at the bottom and she leaned against the wall for a second.

"Come in and I'll make you a cup of tea," said May.

Maisie followed her into the kitchen. She was wearing a wrap-over coat of cerise wool trimmed with a seal-skin collar. Her cloche hat was a different coloured red from the coat and clashed horribly. "Phew!" she gasped flinging open her coat as the heat from the kitchen struck her. May winced. Underneath the coat was a chenille frock of yet another shade of red.

"Nice to see you," said May politely. "Were you passing this way?"

Maisie flopped down into a chair and undid the button straps on her shoes.

"No, dear," she said heavily. "I wasn't passing. I've come particularly because I wanted to talk to you."

May warmed the teapot and reached for the coronation tea caddy. King George and Queen Mary beamed out from the sides of the tin in full ceremonial robes.

"Nice to know 'e's getting better again, poor luv," said Maisie gesturing towards King George. "Thought the poor old dear was a goner this winter. Still, she looks after 'im all right, I don't doubt." She picked up her cup, blew on it, and took a large slurp.

"Yes, I've come because I wanted to talk to you," she said again. "Ma 'as sent me round special. Ruby's looking after the kids so as I could come and see you."

"Well, I'd have come round if you'd asked," faltered May. "If you'd sent a message by Sarah, I'd have come round."

"Ah!" said Maisie mysteriously. "But that's just what we don't want."

"Don't want what?" asked May bewildered.

"Don't want Sarah knowing. And don't want you coming round to the house to talk about it when Sarah, or Charlie, might pop in any minute."

"Is it a surprise, then?" questioned May.

Maisie finished the other half of her cup of tea and pushed it over to May for a refill. "You might call it that," she said ominously. "Certainly it's come as a surprise to all of us. We never thought anything like this would happen."

May began to grow alarmed. "What's happened?" she demanded.

Maisie ladled four spoonfuls of sugar into her second cup and stirred.

"It's about your Sarah," she accused. "There's Something Going On."

"What do you mean? Something going on?" puzzled May.

"That's what we'd all like to know. But there's no doubt about it, none at all. Something's going on with your Sarah. I noticed," Maisie paused and sipped. "I noticed at our Christmas Do that Something was going on. Kept pulling 'er 'and from Charlie's she did. And wouldn't dance properly wiv 'im. Kept making 'im keep 'is distance. Well, that's not right, not at Christmas when you've 'ad a few drinks, is it?" she asked righteously. "We always 'as a bit of slap-up at Christmas, don't we? But not our Sarah, not this year. Wasn't 'aving none, she wasn't."

May picked up a spoon and began to make patterns in the sugar. "That's just Sarah being Sarah," she explained earnestly. "You know what Sarah's like. Half the time she's dreaming away in some world of her own. She's always been like that. Even when we were little. Her ma was always clumping her for dreaming away and not listening." She began warming to Sarah's defence. "And you know what a funny old thing she is with her moods and her fancies—always on about going round the world and doing grand things. She was probably all taken up with some newfangled notion at Christmas. And anyway," she added prosaically, "it's February now. You surely haven't been worrying about this ever since Christmas."

"There's another thing," said Maisie menacingly. "She's been seen out . . . with Someone . . ."

"Someone . . . ?"

"A dark, foreign-looking bloke. She's been seen more than once walking along wiv 'im. In fact . . ." she paused for dramatic effect. "In fact, I meself, 'ave seen 'er wiv 'im. And," she raised her forefinger in the air, "and I might tell you she was so busy talking to 'im, this feller, that she passed right by without seeing me."

"Oh!" said May bleakly, beginning to understand.

"Now then," said Maisie. "We all wants to know what's going on. It's been understood that she and our Charlie are walking out. We just want to know what's going on."

"I think it's something to do with that poor family she's involved with," said May weakly. "You know, that woman who died and left all the children and Sarah had to go up the Charity with them and help sort things out. I think it's something to do with them."

"Ha! 'E didn't look like no widower with a big family to me," said Maisie accusingly. " 'E looked like a foreigner."

"Oh, no! He's not the father," explained May. "But I think he's helping the family too. He works in a market or something, and he takes things to them. That's all it is, I'm quite sure. Just he and Sarah helping out with that poor family."

"Hmm," Maisie looked as sceptical as her round, red face would allow.

"It's only in the way of her duty that she see's him," emphasised May. "He used to work with Mr Alexander on the railway. I don't quite understand. And Sarah promised that poor woman she'd help out after she'd died. The Charity have put the younger children into homes, but Sarah's promised to get the eldest girl through the Labour exam as soon as she can so that the kids can all come home again. That's the only time she sees him, David Baron, I mean. Not the father."

"Ha!" said Maisie swiftly. "Well, at least we know 'is name. David Baron."

May was consumed with guilt. She was trying to help Sarah, and she was only making it worse. The trouble was that, the more she talked to Maisie, the more uncertain she became of Sarah's innocence. She remembered all kinds of incidents, all kinds of little things that suddenly began to have meaning. That time, the first time she had come up to London, and they had gone to Brixton market and had seen David Baron selling purses, Sarah had been terribly upset, more so, surely, than if he had just been a casual acquaintance. And the time, during the wonderful summer, when she had caught Sarah crying for no reason at all. And Fridays—May became guiltily aware of Sarah's changing behaviour on Fridays. At one time she would pop around to see May on Fridays, but she hadn't done that for ages. And once, when May had been given an unexpected Friday evening off, she had hurried round to see if Sarah would go out with her, but Sarah had explained about the Alexanders and how she couldn't let them down. It hadn't worried May at the time but now she remembered that Sarah was all dressed up for visiting with her best coat on and her face powdered and her hair done in a new style, coiled round her head like Miss Bennett's.

"I'm sure there's nothing in it," she said lamely.

Maisie grunted and leaned forward to button her shoe straps over swollen feet. "Well," she said. "We're not 'appy about it. Not 'appy at all. Ma is very worried indeed, I might tell you. It's 'appened before, 'asn't it? It 'appened wiv Sarah's ma. She run off and left poor Maxie wiv a broken 'eart, didn't she? Not that 'e 'asn't done all right wiv Floss," she amended hurriedly, in case it should be thought that Florrie was an inferior addition to the Dance family. "But it ain't right. It ain't right that Maxie should 'ave been jilted all those years ago by Anne-Louise, and now it looks as though our Sarah is aiming to do the same to Charlie."

"What do you want me to do?" asked May weakly.

Maisie stood, held her stomach in with a deep breath, and fastened her wrap-over coat.

"We're going to talk about it, and you'd best come round," she announced stolidly. "We've fixed Friday—seeing as 'ow that's the night Sarah gets Up To Something. It's all arranged. Sid is going to take Charlie out for a game of darts, and we'll all get together and see what ought to be done. You be there."

"Yes," said May nervously. "All right. I'll ask Miss Bennett if I can change my evening off."

"Eight o'clock."

"Yes, Maisie. I'll be there."

Maisie opened the kitchen door and prepared to clamber up the area steps. "Glad the poor old King's all right again," she said socially, trying to leave May on a less sombre note. May nodded.

"Bye then." Maisie's large calves plodded solidly up the stairs. May, looking up after her, could see pink directoire knickers pulled well down over her knees.

"Good-bye, Maisie," she murmured feebly, and went back into the kitchen to start worrying about next Friday evening.

May, unlike Sarah, had never been to a Dance emergency meeting. She arrived early because she was nervous and therefore found that, as more and more Dances arrived, she was pushed right into the centre of the room up against ma's bed when really she had hoped to stay back in a corner where no one would notice her.

Ma gave her a kiss and a hug but, in deference to the solemnity of the occasion, she did not smile. "Sit on the bed, luv. Sit on the bed," she breathed to May, and May had no alternative but to perch on the edge of the slippery pink bedspread.

"Now then," said ma when they were all assembled. "We know what's going on with Sarah and our Charlie. We know that Sarah is Up To Something, no credit to 'er, and we know that our Charlie thinks the world of Sarah and 'as waited for 'er a long time."

There were grumbles and mumbles of assent.

"For a start," said ma, "we don't want our Sarah marrying a foreigner, do we?"

Pa Dance hawked and spat out of the window. "It's like 'er ma, all them years ago," he reminded them. "Going off and jilting our Maxie like she did, and 'im that sweet on 'er." Maxie, standing by the bedroom door, looked uncomfortable but important. It was nice to be reminded that he had survived, with dignity, the turmoils of a broken heart. Then he remembered Florrie, his "second choice" and he turned hurriedly to pat her on the hand because she was looking slightly sullen. Florrie, married to Maxie for twenty-three rollicking, contented, ribald years, sometimes got fed up with being reminded that Maxie had married her on the rebound.

"Not but what's there's something to be said from Sarah's point of view," said ma fairly. "Our Sarah's twenty-four years old, and it's natural she should be thinking about getting settled. She's got to be looking about for a 'usband who's got a proper job and can be thinking about getting married. So we can't blame 'er all that much—even though she's Up To Something."

"But that's not it at all," interrupted May. "It's not like that at all. This David Baron. He hasn't got a job either. He's just like Charlie. He picks up odd work where he can ... I think ..." her voice faltered away as she became aware that everyone in the room was staring at her. She realised she had said the wrong thing. If Sarah was Up To Something with a man who was out of work, it was as good as saying that David Baron was a better man than Charlie Dance, starting as they did with equal chances. And not one of the family would ever believe that a foreigner could top their Charlie.

"Well," said ma, ignoring the interruption. "I thought about it all, and I've decided what must be done."

The family breathed comfortably. The situation was a worrying one, but somehow they had known that ma—and pa too of course—would know what to do. "We've to get Charlie fixed up with a proper job so as 'e can get married. And as there just ain't a job for 'im, the family's got to fix 'im up with a business of 'is own."

One or two of the male Dances, breadwinners, showed consternation. Keeping a family together was hard enough, especially when there were so many kids and one or other of the men was always out of work. Setting Charlie up in a business of his own sounded very expensive.

"Now then," continued ma. "Me and pa 'ave come up wiv a very good idea."

"Don't know why we didn't think of it before," grumbled pa.

"Better late than never, pa. Better late than never," said ma calmly. She laid a swollen, distorted, sausage-shaped hand on her chest and coughed and wheezed for several seconds. Dampness sprang out on her forehead and it was some seconds before she could speak again.

"Old Finnegan up the road is selling 'is 'orse and cart," she announced. " 'E's decided to go out of the old iron business and set up a stall in the Bella. Now," she paused. "What I suggest is this. We club together and buy old Finnegan's 'orse and cart. We can do it up nice, and then Dad and Maxie and all the rest of you up Billingsgate can 'elp our Charlie get started on a nice fish round. There ain't a regular fish round in these streets."

"Ain't we too near the market?" asked Maxie. "Ain't people hereabouts too used to nipping over there early when they wants fish?"

"Well," said pa from the window. "For a start they ain't supposed to buy their fish in the market—it's wholesale—and for another thing if it's brought to the door it's better, ain't it. And we're forgetting the big 'ouses up Kennington Road and in Trinity Square. Those are the 'ouses 'e's got to sell to."

Excitement was beginning to generate within the room. The idea *was* a good one. The purchase of the battered old horse and cart was not impossible if they all chipped in, and the fact that Charlie's round would only be an extension of their site in the market made them feel that the family was branching out, building and expanding into a bigger business.

"It sounds all right to me," said Maisie enthusiastically. A loud babble of conversation broke out, ways and means were swopped and discarded. Ideas for doing up the cart sprang into several minds at once. The types of fish likely to sell in certain areas were mooted and considered.

"Quiet!" shouted pa. "There's a few more things to discuss."

"It's the question of the 'orse and cart," stated ma. "Of where to keep 'em. Now then, we've decided that for the time being we can keep the cart in front of the 'ouse, where the pavement is set back a bit behind the tanner's yard. We can keep it there until the police say otherwise. But the 'orse is a problem. 'E'll 'ave to be kept in someone's garden."

Without exception every eye in the room turned to stare at Maxie and Florrie. Maxie and Florrie were the only Dances who had what could be termed a garden. Several of the others had a small concrete yard bounded on three sides by high brick walls. Some had a balcony in a block of flats. Others looked down into a shop yard filled with old crates and wheelbarrows. Maxie and Florrie had a piece of earth, forty foot long by twenty foot wide at the back of their house. In the middle of the earth was an old lilac tree to which Florrie fixed her washing line.

"It would be lovely!" exclaimed Maisie. "Florrie, your garden would be lovely! 'E could stand under your lilock tree when 'e wanted a bit of shade or when it was raining."

"I reckon I could build 'im a stable, just enough room for 'im to lie down in when 'e was tired," announced Bert.

Ma, pa, Maisie, Bert, and every Dance in the room waited for Maxie and Flo to give their assent. Looking after the horse was going to be a bit more than just chipping in with the money and organising the fish round. They couldn't *tell* Maxie and Flo they had to have the horse. They had to wait until they volunteered.

"Well," said Maxie at last, without enthusiasm. "I suppose me and Florrie 'ad better 'ave the 'orse."

"You're a good boy!" said ma warmly. "You're a good boy, Maxie. And it's right, somehow, that you should be the one to look after the 'orse, you being the one who suffered all those years ago on account of Sarah's ma. You looking after the 'orse is going to make sure that it doesn't 'appen all over again with our Charlie."

" 'Ow are you going to get 'im in the garden?" asked Maisie. There was no back entrance to Maxie and Flo's garden. On either side were other gardens, at the bottom, the corrugated-iron back of a wheelwright's shed. Maxie and Florrie stared at each other, brows wrinkled in consideration.

"I reckon we could get 'im in through the front door," said Florrie positively. "As I remember, 'e's not too big an 'orse, and there's only that one awkward turn by the kitchen door to get 'im through. I reckon we could manage."

"Good!" said ma. "Then it's all settled. Pa will work out 'ow much we've all got to chip in—Maxie and Florrie will pay less because of the 'orse—and wiv luck we'll 'ave Charlie starting on 'is fish round two weeks from now. May . . ." She turned to May who had been stunned to silent awe by the power and administrative efficiency of the family. "May, the next time Sarah's brother comes home on leave, I want you to talk to 'im. Get 'im to stop Sarah seeing this feller, and tell 'im that now it's only a little while till Sarah will be fixed up with an 'usband. In fact it might be a good idea if you 'ad a talk with 'er yourself."

"Well, I'll do what I can," murmured May. She knew that nothing she could say would make any difference to Sarah, but the family's efforts had so impressed her that she felt she ought to try.

Her opportunity occurred on her next half day. She called round to see Sarah just when they were trying to push the horse through the front door. There was no point in trying to get up to Sarah's room until the reluctant beast had been wheedled through into the dark passage. Florrie stood inside the hall holding a carrot before the horse's nose and pa, Maxie, Bert and Sid, pushed and heaved at the animal's behind. Several large flies buzzed fiercely over the sweating heads of both men and animal. Sarah opened her bedroom window and shouted down.

"You won't be able to get in for hours, May," she called crossly. "He won't go in frontwards or backwards."

The horse suddenly decided to throw in his lot with the Dances when it came to winning Sarah for Charlie. He whinnied, threw back his head and then took two nervous steps in the direction of the carrot. May watched with interest while the difficult corner by the kitchen door was handled and twenty minutes later the horse was tethered to the lilac tree tentatively chomping at a wisp of hay.

"I don't know why Aunt Florrie has to have a horse in the backyard," said Sarah irritably when May had come up to her room.

May coughed. "It's something to do with setting Charlie up in a fish round," she said cautiously. Sarah flung herself down on the bed and threw a pile of exercise books onto the floor.

"Oh I know about *that*. It's just . . . the family make such a fuss and noise about anything they do. And we've got to have that horse business twice a day— pushing him in and out through the hall every day. Anyway, Charlie was well enough as he was. He's been getting enough casual work in the markets to tide him over."

"He wants to get settled," said May slowly. "You know he's hoping to marry you, Sarah. It's natural he should want to get settled."

Sarah jumped off the bed and kicked the exercise books. "Why does everyone take it for granted I'm going to marry Charlie?" she asked petulantly. "Nothing's ever been said to me about it. And I don't want to get married, or settled, or anything!"

May breathed deeply and closed her eyes. "Is it something to do with David Baron?" she asked.

She opened her eyes and saw a slow, delicate flush spread up her cousin's neck.

"Don't be silly!" said Sarah with too much assurance in her voice. "Of course it's nothing to do with David Baron. I just see him every week when I go to visit Gertie. And he walks home with me afterwards. That's all." She stared defiantly at May, trying to appear superior and self-possessed.

"He's a friend. Just a casual friend," she said.

May twisted her hands nervously together. "You've been so funny lately. Sort of . . . occupied . . . The Dances have noticed it. And I wondered . . . well I thought it might be something to do with him—with David Baron."

"Well it isn't," Sarah snapped, and then when she saw the hurt on May's face she felt guilty. But how could she explain to May about the excitement, the fear, the delight, the violence of her meeting with David. Every week they quarrelled, every week they shouted at each other about Karl Marx, or the coming election, or Ramsay MacDonald, or whether or not it was right for the voting age for women to be lowered from thirty to twenty-one. And every week David would fire her with excitement, would lift her out of herself, making her feel that she was living in a world where things were happening, where anything was possible. Even to look at him was exciting because he was different—dark and foreign with a moulded face and a strong, vibrant body.

And every week he would surprise her with his sudden changes from vehemence to delight. Once, in the middle of a heated fight, he had turned towards her, grasped her face between his hands and kissed her. Often he would snatch her hand and hold it against his face. Sometimes the tide of emotion between them would grow so great he would just keep saying, "Sasha! Sasha! My beautiful Sasha!" and she was glad they were in a public street where even he had to control himself. For Sarah was quite sure that if ever they were alone together, alone and private and unseen, their passionate reaction would flare into something violent and uncontrollable.

"You like him, don't you?" asked May doggedly.

"Of course not . . ." Sarah began, and then the temptation to confide in someone, just a little, grew too much and she burst out, "Oh, May! He's so interesting! He's got all kinds of ideas, some of them are stupid but they're *different*. And May . . . once, when he had some money, he took Gertie and me to St George's Hall . . . to a concert! May, I never heard music like that before! Not in my whole life! It made me . . ." she flung her arms out in the air, trying to describe in movement the way she had felt. "He makes me feel . . . Oh, May . . . The world is so big! He makes me feel the world is so big!"

May began to feel nervous. She was sorry for the Dances and especially for Charlie, but she was really worried about Sarah.

"Why don't you take him home?" she asked. "If he's that special you ought to take him home to the village to meet your pa and the family."

"I can't."

"Why can't you?"

"I just can't."

She loved her pa, and most things he understood, but she knew that David Baron would be completely alien in the village. Because there were the other things about him, the strange things that frightened her. He stole. Every time he went to the Alexanders' he took groceries, or clothes, or meat, and when she asked where they came from, he said simply, "I stole them." When she protested he refused to listen, telling her she was bourgeois and a servant of capitalist dogma. "In our society of plenty, the Alexanders should go hungry?" he would ask. "No! There's enough for them but the wrong people have too much. I don't take from anyone who is hungry. I take from those who have too much."

He could convince her of anything, but in her heart she knew it was wrong and she knew that in the village his wild words and violent actions would shock and frighten her people. And she loved her village. She couldn't bear to have it, and her pa and her brothers, and her Aunt Betsy and all the good but gullible people, attacked by his sceptical doctrines.

"But what's going to happen?" asked May, distressed. "If you like him that much, but you can't take him home, what's going to happen?" To May, liking someone, and taking them home was the same. If you liked someone, then you wanted to marry them. It was as simple as that. "What's going to happen?"

"I don't know." Sarah turned her face away and fiddled with the lace curtains.

"And what about him? About David Baron? What does he say about it all? You seem to spend so much time talking about things, what does he say?"

"I don't know," Sarah said again. She and David argued and arranged the problems of the world, but they never talked about things like going home to meet their families. And sometimes she sensed that there were areas of background and family in his life that she must not explore—things he would not talk about and did not wish to share with her. Once, when in their absorption with each other they had walked right the way down to Whitechapel, they had encountered a funny little couple in black—the man, old and bent, in a long coat and a flat-brimmed hat from beneath which hung two long sidelocks, the old lady equally incongruous in a bright red wig that was obviously artificial and was only partially covered by a black shawl.

David had suddenly ceased to talk and on his face was an expression she had never seen before—em-

barrassment, irritation, but beneath that a fleeting passage of guilt—as though he were doing something
wrong in walking along with her. It was obvious, from
the cold dislike on the old couple's face, that David
was known to them, and was disapproved of. The old
man had shaken his head very deliberately from side to
side muttering, "Aach! Aach!" and the old woman had
carefully averted her eyes and stared at the ground.
When they had disappeared Sarah waited for him to
give some explanation. None came. He just lurched
angrily along the pavement with his hands in his
pockets.

"Who were they?" she asked.

"My uncle. And his wife." He hadn't turned his
face, just mumbled straight ahead.

"Oh," she said bleakly. She felt hurt because he
hadn't introduced her.

"They're on their way to Shool. It's Friday night.
They think I ought to be going too."

"I see." She didn't see, but she knew she must ask
no more. He had suddenly become very distant from
her, not in temper or rage, but in a silent way, as
though he and the little old couple shared a secret that
she could never understand.

Later she tried to imagine how she would feel if
they had met her Aunt Betsy or Uncle Will up from
the country in their Sunday clothes. I would have introduced them, she thought. Yes, I think I would. But I
couldn't take him down there. I couldn't take him
home to the village.

Now she stared into May's face—good, honest,
simple May—and said again, "I can't take him home,
May. It's no good. They just wouldn't like each other."

Dimly, from the direction of the back yard came the
snort and neighing of the horse. It was a reminder of
the Dances and their scheme for the future of Charlie
and the redemption of Sarah.

"What are you going to do about Charlie?"

"What about Charlie?" asked Sarah blankly. "Charlie's all right. I like Charlie. He's very nice."

"Oh, Sarah!" The distress she felt registered in her

voice and on her face. She looked so doleful that Sarah began to laugh.

"Come on, May," she said, pretending a good humour she did not feel because she suddenly didn't wish to talk about David Baron any more. "There's nothing to worry about, truly. You forget about David Baron. I like Charlie. I hope his fish round works— poor Charlie ought to have some luck. He's been out of work for such a long time." She leapt up and put her arm round May's shoulder. "Come on. We'll go and buy some carrots for the horse!"

They descended the stairs, single file, and May gradually allowed herself to be cheered by Sarah's gaiety. But she wasn't really satisfied, not satisfied at all. And she decided she dare not wait until Peter came home on leave before enlisting his aid. By then it might be too late. She had better write to him at once.

# Nine

THE mail caught up with him in Haifa after a long and frustrating delay due to mishaps that occurred to both crew and ship. The absence of letters and papers from home had been the final irritant in a trip that had superstitiously been labelled "unlucky" by the crew.

They had been forced to put in at Mombasa for repairs to one of the propeller shafts. It had been diagnosed as stern gland trouble and the work had taken so long that the rest of the flotilla had been ordered on, leaving the ship to limp behind as best she could. A day out to sea, when the repairs had finally been completed, a hawser had snapped and hamstrung one of the deckhands who was holystoning the decks. They had put back to Mombasa and waited for a further two days until they were assured that the seaman's condition was no longer critical. When they sailed on they left him in the British hospital, sweating and pain-racked amidst the drenching heat of an equatorial African summer.

Just before they reached Aden two men, a stoker and an able-seaman, had developed a rash and a fever. In all probability both rash and fever had been contracted on a wild shore leave at Mombasa, but the symptoms pointed to scarlet fever or something worse and the quarantine flag had been run up by the port authorities. They had spent three weeks offshore—staring at the dismal, white-hot port and the dusty hills in the background. When the quarantine period was over—it had not been scarlet fever, nor any other apparently contagious complaint—tempers were high and the men alternated between fractiousness and lethargy.

And then, half way up the Red Sea, the propeller shaft had gone again. A temporary repair had been effected—so temporary that the chief engineer had spent the entire passage up the Red Sea in a condition of nervous ill-temper. It was repaired, supposedly properly, at Port Said, and then off the east coast of Palestine it had gone for yet a third time and the chief engineer had gone crazy—swearing and cursing and calling down every kind of retribution he could think of on the heads of all the ship builders and naval port chandlers. They had made for Haifa and before arriving managed to acquire another injury when one of the galley hands badly scalded his arm with boiling water.

Peter, who had thought longingly all the way through the Suez Canal of a rest period in the pleasant town of Haifa, found when the time came to go ashore that he was suddenly too tired. Increasingly in the last few months this same tiredness had beset him so that even the simplest tasks had required a superhuman effort. The thought, now, of pushing and jostling amongst his messmates getting ready to go ashore made his inertia break out afresh.

When he was put on to first watch while the others went ashore he felt no resentment and he watched them donning their tiddly suits and listened to them shouting their shore-leave plans without feeling any resentment.

He had five letters from home. One from his father, one from Aunt Betsy, one from Sarah, and two from May. He opened Betsy's letters first because Betsy's letters told him the things he most wanted to know— about the village, the crops, the weather, the land which every year away at sea made infinitely more valuable to him.

On a summer's day at Richmond he had told Sarah, and May, and Charlie, that he intended returning to the village one day to work the land. He had told

them only half of the truth. For fifteen years of life at
sea had finally convinced him that he was, in fact, a
farmer not a sailor.

As a small boy, reared by his beloved Aunt Betsy
while his father was at the Boer War, his life had been
coloured by the comings and goings of his glorious
Uncle Math—the only man in his life. Uncle Math
with his quiet droll ways and his blue sailor suit and
his infinite patience, always returning from a voyage
with a gift for a small sea-struck boy, and stories of
typhoons and sea monsters and wild countries where
strange men ate one another and, if British sailors
weren't careful, ate them too . . . Uncle Math was the
most wonderful person he had ever known.

Wrenched from this background to live with his
father and stepmother, he had taken refuge in the
realisation that one day he too, like Uncle Math, could
go to sea and be free, leave shrewish, scolding Anne-
Louise and a house made unhappy by the erratic behaviour of a discontented woman, and sail the seven
seas—emulating Math whom he loved as he loved no
other man.

During the war he had enjoyed the sea—he had
been afraid, especially at the Battle of Jutland, but because he was a boy, because it was new and exciting
and everyone was banded together against the Hun, he
had enjoyed it. Mostly he had enjoyed it because he
was, again, sharing something with Uncle Math. They
were on different ships, they were in different seas, but
they were sharing something and they understood
things together that no one else in the family did. And
then Uncle Math had been killed, and he was suddenly
alone on a ship—alone but not alone, for there were
always too many men in too small an area for anyone
to have a chance to enjoy solitude. And it was this,
this lack of a chance to be alone that finally became
unbearable to him. His grandfather had been a shepherd, his father a countryman who worked alone. The
habit, the need for isolation was inherent in him.

He enjoyed the night watches—the time he could
stand alone on deck with sea and sky and nothing else.

But for the rest, the overcrowding below decks, the enforced sharing of personal intimacies, the lack of any privacy whatsoever—in latrine, hammock, and mess—made him long with every passing year for the loneliness of woods and meadows.

He could not leave the sea. He had signed on as a regular sailor and in any case there was just not sufficient civilian work in post-war England. And he was now caught irretrievably in his own childhood ambition. The family and the village now accepted that his worship of Mathy, and his small boy's desire for the sea must be indulged. His Aunt Betsy was proud of him—he was a loving link with her husband. And slowly the family had forgiven him for running away from home and joining the Navy. "You were a bad lad," they would say tolerantly. "Worrying your poor pa the way you did. But there, if the sea's in your blood, there's nothing you can do about it." And they would smile chidingly as though they were amused but secretly proud of what he had done. After all, were they not the very best of Englishmen? The strongest, the toughest, who for generations had worked with their hands in the soil. And those who left the soil became sailors, or fighters, the very best there were. They didn't say any of this, it would have been immodest, but it was there in their smiles and jokes and chidings— a pride that Peter was one of them, one of the tough, wholesome ones.

He had made his plans. Quietly, over a long period, he had designed his future. His pay was frugal, but he had saved as much of it as he possibly could. His only obligation was to his sister, Harriet. He set aside something to help pay for her upkeep in the home, feeling it was his duty to take some of this burden from his father. And aside from that and the few presents he bought for his family, he saved all the rest of his pay. The time, now, was not far short of the realisation of his dream. He intended to buy the meadow that his father rented and, as he had told Sarah, to turn it to a profitable, rotational holding. At night, swaying gently in the hammock against the roll of the sea, he would lie staring at the deck just over his head, and he would plan in detail the functioning of the meadow—where he would put the poultry houses (eggs and table fowl), how many extra hives he could accommodate, the soft-fruits, the greenhouses and cold frames (cucumbers out of season, asparagus, tomatoes all the year round). No pigs, he would think. Pigs take too much room and there's not enough profit. No, I've got to specialise—things that aren't easy and that are much better than other products of the same kind.

The sea had taught him much. It had taught him to be self-reliant, to be practical, and to plan in detail. He knew he needed more money than just enough to buy the meadow. He needed money to carry him for the first two years, and he had planned accordingly. He needed specialised knowledge—more than the knowledge that any country boy is born with. He knew soils and crops and animals, he had worked with them from childhood, but this was not enough. During every spare moment, during make-'n-mend afternoons when he was supposed to be engaged in personal maintenance, he would read and study every kind of book and agricultural paper he could manage to have sent him from home. He read about pests and greenhouse heating and hybrid strains and poultry diseases and specialised feeding and manure. Whenever it was possible on shore leaves, he traveled outside the ports— eschewing the bars and brothels where his messmates banded together in protective enjoyment—and looked at the surrounding land, the farms, the coolie patches, whatever the local form of agriculture happened to be. He had studied the fruit farms of the Cape and Australia, the tea plantations of Ceylon, the paddy-fields of China. The knowledge he gleaned from his visits in all probability would be of little use on his own land, but looking at other people's farms made him feel closer to possessing his own. And the time when he could realise his ambition grew closer. He had decided that on his next leave he must begin to make enquiries about the purchase of the meadow, perhaps put down a holding fee and tell the family what his plans were to include.

At the back of his mind was the thought of Harriet. He envisaged a future composed of a successful small holding and a cottage where his Aunt Betsy could come and live once her own family had left her. And then he could have Harriet out of the home to come and live with him. It was still a nebulous plan, but it made the purpose of the meadow, the saving of his pay all these years, a real reason for looking forward.

He read Aunt Betsy's letter and was reassured. It still rained, the soil was good, no one else had bought the meadow. He read his father's. The family were well. He read Sarah's which was full of notions and ideas and comments on the people they both knew. He grinned when he read Sarah's letter because it was so much like Sarah—beautiful and humble and funny and frustrated all at the same time. He was sometimes honest enough to adimt that if Sarah had been given the chance of going to sea, if she had been a boy, she would have made much more of it than he had. She would have been a petty officer by now instead of just an able seaman. She would have been a petty officer, and she would have married a Spaniard, or a Japanese, or a Tahitian, and she would have curios from every part of the world and a good working knowledge of the language of every country she had visited. She would have seized every opportunity that life at sea offered. He sometimes felt sorry for her, fighting her own frustration under the tyrannical rule of Miss Bennett.

When he read May's letter—the one about Sarah—he felt even more sorry for his sister. Not because she was going out with a "foreigner" but because she was hemmed in, trapped by good, kind, well-meaning people who wanted to love her and keep her close in their own safe worlds. At first, after reading the letter, he wasn't worried about the "foreigner." He knew that for Sarah there would always be "foreigners," or funny people, unacceptable eccentrics who would upset the Dances and the family and the village, but who would be irresistible to Sarah. Later, towards the end of his watch, the thought of Sarah's entanglement began to fidget at his mind. Sarah, on her own, would not do anything too wild. But Sarah, pressured by the Dances, all stifling her and trying to chain her quicksilver brightness to their own solid worthiness, might be pushed into foolishness, into something irrevocable she would come to regret.

Not long until I'm home again, he thought. Then I'll talk to Sarah. Lots of things to do next time I go home. Begin negotiating the sale of the meadow, persuade pa to let me do what I want with it—we might even start some of the soft-fruit bushes already, before the sale. Talk to Sarah. See what I can do about Sarah.

He felt tired again. Just thinking about all he had to do made him feel tired again and he was glad he had to wait before he could go ashore.

He had a special plan for this trip. He had read somewhere about a farm inland from Haifa, over towards the Sea of Galilee where a settlement of refugees were experimenting with land. He wasn't particularly interested in the reason for the experiment but he wanted to see what people, who had no previous knowledge of farming and agriculture, could do with enthusiasm and the will to experiment.

Haifa was a pleasant port—even from offshore it was a pleasant port—hills and white buildings and the golden dome of the Bahai temple. He got through the turmoil of the quayside and asked a white-helmeted member of the Palestinian Police Force how he could get to the collective farm. The policeman eyed him curiously. It was unusual for a British able seaman on shore leave to ask the directions to a kibbutz but he directed him to the bus station and told him he would have to walk at the other end. He was glad to sit down on the bus. He felt tired again.

It was a strange country for farming, he reflected, as he gazed out of the window at the moving landscape. Much of it, most of it, appeared to be arid. Dusty scrub, some grass and olive trees with sheep and goats tended by Arab herders. But when they passed one of the Arab villages—stone houses clustered round a spring and a well—the soil looked rich and there were patches of good corn growing. The landscape was beautiful in a dry, distant way and when the bus moved up into the hills the terrain became much greener, the soil alight with wild flowers. He was not very interested in the sweep of the land around him—only in the soil and in what the inhabitants had done with the soil.

The Arab driver of the bus put him off before the bus reached Tiberias and pointed south towards a track leading through the hills. He began to walk, still feeling tired but his spirits lifting because he found himself alone, walking through hills covered in blue and yellow flowers, with birds wheeling overhead and, on his left far distant, the huge tranquil water that was the Sea of Galilee.

It was a long walk, very long, and once or twice he sat down on a rock and wondered if he ought to turn back. A cart came along pulled by a skeletal pony and driven by a young Arab boy with vivid blue eyes. Peter, claiming the right of British supremacy, stopped the boy and asked for a lift. The cart could only be going one way in this open country.

The boy said little—yes, he knew where the farm was, and no, he didn't work there. Just before Peter climbed down from the cart the boy stared hard at him and said, "Many British here, during the war." Then the cart turned off straight onto unmade soil and Peter began walking again, towards a deep, large patch of vegetation that lay a little way ahead.

When he saw the farm his tiredness dropped from him. It was lush, the rich, deep green of a fertile soil. There were trees, olive, and orange, still bearing fruit, and in the distance what appeared to be a grove of palms. Immediately ahead of him was maize, avenue upon avenue of tall, green maize shoots, succulent and strong and standing nearly up to Peter's shoulders. He reached up and fingered the fleshy sheaths and could tell the crop was healthy by the feeling of moisture beneath the leaf fibres. Two men watering the crop stiffened when they saw him and began to walk quickly forward. He smiled and nodded and waved his hand at the crop and then one of them said "Shalom" and beckoned him further into the field. He crumbled some soil between his fingers. It was rich and loamy and the man who had spoken came up to him and said in heavy guttural English, "Good?" Peter nodded again. The soil was good, and a wave of longing for his own soil smote him afresh. Not long, he thought, not long now and I shall be working my own land.

"From Haifa?" the man asked.

"Yes."

They were joined by the second worker. At the foot of one of the maize shoots lay a blue handkerchief tied into a bundle. It was opened and Peter was offered an orange, a piece of cheese, a hard-boiled egg and some olives. He accepted the orange because he was thirsty, but the two men insisted that he take the rest of the food as well. They sat on the ground in the shade of the maize and when they had eaten they drank water from an earthenware jug. Then they lay back on the ground, tilted their blue canvas hats forward over their eyes and went to sleep. Peter, with an extraordinary sense of well-being and contentment, joined them.

When he woke it was no longer so hot and he could tell from the position of the sun that it was late afternoon and he should already be on his way back to Haifa. The men had gone, but the water jug and another orange lay beside him. He drank thirstily, put the orange in his pocket and began walking back along the track.

He tried to recognise landmarks so that he could encourage himself with how much further he had to go, but the landscape was much the same all along the road and he could not remember where it was that the Arab boy had put him off, or picked him up. When he came to the point where he could see Galilee once more he knew he must be half way.

And then he began to sweat, to sweat so badly he had to sit down, then lay down while great drenching spasms of perspiration flooded over him, saturating his clothes, running into his eyes, making his body flame with wet heat. It wasn't hot any more. That's what he couldn't understand. Often, at night on board ship, he became drenched in his own sweat in just this way. But then it was because of the small, stuffy mess deck filled with sleeping men. Now it was cool, the pleasant cool of early evening in the hills of a hot country and there was no reason why he should sweat like this.

When he started to walk again he could feel his clothes drying on him and he shivered. He lifted his tunic and studied his chest and stomach to see if there were any sign of a rash, wondering if he had caught the complaint of the two seamen who had put the ship into quarantine at Aden. In the dimming light of the evening he stared hard at his own body, still drying out from his perspiring chill. There was no rash, no redness or patches that might turn to redness. No outward indication of anything wrong.

The track seemed incredibly long, and the second half much longer than the first. When he reached the road he was glad to sit down and wait for the bus. He didn't care how long he had to wait providing he could sit down.

He could just see the bus appearing way down on the winding road at the foot of the hills when the sweat broke out again. This time it was worse, so bad that his breathing became impaired and he lay in the scrub at the side of the road gasping, trying to drag air down into his lungs and aware all the time of the clammy wetness breaking out over his skin. He managed to drag himself upright as the bus came up—he dared not let it go—and as he tried to mount the platform the driver looked and saw he was ill. He leaned over and hauled Peter's six-foot frame into the bus, shouting at a couple of Arabs to move and make room for him. The effort of getting on began the chill all over again. He sat sprawled just where the driver had thrown him, gasping and coughing for breath, for air to blow away the terrible drenching of his body.

"You all right, mate?"

He opened his eyes and saw the comforting sight of a homely British face over a khaki shirt—one of a small group of soldiers returning to Haifa.

He nodded, afraid to speak in case it started again.

"Where are you going? Haifa?"

He nodded again.

"We'll see you're all right, mate. We'll get you back on your ship." He tried to say thank you but the air in his lungs ran out again. At the back of the bus were three nuns in the white robes of one of the Holy Land orders. He hoped that he would not have another attack in front of them.

When they arrived at Haifa he felt better. Two of the soldiers took him into a small, smelly Arab bar and bought him a glass of brandy. He felt better when he had drunk it and then they walked down to the quay with him and waited until the liberty boat came out from the ship.

On board he went straight down to the mess and leaned back heavily against the mess steps.

"Where's the killick?" he gasped. Two of his messmates looked up at him and in the light of the cabin took in his feverish face and swaying form.

"Christ, Whitey! You'd better lie down! The killick's not back yet. You all right?"

"Don't feel good," he said. He tried to unstow and hang his hammock but couldn't manage and they did it for him. He supposed he ought to report to someone but with the leading seaman not back he decided it could wait until morning. All he wanted to do was rest—to sleep.

"I expect it's just the heat," he said to the anxious faces of his messmates. "I walked too far—up in the hills. Should've had more sense."

"Bloody crazy, you are," said his mate unsympathetically. "Why the 'ell do you want to go traipsing around the country every time we put ashore? Why can't you come into town like the rest of use and 'ave a good time? Shouldn't be surprised if you'd caught something nasty up in them hills. Something nasty and we'll all be put in bloody quarantine again."

He closed his eyes, too tired to argue or to reassure his mate. He didn't even know if he was ill. He'd had the sweats before—lots of times—but not like this. And he didn't really feel ill—just hot and strange and tired—terribly tired. He gave himself up completely to the tiredness, blocked out all the noises and disturbances of the mess, and went to sleep.

In the morning he felt fine. He couldn't believe that he had been so feverish, so sweat-drenched on the previous day. He tried to think what it could be and then he remembered the two men on the farm and the earthenware jug of water. They were all warned about the dangers of drinking water in Arab countries and he had drunk twice, deeply and long. He cursed himself for being so foolish but felt better because now he knew what had made him so bad. He grew steadily more cheered as the morning progressed and when the divisions were called he went up on deck feeling buoyant and light-hearted because he was not, after all, seriously ill with some kind of tropical fever.

They stood to attention on deck, the offshore breeze lightly lifting the back of their collars, hats set smartly forward on the front of their heads. It was warm and fresh and very pleasant and the captain and the first mate made the inspection in an easy, relaxed way, without too much critical attention to detail.

They were nearly up to his division when he felt the cough rising in his throat. He was amused because he often found—as many of them did—that it was always at divisions that one wanted to cough or sneeze or scratch one's nose. He held the cough back, waiting until they had passed him by but this time they didn't pass. The captain stopped in front of him.

"Your uniform's sloppy. It doesn't fit you properly, man. Too big. Make sure you change it or have it altered."

He opened his mouth to say, "Aye, Aye, Sir," but the cough came out instead. Only it wasn't a cough. It was a bright jet of blood and then he did cough and this time it was more blood, showering out on the deck in front of him and he could feel himself beginning to choke, feel his lungs and nostrils and throat blocked with blood. He slumped forward down on to his knees, holding his lanyard away from his chest, fighting agonised against the blood clogging the whole of his inside.

Then his messmates on either side caught hold of him and he heard the first mate shouting for the chief petty officer to signal for a doctor.

After the conversation with May, her relationship with David Baron changed. She could no longer pretend that he was—as she had told May—"just a friend." The arguments, the fights, the ideas they had together, these were important, but now she had to admit that more important were the swift kisses, the way he smiled at her and grasped her shoulders, the way her stomach knotted inside every Friday when she saw him waiting for her outside the Alexander flats.

She couldn't take him home, but she wanted to. She wanted, on this one occasion, to be just like May. To adore, and be adored, to do everything properly, to have her feelings for him blessed by the approval of family and friends.

After talking to May, after the inauguration of Charlie's fish round and the unspoken but keenly felt pressure of the Dance family the friendship between them became more intense—so intense it was sometimes unbearable. It was as though David, instantly recognising the change in her, responded quickly to her lack of restraint.

Now they met on two evenings a week and they ceased to pretend that they were going to see the Alexanders. They began to avoid places where they might be seen by people who knew them. They crossed over to the other side of the river and the first time he held her hand she didn't pull away.

At the end of April he took her to another concert, only the second she had attended in her whole life and this time, with her emotions towards him no longer controlled, she found the soaring introspection of the music more than she could bear. It was Brahms. She made a careful note of that because—afterwards—she felt she never wanted to listen to it again. It was big, painful music during which she became hurtfully aware that he was beside her, that his arm was touching hers, that if she turned her head she would see his rich, curved features and intense face.

When they left the concert hall he didn't speak to her, just walked towards the tram stop and pushed her on in front of him.

"It's going the wrong way," she faltered.

"No."

They had to change onto another tram, and this time she didn't ask where they were going. She was frightened of him but in her stomach was the knotted excitement that his presence always induced. He sat opposite, staring at her face, her throat, her body covered in her best blue coat. His eyes were hot and darker than usual and it finally seemed that she could feel them on her body, touching her as though they were his hands.

They got off the tram somewhere down towards Bow. He didn't touch her. He didn't have to. He made her walk in the direction he wished merely by the heat and distant pressure of his body. She knew if he touched her she would cry out.

When they came to a small street of terraced houses with front doors opening straight on to the pavement, he took a key out of his pocket and walked up to one of the front doors.

"Where are we?" She began to tremble.

"My home."

It was like a douche of cold water. Shock took the breath away from her. The last thing she had wanted or expected—especially on this evening—was to be taken to his home, to have to be guarded and civil to his family, of whom she was a little afraid—without any preparation, any chance to question him about them.

"But . . . I don't think . . . I shan't know what to say to your family."

He opened the door, drew her into a tiny, narrow hallway, and closed the door behind him.

"None of my family are here this evening," he said abruptly, and then he kissed her.

It was the most terrible feeling she had ever had. This wasn't like the times he kissed her in the street, not even like the time they had stood close together during the strike. This was a terrible, fierce drowning, a pressure of their bodies, mouths, hands, of their faces moving frenziedly against each other, of her hair released by his hands pouring over his neck and hers, wound round both of them, of his muttered, feverish, "Sasha! Sasha! My beautiful Sasha!"

There must have been a door just behind her, for she felt it open against the pressure of her body and somehow they were in a small room which was lit very dimly from a distant street light shining through the lace curtains. She could just make out his face, his expression was one of complete, ungovernable emotion.

"Sasha! Sasha!" he gasped, and her coat was on the floor and the top of her dress was unbuttoned and her plain, old-fashioned cotton chemise and "sensible" vest were suddenly pushed away from her shoulders and she felt his mouth, his hands, his face burning into her body, kissing her . . . kissing her hair and neck and breast. She felt wetness fall on to her shoulder and she saw that he was crying.

"Beautiful, my Sasha! Oh, so beautiful!"

And she knew she was beautiful. She freed her arms from her dress and raised them over her head, and she knew she was beautiful. She knew her hair was soft by the way he kissed it and wound it around his face. She knew her shoulders, and her throat and breast were smooth and lovely. His lips were very heavy, very warm, and they were trembling. The trembling spread to his hand and then to the rest of his body and every time he kissed her he murmured, "Sasha" into her flesh.

She found she was capable of things she had not believed she could do—she was able to undress with grace, with a seductive, gentle movement that turned her full body into that of a lush, wild creature. She was able to smile at him, without shyness or humility, so that her smile was an enticement, an invitation. She was able to lift her hair away from her shoulders, stretching her arms, arching her body, feeling music and emotion and power flowing from her, capturing and ensnaring him—he, who was so much stronger, more powerful, more wild than she.

Her gracefulness made him, in turn, clumsy and awkward. He fumbled with shaking hands at his coat and shirt. He was reduced to a supplicating passion that was only aware of the need to capture her, to subdue and tame her to his own emotional needs.

When his arms locked round her, when his chest met her breast, there was a quick indrawing of breath—soft cry at the conflict of flesh between them. He drew her down beside him and his body was as she had always known it would be, full and strong and very smooth.

Her eyes had grown accustomed to the dim light from the street lamp. Over his trembling shoulder she could see the fantasy shapes of the room, the heavy furniture, the ugly china and ornaments, the photographs standing on a table just behind the sofa, a photograph that was just close enough for her to see ...

He sensed her sudden withdrawal from him, sensed that she was no longer completely submerged in the desire that had carried both of them this far.

"Sasha?"

She didn't answer, but she was quiet, so still, that he knew the moment when he might have loved her had gone.

"Sasha?" He turned to follow the direction of her gaze. She was looking at the photograph, the big one of his mother, father, brothers and himself. She reached up and lifted it down from the table, turning it into the light so that she could see it better.

She knew it was his father and mother, and she knew it was him as a child standing in front of them. She became burningly aware of where she was, of what she was doing. Her gracefulness vanished. With ugly movements she tried to put her clothes on and hide her body from him at the same time.

"No! Sarah, no!"

She was crying, very very quietly. "This is your mother's house. This is her parlour, her sofa, her photograph."

"I know, Sarah! I know," he moaned. "But I love you so much. I love you so much."

She tried to fasten her dress and found that some of the buttons had been torn off. She controlled her crying and said in a tight aching voice,

"I'm sorry. I should not have done the things I did. I want to go home now."

"I can't let you go home. Not like this! Not like this, Sasha!"

She buttoned her coat. Her hair was tangled and wild and she had to grope about on the lino and find her hairpins before she could pin it up in some kind of order. She wanted to tell him how sorry she was, how wrong to make him want her, how cruel to provoke his desire by her shameless behaviour.

It was the photograph, but how could she explain it to him? It was the photograph of the family, and more especially of his mother and father, two strange, outlandishly dressed people, obviously foreigners, obviously different and yet, oh so much the same as her own father and mother. So tired, so poor, so worn out with hard work and children and trying to retain their pride. They were exactly the same in this way as her own people. For all their differences they were the same and she had suddenly felt that her own father and mother were watching her. She began to cry again, so softly it was hardly noticeable.

"I don't want you to come home with me," she said. "I want to go home alone."

She fumbled for the catch on the front door and turned back before she opened it.

"I'm sorry," she said. "Please forgive me. But it's your mother's house, you see?"

She went on crying all the way to the tram.

He came and knocked on Aunt Florrie's door for her the following day after school. Aunt Florrie wouldn't ask him in and the cold dislike of the Dance family must have registered because when she came out of the house—in response to a belligerent and surly message relayed by Aunt Florrie—he was standing nervously a little way up the street waiting for her. She was embarrased and didn't know what to say. The memory of last night had grown worse with every passing hour.

"I want to talk to you."

"Not here."

"Walk up to the river with me. I must talk to you." He was white and there were heavy shadows under his eyes. He grasped her hand when they were only just round the corner from Florrie's but she felt unable to do anything about it. They were only a short way into Trinity Square when he turned her to face him.

"Sasha," he said hoarsely. "You must marry me. You must marry me as soon as we can arrange it. We will go to the Town Hall, we will be married in a civil ceremony, and then we must move away to a new part of London—you away from these wretched people," he waved his hand in the direction of Aunt Florrie's house, "and me away from my family."

She wasn't surprised. It was as wild and as unpredictable as everything else about him.

"It's the only way," he said, growing excited. "It's the only way we can ever do it—quickly and without thinking."

"You know we can't," she said tiredly. "We can't do it like that. People like you and me are too ... too ordinary to do things like that."

He seized her hands, gripping them so fiercely that the bones of her fingers scrunched against one another.

"That's just it! Don't you understand, Sarah? It's because we're so ordinary that we must do it this way. If we try to work out everything in the proper way, we won't be able to do it, we'll never be able to marry. Don't you understand, Sasha! It has to be done first, and thought about afterwards!"

She began to understand, to realise what he was trying, inarticulately, to explain.

"But, my family," she faltered. "No, not my family, but my pa. He's done so much for me. Helped me to be a teacher ... and he loves me so much ... it would hurt him so dreadfully ..."

He wrung her hands up and down. His face was screwed into an agony of trying to make her understand.

"Sarah! Sarah! Once you start thinking of all the reasons why you shouldn't marry me, you'll never stop! There's my family too. Do you know anything about a Jewish family, Sarah? Do you know how terrible it will be for my family—their son to marry a gentile? They will not believe it, and when they believe it they will never want to see me again."

"What shall we live on? If I have to leave my job, and you leave your father's business, what shall we live on?"

"Stop it, Sarah! Stop it!" he shouted. "You're destroying it all, you're killing it! You know I'm right, don't you? You know I'm right. If we even stop to think about it, it will be more than we can manage. If you want me, you must marry me now—without planning and without thinking. And Sarah," he smiled suddenly—a wide, big smile that made her heart lurch and ache with loving him so much, "Sarah, you know it will be all right. Deep down you know it will be all right. Our families won't want us. Our friends? We shall have to make new friends. And I don't know how we shall live, or where. But it will be all right, Sarah! It will be all right because we're the same, aren't we? We're the same. And we'll fight and I'll frighten you because I'm wild sometimes, but you're never alone with me, are you? I know how you feel about things, I can follow you up there, can't I? When you're up there with thoughts, or music, or ideas, I'm with you, aren't I? Aren't I, Sarah! Aren't I the only one you've ever met who's with you, right there with you?"

"Yes, you are!"

"And whatever else goes wrong, that's why it will be all right for us. That's why I love you, why you're beautiful, why with us it will never be dull, or dead, or stale like it is with everyone else. Come on, my Sarah, my lovely Sasha! You've never lacked courage before. Lots of things you haven't got, but courage isn't one of them. Marry me, Sasha. Marry me!"

"Yes . . . perhaps yes . . . perhaps you're right. I think you're right. But you must let me think." She wrenched her hands away and put them up to her face, pressing the sides of her forehead as though trying to hold all the wild ideas inside still. "You must let me think . . . just one night, David, one night to see if it's all right. You had last night to think. Give me one night too."

He hesitated, his eyes burning into her face, willing her to agree with him.

"I promise you, David. If I say yes I shan't back out before it happens. You know that. If I say yes it will be final. You know that, dear dear David! You know that, don't you?"

"Yes, I know."

"So you must let me think. Think without you standing in front of me holding my hands. Think what it would be like to spend the rest of my life with you, or without you."

He caught her into his arms and held her tightly, crushing her shoulders and talking into her hair, oblivious of the passers-by.

"You know I love you, Sasha? I love you so much and I need you. I need you because you're all the things I'm not. Please, Sasha! When you're thinking, remember how much I love you. No one will ever love you like this again. You mustn't throw it away, Sasha! You mustn't throw love like this away."

She kissed him. She put her arms round his neck and kissed him without thinking about who might be walking by in the street. It could be the Dances, Charlie, or May, or even Miss Bennett, but she didn't care. She kissed him.

"I love you, David. I love you so much!"

He held her hard for one more moment and then he let her go. "I'll come round tomorrow evening," he said. "I'll come round, and then we'll decide what to do next."

She turned and walked back in the direction they had come from. She had asked for time to think, but already she knew what she would do. She wanted to think because she had to know if she could face up to all the things that marrying David Baron would mean. She had to know if the guilt of walking out on the Dances would be bearable. She had to know how mean she would feel at the removal of her financial contribution towards her brother's education. And, more personally, she had to know if she could face up to a future so hazardous that it was possible they would neither of them find regular employment. Once she had looked at all these things, and had faced the very worst that life with David Baron could mean, then she could tackle anything. She was so strong that once she knew what could happen, she would not hesitate to take a chance.

For she sensed that, just once or twice in everyone's life, a chance—like this—must be taken if one was to retain any kind of spirit or fight. For most of the time she was, and would be, sensible and reliable, aware of her duty and her place in the world. David Baron was right. Sometimes, by instinct, he arrived at the correct solution to life while she, trying to reason and deduce by logic, failed to see that the unplanned, foolish, seemingly disastrous course of action, was often the only one there was.

She was reasoning now, she grinned to herself. But beneath the reasoning was the warm, glowing, cherished feeling of a woman who knows she is loved.

When she arrived home she found the telegram from her father. Peter had been taken seriously ill on his homeward voyage. He had been rushed to the naval hospital at Portsmouth and was about to be moved to a sanatorium in Kent. He had advanced tuberculosis, and would she please come home at once.

# Ten

THE sanatorium was at Benenden in Kent, and it made him feel good just to know that he wasn't too far away from the village, from land and woods that he knew. He liked the sanatorium. It was quiet and he was able to sleep a lot. The doctors had told him he was seriously ill, but that with care and rest he would probably get better. They had assured him that consumption was no longer a killer—lots of people recovered from it nowadays, and he mustn't be frightened or influenced by all the tales and stories he heard.

He wasn't frightened because he knew he wasn't really as ill as they seemed to think. He didn't feel ill. He had no pain, and apart from feverish sweats that broke out at frequent intervals he had very little inconvenience. He was just tired, that was all, so very, very tired.

It was nice being at Benenden. His father came to see him a lot, and so did Anne-Louise, his stepmother, whose natural sharpness was always subdued in the presence of severe illness or death. Betsy came as often as his father, and so did his brothers and cousins.

May—poor, frightened, little white-faced May—came every week, spending her meagre salary on the fare down from London and on expensive presents for him. At first, when she used to come and there were other people present, she just sat quietly by the bed looking at him, but then she grew bolder and would hold his hand all the time she was there. He kept telling her he wasn't all that ill. When his visitors had gone he was able to get out of bed, put on his dressing-gown (a present from May) and stroll up and down the ward laughing and chatting to the other patients. But May seemed to take no comfort from the news. She still sat watching him and stroking his hand.

Sarah came too. Every week. Helping him to sort out the muddle of official papers and documents from the Navy and assuring him that he wasn't to worry about Harriet and the money for the Home. It was all taken care of. Sarah was a great comfort to him. She was so controlled, so steady and strong and quiet, and . . . Sarah . . .

He was there for four months, and he liked it very much. From the windows of the ward he could see green, and watch the rain falling on trees and shrubs and grass. And in the morning, very early, the birds woke him; the lovely soft stillness of the country and the birds waking him in the morning. When it was hot, bees came in through the windows and sucked pollen from the flowers standing in hospital vases, and he would lie, watching them buzz from rose to gladiola, from carnation to delphinium. He had lots of flowers but the ones he liked best were the ones Aunt Betsy brought him—the ones she picked from the hedgerows and the edges of the fields—poppies and cornflowers, and dog roses, and agrimony and water mint from along the banks of Sandy Bottom. And mixed in with the flowers were grasses and weeds where dear Betsy had been in a hurry to pick and hadn't sorted out all the bits and pieces.

At the end of August they told him they were sending him to the Chest Hospital at Bethnal Green. This wasn't a bad sign, on the contrary they had great hopes for him because at the Chest Hospital all kinds of new successful treatments were being put into operation. In all probability he would have the new "collapsed lung" treatment, and this meant the diseased lung would be able to rest completely and get well while the other lung did all the work. He was sorry to leave Benenden and the countryside but, as he told Sarah privately because he didn't want to worry his pa, he thought it was as well that more drastic treatment was going to be taken. He didn't truthfully feel any better and the tiredness didn't get any less.

At the Victoria Park Chest Hospital he was examined with a thoroughness that was frightening and exhausting, but in a funny way it cheered him tremendously because he felt that at last something decisive was being done. He admitted to himself that, during his last weeks at Benenden, he had become frightened that he wasn't going to get better. He still didn't feel ill, but one look at his body, growing steadily thinner, made him wake up in the middle of the night wondering if he was going to die.

Now, at the Chest Hospital, he knew he was not going to die. The whole place bristled with efficiency and an air of comprehensive knowledge. They were going to do things to him, it might be uncomfortable and it might take a long time, but he was not going to die.

His father and Aunt Betsy couldn't come quite so often. It was a long and expensive journey from the village, and he never forgot that there was poor Harriet to go and see as well as him. Every month, for the last nineteen years, his father had gone to see Harriet on the first Sunday of the month, and it was an unwritten rule of the family that whatever else happened, Harry should never be forgotten.

Sarah and May came as often as the hospital permitted, May more than Sarah, of course. And slowly the strangest thing happened. He found he watched the door of the ward, hoping she would come in, feeling ridiculously pleased at the sight of her small, worried face over the shabby coat. Her soft curly hair wisping out from the ugly cloche hat that she wore. She came on her days off, and sometimes she came when it wasn't her day off but she chanced snatching a few hours which she wasn't really entitled to. Once she hurried in all out of breath with her apron still on under her coat. Sometimes, when he was expecting her and for some reason she couldn't come, his sense of deprivation and disappointment was out of all proportion to the fact that it was only little May who was coming to see him.

When she had come to visit him in Benenden, and had sat holding his hand, he hadn't minded too much because he was fond of May, and he knew she felt better holding his hand. He hadn't wanted to hurt her. But now he needed her hand. He clung on to it all the time she was there and he felt lonely and miserable when he watched her walking away from him up the ward. He tried to understand why he felt this way. He didn't lack for visitors, or for family who cared for him and wanted him to get well again. But May was special, because for her he was the only one. To his father, and Sarah, and Betsy, he was one of several, well-loved and important people. May was the one to whom he was infinitely dear.

Because she didn't talk very much, her visits usually meant that he talked, and slowly, over a period of time, he told her about the meadow, about the money he had saved and what he was going to do with it. It was going to take longer now, but the plan was still there. All the work and ideas he had prepared for the meadow were still good. He showed her his post-office book with the money he had saved and asked her how much she thought the Tylers would want for their meadow. In the ordinary way—if he had still been at sea—he would never have shared these things with her. But now her love had ceased to be a gentle burden to him. Now her love was what stopped him being afraid in the night when, foolishly, he wondered again if he was going to get well.

And then, one day, when he was talking about the meadow, about the soft fruits and the hot-houses and the luxury crops he was going to grow, he looked at May's face and saw that she was crying. Soundlessly, without movement she was crying. And he knew then that he wasn't going to get well again.

The doctor had arranged to see Jonathan on a Wednesday morning but he agreed to alter the time to later in the afternoon so that Sarah, if she hurried over straight after school, could be there with her father. May had wanted to come but it was family only. The night before they saw the doctor she made Sarah promise to telephone her from the hospital, telephone her on Mr Bennett's special private telephone in his study.

"But what will he say?" asked Sarah. "And what will Miss Bennett say? They might not like you having a call on their telephone, May."

"It doesn't matter," said May stubbornly. "It doesn't matter what they like. And anyway, they'll probably be out. Or he will. It's magic lantern night at the Mission Society and he always goes to that with his slides of Ceylon."

"All right," said Sarah wearily. "I'll telephone you. But it won't make any difference, May. It only means you'll spend the evening worrying, frightened to move away from Mr Bennett's room in case you miss it."

"You telephone me!" cried May, a faint note of hysteria in her voice. "You understand, Sarah! If you don't I'll never forgive you. Never!" She was always so calm and quiet when she went to see Peter, but now, with Sarah, she was overstrung and imperious. Sarah, at first startled to see the change that Peter's illness had wrought in her cousin, now accepted it with a profound sense of pity. If only May could fight like that for herself.

"I'll telephone," she promised tiredly. "I'll telephone as soon as I can."

She arrived a few minutes late at the hospital and her father didn't see her at first. He was waiting outside the main door, wearing his best suit and a blue striped shirt with a starched collar carefully studded into place. His hair, which was white now, was flattened down with water and he held his stiff, black Sunday hat between hands that were gnarled and brown from working with animals and plants. He was still tall, but his shoulders were stooped forward and his face was older than it should have been.

"Hullo, pa." She held her face up and he kissed her.

They smiled brightly at one another, pretending that everything was normal. "I'm sorry I'm a bit late."

"We've plenty of time, lass. Plenty of time. I got an earlier train. Didn't want to leave anything to chance."

It was nice and safe, talking about trains and times and delays. It held off the thing they were very soon going to have to face.

She put her hand through his arm and they walked slowly along the corridor until they came to the sister's office. Then they sat on two wooden chairs, her father turning his hat between his fingers, until the doctor came out to see them.

"Mr Whitman?" Jonathan stood up. Beside the white-coated doctor he looked what he was—unsophisticated, clumsy, a countryman who was about to hear that his son was going to die.

"Please sit down. You too," he nodded to Sarah. They all three sat.

"I expect you know, Mr Whitman, that we haven't been very happy with the progress of your son. We hoped, when he came from the sanatorium, that we could do something for him. But his lungs are much worse than we thought."

Jonathan cleared his throat. "I thought," he said slowly. "I thought you were going to do this new thing. I thought you were going to collapse his lung so that it could rest."

The doctor stared down at a brown folder he carried in his hand. Sarah noticed "Peter Jonathan Whitman" written in red ink across the top right-hand corner.

"It's no use in this case," the doctor said quietly. "I'm afraid both lungs are badly affected. Your son has had two haemorrhages. The next will probably prove fatal."

The room was very quiet. No sound at all, not even in the distance.

"I'm very sorry," said the doctor.

"Yes."

He fumbled with the folder again. "I don't wish to add to your distress at this time," he continued. "But of course we cannot keep him here. We are short of beds, and we are concerned with treatment, not . . . not intensive nursing. We have made arrangements for him to be transferred to the Infirmary tomorrow morning. He will be well looked after there. Every care will be taken of him."

"No!"

The doctor looked startled. "I beg your pardon."

"My son isn't going to the workhouse to die. He'll come home. He's my son. He'll come home. That's where he'll die. At home amongst his family."

The doctor looked embarrassed. "Now really, Mr Whitman. You can't call the Infirmary the workhouse. It's not the same thing at all. I assure you the care is very good there."

"He'll come home. He'll come home now, with me."

"But you can't do this," said the doctor irritably. "As I recall from your record you have other sons at home, one of them still at school. The disease is highly contagious. I cannot stress that point too strongly. Highly contagious. Nursing a consumptive patient demands the strictest care if the bacillus is not to spread."

"He will have every care. I shall see to it. My family and I will see that he is loked after, and that the disease does not spread."

"How?" snapped the doctor. "How will you ensure that the strict precautions necessary in a case of this kind are observed?"

"We can manage," Jonathan answered simply. "People like us know how to manage."

Frustration showed on the doctor's face and Sarah, in a detached manner, felt sorry for him. He was so used to having people obey him without question that, faced with her father's stubborn simplicity, he did not know how to deal with the situation.

"It will be all right," said Jonathan quietly, as though trying to reassure him. "We've had sickness and trouble before. We know how to manage. You tell us some of the rules and regulations and we'll obey them in our own way. We'll see everything is done properly."

The doctor just stared at him.

"I can't let him go to the workhouse to die! He's my son!"

The tired, hazel eyes gazed into the doctor's face and

the younger man looked from Jonathan, to the girl
sitting beside him, the girl with identical hazel eyes,
brighter, softer, but reflecting the same obstinate assurance, the same pride. They were irritating. They
were stubborn, and the stubbornness came from a belief that they were right. But they were good people, he
thought suddenly. They were good, and they were
fighters.

"All right," he said slowly. "If you want to take him
now, this afternoon, I will arrange with the sister to
begin getting him ready. He can still walk of course—
do most things in fact providing he can go slowly and
rest a lot. If you would rather wait I will arrange for
his bed to be held until the end of the week."

"I'll take him now. While I've my girl here to help
me."

The doctor nodded, lifted a brass bell from the sister's desk and rang. Almost immediately she hurried
starchily into the room and she and the doctor entered
into a quiet, detailed conversation over in a corner of
the room.

Sarah looked at her pa. He was sitting tired and
slumped, the lines of his face sagging and the hands
holding his best hat shaking a little.

"You all right, pa?" she choked.

He nodded, but his mouth and his cheeks began to
move and she saw his eyes blur over red. She put both
her hands over his and said, "Oh, pa! Dear dear, pa!"
and he very briefly covered his eyes with his hands for
a second. She saw his lips move and knew he was
praying, and she who had almost discarded the God
she had grown up with, who had moved so far into a
new life where the old rules were not so important,
found that her father's God was still there. The God of
the village was still the one to pray to.

"I want you to see about getting a taxi-cab, Sarah.
We shall take a taxi-cab to Victoria Station and you
shall help me get him on the train. I shall be all right at
the other end because old Deacon will be there and
he'll help me get the boy home in his carriage."

The doctor came over to them and Jonathan stood
up.

"If you'll come with me, Mr Whitman. I will go through, in detail, the things you must do when you get him home. Sister here will give any assistance to your daughter."

She watched her father following the doctor through into a far room. He walked clumsily, as though he were unsure of himself in these efficient, antiseptic surroundings. She remembered May, and the slip of paper with the Bennett's telephone number that she carried in her bag.

"Please, would you help me to make a telephone call?"

The sister nodded. She was formidable but kind. She held her hand out for the piece of paper and then she lifted the mouthpiece down from the hook and waited for the operator.

How strange, thought Sarah, I'm making a telephone call at last. I always wanted to telephone someone and here I am, about to talk to May on a private telephone.

May's voice sounded odd. Sarah wondered if it was the telephone, or if May had been crying.

"What's happened, Sarah?"

"Pa's taking him home. We're taking him home now, in a taxi to Victoria Station." She heard May give a little gasp and realised, too late, that she had cruelly said the wrong thing. For a second May was allowing herself to believe that Peter was so much better he didn't have to stay in the hospital any more.

"There's nothing more they can do for him, May," she added quickly. "Pa's going to look after him at home."

May didn't say anything.

"May? Are you all right?"

"Yes."

"I'll have to go now. I've got to see about a taxi and everything."

"Yes."

"You'll be all right, won't you?"

"Yes."

"Good-bye then, May."

There was no answer. Just the click of the replaced receiver.

She had made her first telephone call.

When she finally arrived home May was waiting for her. Sitting on Sarah's bed in hat and coat and with her ridiculous squirrel tippet (passed down from Mrs Fawcett) round her neck. On the floor was May's papier-mâché suitcase tied round with string. Sarah, physically and emotionally exhausted from the strain of seeing her six-foot, emaciated brother on the first lap of his journey, realised the day was not yet over for her.

"I'm going home, Sarah. Back to the village."

"Not now, May. You can't go now, this very minute."

"I must," said May simply. "He might die at any moment, mightn't he? I mustn't leave it in case he dies before I can get home."

Her thin little face was quite calm and showed no trace of anguish or tears. She was as resolute as Sarah's father had been before the doctor.

"I'll be needed at home," she quietly. "Your ma's got the boys to look after, and Uncle Jonathan will need some help. I know he's on early work with the post round, but he won't be able to manage on his own. I shall do a bit of temporary work in the village—maybe a few mornings at Fawcett's if they want me—and the rest of the time I can help look after him."

Sarah was aware of shame—shame at feeling tired and miserable and worried about how she was going to cope with the next few months. She felt shame because May was thinking of nothing except what she was going to do for Peter.

"I wasn't going to leave pa to manage on his own," she chided gently. "I'm going to ask Miss Bennett for unpaid leave of absence. Pa and I have worked it out. I shall go home and take most of the work from pa."

"No, that's silly," said May practically. "It doesn't need two of us. And it's more sensible if you go on earning money because you earn more than me."

She was right of course. Even with Peter dying and

the family quietly ravaged with its private grief, there were still the prosaic things to be attended to, the money and the cost of nursing a sick man.

"And anyway," said May distantly, "it doesn't matter what you or your pa decide to do. I'm going home to Peter."

She sat very quietly, her feet tucked neatly together and her hands all stubby and red from housework folded over her handbag. She had had nothing from life except her own capacity for loving. And now even the object of that selfless loving was to be removed.

"There's just one thing," she continued, taking a note from her handbag. "There was no one in at the Bennetts' when you phoned, so I just walked out without waiting to tell them. I want to get the evening train down you see."

"You haven't told them!"

"I've written my notice," said May holding out the note. "And I'll have to forfeit my month's pay of course. I was going to leave my notice on the mantlepiece but I thought it looked rude so I wondered if you'd take it round there for me."

"Oh, May! Whatever has happened to you?"

This, more than anything, brought May's metamorphosis home to her. That her quiet, nervous, obedient cousin would wildly fling protocol and training to the four winds made Sarah realise the extent of her distress.

"I know I shall lose my character," said May. "But I'll worry about that after . . . after . . ." A wild sob burst from her, a terrible uncontrolled noise that was worse because it came from May. She clutched at the squirrel tippet, her face screwed into unbearable anguish. Then she stood up and picked up the suitcase.

"I'll miss the train if I don't go now. Explain to the Bennetts, won't you?"

Sarah followed her down the stairs. When they got to the bottom Florrie came out of the kitchen with a packet of sandwiches. Her fat, red face was full of good-natured concern.

"There you are, luv," she said pressing the packet into May's hand. "You've had nothing to eat this evening I'll be bound. And there," she fumbled in her apron pocket and pulled out ten shillings. "That's from your Uncle Maxie to buy something for the boy. Get him something nice and if you need anything, you or young Peter, or Sarah's pa, now you let us know."

She kissed May noisily on both cheeks and then May went out of the door and Sarah watched her trudging up the street with the battered old suitcase in her hand.

Now I'll go to the Bennetts', she thought. I'll get that done, and then this dreadful day will be over. She climbed the stairs to her room, picked up May's letter, and began to walk to Miss Bennett's.

In spite of her grief, in spite of her tiredness and despair, she was interested to see the inside of the Bennett house. She had a confused idea of what it must be like, drawn partly from May's description and partly from her own imagined pictures of what Miss Bennett would demand as her home background. The only part of the Bennett house she had ever seen was the kitchen, and that very briefly when she had been waiting for May.

She climbed the steps to the front door and rang the bell. The hall light was on but that could possibly be May who had switched it on—all electric!—before she left the house. She had to ring twice before she heard someone moving inside, someone moving with an odd, irregular step, and then the door opened and a funny little man stood there. She couldn't see him properly because the light was behind him, but his outline was funny. He was small and his ears stuck out and he appeared to have a pointed head.

"Yes?"

"I'm sorry to trouble you. I'm May's cousin. I wondered if I could speak to Miss Bennett."

He tutted fussily. "My sister is not back yet. And I don't know where May is, don't know at all. I wanted some cocoa but I can't find her anywhere in the house."

Sarah cleared her throat. "That's what I've come about. I'm afraid May has left—a sudden family emergency—she was unable to let you know."

He paused for a moment, staring hard at her. She felt at a disadvantage because she could be seen clearly in the light coming from the hall, but he could not be seen at all.

"You'd better come in," he said suddenly, turning and leading the way towards the back of the house so that she was left to shut the front door and follow him. She was vaguely aware of a huge hall papered in brown lincrusta and an Indian dinner-gong standing by the bottom banister rail. Then she had to hurry up the stairs in the wake of the funny little man with the irregular step.

She was surprised as she watched him walking up the stairs ahead of her. He had one leg shorter than the other and he wore a heavy surgical boot. Fancy May never telling me that, she thought. How odd that she should have forgotten to tell me that.

"In here," he said, opening a door on the first landing, and Sarah recognised the room instantly from May's description as Mr Bennett's study.

There were all the things just as May had described them—the carvings and the brass statues, the umbrella stand made out of an elephant's foot, the ivory tusks along the overhang, the inlaid table and the japanned fire screen. And the walls were covered in books all nicely set under glass.

"Sit down," he said. Now she had a chance to look at him in the light she saw that his head wasn't really pointed. He had very tight curly hair of a nondescript brown that grew to a wiry point on the crown of his head. His face was small, but not thin.

"You teach at my sister's school, don't you?" he asked.

"Yes, Mr Bennett. My name is Sarah Whitman."

"What's happened to May?"

She took the note out of her pocket and handed it to him. "This is for Miss Bennett. I'm afraid it is May's notice. She had to leave very suddenly because my . . . one of her family has been taken seriously ill and she's had to go home."

"It's your brother, isn't it?"

She was abashed. She had lied to try and save May's character for the time when she would be needing another job, but Mr Bennett appeared to be fully acquainted with the family news.

"I know all about it. She used to talk to me when she was cleaning my study. He's bad, is he?"

Sarah nodded, and the day's tiredness washed over her. "He's going to die," she said wearily.

"I'm sorry," said the little man. He limped over to a lacquered cabinet and rummaged in the back until he found a bottle. "We don't drink, my sister and I," he pontificated. "But I keep a little brandy for medicinal purposes. I shall join you if I may."

He handed her a glass, and poured one for himself. It scalded and hurt her throat but almost at once she felt better.

"I've had to give May one or two of these since your brother's been ill," he said smiling, and a warm sense of gratitude that had nothing to do with the brandy spread through her breast.

He frowned. "It's really too bad though. I don't know what Amelia is going to say. And I wanted my cocoa."

"Perhaps," said Sarah tentatively, trying to soften the blow of May's desertion a little. "Perhaps I could go and make it for you. I think I know where all the things are kept."

"How nice!" he beamed. "How very nice. You won't take too long, will you?" She hurried down the stairs, and then down again to the basement kitchen. It was all very dark. The whole house was dark in spite of the new electric light. The lincrusta was brown, and the paintwork, and most of the wallpaper was heavy and embossed with dark red and blue tapestry flowers. There was plenty of brass—May had always complained about the brass, so much of it to keep clean—but even that didn't do much to alleviate the general gloom.

When she went back to his study with cocoa he bounced up and down on his chair several times, obviously trying to make himself comfortable, and then she realised that as well as one leg being shorter than the other, he had a very slightly twisted spine.

"How kind," he said again, and sipped the cocoa appreciatively.

On the walls were several photographs—groups of Indians with Mr Bennett seated in their midst, the verandah of a bungalow with Mr Bennett standing on the steps, a huge banyan tree with Mr Bennett resting beneath its shade. And a painting of the Taj Mahal, and another of the panoramic vista of the Himalaya.

"Have you actually *seen* the Himalaya?" asked Sarah.

"No. My Calling was in Ceylon. The painting was given to me by a very dear pupil of mine who had served up near the frontier. A dear pupil, a dear pupil," he reminisced. "He was later called to Batowana . . . Bechuanaland, you know."

"Oh, yes . . . I know," breathed Sarah. She hadn't forgotten any of the horrible day, or what had happened, or what was going to happen. But here, in this funny little man's study stuffed with curios from foreign parts, she felt as though it were a little island of time, of strange excitements that were nothing to do with the everyday world outside.

"He went to help on a new mission . . . on the edge of the Kubango marshes . . . a very primitive people . . . very primitive."

She waited to hear what had happened. Had his friend been eaten by the primitive people? Or sacrificed to a heathen god? Or just merely died in some dull ordinary way like sleeping sickness or a snake bite? A shudder of delighted anticipation swept over her.

The front door slammed and she was amazed at the speed with which the little man moved. In one galvanised action he had pushed the bottle of brandy to the back of the lacquered cabinet, opened a drawer of the desk, placed the glasses and the dirty cocoa cup inside, and returned to his chair.

"Up here, Amelia," he called.

Sarah stood up. She deduced that it would not be wise for Miss Bennett to catch her sitting in Mr Ben-

nett's study. Miss Bennett came in, froze, and slowly
peeled her gloves from her hands, staring hard at Sarah
all the while.

"Miss Whitman? How extraordinary."

"I have come on behalf of my cousin, Miss Bennett.
She has been called home suddenly on a serious family
matter. She apologised for the inconvenience and asked
me to hand you her notice . . ."

Miss Bennett's face blanched and Sarah looked
away. She heard Mr Bennett give a nervous cough.

"You mean, Miss Whitman, that your cousin has had
the temerity to walk out of this house without any
notice whatsoever?"

"I'm afraid it was unavoidable, Headmistress." She
had forgotten that she was not here on school business.
In Miss Bennett's presence she was immediately reduced to the subject position of employee facing em-
ployer.

"That girl! Unreliable and bad-mannered! How dare
she? How dare she?"

She strode across Mr Bennett's study with a wild,
man-sized stride, and the little scholar leapt well back
to keep out of her way.

"Perhaps one of the senior girls at school could help
out temporarily," suggested Sarah timidly. "I am sure
Gertie Alexander would be very pleased to earn a
little money."

"I don't need you to tell me how to employ my
domestic staff!" snarled Miss Bennett rudely. "Your
family have done enough. I was foolish to consider taking on one of your relatives, even in a menial capacity.
I should have remembered your own record at school."

Sarah suddenly felt she could take no more. The
day had been too much. She turned round and hurried
towards the door, muttering "Good Evening" and then
she walked down the stairs as quickly as she politely
could. While she was fumbling with the latch she heard
the bobbing little walk behind her again accompanied
by a furtive, "Ppst! Ppst!"

"Good-bye, my dear Miss Whitman. Please send my
kindest regards to your cousin. And I hope the Lord
comforts you all in your hours of distress."

"Thank you, Mr Bennett. You've been very kind."

He smiled, leaning heavily against the frame of the door with his strange twisted body balanced at an uncomfortable angle.

"Perhaps Miss Whitman, when your tribulations are eased a little, you would care to come to one of my magic lantern evenings. They are considered entertaining, you know. I have some very gifted speakers. Colleagues and friends from Callings all over the world."

"I should like that," said Sarah politely.

"Good-bye then, my dear young lady."

A door upstairs slammed violently and Sarah heard Miss Bennett's voice call, "Bertram! Bertram! I wish to speak to you at once."

His face blanched. He whispered, "Good-bye" once more, and then quickly shut the door.

In spite of her terrible day she still had sufficient compassion to feel sorry for him.


They did, as Jonathan told the doctor, manage all right.

The front parlour was stripped of its furniture and the bed put in the window so that Peter could look out and see the hedgerow opposite and the fields rising behind.

It was the beginning of December when he came home, and for a short while he ate with the family in the kitchen. But once Christmas was over and the feeling of winter conviviality had passed, he ate alone in his room, plied with all the good things the village could provide, the fresh eggs and cream, poultry and butter, fruit and honey, and still, in spite of it all, losing what little flesh remained on his body.

They were a practical family—they would not have survived otherwise—and all the things the doctor had told them to do were carefully observed.

At the top of the garden, behind a screen of elderberry scrub, Jonathan built a rough brick stove and every evening the soiled handkerchiefs—which they could not afford to throw away—the bed linen, and Peter's night clothes were boiled in an old zinc bath filled with soda and disinfectant. His cup, saucer, plate,

knife and fork, were scalded in hot water every meal
and then taken back into his room to wait for the
next time of using. He had visitors, but no one with
young children, and his visitors, apart from Betsy,
Anne-Louise, May, Sarah and his father, kept well
over to the other side of the room. The house, the
family, changed its pattern of life and adjusted to
centre round the dying man in the front parlour. The
necessity of caring for him, the extra work and money
needed, were a salve, a useful therapy that helped to
exorcise their spiritual grief.

He knew he must be dying, but he fell into a
euphoric condition of sleep and gentle walks out into
the garden in his dressing-gown, and peaceful contemplation of the woods and fields about him, and it
was hard to believe he was really going to die for he
felt no pain.

At first he was alone at night, just for the first
couple of months, but after the next haemorrhage he
had someone with him all the time. The haemorrhage
came when he was on his own at night, the choking
and the terrible clogging with blood of his lungs and
throat and stomach. He tried to sit up, feeling it would
ease the scarlet flood, get it away from him so that he
could breathe again, but as he struggled and fought with
the bedclothes and with his own body, it had just made
everything worse.

Some miracle of paternal instinct had made Jonathan hurry down the stairs, lighting the candle as he
came, and he had been in time to hold his son's head
up so that his chest could clear of the blood swamping
through it. After that Jonathan had bought a small,
collapsible canvas bed to stand in the corner of the
room, and someone stayed with him every night—if
not his pa, then Aunt Betsy, or May—getting up whenever the night sweats soaked over him and mopping his
body dry with an old towel.

Anne-Louise had sat with him for one or two nights.
Even her self-absorption could not remain detached
from the seriousness of his condition. But he found her
nursing clumsy and painful. She had lived so long

without giving that now, in the presence of a sad sickness, she did not know how to express love in terms of gentle ministration.

May was the one he needed most. May was the one he would cry to in the night, "Help me, May. Help me!" With his father and his Aunt Betsy, and with everyone else, he knew he must not show his fear. He must not add to their distress and he told himself that when the time came he would try to die quietly and with as little trouble as possible. But with May he did not have to pretend. With May's arms round him, and the sweat soaking her body as well as his, he could cry and bury his face in her shoulder and tell her he was afraid. "Hush, my dear, hush. You won't die yet. I won't let you," and "Don't leave me, May. Please don't leave me," and "I won't leave you, Peter, my love, my dear. I won't leave you. I'm here beside you. I'm holding you. I won't leave you."

He wished so much that May could sit with him every night, but the strain on her was too much for him to ask, even of May who gave so easily that he took without thinking. It was just that he needed her so much.

When Sarah came down he gave her his post-office book—all the money he had been saving for the meadow.

"For Harry, Sarah," he said. "The money's to be used for Harriet—to buy her things in the home and to help pa with the upkeep—just as long as it lasts."

Sarah had taken the book without a word. Later she had brought him a form to sign authorising her administration. She attended to all that kind of thing. That's why he had given Sarah the book. You could rely on Sarah to sort it all out.

He watched the winter pass, the bare shapes of the trees against a grey sky, and then the snow, and the frost on the window pane and a fire burning in his room all the time. He watched the birds, robins and finches and bunting, and flights of big cawing seagulls that flew in when the weather was bad on the coast, and then spring came and the hedgerows opposite

turned yellow with lambs' tails, and then the hawthorn
and the blackthorn, and the breeze blew through his
window smelling of light, delicate flowers and the new
grass on the hills to the north. May knew how much
he needed the spring. She dug up roots of celandine
and violets and planted them in an old egg crock for
him, and when they died she replaced them with primroses and stitchwort and even a few early bluebells that
she found in a warm, sheltered patch of wood.

And May understood how he wanted to see the
things that were happening in the meadow, the eggs
all warm and soiled straight from the hen-run, and an
early, adventurous bee that she trapped in her hands
and fetched in to show him. And when the flowers on
the strawberry plants turned into tiny, hard, green
fruits, she picked a large spray and set them by his bed.

It was May's idea that they should buy the cane bed
for him. She and Jonathan and Sarah, put their money
together and bought it, a straw-coloured garden bed
that could be lifted very easily and taken into the
garden and up to the meadow. When June came and
the weather was warm, May and Jonathan would wrap
a blanket round him and Jonathan would lift his son's
six-foot frame as easily as he had lifted him when a
child. Gently, taking care not to bang his legs and
shoulders on the narrow doorways, he would carry
him up to the cane bed and the boy would lie there
on the ground he loved so much.

Towards the end of June it became too hot, and he
found that after an hour or so he couldn't bear it any
more. "Take me in, pa. Take me in," he called fret-
fully, and as his father started to lift him, he felt the
blood come up again, felt it choking and smothering,
salty and unbearably hot. He saw the blanket stain
red, and the cane of the chair, and specks of blood
showering all over the grass of the meadow. He saw
his father's white face, and over his father's shoulder
he saw May begin to run towards him with her hands
full of flowers.

Then he died.

She saw May at the burial of course, but she didn't have time to talk to her properly. They were so hemmed round by family, and friends, and visiting preachers who all wanted to ask a prayer by the graveside, that private conversation was impossible.

She didn't cry at the burial. She had done her crying away from home, upstairs in Aunt Florrie's house where no one could see her. The weekends she had spent in the village helping to look after Peter had been too busy and concerned with the physical things of illness to allow time for tears. But she had wept a lot during the weekdays at Aunt Florrie's, mostly for Peter, but a little for herself too. She'd been dreading the burial. Family burials, like weddings and birth blessings, were attended by the family in all their strength and she was afraid that the massed presence of all the relatives would prove the final harrowing strain on her grief. But she was troubled only twice, when the coffin was borne in on the shoulders of Uncle Frankie and three of her brothers—such a thin coffin—and when she caught sight of May, unbelievably small and lost, and looking white and ugly in her passed-down mourning.

Briefly, in the scullery, when they were refilling the teapots for the leviathan funeral feast, she said to May, "Are you all right, May?" knowing it was a foolish question but feeling that somehow she must let May know that she was aware of the extent of her personal loss.

May swirled water round in the pot and threw the old tea-leaves down the sink.

"I'm all right," she answered, without expression.

"What are you going to do about work?" Sarah asked diffidently. "Would you like me to look around again?"

"I'll go on at Fawcett's for a couple of weeks. I haven't decided what to do yet."

She was forbidding, so stiff and reserved and unlike May that Sarah made no effort to continue the discussion. They filled the teapots and returned to the parlour which had been scrubbed and cleaned and was no longer the refuge of a dying man.

For the rest of that day, May was just as distant. She said good-bye to Sarah in a manner so disinterested that it was almost as though she disliked her cousin, and in the weeks that followed she made no effort at all to contact Sarah.

So it was with surprise that Sarah returned from school one afternoon to learn that May was waiting in her room.

"Broken, she is! Just broken by your poor brother's passing-on," whispered Aunt Florrie dramatically in the hall. "She looks dreadful. Haven't ever seen 'er looking as bad. You don't think she's caught it, do you?"

"The doctor looked at all of us just after ... just after he died. He says we're all fine."

"Well," said Florrie with relish. "Your cousin certainly ain't fine. She looks as though she's going to pass on too. I'll bring you up some tea as soon as I can," she finished hastily, obviously intending to have another look at May as soon as she could.

"No. That's all right. We won't want any." Sarah hurried up the stairs, sensing that one thing May would not want would be Florrie sitting on the bed with them for a nice harrowing reenactment of the last few months.

May was terrible. She sat small and cowed, all life beaten out of her, a piece of helpless flotsam dressed in black. The papier-mâché suitcase was black as well.

"I've run away, Sarah."

"Oh, May!"

"I don't know what I'm going to do, Sarah."

"May, darling. You'll be better. I promise you one day it will feel better. It won't hurt so much." She put her arms round her cousin and hugged her. And she smiled thinly to herself at her own words because even through the grief of losing Peter, even through the pain and bewilderment of the last year, she had still not got over losing David Baron. When she had time to think about it, the hurt was still there. And May's loss was so much more irrevocable, so completely and utterly final. May would never see Peter again. She could not walk along a street and wonder if perhaps there might be a chance encounter, or a message relayed from someone they both knew. Peter was lost to May, ruthlessly and dreadfully.

"I'm going to have a baby," said May timorously.

The breath left her lungs and a sharp pain, as though she had been struck in the stomach, lurched inside her. She heard the words but they didn't make sense. Someone else had said them, or she had imagined them. Whatever May had said it wasn't that.

"I'm going to have a baby," May said again. "I think I'm going to have it in November. I don't know. I'm not sure quite when because ... you see ... I'm too frightened to go to the doctor. I couldn't go at home, could I? They'd all find out. The village would all find out."

"But you can't be, May. You can't be! You don't know what you're talking about ... Why, Peter ..."

Silent, un-crying tears ran down May's face. "He was so afraid, Sarah. At night he was so afraid. And he needed me so much ... so much. Even at the end ... even when he was too weak to move he liked me to hold him in my arms ... just to lie and hold him while he cried ..."

Beneath the shock was a huge, aching admiration for May. Admiration—and envy—because May had not, and could not, be dissuaded from her chosen path. She had loved Peter to the exclusion of everything and everyone else. She had loved Peter more completely, more fully, than Sarah had ever loved David Baron. She tried to absorb the fact that May ... that Peter had loved as she and David Baron had nearly loved one night last summer. May, undeterred by questions of the future, or family, or even the question of catching tuberculosis herself, had overwhelmingly succumbed to the needs of the man she loved.

"Oh, May!" she said, believing at last.

"Only I can't stay there, in the village. I can't. I don't know how I'm going to tell them. And I don't know what I'm going to do. You'll help me, won't you, Sarah? You'll help me!"

"I'll help you." A swift remembrance of Mrs Alexander swept through her mind ... Mrs Alexander so desperate that she had succeeded in killing herself ... and a knowledge that May would never understand the fear that drove a woman to such lengths.

"They'll have to know," she chided gently. "You'll have to tell them, May. Your mother, and my ma and pa too."

"I can't." She began to shake. "And I can't ever go back to the village. You know what they're like, Sarah. They'd never let me forget, and the child ... Sarah! Don't make me go back! I can't go back! Not ever! Please, Sarah, help me ... You're the only one who knows what to do. Help me!"

She wiped her cheeks and the colour from the dyed gloves came off on her face. "Help me," she said again.

"I'll help. We'll sort it out somehow."

"You won't make me go back?"

"You won't have to go back, dear."

"I want to keep the baby. I don't want it to be sent away. I want to keep the baby."

"We'll manage. We'll get a room, or a small flat, and between the two of us we should be able to manage." In her heart she said, forgive me, Peter. The money you saved, your money that was meant for Harry—I'm going to have to use it. But Harry doesn't need it as badly as May does. We're going to need it, Peter, so forgive me.

"I can take in sewing and washing until the baby's old enough to be left," said May eagerly. "Or perhaps I could get a job in the evenings when you've come home from school. And it won't cost much at first, will it? Not a tiny baby. And when it's bigger and needing more, than I shall be out working."

"We'll plan it all out in the morning."

From outside the door came the rattle of cups and Florrie's cheerful, "Yoo-hoo!"

"You can stay here with me this week. Florrie won't mind. And that will give us a chance to sort things out."

Later, when May had finally been soothed to sleep, she lay awake, pressed narrowly against the wall in the single bed shared by the two of them. And she faced up to the realisation that any tiny hope she ever had about seeing, or loving, David Baron again was gone and must irrevocably be renounced.

She was now too fully committed to her family.

# Eleven

THEY were bad times—the thirties—but somehow they managed to get by.

The maelstrom of the depression became worse and drastic economies were made. M.P.'s salaries were cut. The Navy's pay was cut. Schoolteachers' pay was cut—by fifteen per cent which didn't help Sarah and May and young Anna very much.

They should, by right, have been miserable and poor and crushed with despondency. They had very little money and May, after the baby had been born, had been ill for a long, long time. They lived in an attic flat in Brixton and the landlord was belligerent and menacing and had warts all over his face that made him look quite terrifying when seen in a dim light. May, and to a certain extent Sarah too, was in disgrace at home in the village. May had been home once with Sarah and Anna, but the giggles and stares from everyone they passed in the village had reduced her to tears and she had never gone home again. Even worse than village gossip was the gentle hurting love of Betsy, and the silent guilt of her Uncle Jonathan who felt that May's situation was somehow his responsibility because Peter had been his own son.

They should have been miserable, but they were not. It was as though, having reached the very ultimate in despair, nothing could ever be quite so bad again. By comparison with the death of Peter, the birth of the child, the illness of May (and for Sarah the irrevocable loss of David Baron), whatever else happened could only be better. And strangely enough, it was better.

The flat had a bedroom, a living-room, and a kitchen that had no window or ventilator. When they were cooking or boiling the washing they couldn't see across the room because of the steam and the bedroom had green mould growing all over the walls except when once a month they scraped it all off. But in spite of the kitchen, and the mould, it was a nice flat. Charlie had got them one or two pieces of second-hand furniture and brought them round on his fish-cart. And Anne-Louise—grudgingly—had sorted out a few bits to help furnish. Betsy had made several rag rugs and had given them the old lino from her upstairs back bedroom. It was horrible getting into the flat—past Old Krelli with his warty face, always snooping and waiting about in the hall—up three flights of stairs that led straight into the steamy kitchen. But once up there, once up in their own small home with their precious things about them, it was nice and warm and cosy and . . . theirs.

They just about managed to skate along on the money that Sarah earned and the little that May could pick up from time to time. In the years since Peter had died, Sarah had fervently blessed the impulse that had made him hand over his savings book to her. That money had kept them going when May was ill, and had been the means of them getting, and making, the flat a home.

May had tried extra ways of earning money. Evening cleaning when Sarah came home from work; taking in washing (they'd had to discard that idea when the steam in the kitchen got so bad that even Old Krelli had come up to complain); going out as a daily cook and taking young Anna with her. Anna was no problem. Anna (May had insisted on calling her that after seeing Garbo in *Anna Karenina*) had been born as old as May and Sarah. She knew she must be quiet when the girls were both out. She knew she must be unobtrusive when she went with her mother to work. She knew she mustn't let her ball or teddy-bear roll down the stairs into Old Krelli's domain. It wasn't Anna that made outside jobs difficult for May. It was May herself who—although she would never admit it—was no longer strong enough to stand the strain of heavy, over-wearing housework—especially with the added worry of Anna, and the money, and feeling that she ought to do more than her share at home because Sarah was really keeping them.

With Peter's death May had lost some of her endurance, the strength that her will power had been able to produce, even when her body was tired. Peter had taken everything May had been able to give and her physical stamina was never to be the same again.

And then May, who had thought she was incapable of doing anything but housework, found that necessity produced hitherto unsuspected talents. Her own sister Mary was the trained dressmaker of the family, and Sarah usually made the clothes for herself, May and Anna. May had never thought of herself as a dressmaker until she saw a notice in the sweet-shop window asking for a dressmaker to make costumes for the Butterflies-in-the-Rain Dancing Academy.

That night, after a frenzied and hysterical interview with Madame Parker who ran the academy, she and Sarah had unwound fifty yards of seaside-rock-pink tarlatan and began to make twenty-five ballet dresses for twenty-five fat fairies. May would be paid ninepence a dress, and they all had to be ready for the following Friday—four days away. At midnight on Thursday Sarah and May felt ill every time they looked at anything pink. The flat was smothered in small scraps of satin and tarlatan that stuck to everything and the fat fairies' dresses were hung up all around the picture rail. Anna, who had begun by making a replica of a fairy's frock for her teddy bear out of the scraps suddenly said,

"I don't *ever* want a pink dress," and Sarah and May had vowed that she should never have one.

The dresses had been delivered on time, and May had returned with an order for ten black satin tap-dance dresses (with matching black satin knickers to be embroidered with spangles). This time Sarah didn't have to help so much. May had gained confidence and had learned from working on the fairies' dresses with

Sarah just how she could "throw" a stage costume together quickly. They still had their panics when they
both had to drop everything and sew like mad—thirty
golliwog costumes turned all three of them against red
and black for some considerable time—but the money
came in fairly regularly, and mostly May was able to
work on her own during the day. Anna became adept
at picking up, and passing, pins, and also proved useful as a model for the "tots" costumes ("three little
kittens who had lost their mittens"). She suffered fit-
tings with scowling resignation.

They were happy for many reasons; because they
were still only young and it is hard to go on being
miserable indefinitely when you are young; because of
the Dances and especially Charlie—Charlie who moved
them into the flat on his fish-cart—Charlie who came
and distempered the living-room walls for them—
Charlie who picked up a collapsible pram cheap in the
Portobello Road when Anna was still a baby—who
bought them a wireless and changed the accumulator
every fortnight regularly for them. Charlie who bought
them at least one free fish dinner a week and more at
the end of the month when Sarah was waiting for her
pay. It was Charlie who had carried May up the three
flights of stairs when she came out of hospital and was
too weak to walk—Charlie who still thought of Sarah
as "his girl" (only he could see that she couldn't leave
May and Anna and get married yet awhile). It was
Charlie, too, who was able to vanquish Old Krelli.
Charlie was the only one not afraid of Old Krelli.

He had come round one afternoon to find young
Anna waiting on the doorstep, huddled into a corner
of the porch and clasping her bear under one arm. She
had made her once-a-week foray to the sweet shop on
the corner to spend her "Sarah's penny" (a sherbert
fountain or a packet of confectioner's cigarettes!).

" 'Ullo, Annie love. What are you doing 'ere?"
asked Charlie.

"Waiting."

Charlie twisted her nose between his thumb and

forefinger and she wrinkled up her face at the smell of fish. "What you waiting for, love?"

"Sarah and Mummy."

Charlie scowled. "You can go in, Anna love. You know how to reach the knocker. You can go in and upstairs on your own, can't you?"

"Not past Old Krelli," said Anna stoutly. "He might get me."

Charlie had begun to laugh, and then the sight of Anna's small, upturned frowning face had suddenly hurt him. She was so much like Sarah to look at. Her eyes were blue like May's, and her hair the same light brown as Peter's had been, but everything else about her was exactly the same as Sarah, the shape of her face, the smooth forehead and high cheekbones, the large soft eyes that bore the same expression as Sarah's, even though their colour was different. He reached down and hoisted her up onto his shoulder, then he beat a rumbustious tattoo on the door-knocker. After several minutes, several creakings and grumblings and groanings, the door was opened a couple of inches to reveal the terrible face of Old Krelli.

" 'Ullo, Mr Krelli!" he said noisily, pushing past and striding through the hall to the foot of the sairs. "Not like you to take so long to get to the door. You're usually in the hall, aren't you?"

Krelli had scowled and mumbled but Charlie was already on his way up the stairs. And every time Charlie came round after that he made a point of showing Anna and the girls that Krelli must be fought rather than feared. "Waiting in this cold hall again, Mr Krelli? A man of your age should be careful. A bad cold could be the death of a man your age," and "My word, this hall's a dark old place, Mr Krelli. I shouldn't be surprised if one day you tripped and broke something and had to lie here all day." The girls watched, fascinated, and had seen Krelli curse and swear and mutter, but move back into his dark basement kitchen. And there he would stay until Charlie had gone.

They were happy, too, because they were free. They had no mistress, or kind landlady, or member of the

family living with them, and they were free to do as
they pleased and go (subject to the limitations of
finance and leisure time) where they wished. And the
place they went to most was the pictures!

Before Peter's death they had gone only rarely to
the pictures because the influence of the village was still
strong upon them and they both felt guilty about the
amount of enjoyment they received in the dark euphoria
of the picture palace. Pictures, like pubs and gambling
and make-up, were worldly and therefore wicked. They
had gone once or twice during May's pregnancy (hence
the name) and then when May had been so ill they
had been able to do nothing except work and look after
the baby.

When Anna was ten months old, and May was better
but spending a lot of time staring into the middle-dis-
tance and crying, Sarah had suddenly said one evening—"Let's go to the pictures!" May brightened immediately, then her face had dulled over again and she
said, "What about the baby?"

"We'll take her with us."

"We can't!" said May astonished. "Supposing she
cries?"

Sarah had already picked up Anna and was wrap-
ping her in a shawl. "She won't cry. She never cries
when Old Krelli's around. She knows she mustn't. She
only cries when she's hungry. We'll take a bottle for
her."

May, protesting only slightly, had allowed herself to
be swept along to the pictures—to be lost in a world
of pleasure and romance and nostalgia. That first film
was *The Love Parade;* Jeannette MacDonald ("How I
*wish* I had called Anna, Jeannette"), cool, blonde, and
beautiful, and Maurice Chevalier, French, roguish, and
charming. May, who had known what love really was,
who knew the agony and pain and misery of an un-
stinted adoration, still found the gay, sweet, brittle
romantic love of the pictures believable. Or perhaps it
was that she couldn't ever bear to think about real love
again.

Young Anna had not cried. Her eyes had absorbed

with interest the new surroundings. She had listened fascinated to the sounds of the screen, and of the theatre organ in the interval. When she grew tired she went to sleep. By the time she was three she was a keen connoisseur of the picture palace and complained if she missed a visit. She never actually saw the end of a picture. She had always gone to sleep by then, clutching her sherbert dab in her hand and dropping the toffee spoon onto Sarah or May. They usually came out of the pictures covered in sherbert and with the toffee stuck to one or other of their coats.

Their favourite place was the Trocadero—two pictures, a stage show, and the organ in the interval, all for sixpence. And then out to the delicatessen on the corner to buy pease pudding and faggots for supper. Anna woke up then and was able to stare sleepily over Sarah's shoulder and ask for a "sausage with red skin."

They saw them all, and the pictures became their escape, and their own private dreams. There was Chaplin, and Jackie Coogan in *Tom Sawyer,* and Jack Buchanan and Anna Neagle—*Goodnight, Vi-enn-a!*— And Garbo again, in *Grand Hotel.* And Charles Laughton staring out of his palace window looking very sad because Anne Boleyn was going to have her head cut off, and then looking angry because Elizabeth Barrett wouldn't drink her porter. May cried dreadfully when poor Henrietta was held down on the floor by Mr Barrett until she promised not to see her soldier again. Sarah just became impatient. "Stupid creature," she muttered. "Why doesn't she just walk out and get a job of work and then marry him?" But she felt a lump in her throat just the same. Sarah liked the Thin Man films best because Myrna Loy, cool, brunette, and beautiful, was just the kind of person she would have liked to be herself.

For Sarah, the pictures were more than a means of escape. They exorcised her frustrations and soothed the desperate sense of wasting life that sometimes she could hardly bear.

She knew May was a better person than she was. May was kind, and gentle, and good. She loved without reserve, and no one could help loving May in return.

But sometimes, in the middle of the night, Sarah would wake and stuff the edge of the sheet into her mouth to stop from crying. "I'm nearly thirty," she would choke into her pillow. "Nearly thirty, and nothing has happened to me! I haven't done any of the things I was going to do. I haven't been anywhere, or done anything exciting. I shall stay at that horrible school, watching Miss Bennett's hair come down when she thrashes the children. And one day I shall be like Miss Enderby, frightened and twittery and terrified of losing my job before I qualify for a pension." And her body would grow hot as she twisted and turned in her bed, unable to sleep, thinking of the time she had already wasted, of David Baron, of Charlie Dance. She would look across to May's bed, and then to Anna's. I'm trapped! Trapped! she would scream silently to herself. May and Peter between them have trapped me!

In the morning her guilt would be so bad she would get up early and bring May her breakfast in bed. All the way to school she would recite to herself her string of good fortune—It could have been me with the child—if David Baron and I . . . it could have been me. Or it could have been me that got consumption and died. And we've got a lovely flat, and I don't have Aunt Florrie checking up on me any more. And Anna! I wouldn't be without Anna! For Anna belonged to both of them. The child herself could not differentiate between Sarah and Mummy. Mummy was the one who made the nice dinners and sewed. Sarah was the one who gave her her weekly penny and read her stories. They both took her to the pictures, they both carried her home afterwards. They both cleaned her up when she was sick on the tram. Mummy was the one who made her the pretty dress to wear down to Grandpa's. Sarah was the one who took her. Sometimes, to Anna, it seemed that Mummy and Sarah were the same person. They were certainly the best people in the world. She hadn't made up her mind about men. Some were nice, like Uncle Charlie and Grandpa, and some were terrible like Old Krelli and Henry VIII (or was it Charles Laughton?). But it didn't matter too much about men. The world was really composed of Mummy and Sarah.

"No, I wouldn't be without Anna," Sarah vowed fervently on her way to school, and tried to suppress the shouted urge that she wanted something more ... something more from life than growing old at the school and looking after May and Anna until ... what?

She became increasingly aware of the passing of time and it was marked by the physical events of the school. Gertie Alexander had turned from a thin, undernourished child, to a thin, undernourished seventeen-year-old drudge. Sarah had kept her promise to Mrs Alexander. Gertie had taken the Labour exam and had left school at thirteen in order that the family should be reunited. Sometimes, when she saw Gertie toiling with the responsibility of looking after her family, Sarah wondered if she should have broken her promise to the dead woman. If the other children had remained boarded out, at least Gertie would have had some chance of a life of her own. Mr Alexander was still out of work and the family income was dole and the wages of sixteen-year-old Sammy who (and there was a kind of poetic justice in this remembering the incident of the horse dung and Miss Bennett's bicycle) was stable-boy for the milkyard's horses, and fifteen-year-old Maud who had just begun work in a button factory.

The youngest of the Alexander children—the rickety baby who could scarcely remember his mother—was now in Sarah's class, and every time she looked at him she realised, again, that time was passing quickly, too quickly.

Once a week Gertie Alexander took the tram to Brixton and spent the evening with Sarah and May and Anna. Sarah was always touched when she saw how important this evening was to Gertie—how the girl dressed up, looked forward, made an exciting outing of her once-a-week social visit. She listened enraptured to May's account of the latest pictures and stage show at the Troc. She admired and fingered whatever costumes were being made for the Butterflies-in-the-Rain Dancing Academy. Sarah and May were her safe link with a big, exciting, glamorous world. Were they not the first people who had taken her into a tea shop?

As well as looking after the family, Gertie spent two mornings a week charring at Miss Bennett's. She said she didn't mind charring there because Miss Bennett was out at school. "And Mr Bennett's ever so nice," she said informatively to Sarah. "Ain't he nice, May? You worked for 'im, didn't you? And wasn't 'e nice?" May would nod, but not say very much. She didn't talk about that period of her life very much. She talked about Anna, and the pictures, and about when they were all young. But she didn't talk about the immediate years before Peter's death.

One evening in the summer of 1934 Gertie turned up with an air of suppressed excitement and a large white envelope addressed to Sarah and May.

"From Mr Bennett," she said, her washed-out face suffused with a gentle glow of warmth. "About his magic lantern lecture. It's an invitation, and what do you think?" She paused and waited importantly, staring from May to Sarah and defying them to steal the pleasure of her announcement.

"He has put me in charge of Refreshments," she said. "I'm to have a girl to help me and I am to do it all myself. Take the money. Buy in the tea and biscuits, make the cakes. Look, my name is on the invitation card!" Unable to wait she took the envelope from Sarah's hand and ripped it open. Inside was a large white card embossed with black lettering.

Six Years in Ceylon
By Bertram Bennett, B.A.Cantab.

Reminiscences of a Ceylon Teaching Mission.
Illustrated with slides. To be given in St Stephen's Hall
on 20 August at 7 p.m.

Admission free. A silver collection will be taken
for the Overseas Mission fund.

And down in the bottom right-hand corner, "Refreshments, Miss G. Alexander."

"Just look," breathed Gertie, gazing enraptured at her name in print, and then as she handed the card back to Sarah, "Oh, Sarah. There's something written on the back."

In a fine, spidery, academic print, Sarah read:

My dear Miss Whitman,

Perhaps you will remember, some years ago at the time of your family bereavement, my invitation to you to attend one of my Evenings. In view of your further Family Trouble I have hesitated to do so before, but as it is possible that I shall soon be accepting another Calling, I presume to intrude upon your domestic privacy and invite you and your cousin to the occasion described overleaf.

I am sure you will find the lecture most edifying.

Bertram C. Bennett.

"Good gracious me!" said Sarah. "How very extraordinary."

May took the card from her, read the printed type, then turned over and read the note. Her face became instantly withdrawn and blank.

"I don't wish to go," she said tonelessly. "I think magic lantern slides are very old-fashioned. Who wants to see them now anyway when there's the pictures?"

Gertie's face clouded over with disappointment. Too young to understand the turmoil in May's heart at the reference to Family Trouble, she saw only that her name on the printed card was being rejected.

"I'll come," said Sarah hastily. "I would like to come, Gertie. I'll write a little note to Mr Bennett and you can take it on your next cleaning morning."

Her acceptance was partly to soften May's words, but only partly. She remembered funny little Mr Bennett—crippled leg, twisted spine, and pointed head—how frightened he was of his sister, and how eccentrically kind in the matter of the secret brandy. She was fascinated by the Bennett *ménage*—the weird combination of strange, studious little man, and terrifying, uncontrollable Miss Bennett. She was fascinated and curious.

And although May was right about magic lantern slides being old-fashioned when there were the pictures to go to, Sarah was nonetheless always aware (as May

was not) that pictures were make-believe. They were
made in a place called Hollywood and everything was
false and the things that happened were not really happening. Whatever Mr Bennett's slides and lectures were
like, it would be real—because he had been to Ceylon.

When the time came she didn't, after all, go alone.
Anna, captured by the phrase "magic lantern," announced that she wished to accompany Sarah to the
lecture. In an apricot muslin dress, made from scraps
left over from four powder-puff costumes, and with a
small paper parasol that Charlie had given her, she set
off beside Sarah towards the "magic lantern."

The St Stephen's church hall had a raftered roof and
rows of narrow wooden chairs set each side of a gangway. The magic lantern projector stood at the back of
the gangway and Mr Bennett was hopping agitatedly
between the projector and the magic lantern screen. He
was wearing a very old-fashioned biscuit-coloured alpaca jacket and the lightness of the jacket made his
heavy surgical boot stand out even more. When he saw
Sarah he turned rather pink and a gratified smile spread
over his face.

"Miss Whitman! How nice!" he exclaimed. "I hardly
dared to hope that you would abide by your acceptance.
I know your duties are onerous . . . onerous." He suddenly thrust his hand towards her and Sarah, who was
holding Anna with her right hand, had to let go quickly
in order to meet the courtesy of shaking hands. "How
nice, how nice!" he said again, then looked down at
Anna and asked,

"And this is . . ."

"This is Anna, my niece."

Mr Bennett wrinkled his face up into an expression
Sarah could not begin to understand. "Little May's
child," he murmured reflectively. "Of course, little
May's child."

He stared hard at Anna, then at Sarah. "You are
very much alike," he said after contemplation. "Very
much alike. But then, of course, you are related on
both counts are you not? Through your brother and
through your cousin."

She was surprised. Anna's relationship was a strange

and slightly complicated one—Anna was both niece and cousin to her—but it was hardly the kind of thing she would have expected a stranger to remark upon, or to be interested in. And, upon reflection, she wondered how Mr Bennett had known enough to work it all out.

"Please," said Mr Bennett importantly, leading them forward down the gangway. "Please sit here in the second row. Very good seats. You will see the slides clearly and have no trouble in hearing my lecture . . ." He ushered them in with a little bow, then bustled busily back to the projector.

"He's like a gnome," whispered Anna noisily. "He's like the gnomes in the Grimms' book. And like the rabbit in Alice."

"Ssh."

"Why has he got a funny shoe?"

"Because he's lame."

A gentleman in a clerical collar suddenly stood up, rapped on the back of a chair, and called for silence. Then Mr Bennett hopped to the front of the hall.

"During my six years in Ceylon, I was fortunate enough to explore the jungle interior, and to do some research with the nearly extinct, ancient people of Ceylon, the Veddah . . . still living very primitively . . . much as our own Stone Age ancestors must have done. This evening I want to tell you something of my work amongst these peoples . . ."

The slides were bad, indistinct and colourless, but the lecture, to Sarah's surprise, was enthralling. Indeed it was misnamed because it was quite obvious that, though Mr Bennett had been sent to Ceylon to teach the people about God, he had actually spent most of his time studying the history, languages and customs of the hill people.

As Sarah listened the mental image of Mr Bennett— as a frightened, crippled eccentric—began to fade and in its place emerged a rather wild little man, plunging through the jungles of Ceylon, avoiding crocodiles and herds of elephants, fording the great Mahaweli Ganga— and all the while taking copious notes and rushing back to the mission to do a little more study in between leading prayers and teaching the heathen.

Anna sat quietly beside her. The "magic lantern" was disappointing and not nearly as good as the pictures. But she loved to watch people, especially unusual people, and although not understanding everything that Mr Bennett said, she was capturing, alongside Sarah, the visions of jungles and leopards and strange people up in the hills. They were both sorry when the interval came.

"And after the refreshments," said Mr Bennett flatly to his audience, "I shall continue my lecture with a description of some of my work in the mission."

A rattle of tea trollies heralded the arrival of Gertie, her sister, and another young woman whom Sarah recognised from school. Gertie's face was furrowed with responsibility as she presided over two large tea urns and several plates of paste sandwiches and rock-buns. Sarah took a cup of dark brown scalding tea and Anna gnawed politely at a rock-bun. And almost immediately Mr Bennett popped up in front of them.

"Well?" he asked anxiously.

"I think it's wonderful, Mr Bennett! All those interesting things you've seen and done—the places you've been to—and the people! All those lovely people—all different, and exciting, and so ... interesting!"

He flushed. "How kind! How very kind!" he said, staring intensely at her.

The second half of the lecture lost its brightness. Mr Bennett obviously tried very hard to be an inspired missionary, but his heart wasn't in it and the last part of his talk tailed off into a mumble of mission routine that ended suddenly with a loud, "Let us close with a prayer for all our brothers overseas."

When she and Anna went to file past him with a muttered "Good evening ... Good evening," he drew Sarah quickly to one side.

"I am walking in your direction, Miss Whitman. If you would be prepared to delay your departure for just a few seconds, I should very much like to discourse with you—on one or two of the points in my lecture."

She was a little embarrassed, but her natural good manners—and also a sense of pity—made her stand to one side while the rest of the visitors filed past him and out into the street. She saw him cross over to Gertie, and then saw Gertie's face blush as he pressed a ten shilling note into her hand and she felt again—as she had five years ago when she learned he had been giving brandy to May—a sudden glow of gratitude because he was generous to people who needed generosity.

Outside he made a point of meticulously walking on the outside of the pavement, and every time they crossed a road or turned into another street he would dart about, tripping and bumping into her so that he was, again, on the outside. She felt ashamed and ridiculous because she was so much taller than he was and she felt she ought to be walking on the outside looking after him.

"I couldn't mention everything in my lecture. There wasn't time. So many things one wants to describe, the birds, and the turtles, and the flowers! Lilies and hibiscus and poinsettia . . . all so beautiful . . . so beautiful. And the people are beautiful too. They wear sarongs you know, not saris like in the rest of India, men and women both wear sarongs, blue and white and green. You see them bathing in the river, their hair and the colours of the sarongs all shining and wet."

"And the elephants?" said Anna, captured again by Mr Bennett's words.

"The elephants too," he replied, in exactly the same tone of voice because he did not know that children should be spoken to in a different way from adults. "An elephant bathing in the river is one of the most relaxing sights in the world."

"You must miss it all so much!" exclaimed Sarah. In just a few sentences he had once more made her forget that he was a funny, embarrassing little man. She was no longer sorry for him. Just envious because of all the things he had seen and done.

"I wonder, Miss Whitman," he said stiffly, "if you would care to accompany me to a lecture given by a friend of mine—it is at the British Museum—he has recently returned from China—from the northern provinces—you may find his lecture of even greater interest than mine."

She paused for a moment, not because she didn't want to go to the lecture, but she felt awkward about going with him. When he saw she was hesitating he said quickly, "I shall not have many more opportunities for lectures in this country. Just one or two, no more. I am accepting another Calling, you know."

"Back to Ceylon?" she asked wistfully.

"In Baluchistan, Miss Whitman. On the north-west frontier. Afghanistan . . . the mountains . . . Pathans . . . and the deserts of the north!"

"And the Khyber Pass! And the raiding Afghans swooping down from the hills!"

Mr Bennett coughed apologetically. "I shan't be very close to the Khyber Pass," he explained. "A friend, an old colleague, runs a small private mission towards the south of the country. It has long been my ambition to join him and now an inheritance—a maternal aunt you know—a small legacy has enabled me to fulfil my wish."

To Sarah it was a world which one read of, but never really encountered—a world where people were left "small" legacies that enabled them to travel halfway round the globe and explore the lands and peoples of the north-west frontier.

"I have been, for some considerable time, endeavouring to prepare myself for such an eventuality," explained Mr Bennett. "It is a land of many languages—too many for one person, but I have managed to acquire a working knowledge of Urdu and Brahui. And recently I have begun my studies on Baluchi—some of the native Baluchi tribes are very interesting—very interesting indeed . . ."

She was filled with a growing, unashamed envy—an envy that was a fretful pain because Mr Bennett was able to do all the things she wanted to do—all the things she could do so much better than he. It's not fair! It's not fair! she thought. I'm trapped here! I'm going to have to spend the rest of my life putting up with Miss Bennett—taking all her spite and tempers while he goes gadding off to Baluchistan!

"There's a man staring at you," said Anna, suddenly

breaking into her rancorous thoughts. "Over there. He's been staring at you all the time."

In a dream—a confusion of sight and sound that was Baluchistan, and Miss Bennett, and Ceylon, and the northern provinces of China—and an evening just over five years ago that she tried to forget, she saw him . . . saw David Baron walking towards her looking fatter, and well dressed, and holding, as she was, a small child by the right hand.

They advanced towards one another and in her heart she felt confusion and sadness, and also an overwhelming sense of annoyance because whenever she had imagined this moment, the time when they would accidentally meet again, she had envisaged it as just the two of them in some quiet place together where they could talk softly like old, safe friends. Instead she was trapped—hemmed in with Mr Bennett on one side and Anna on the other.

When they came face to face neither of them knew what to say. He stopped in front of her and just stared, his eyes as warm and wild as they used to be, his olive skin and smooth, moulded face just as she remembered.

"Sasha?" he said at last. "Sasha. How are you?"

She nodded.

"You look well, Sasha. Are you well?"

"I'm well."

"You're still teaching?"

"Yes."

The colour came and went several times in his face. He looked guilty, happy, confused, uncertain.

"This is Mr Bennett . . . Mr David Baron." It was all so wrong, meeting with him after all this time in the presence of Mr Bennett and Anna and the other small child. Mr Bennett had stopped jigging about and was standing very still to one side staring hard at David Baron. When Sarah introduced him he muttered, "How de do," and relapsed into silence.

"And this is my niece, Anna," she went on. "My brother died you know. This is his daughter. She lives with me."

There was a long uncomfortable pause when neither of them knew what to say.

"I joined my uncle in his business," he blurted suddenly. "Soon after . . . about five years ago. The leather business—like my father—quality handbags and handmade shoes and gloves. We've expanded—have a factory now, my father and three uncles and my brothers and myself—a family business—very successful. We've been making a lot of money . . . expanding in spite of the slump."

"How nice," said Sarah bleakly.

"My mother and father—they're very happy now." He smiled nervously at her. "I was always a firebrand, wasn't I? I caused them a lot of trouble—made them worry . . ."

Anna and the small boy were warily sizing each other up. The little boy was younger than Anna, probably no more than three. Sarah stared down at the child.

"My son . . ." he said faintly. "I married . . . My uncle's wife had a younger sister . . . I . . ."

"How wonderful!" she said gaily. "Such a lovely little boy! His mother must be so proud of him . . . and of you too now that your business is doing so well. How wonderful! How really wonderful that all those bad times are over! I still see the Alexanders you know. They're doing very well too! Gertie looks after the family—you remember Gertie, don't you—and Sammy and Maud are working. Gertie comes to see us every week. She helps Mr Bennett. Gertie is a great friend of ours. I'll give her your regards, shall I? I'm sure she'll be thrilled to know I've seen you. But I must go now because it's late and Anna should be in bed. It has been nice seeing you again . . . lovely . . ."

"Sasha . . ."

"Good-bye!" she sang brightly. "I do hope everything goes well for you."

She strode on, dragging Anna so fast the child had to run. She couldn't see where she was going, her eyes were blurred but she was conscious of Mr Bennett pattering jerkily along beside her.

"Miss Whitman! You are going in the wrong direction!"

She smiled brilliantly at him. "How silly. Of course

I am." They turned down the next side street and once again he hopped round so that he was walking on the outside.

"It's many years since you've seen him, isn't it?"

"Who? Seen who?" she asked.

"David Baron."

She shrugged and made the smile come back to her face, the bright arched smile that showed she didn't care. "Oh, yes. Some time I suppose."

There was a thin film of sweat across Mr Bennett's forehead and he was panting slightly. "Miss Whitman. Do you think you could slow down a little ... my leg ... it's difficult."

"Oh, I'm sorry! Mr Bennett, how thoughtless of me!" She stopped walking altogether for a moment and, through her own pain, she saw how her frenzied flight from David Baron had put too much of a strain on the little cripple. He was still trying hard to behave like a man—dodging round on the outside and taking her arm when she stepped off the kerb. But he was obviously suffering from having to drag the heavy boot along too fast.

"Perhaps if we could walk slower," he suggested. She forced herself to a calmness she did not feel. Anna was puffing too and her apricot-coloured straw bonnet (also renovated leftovers from the dancing academy) had slewed to one side in the chase.

"You mustn't mind too much," said Mr Bennett quietly. "When times are bad and everyday life is difficult, it is a natural thing for a man to lean on his family. There is a great comfort and security in a family. It is easy to give way to the pressures of parents and grandparents and let the family guide your life. You can surely understand that, Miss Whitman? You who have such a big, loving family can surely understand David Baron's family too. For people like him, and like you, the family is the most important thing there is."

Someone else had said the same thing years ago. Someone had said to her a long, long time ago, the very same thing ... "That's all that people like us have . . . nothing else . . . just each other." It was Mrs Alexander, tired and dying and clinging to the comfort of her family.

"It's not that," she choked to Mr Bennett. "It's not just him getting married and having a son. It's all his ideas, all the things he made me believe too. He didn't mean them. He was lying!"

"He meant them, Miss Whitman. He meant them. He probably still believes in them. But it is hard for a man to go on fighting and believing for the whole of his life. Especially when he is alone."

"But I couldn't do anything else!" she cried. "I couldn't do anything else! The family needed me, I couldn't go off and leave them! I couldn't!"

She turned to stare entreatingly at him, and then she realised who he was, and that he knew nothing at all about her, or about David Baron and the past. Later, upon reflection, she saw that he must know more than she realised. That he knew a whole lot more about her and her family, about May and Peter and everything that concerned them, and her.

"I'll get on a tram here," she said abruptly. "It's rather a long way for Anna to walk and it's getting late."

He quickly withdrew behind his shell of meticulous pomposity. He held out his hand and made a little bow over it. "The lecture, Miss Whitman. The lecture at the British Museum on the northern provinces of China. It is in two weeks' time and I shall take the liberty of ordering a ticket for you. If you would care to wait for me on the steps of the British Museum at six o'clock, two weeks from tonight, I shall be delighted to introduce you to the land of Green Ginger!"

"Thank you." She wasn't really sure whether she was going or not.

For the first time that evening he looked nervous and afraid of something. "I think, Miss Whitman, with your permission, it would be as well if my sister was not acquainted with our forthcoming expedition. She is . . . highly strung you know . . . highly strung. There is no need for her to be bothered with such a trivial matter."

"No, of course not. And thank you, Mr Bennett, for a very interesting evening." They shook hands again and she was thankful to see a tram coming because she couldn't have borne talking to him any more. She was sorry for him, and he was kind and interesting, but she wanted to get away from him to where she could tell herself she didn't care about David Baron.

"Good-bye, Miss Whitman. Until the British Museum!"

They climbed onto the tram and Sarah sat staring blindly ahead of her, feeling old and ugly and somehow betrayed.

"He's still there," said Anna who was kneeling up on the seat staring out of the back window. "He's still watching us. I'll wave." She waved amiably to Mr Bennett, a small, sad figure standing in a pool of light reflected from a street lamp, and went on waving until he could no longer be seen. Then she put her head against Sarah's arm and went to sleep.

When they got back to the flat Old Krelli was waiting in the hall as usual. Anna, roused from a deep sleep, whimpered slightly at his nightmare form in the gloom and clung close to Sarah's side as they climbed the stairs. The lower stairs were steep, dark, labyrinths of horror and Anna had a nightmare at least once a week where Old Krelli chased her up the dark stairs. In her dream the stairs went on and on without a top to them and she ran silently—hoping that Old Krelli wouldn't hear her if she didn't scream—upwards and upwards and upwards. Sometimes, like tonight when she was half asleep and the real life became confused with the dream world, she grew afraid that the stairs really would go on for ever. But it was all right. As they reached the third flight she saw light from the kitchen window spilling out onto the stairs and then she heard a big, booming laugh coming from behind the kitchen door. Relief flooded her small form.

"Uncle Charlie's here!" she said happily.

Charlie, dear, dear, darling Charlie! Charlie who leaned on his family, and was part of them, but who still retained his integrity, who believed in things, and was loyal and loving and faithful. Charlie who was always there when she needed him, who got nothing from life and still less from her whom he had loved all these years. Dear, dear, wonderful faithful Charlie! Their steps quickened, Sarah and Anna, both needing Charlie because he was solid and real and loyal.

May was crawling over the floor cutting out costumes from tinsel gauze. Her hair was dishevelled and she had pieces of tarlatan stuck all down the front of her Miss Muffet print frock. But she looked happy and excited.

"Sarah! Charlie's got some wonderful news for us. We're going to have a holiday!"

Charlie beamed and looked gratified. "You can pack your bags, girls. You're off to Brighton for the week!"

"Brighton! But we can't afford . . ."

"You're going to Brighton! On Saturday. One of the blokes in the market, his sister does cooking and attendance down at Brighton. I've taken it for you girls for the week. She's been let down and she's got a last minute vacancy!"

"But Charlie, the money . . ."

Charlie held up a large, imperious hand. "My treat!" he said grandly. "And I've already paid for it so if you want to get proud you're just wasting my money. You girls can buy your own food and Mrs Mullins will cook it and do the washing-up and keep the room clean for you. You goes on Sunday, and I'm going to 'ave a little trip too because I've fixed me fish round with Maxie and I'm going to come down on Thursday and spend three days with you all."

"Oh Charlie!" Sarah's eyes blurred over with tears again. "Charlie, you're lovely! I don't know what we'd do without you. All these years you've been so kind and good and we've never really appreciated you."

"Oh, don't be a nana!" said Charlie embarrassed, but he looked pleased and happy too. Making Sarah happy was what he wanted to do more than anything else in the world, but sometimes it was difficult.

"It's just worked out right!" said May excitedly.

"You've this week, Sarah, before the new term starts, and you've done all your visits to your ma and pa, and we're up to date with costumes—when I've got these dragonflies done. It's just worked out right!"

It had worked out right. In a different place, where there was sea and lots of different things to do and go and look at, she could forget all about David Baron. She smiled radiantly at Charlie. She was thirty years old. She had wasted too much time dreaming and thinking of David Baron and looking after her family. At thirty it was time she started thinking sensibly— like the Dances were always telling her—thinking sensibly and planning for the future.

She smiled again at Charlie and saw his face flush, and his blue eyes brighten because it was Sarah, his girl, whom he had made so happy.

# Twelve

IT was a hot week. A scorching, bright hot week that made their noses peel and the sea a constant invitation.

They left Mrs Mullins' small terraced house at the top of a steep hill every morning and began the long trek to the beach, white canvas hats pulled well forward to shade their eyes, and their shoes, newly whitened the night before, leaving little showers of blanco on the pavement. By the time Tuesday came—greatly daring—they left their stockings off. Sometimes they took a basket of fishpaste sandwiches and bananas, and other days they sat on the beach by the Steyne and at midday walked up to the Pie Shop and ate hot meat pies straight from the oven on their way back to the beach. Anna, on her first trip to the seaside, was fascinated by the beach and liked to spend as much time there as possible.

They bought her a bucket and spade, and a rubber duck that, when blown up, bobbed about on the waves with a one-sided tilt. When they saw her small face brighten with suppressed pleasure and excitement they both wanted to cry—she was such a funny little girl and most of the time they forgot she was a little girl at all because she had learned—of necessity—to be independent. She knew that the most serious and important things in life were earning a living and not being a nuisance to people.

In her small, serious way she became almost delirious over the sea. All day she plunged up and down in the waves, trying to climb on the back of the rubber duck, and only coming out of the water to take her place on the end of the queue for the pony rides.

The three of them quickly came to a compromise over the holiday. They agreed that all day should be spent on the beach as Anna wanted, but that in the evening Anna must do what Sarah and May wished—without complaint. And so, once they had toiled back up the steep hills to Mrs Mullins, eaten their cooked tea, washed, and changed their frocks, they would hurry down into the town again—to the West Pier to see the Pierrots, or to the theatre, or the Variety, or the pictures. And although Anna always went to sleep and had to be carried home afterwards, she was able to open her eyes long enough to see the lights—the chains and loops and garlands of brilliant gleaming colours that lit the dark evening all along the sea front.

By the time Thursday and Charlie came, they were bright and vivacious with glowing relaxed faces and arms lightly tanned up to where their sleeves began. He leapt off the train, kissed them all, put Anna up onto his shoulders, looped an arm through each of the girl's, and set off leaving his suitcase on the platform. And the first thing he said after "Hullo" was, "Fish for tea tonight, girls! I brought four nice haddocks straight from the stall!"

The holiday had been good up until then, but with Charlie's arrival it turned into a brimming, never-ending interval of excitement and gaiety. Dear, generous, big-hearted Charlie took them on the small railway to Black Rock, to the competitions on the pier, bought them cockles and whelks and candy-floss from the beach stalls, took them to Madame Tussaud's, and the Regent's Palace, and through the Lanes looking at the old junk shops.

Charlie rolled up his trouser legs to paddle and then fell over in the sea. Charlie got his face so scorched the first day that he spent the rest of the holiday looking like one of his own lobsters. Charlie walked through the town with them encouraging them to "dream" buy—to choose dresses and furniture and hats and jewellery from all the beautiful things in the windows. And

Charlie, on their last day, bought May an emerald green taffeta evening dress.

They were staring into the shop window, and the green dress was right in the centre. It had puff sleeves and a sash, and the skirt was flared and cut on the cross. "Isn't that *beautiful*?" breathed May. "It's like the evening dresses Myrna Loy wears. It's beautiful!"

Charlie stared at the dress, and then at May. "You know, May," he said thoughtfully. "You're a bit like Myrna Loy to look at. I never saw it before, but you are. Come on, let's go and see what you look like in the dress."

May giggled and went to walk away from the window but Charlie took hold of her arm. "Come on now, you two. I'm going to buy both of you a party dress. Let's see what they've got inside for Sarah, and May, you shall try on that green one."

"Oh, Charlie!"

"The frocks are lovely, Charlie. But we'd never wear them!

"Yes you will," boomed Charlie. "You'll wear them tonight on the Palace Pier. We'll go dancing. And you can wear them again at Christmas—at our place when we has our Christmas party. That's two times you can wear them and we haven't even *tried* to think."

"No, Charlie. The money . . ."

"We've got lots of frocks, Charlie. And it isn't right."

Sarah was more bothered than May. May was being swept along by Charlie's unbounded enthusiasm and was forgetting that girls didn't allow men to buy them dresses—not even when the man was Charlie.

"If you don't come in with me, I shall just go in and buy them without knowing sizes or anything. I shall buy whatever takes me fancy!"

His red face brimming with mischief he pushed the door of the shop open and went inside. And Sarah, May, and Anna hurriedly followed after him.

Sarah needn't have worried about him buying her a dress because there just wasn't anything she looked right in. She was too tall and her face too finely carved

to look right in any of the pink and blue and yellow
puff-sleeved dresses with velvet bows and diamanté
trimmings. She tried on everything there was in her
size and even Charlie—with his bad taste and his love
of bright colours—was forced to admit that Sarah
looked awkward and ungraceful in the satins and taf-
fetas and marocains. May, in the emerald dress was
pretty and small and just like Myrna Loy. Charlie, for
once, didn't know quite what to do.

"We'll go somewhere else for the dresses . . . no . . .
we'll get the green one here and we'll get yours at
another place, Sary . . . yes, that's what we'll do . . ."

"We'll see," said Sarah. She was relieved because
she didn't really want Charlie to spend his money on
buying her a dress. But later, after a heated argument
and a promise that when she got back to Brixton she
would look around for a frock to match May's, she felt
strangely disappointed and depressed. It *would* have
been fun for them both to have dressed up in Charlie's
new frocks instead of May wearing the shining green
while she made do with her blue *crêpe de chine*.

That afternoon May disappeared from the beach for
a couple of hours. She muttered something about last
minute shopping and getting a present for Ma Dance,
and then hurried off, tactfully leaving Charlie and
Sarah together on the beach with Anna bobbing up
and down a few feet away from them in the sea.

"Ain't it a lovely holiday, Sarah?"

"It's wonderful, Charlie. Just wonderful! And you've
been so kind to us—not just to me, but to May and
Anna as well."

He coughed and fidgeted in his deckchair, and she
wondered if at last the moment had arrived—the
moment after all these years when he would actually
put their marriage into words . . . into a definite practical proposition about time and place and ways and
means. She felt a little nervous, a little trapped, but
she knew she was going to say yes. She had dreamed
for too long. The time had come when reason and
common sense must govern the rest of her life.

"I love doing things for you," he mumbled shyly—
and she waited.

But the day was too hot, and the atmosphere too balmy and relaxed for anything unusual to happen. She turned and smiled at him, and he flushed and looked pleased, and then they lay back in their canvas chairs with the easiness of old friends, dozing, and listening to the shingle moving in the waves and the cries of children splashing in the sea.

They were woken by May—standing over them with three ice-cream cornets melting in her hand—a new May, a startling May, a bold, brazen modern-looking May.

"May! What have you done?"

"Had my hair cut," said May cheekily. "Do you like it?"

Round May's small, sunburned face curled short dark hair, nicely waved over one side of her face in even ridges, and ending in flat curls close to her head.

"Oh, May! What will your ma say? Aunt Betsy! What will she say?"

May sniffed. "I don't care. I'm grown-up. Surely I can have my hair cut if I want to."

It was silly really—they had faced the disgrace of Anna's birth together without flinching—Sarah had bravely stood before the family and told them that May was going to have a baby and that Peter was the father. But the thought of letting the family and the village see May with her hair cut filled Sarah with trepidation.

"I think you look very nice," said Charlie slowly. "You really look like Myrna Loy now—just like her . . ."

All the way back to Mrs Mullins, Charlie and May and Anna were laughing and talking together. But Sarah was rooted in silence, wondering what on earth had possessed May to do such a thing and what—not only May's mother would say, but also Anne-Louise, Sarah's mother.

They went to the Palace Pier that night, although neither Sarah nor May knew how to dance. But Charlie, undeterred, jogged alternately with each of them, doing the same step regardless of whether it was a tango, or a foxtrot, or a twostep. And May, in the emerald dress, and with her new short hair, found when it was her

turn to sit out, that she was approached more than once
by various young men all wanting her to dance. She
didn't of course, but it was lovely to be asked and she
began to enjoy the sitting out dances more than the
jigs with Charlie. She could never remember being so
popular before and felt quite sad and depressed when
the last waltz was played and then the lights were
turned up for "God Save the King."

"Hasn't it been a lovely holiday!" she breathed when
they were walking back up to Mrs Mullins' in the
sultry evening air, the light of the piers effervescing
behind them against the night sea. Charlie and Sarah
were strangely quiet.

"A lovely holiday," she said again.

The following week Sarah went to the lecture at the
British Museum, and the week after that she went to
another—this time on the ancient people of the Tigris
and Euphrates rivers. Then she went back to the
British Museum with Mr Bennett because he wanted to
show her some interesting scarabs in the Egyptian
rooms.

She didn't really know why she kept going to the
talks and lectures with him. He was an odd little man
and although she felt sorry for him—not merely because of his physical disabilities but because of his
obvious terror of his sister—her pity was not the sole
reason for accepting his invitations.

She had a sense of time closing in about her—of
the best and most intelligent years of her life coming
to an end. Soon, in a couple of years or so, she would
marry Charlie. Anna and May would probably come to
live with them, and they would all settle down into a
comfortable, well-ordered pattern—yet another unit of
the vast Dance tribe. But before it happened she must
learn as much as possible . . . accept every invitation . . .
talk to every new person she could . . . seize every
opportunity that life offered. And Mr Bennett offered
her one or two very minor such opportunities.

After the first lecture she was surprised to find herself introduced to the "friend back from China," introduced, and then invited to a house in Bloomsbury

where several people drank—appropriately enough—
China tea and conversed on Ming dynasties and different ethnic groups of the land. She was fascinated, and
at the same time appalled at her own ignorance, feeling hopelessly inadequate before all these learned peo-
ple. Mr Bennett however seemed unaware of her shortcomings and after that she was always included in the
introductions and invitations that followed the various
talks. When she wasn't feeling sorry for Mr Bennett,
or was amused by him, she was vehemently and bitterly
envious of him. He had the money, the learning, the
opportunity, to do all the things she wanted to do. And
increasingly, in his strange little circle of professors and
missionaries, reference was made to his new Calling—
the interesting aspects of Baluchistan that he would
shortly be able to study for himself.

Once, walking back from a lecture, he had astonished her by asking if she had seen the young man—
Mr Baron—again, if they had had occasion to com-
municate.

"No," she had snapped, angry because she hadn't
wished to be reminded, and because she didn't see
that it was any of Mr Bennett's business. In fact it
wasn't strictly true. There had been a one-sided com-
munication—through Gertie Alexander. Gertie on her
once-a-week visit had reported that—after all these
years!—David Baron had been round to see them.

"And he asked after you, Sarah," she said with interest. "He wanted to know what had happened to you
and where you were living—your actual address—he
wrote it down on a piece of paper."

Sarah felt something cold move in the pit of her
stomach.

"He said he'd like to come round with me one evening, to see you and May and Anna. He asked if it
would be all right."

"It won't be all right! I don't want to see him again.
Not ever!" She jumped up and went into the dark old
attic kitchen with Anna to make welsh rarebit for
them all. She could hear May and Gertie talking very
softly and she took a long time getting the supper, long
enough for the pain and the panic to subside and long

enough for her to get David Baron right back in per-
spective again, an irresponsible young man who brought
nothing but trouble into people's lives. She compared
him, as she had many times, with Charlie. Charlie was
a giver, a faithful loyal, constant giver. David Baron
was a taker and would always be a taker.

By the time she and Anna carried the welsh rarebit,
and the pickles and tea into the living-room, they were
talking about something else and the subject was never
brought up again.

Sometimes she wondered why Mr Bennett kept inviting her to things. It was most odd considering the
risk he ran—the risk that his sister might find out.
About every third occasion he stressed the need for
discretion—"No need to cause anxiety to poor Amelia.
She has so many anxieties and responsibilities with her
school duties . . ."

Mr Bennett's euphemistic "anxiety" caused Sarah
some considerable anxiety of her own. Miss Bennett's
reaction, if she discovered that her brother was frequently in the company of Sarah Whitman, made the
old familiar fear—partly the fear of losing her job but
much more the fear of Miss Bennett's uncontrollable
violence—to settle over her again. Ten years under
Miss Bennett's jurisdiction had certainly effected an
uneasy truce between them, but Sarah was never left
in any doubt that the headmistress watched—and enjoyed—every large and small mishap of Sarah's teaching career.

She came to the conclusion that Mr Bennett was
lonely, in spite of all his academic and scholarly friends,
and that he was attracted to her by whatever quality it
was that always had attracted older people to her. She
didn't know what it was, only that older men and
women (with the exception of Miss Bennett) had always liked her very much.

Sometimes he asked her about her family, about
their strict, non-conformist views and about their mode
of worship. Once, when she tried to explain to him the
way her people in the village lived, he had surprised her
by saying, "You love your father very much, don't
you?" He often said strange things like that—small,

preceptive things that made her uneasily aware he had a keen, sensitive instinct about people.

At the beginning of November she had a letter from him.

My dear Miss Whitman,
  I wonder if I could presume upon your valuable time and ask you to visit me here at my home on Saturday next at 3 p.m. in order that a certain matter may be discussed. Amelia will be opening a Christmas Bazaar and will be absent from 2:30 p.m. until approximately 5 p.m. Please do not get here early.
                                    Your sincere friend,
                                        Bertram C. Bennett.

She showed the letter to May.

"I think I had better go, May," she said thoughtfully. "I know we were all going to the matinée at the Troc, but I think I'd better go as he's asked so specially. I'll get Charlie to take you both."

"There's nothing to stop Anna and me from going on our own," May snapped. Sarah couldn't see her face because May was bent over the sewing-machine, but she sounded very cross. Sarah didn't say any more. She had noticed that since May had cut her hair she had changed. She didn't seem gentle and contented any more.

Mr Bennett answered the door before she even had time to knock. He was wearing his "lecture" jacket, the biscuit-coloured alpaca, and his hair was brushed to an exceptionally neat point on the top of his head.

"Miss Whitman! How nice!" He held the door open for her and then led the way upstairs to his study. Sarah, staring about her, decided that the house hadn't changed one fragment since she was last in it five years ago. It was just as gloomy and the ornaments were all in exactly the same places.

"Sit down. Sit down, Miss Whitman." Sarah sat, but Mr Bennett didn't. He walked over to the fireplace, clasped his hands behind his back, and cleared his throat.

"Miss Whitman. Over the past few months I have been watching you very closely, very closely indeed. I

was, of course, not unaware of your potential and your
abilities. I may say," he rocked up and down on his
surgical boot a little, "I may say that over the years I
have followed the vicissitudes of your career and domestic circumstances with the greatest of interest."

Sarah, without knowing why, began to feel nervous.

"I have watched your demeanor in learned circles,"
he continued. "And I have been impressed with your
ability to learn as well as to teach. I have further noted
that you have excellent health and a tidy, businesslike
mind. In addition you do not shy from accepting responsibilities—heavy responsibilities."

She had never had so many compliments paid her
before, and they were the best kind of compliments.

"I have thought long and seriously before coming to
a decision, Miss Whitman. And I have spent much time
in contemplation and prayer before finally concluding
that my course of action is the right one."

"Yes, Mr Bennett?"

"I wonder, Miss Whitman, how you would feel about
accompanying me to my teaching mission in Baluchistan?"

She knew then that his eccentricity had carried him
too far. His yearning for the knowledge and peoples of
other lands had made him lose all sense of exactly
what, and who, was needed on a teaching mission. Because he, with his legacy and the friend's private mission, could indulge his extravagances, he had lost all
sight of the basic requirements of a qualified teaching
missionary. She was touched to think he believed her
suitable for such a post, but at the same time sorry
that his isolation from the world had resulted in such
a lack of judgement.

"I am most flattered," she said gently. "And believe
me, Mr Bennett, there is nothing in the whole world I
would rather do than explore Baluchistan as part of
your mission team. But—even in a privately run mission—certain basic essentials are required . . . and I
have none of them. I have no knowledge of the language, or the peoples. And above all I am not equipped
to teach mission work. I have no experience of mission
work, have never even belonged to a mission group in

this country. We both know, Mr Bennett, that to take a post abroad one must have been associated with overseas mission work in some way."

She tried to speak as kindly as she could, anxious not to let him see how silly and pathetic he was. A slow flush spread up his face.

"You appear to have misunderstood, Miss Whitman," he said stiffly. "I was asking you to come as my wife."

For one wild, delirious moment she wanted to say "yes," even before the full significance of his proposal struck her. While shock and incredulity were registering inside, something else was saying, Accept! Accept! This is your chance! This is the way out of the trap . . . to see all the things you've always wanted to see . . . to escape being like all the others . . . Accept! Accept!

"I am aware, naturally," Mr Bennett was droning on, "that the match may seem a little strange to you . . . our difference in stations . . . your religious background . . . very non-conformist—very non-conformist indeed!"

She could get away from the school—get away from Miss Bennett and pathetic Miss Enderby, and the poverty and wearing sadness of children suffering from malnutrition. She could travel half way round the world—seeing, exploring, having wild, incredible adventures!

"And of course I am not a young man," he said, suddenly very humble, so humble that she stopped thinking and looked at him. His pomposity had vanished, and was replaced by stumbling sincerity. "I'm forty-seven," he said anxiously. "And you are only thirty. I know that. I found that out like I found out all the other things. I listened to your cousin, May, when she worked here, and then I listened to Gertie Alexander. And I listen to Amelia too, when she talks about you."

His face flushed even brighter and he brought his hands round in front of him and held them tightly together. "Seventeen years is a lot. And I'm not . . . not a strong man . . . I have never been robust. I am not a man you could be proud of . . . not to look at. I could not be to you what a young man could be. But I would be very honoured if you would be my wife . . . I would teach you everything I know—all the learning I have acquired in thirty years . . . I would try to make you happy . . . to the best of my ability . . . I would like you to be my wife. I would like it very much."

He was eccentric and pathetic. But he had dignity too, and sincerity. She was shocked at the path her own greedy thoughts had been travelling on. He did not deserve that.

"I'm sorry . . ." she said softly, but before she could continue he interrupted.

"I don't want to know now. I don't want your answer right at this moment. If you think about it you may see it's a good idea. Please go away and think about it."

"It would be unfair. If I went away you might think I would change my mind."

"But you might! You might!" he answered eagerly.

"No."

"There isn't anyone else! I know there isn't anyone else! Not since you learned Mr Baron was married." She stared at him aghast. "I know all about you," he continued feverishly. "I know you loved him. But he's married now. And you'll never marry the other one— the fat one with the fish-cart. If you'd been going to marry him you'd have done it years ago!"

"I don't want to talk about it!" She couldn't believe it was Mr Bennett talking like this. All his control, his pedantic eloquence had vanished. He was hopping up and down the study, wringing his hands together, his face flushing red and white by turn.

"You'd be wasted on him! Wasted I say! Like you'd have been wasted on the other one!"

"Stop it, Mr Bennett!"

"I want you to marry me, Sarah. I want you to look after me. I want you to come to Baluchistan with me!"

"Stop it!" She jumped up from her chair and ran across the room. Stumbling he came after her, reaching out to catch and stop her. His hand—trembling— grasped her arm and she pulled herself away.

"I want you. You're not for him! Not that big, strong fellow! I want you!"

She wrenched the door open. "I'm going, Mr Bennett!" She felt sick, and shaken, and she was ashamed because there was also a small sense of rising excitement in her. It was as though Mr Bennett had released a bizarre, hitherto unsuspected aspect of her character.

"Don't say no!" he shouted over the banister rail as she ran down the stairs. "Think about it, Miss Whitman, think about it!"

She slammed the door, ran down the steps to the road, and then continued running along the pavement, trying, by physical movement, to work off the revulsion, the shock, the . . . fascination . . .

All the way home on the tram she could feel where his trembling fingers had rested on her arm and small, icy tendrils of disgust crept over her body. Then she realised the disgust was not only disgust. Some of it was excitement, weird, nasty, attractive excitement . . .

She began to giggle nervously when she got off the tram. The whole incident had been embarrassing but, back on her home territory, she began pretending to herself it was all a joke—fancy being asked to be a missionary's wife. She wondered what she could say to May when they came back from the pictures. May would want to know why he had asked to see her and she didn't want to tell May anything of what had happened.

She stopped on the way home and bought a tin of baked beans as a treat for Saturday tea when the others came home from the pictures. And going up the stairs in the flat she was glad they were out so that she could spend a couple of hours composing herself.

Only they weren't out. When she opened the sitting-room door, Charlie and May were sitting together on the sofa holding hands.

They sorted it out all right. They sat up until three o'clock the following morning, talking, crying, trying to explain what had happened. How it wasn't anybody's fault.

Sarah's sense of loss was bewildering. For so many years Charlie had been *her* Charlie, she couldn't assimilate the fact that now he was May's Charlie.

Charlie kept making fresh pots of tea and May was crying nearly all the time, asking Sarah to forgive her. She hadn't meant it to happen and if Sarah hadn't caught them she would never have told Sarah.

Charlie looked sheepish and said he hadn't meant it to happen either. He had always wanted to marry Sarah, had always loved her, worshipped her, idolised her. Only one day he saw May in a green taffeta evening dress and she looked just like Myrna Loy and she was so pretty and little and he didn't feel nervous when he was with her.

"If I hadn't caught you, what would you have done?" Sarah asked. "Would you have married me, Charlie? Would you have married me and had May and Anna live with us?"

"I suppose we'd have just gone on . . . like we are now . . ." he muttered. "The four of us . . . you and May and Anna living here, and me with ma and pa."

"You'd have let me go on thinking . . ." She couldn't take it in . . . couldn't believe that Charlie, who had loved her since she was fifteen, didn't love her any more. Charlie was loyal, loving, faithful. He wasn't like David Baron. Charlie, once committed, remained committed, and nothing could change him.

"I don't know what I feel," said Charlie unhappily. "You're still special to me, Sarah. You always will be. It's just . . . May's suddenly different to me now . . . it's as though she's a person I never knew before."

"What are you going to do?" She felt betrayed . . . and lonely. She felt so lonely she didn't see how she was going to get through the rest of her life on her own. Pride would make her pretend she wasn't lonely, but a terrible sense of desolation had already gripped her and she was afraid. She had felt betrayed when she had learned that David was married, but this time it was different. Charlie, reliable, constant Charlie had betrayed her and nothing, no one, would ever be the same again.

"We thought we'd like to get married," said Charlie humbly. "If you don't mind."

She laughed so much they had to slap her face and then she began to cry again and Charlie got up and made another pot of tea and they started it all over again.

"It's Anna too," said May pleadingly. "Anna needs a father and Charlie's the one man she trusts and loves."

She was going to lose Anna too! She hadn't thought of that. It was almost worse than losing Charlie. Anna was her child just as much as May's. She had taught Anna to read, she told her stories, she took her to the village. May knew lots of things about Anna, but Sarah knew other things . . . that Anna was bright and intelligent and must be taught how to fight.

"Where will you live? Where will I live?"

"If you want the flat we'll go."

"Live here alone? Without Anna? And Old Krelli downstairs?"

"Couldn't you go back to Aunt Florrie's?"

It went on and on. And they were tired, and unhappy, and confused. But even though Charlie and May were consumed with guilt and a sense of betrayal, nothing could conceal the fact that they were delighted because they had discovered they loved each other and could live happily together. It wasn't the love May had once known—she was incapable of living at that pitch of ecstatic sacrifice again. This was a warm, cherished, safe love. A Charlie love.

And in the end there was nothing Sarah could do but accept it. Because it was obvious, whatever she said or did, it made no difference. Charlie and May were in love, and in their quiet, humble, Charlie-and-May fashion they were going to get married and no one could stop them.

She had to accept it.

The following day she went round to Mr Bennett and told him she would accompany him to Baluchistan as his wife.

# Thirteen

MAY and Charlie were married three weeks later at Brixton Registry Office. After the wedding they waited—Sarah, Anna, Maxie Dance, and the bride and groom—in the bitter November wind for the tram to take them up to Kennington where Ma and Pa Dance were giving a nuptial tea.

In contrast Sarah's wedding was to be at home in the village just after Christmas, and was to be the event of the year.

The family couldn't believe the honour and prestige that was falling upon them—Sarah—to marry a missionary and preach the Lord's word to the heathen in Baluchistan! Nothing like it had ever happened before in the history of the Pritchards or the Whitmans and they took it as a tribute to the village in general, and to the family in particular. They could have wished that Mr Bennett worshipped in the manner that they worshipped, but allowances had to be made and this point was overlooked when Mr Bennett graciously said he had no objection to the usual private marriage blessing of the Meeting folk being celebrated after the more formal ceremony in the village church.

Sarah had at first been afraid that her mother, envying her good fortune, would allow her jealousy to crystallise in spite. She knew—had known even as a small child—that Anne-Louise bore none of the usual maternal feelings towards her only daughter. She was jealous of Sarah and had done—would do—everything to prevent Sarah's fortunes being better than her own.

But when Sarah, accompanied by Mr Bennett—Bertram—paid her first visit home to the village, Anne-Louise had stared at the little man, noting his crippled foot and twisted spine, had seen that he was older than Sarah, shorter than Sarah, and had then graciously extended her hand and smiled at him.

"Sarah's a very lucky girl!" she said with affection. "I can't tell you what a relief it is to her father and me to know that someone will be taking her in hand. She's been quite a problem to us, I can tell you ... quite a problem."

At one time it would have hurt and embarrassed, but Sarah had outgrown her mother now. She knew that if Mr Bennett had been tall and young and strong, her mother would scarcely have been able to control her venom. As it was, Mr Bennett was obviously second best—even with Baluchistan thrown in—and was therefore good enough for Sarah.

Everyone was delighted. Aunt Betsy because Sarah's impending marriage allayed her fears that May had "stolen" Charlie from Sarah. Everyone had thought that Sarah would one day marry Charlie. That she had chosen a crippled missionary was exactly the kind of thing one would expect from Sarah. Aunt Betsy just felt relieved and happy that everyone was matched—and especially that her own daughter was now respectably married and her granddaughter had a father. Betsy was content.

And Jonathan was delighted—almost. His son had died, his elder daughter was in a home, but now this child—his favourite and best beloved—had done more for herself than he had ever hoped. Only ... when he saw Mr Bennett—Bertram—he began to worry, just a little.

"It's what you want, lass, is it?" he asked anxiously. "I mean, you've thought about it, have you? You're sure he's the right one for you? You'll be happy with him?"

"It's what I want, pa," she answered woodenly.

They were standing at the top of her pa's garden,

looking over the hedge into the meadow at the shuttered hives.

"I'm not against him! Don't think that," Jonathan said quickly. "Just, I'd always thought of someone more . . . younger . . . more like you, lass."

"I don't mind what he's like, pa. I'm strong. I can take care of him."

"If you're sure, lass. If you're sure . . ."

He knew there was something not quite right, but the gap between them was now greater than the love. She was older than her father.

It was strange, the way people reacted to the news of her forthcoming marriage and her departure for Baluchistan.

Miss Bennett had not spoken or looked at her since the evening she had been acquainted with the news of her brother's engagement. Sarah, knowing Mr Bennett's terror of his sister, had offered to tell Miss Bennett herself.

"Oh no!" said Mr Bennett cheerfully. "I shall quite *enjoy* telling her. You will leave school of course—this term. I know you are supposed to give notice but there's nothing she can do as you're marrying me, is there?"

"But . . . you've been so anxious that she shouldn't know anything about us meeting . . . so concerned that I shouldn't mention it . . ."

Mr Bennett beamed. "That was *before*," he explained. "I have you now. I don't belong to her any more. And you're as strong as she is."

"I see," she answered, but she didn't see at all. Mr Bennett was such a strange and incomprehensible mixture that she understood less and less of him.

Miss Enderby had cried when she heard Sarah was leaving. "I'm happy for your good fortune," she sobbed. "But I did hope you would stay on until my retirement. I don't think I can bear Miss Benn . . . the school without you."

Sarah was surprised. She had always thought Miss Enderby was in favour of the headmistress's attitude towards her.

"It always made me feel better when you stood up

to . . . things. I wanted to, you know. I did want to."
She stared anxiously at Sarah. "Some of the poor children—I felt so sorry—but I didn't dare do anything.
You were so brave. I don't know what I shall do
without you."

"You'll be all right, Miss Enderby," said Sarah,
touched. "I will write to you if you like . . . tell you all
the interesting things I see."

"Would you?" said Miss Enderby cheering a little.
"It would give me something to look forward to. And
I could write to you on Sunday afternoons, before
Evensong. Sunday is such a long day . . . such a lonely
day . . ."

Sarah felt again the surge of relief that she was
escaping. Anything—anything at all was better than
staying at school and following the path of Miss Enderby.

Gertie Alexander cried, and then all the Alexanders
came round and cried, and she promised to write to
them too.

The Dances cried—noisily and jovially—and May
looked guilty and said she hoped Sarah going away
was nothing to do with her and Charlie getting married.

Anna didn't cry, and that was terrible. Her face
buttoned tight and she went about being carefully controlled until at last, just before the wedding, she finally
brust into tears.

"I don't want you to go! Please don't go! Let's live
together like we did before."

"We can't, darling," Sarah choked. "You live with
Mummy and Uncle Charlie now."

"I don't want you to go," she sobbed. "I don't want
you to go."

She looked at Anna's small face and she saw Peter—
Peter telling her how he was going to run away to
sea—Peter saving up the money for the fare to Chat-
ham, stuffing the money under his mattress—Peter
lying emaciated in the hospital, telling her all the
practical things that must be done when he died.

Anna quietened. She controlled her sobs and the

following day her face was set firm against any further emotion.

Sarah enjoyed her month in the village. It snowed just before Christmas and the woods and fields turned into a silent landscape, broken only by the prints of birds and foxes.

She walked at lot—tramped for miles on the hills she had not really had time to explore since she was a child. Sandy Bottom had become a stream of silver running between snow banks. Every morning she looked out of her window and saw the trees had turned to crystal in the night. She pretended, whenever the arrangements for her wedding allowed, that she was a girl again, living in the cycle of the seasons.

I shan't see the primroses this year, she thought one morning when she had discovered a small clump of aconites growing in a sheltered corner of the wood. I shan't see the primroses, or the trees beginning to bud, or the hares come out to box. I shan't see any of those things for a long time.

The day before the wedding the cottage was invaded by Dances. Anne-Louise and Auntie Florrie, reunited after an interval of several years, gossiped incessantly and the tiny rooms became hot, overcrowded, and noisy. When, on the evening train, Gertie Alexander arrived (face crimson with excitement and brides-maid's dress packed into a large cardboard box) Sarah felt she could stand no more. She took Gertie up to her bedroom, showed her which bed she would be sleeping in, and then said, "I'm going out for a while, Gertie. Just up to the village. Tell the rest of them I'll be back soon."

"Sarah . . . there's something . . ."

"I shan't be long, Gertie. I just have to go out!"

"But . . ."

She had her hand on the door, anxious to get away before Gertie started talking and kept her. She didn't want to talk to Gertie or anyone. "Shan't be long," she said again, quickly.

"I've got a letter for you . . . from . . . someone . . ."

When she turned round Gertie was holding an envelope in her hand. She looked uncomfortable, and uncertain, as though wondering just how Sarah would react. Sarah took the envelope from Gertie's out-stretched hand and stared down at the heavy, black writing. Se knew, even though she had never seen his writing before, who the letter was from.

"He was ever so upset," said Gertie nervously. "He comes to see us sometimes—only I never mentioned it because you said not to. And he always asks about you. And I told him, like, that you were getting mar-ried. And he really was ever so upset—he said he was going to come down here and talk to you but I said you wouldn't like that. You wouldn't have liked that, would you?"

"No." She had a cold sensation in the pit of her stomach at the thought of David Baron storming into the cottage and making a terrible scene in front of all her family.

"In the end he said all right, he wouldn't come, but I must promise to give you the letter . . . You're not cross with me, are you, Sarah?"

She managed to smile. "Don't be silly, Gertie, of course I'm not cross. I expect it's just a letter to wish me good luck."

Gertie looked doubtful.

"I'm sure that's all it is. So you forget about it and hang up your dress. Look, I've put a hanger here on the cupboard door for you. Unpack it now and that will give plenty of time for the creases to drop out."

She was aware of the letter, huge and heavy, in her right hand pocket, but she forced herself to chatter gaily to Gertie while the pink moss crêpe was shaken out of its tissue paper, hung, and its finer points noted and admired. When Gertie's nightdress had been neatly folded under the pillow on her bed, Sarah felt free to escape. She led Gertie down the stairs and into the kitchen. As she pushed her way through the hubbub of family and friends, she realised that her hand in her pocket was clasped rigidly round the letter.

Outside she leant against the back door for a moment and breathed deeply. The air was crisp and stung her hot cheeks. In the light from the kitchen window she made her way across the yard to where

her brother's bicycle was standing and she crouched
down and carefully unscrewed the front lamp. Then
she scrunched down the path into the lane, walking
towards the stile that led to Tyler's fields.

There were footprints in the snow as far as the stile,
but once she had climbed over she was treading on
clear, unbroken snow—not even a bird or rabbit track
broke the sugary white surface. The trees on each side
were hung with white filigree and icicles, and when she
reached the fields she saw that the moon cut a swathe
of light like a river across the expanse of snow.

She didn't want to open the letter. While it was still
unopened she could pretend that it was a good letter—
that it contained warm and comforting news that would
somehow make everything come right again. With the
letter in her pocket she had a link with him. She was
alone, and yet not alone. She trudged across the field,
breaking the surface and sinking deeply into the snow
in several places where it was deep. The cold air nipped
at her fingers—she had forgotten to bring her gloves—
and made her face glow. When she reached the other
side of the field she climbed up, sat on the gate, and
took the letter from her pocket.

Heavy handwriting, definite like he himself was,
sloping to the right and with wild, generous strokes
reaching up and down. She held it for a while longer,
then opened the envelope, switched on the bicycle lamp,
and read.

Darling Sasha,
    You can's do this to me! It's a terrible thing to
marry that old man and you mustn't do it, not when
I love you so much! I nearly go mad when I think of
you and him. He's crippled and old and he mustn't
marry you—you mustn't marry him! Please, Sasha!
Don't do this to me. Don't make me suffer like this!
I beg you, come back to London and see me, talk to
me. I won't force you to do anything you don't want
but you must see me and talk to me. Please! Just see
me! Don't marry him. Don't go to India. Please,
Sasha! I can't bear it if you marry him!
                    Please, Sasha, Please!
                                        David

Agony twisted her cold hands and made her crush the paper into a ball. How could he! How could he do this just before the wedding! Offering no solution, not even saying he was sorry he had married someone else . . . no mention of his wife, his son. Just telling me not to do it! Saying he can't bear it if I marry someone else . . . telling me to come back, stay as I am, go on waiting and hoping for something that can never happen! How could he! How could he!

Her throat began to hurt with unshed tears, and then when she remembered him—his face, his warm mouth, his excitement and vitality, a low moan burst from her, a bitter, anguished noise that ended on a sob. Tears began to flow down her cold cheeks, "So selfish! He always was so selfish!" she sobbed, and she hunched her body forward, clutching her hands round her waist to try and stop the pain that had settled there. "Not helping me . . . just when I thought I could manage everything . . . make my life come right . . . do something instead of waiting . . . Oh, David!"

She ceased trying to fight her grief. She surrendered to the desolate pain that his letter had aroused after years of fighting it, not thinking about it, controlling it. She let her whole body shake with sorrow, allowed tears to rain unchecked down her face and neck, rocking to and fro in a rhythm of despair.

She did not know how long she sat there, but after a while she heard the sound of her own weeping die away and, her mind emptied of everything, she became quiet—sunk into an apthy of emotional exhaustion.

On the far side of the field a small, dark shape appeared, stopped, moved, and loped towards her. Drained of all feeling she sat motionless and watched the fox trotting across the snow, lifting his paws daintily into the air and shaking them free from snow every few paces. When he saw her on the gate he paused again, ears and brush standing up taut, ready to dash at the first sign of danger. Sarah didn't move and the fox relaxed, changed his direction and passed close in front of her on his way to the other side of the field. She caught a glimpse of his eyes shining in the moonlight, and then he disappeared into the trees.

She climbed down from the gate, scooped up handfuls of snow and held it to her eyes. She remembered the bicycle lamp and hastily switched it off. Mustn't waste Bobby's battery. They were expensive. When she felt her face was less swollen she dried it on her handkerchief. Then she dug a hole in the snow, tore the letter into small pieces, and buried it.

"I don't suppose I shall ever forget him," she said softly to herself as she trudged back to the cottage. "I don't suppose I shall ever forget him."

## Fourteen

THE one thing she had not expected from Karachi was the scent of roses. She was prepared for everything else. Mr Bennett had told her all about India, about the beggars and the smell of burning dung, about the red stain of betel juice, and water buffalo blocking the traffic in main thoroughfares. He had told her especially about the smell of India—of urine and scorched earth and spice—the smell that she had sampled in varying degrees at Aden and Port Said. But the first smell that really made a conscious impact on her was the smell of roses.

When the ship docked Mr Bennett hung excitedly over the rail peering down at the confusion of figures on shore. "He's there!" he shouted suddenly. "Amos is there! Look, Sarah. Down there to the left. There's Mr Scavener!"

Sarah tore her eyes away from the sails of the native fishing boats that seemed—dangerously—to lie littered all around the harbour in the leeway of liners and merchantmen. She stared down in the direction of Mr Bennett's trembling hand and saw, amidst the hawsers and cables and shouting coolies, a tall, thin, cadaverous figure in a crumpled suit and a solar topee.

"Amos Scavener! My very dear friend! He has come all the way down from the hills to meet us!"

Mr Bennett's excitement grew more and more uncontrollable. He gripped and ungripped the ship's rail several times and when they finally went ashore his entire body was shaking. He grasped her arm so tightly she could feel his small, hard fingers biting into her flesh.

"You will like him, Sarah. Such a brilliant man. Such a brilliant scholar!"

She thought perhaps he would leap forward to greet his friend privately but he held firmly to her arm and made her walk beside him.

"Amos!" he said to the skeletal figure standing before them. "Amos, this is my wife!"

Mr Scavener did not smile. He lifted her hand in his and stared sombrely into her eyes.

"I cannot tell you, my dear Mrs Bennett, what a gift and inspiration you are going to be to us in our work. When Bertram wrote me of his excellent notion I felt it was the answer to all our needs. I myself have intended to seek a companion for my work, but time simply has not allowed . . . not allowed . . ."

"Thank you," said Sarah simply. Mr Bennett was still holding tightly to her arm. She had the feeling that at any moment he was going to turn her slowly round and ask her to remove her hat so that Mr Scavener could study her better.

Mr Scavener turned to his friend. "Did you bring copies of the records from the museum . . . the ones of the Baluchi tribes?"

Mr Bennett dropped Sarah's arm. "All here . . . also some interesting papers I find were previously overlooked . . . details of the Arghun invasion and the driving of the tribes further east . . . I think you will find some new data that may be relevant to Tynan's paper . . ."

They wandered ahead, Mr Scavener's steel-thin body bent sharply over the frail one of Mr Bennett. They looked incongruous and bizarre together but Sarah forgot, almost at once, to notice them. Overhead, kites were falling and lifting, big black birds against the brilliant white sky. The smell was there again but she didn't notice it much. It was similar to Port Said and Aden and she was too busy staring at the porters and coolies and beggars to think about it. Again the rising excitement that she had experienced at every port of call along the voyage bubbled up inside her, excitement compounded of strange tongues and strange faces. Mr Scavener led them to a horse-drawn victoria, turned and addressed the porters in fluent Urdu (all she could recognise was that it *was* Urdu) and then helped Sarah up into the carriage.

"Tonight we shall stay with mission friends on the outskirts of the city. I considered it too much to commence the train journey immediately after landing and thus we shall have a chance to compose ourselves before ascending into the hills."

She smiled, and nodded, gazing straight past him to where a handsome but dirty Baluchi led a trail of donkeys along the road. Behind him walked the draped and concealed figure of a woman in a *burqa*, and behind her a small convoy of cars hooted and screeched with resentment at having to go the pace of the donkeys.

After a while she completely forgot about Mr Scavener and Mr Bennett. Several times the victoria came to a halt while a camel caravan, bells ringing and stomachs grunting, wandered across the road. The camels, and the women—those not covered in the *burqa*—wore intricate ornaments of shells and blue beads. Many of the men were wild and incredibly handsome, some in turbans and baggy trousers, some in loose tunics that reminded her of figures from the Old Testament. The entire city was noisy, confused, hot and dirty.

And then, when they reached the outskirts of the city, she was suddenly overwhelmed with the scent of roses—masses and masses of roses growing in the gardens of the surburban villas. Roses, some that she could see and others concealed behind courtyard walls, that filled the Indian spring with cloying, overpowering perfume. She leaned forward, colour flooding up from beneath the shantung collar of her dress, unable to still her enthusiasm any longer, and she placed her hand on Mr Bennett's knee.

"The roses, Bertram! Smell the roses! Who would have thought India could smell of roses!"

The two men blinked myopically at her. Mr Scavener bared his teeth in polite acknowledgment of her comment. Mr Bennett blinked again, then smiled suddenly. "You look very happy, Sarah." He pressed his hand over hers as it rested on his knee and hastily she snatched it away from him.

"One is not blessed with the savoury scents too often in this land," said Mr Scavener. "But certainly the roses are agreeable—very agreeable."

"I didn't think there would be roses in India."

Mr Scavener stared uncomprehendingly. "But yes. In the spring, especially up in the hills, in Quetta, there are roses and flowers in the gardens."

"Are there roses at the mission?"

"Eh . . . no . . . I think not."

"How big is the mission?" She had asked Mr Bennett the same question but, extraordinary though it seemed, it appeared he had never bothered to find out from Scavener. She had thought that, on arrival, it would be one of the first questions Bertram would ask, but instead he had passed the ride talking of Puzh Rinds and Mir Chakur and the Arghun invasion.

Mr Scavener's eyes avoided hers. "The mission is only small as yet. This is a difficult country in which to spread the Lord's word. The people are stubborn and concerned with the old ways."

"I'm afraid," she murmured nervously, over the sound of the trotting horse and the carriage wheels, "that I am not going to be able to help very much, not at first. The language you see. I had so little time to prepare and although I have been trying to learn Urdu on the ship, my knowledge is still very sparse."

"It is of no account," replied Mr Scavener. "The children can understand English. And of course your assistance to us, to your husband and myself in our work, will be invaluable."

She was puzzled. From the missionaries she had spoken to on the boat she had gleaned a positive idea of what life would be on a mission station—a babble of strange tongues and a philosophy entirely alien to the one she had been reared in. Many people, mostly very poor and practically all illiterate, taking every advan-

tage that the mission offered but giving nothing, and
especially not their loyalty, in return. Mr Scavener was
giving little or no indication of the work and the teaching of his mission. He spoke of her help, but told her
nothing.

"How many pupils do you have at the mission?"

"Ah! We have arrived! There is the good Mrs Hadley to welcome us and, no doubt, to offer some welcome refreshment."

The victoria had stopped before a faded brick bungalow with a corrugated roof. A verandah flanked the
doors and windows, and waiting at the top of the
steps was a stout woman in a grey wrapover dress and
buttoned canvas shoes. She wore thick pebble glasses
and when Sarah came close to her she saw that Mrs
Hadley had a dark moustache on her upper lip.

"Welcome! Welcome!"

There were introductions and confusion, and boys
lifting luggage from the victoria, and a glass of luke-
warm lemonade on the verandah before Mrs Hadley
took Sarah into the bungalow and showed her to a
room with a double bed against the wall.

"I hope you won't mind, my dear, if you share my
room with me. I am a little short of accommodation—
I have other friends staying, waiting for the ship to
sail—and if your husband and Mr Scavener have no
objection to sharing the other room it will simplify
matters considerably."

"That will be lovely!"

Mrs Hadley stared curiously at Sarah. "Have you
been married long, my dear?"

"We were married in January and sailed immediately
for Karachi. Mr Be . . . my husband had already made
his plans for coming here so the wedding had to be
fitted in with the existing sailing dates."

"I see." She obviously didn't see, and was unpleasantly curious. "You are rather younger than Mr Scavener expected I think. He and Mr Bennett have been
friends for so many years . . . I believe Amos was expecting someone of their age. And . . . of course . . .
your husband is not . . . not a strong man . . ."

"I think I would like to wash," said Sarah woodenly,

and Mrs Hadley, forced by convention and good manners, turned reluctantly away and called for the boy to
bring water.

What a hateful woman, thought Sarah as she sponged
the dried sweat from her body with cold water. What a
horrible, inquisitive woman! The recollection that she
would have to share a bed with Mrs Hadley made her
shudder and, in spite of the heat, her skin came up in
small, chilly bumps. And then she reflected that, had
she not been sleeping with Mrs Hadley, she would have
been sharing a bed with Mr Bennett, and her relief was
so great she forgot all about Mrs Hadley's moustache
and her unhealthy curiosity.

The mission consisted of a large one-storeyed building built around a compound. Faded stucco peeled
away from the brickwork and the slatted roof was
broken in several places. The compound, when Sarah
saw it for the first time, was turned into a mess of thin
red mud by a late spring rain squall. The entire building was sprawling and shabby—but Sarah loved it because it somehow captured the mood and essence of
north-west India just as she had imagined. Familiarity
with the mission never removed this first impression of
mystery, of brightness and darkness curiously combined, of something which, to incurably romantic Sarah,
was akin to the Arabian nights.

The area round the compound was bordered by very
high, curved stone arches. In the summer, columns of
brilliant sunlight marked the verandah with bars of
light and when one stepped out of the shade the heat
was like a blow on the body. Small lizards and occasionally a scorpion basked on the dust of the compound
and Sarah would call a boy to crush the scorpions and
remove the vicious-looking bodies. At night—the huge,
beautiful, sad nights of India—the moon shone down
through the arches enhancing their mystery all the more.

One side of the compound was devoted entirely to
the servants' quarters—and there seemed to be many
more people living in the servants' quarters than were
ever seen working about the mission. At the front of

the building there were no closed quarters at all—the shadowy, tall arches led straight through into the compound, forming a baked, scented cloister and this, explained Mr Scavener, was the area used as the schoolroom and place of worship. The remaining two sides of the quarters provided the living area for Mr Scavener, Sarah, and Mr Bennett. Mr Scavener, without consultation with either of them, had provided a separate room for Sarah.

It took two and a half days to get up from Karachi and when Sarah arrived at the mission she was too exhausted to do more than glance at the building very briefly before she lay down in a bedroom surprisingly cool and shuttered against the glare of the sun. She, who had always been so strong and well, fell victim to the first of the feverish bouts that the Baluchistan summers were continuously to bring her. The railway journey across the Sind desert and plains had been unbearable—full of thick, choking dust and with the white glare of the sun-scorched sand hurting her eyes, even when she closed them. When at last the train moved up into the hills it became cooler but her head still ached and she found the wild, rugged landscape depressing.

Mr Bennett and Mr Scavener had not stopped talking since they left Karachi and their dry, clipped tones began to irritate her so much she wanted to scream. Fragments of sentences, phrases and odd words, filtered through the glare and the heat that surrounded her ... "structure of tribal society ... Mrattas largely descended from the Humayan captives ... the seven clans descended from Rind compatriots ..."

When they eventually descended from the train and climbed—amidst noise and a confusing babble of tongues and animal cries—into an old and badly sprung Austin, the change in temperature made Sarah shiver. It was not really cold, just cooler than the train journey had been, but the perspiration drying on her body made her feel damp and chilled. For a while the road was fairly good, then it degenerated into a track of potholes and rocks, sweeping around bleak, dun-coloured hills with occasional patches of green marsh showing wherever a little water rested beneath the surface of the rock. The ancient Austin bucked and jolted all over the road. She folded her arms tightly across her stomach and pressed her lips together, fighting the nausea and lurching sickness that every fresh bump brought. When, later along the road, the driver stopped the car in order to let the engine cool, she could contain herself no longer and she crouched behind a rock and was painfully sick.

She was climbing back into the car when the chilly remembrance of May being sick before Anna was born smote her. Please God, no, she thought desperately, not from that one time. Please, God, don't let me be pregnant from that one dreadful time!

By the time they reached the mission she was past caring whether she was pregnant or not. All she wanted to do was lie down in the darkness with a damp cloth across her aching eyes. Mr Scavener's allocation of separate bedrooms for her husband and herself was the first action—in her eyes—that won him any favour at all. She went straight to bed and stayed there—feverish, sick, and shivering for three days.

On the fourth day she woke early feeling rested and calm. There were noises outside, but they were the noises of the country, the noise that is really a silence with insects and birds and animals echoing in quiet air. Across the compound she could hear pots being clattered and two men quarrelling in a tongue she could not recognise. Clean sunlight slatted through the blinds and made patterns on the numdah rugs scattered over the floor. She sat up slowly, put her feet experimentally to the floor and was relieved to find that the nausea had left her. She crossed to the window and looked out between the slats of the blinds.

An eerie, bleak, wild landscape—sun-scorched, wind-scorched, desolate and bizarre—like a different planet or the other side of the moon. In the distance, sharp impossible mountains blurring into the blue mist of early morning. In the middle distance, gullies, dried water-courses and miles and miles of sweeping scrub and rock. It was . . . beautiful . . .

She dressed as quickly as she could, already forgetting that she had been ill, and hurried out into the compound, then out through the arches to stand on the road in front of the mission, staring out at Baluchistan.

It was empty. The country was empty, and huge. At first glance everything appeared to be brown and ochre, but when one stared hard, slowly and with concentration, the colours changed. There was red, and white, and yellow, and here and there a splash of sage green where a thorn tree fought to take moisture from the rock. To the left of the Mission was the Dak Bungalow, then the road curved down into the brown mud huts of the village with an occasional galvanised-iron roof showing—a sign of wealth. The village appeared to be prosperous by Brahui standards, two wells and some *karezes* indicated a good supply of water, patches of corn were growing and there were several small groves of vines and apricot trees. It seemed to be a little oasis of wealthy vegetation in the middle of a barren, brown landscape. A goat wandered by the side of the track stopping to nibble at the odd tufts of dried, dead grass. And a thin, high-pitched wind sang softly around the hills and mission.

The more she stood and stared at the landscape, the more she had to fight an overwhelming desire to walk forward, step off the road and lose herself in the vast nothingness of the mountains. The wind and the emptiness lured her forward, beckoning her into a strange world of hills and white sky.

"Memsahib?"

She turned. A fat, cheerful-faced woman in a voluminous dark skirt and winding top robe stood grinning at her. Sarah vaguely recognised the face from brief visits to her bedroom over the past three days.

"You are better, Memsahib?"

"Yes, I am."

"I am Lili, Memsahib. You go to your room and Lili will bring you tea."

She grinned again and Sarah smiled back, suddenly feeling weak and shaky. When Lili brought the tea to

her room she sipped appreciatively and for no reason
at all began to feel very happy. Lili was obviously in
no hurry to depart.

"Sahib Scavener is very pleased you come. Now he
has someone to work with, and someone to look after
his papers."

"I can only speak a little Urdu. And I do not understand Brahui, or Pushto, or any of the languages
needed for the mission."

"We speak English, Memsahib. Everyone on mission
speak English." She nodded and beamed at Sarah, and
Sarah found she liked the fat, dark woman in the same
way that she liked Ma Dance. Her hands were dirty
and so—probably—was the rest of her, and there was
an unpleasant odour of animal fat that wafted out from
the voluminous robes whenever she moved.

"You want breakfast here, Memsahib? Or with
Sahib Scavener and Sahib Bennett?"

"I'll eat with them."

Lili smiled, picked up the tray and shuffled cheerfully from the room. Outside the door Sarah caught a
glimpse of a small, fat-faced boy leaning against the
wall. When Lili came out of Sarah's room he trotted
along the passage after her.

When she went into the breakfast room it was as
though the last three days had never happened. Mr
Scavener and Bertram were still engaged in scholarly
conversation, still bandying records and theses back
and forth between them. They stood when she came in.

"You're better, my dear! I'm so pleased, so pleased."
Mr Bennett came round the table and kissed her but it
was all right. The kiss was a dry, brushing of the
cheek and intended as no more than a public acknowl-
edgement that she was his wife.

"You must take a little more care in hot countries,
my dear Mrs Bennett. Take plenty of quinine, and rest
when it is too hot. It is really a case of acclimatisation."

"I feel quite well again, thank you." She did feel well,
and she still had the sensation of well-being and contentment that had struck her earlier on. She was fired
with enthusiasm and love for her new country and her
new work. "I feel quite well enough to begin my duties.

I know, of course, I shall not be of great help until I am better able to understand the language. But the sooner I start, the sooner I shall learn to talk to them."

Mr Scavener waved a knife in the air. "They can speak English," he replied without interest. "You can attend morning prayers with us, then—if you are quite sure of your recovery—you can come along to my— our—study and we can introduce you to the collation of the papers and the research we shall be doing."

"But . . . the school . . . the mission teaching," said Sarah puzzled. "When am I supposed to contribute to the school?"

For the first time since she had met him, Mr Scavener looked uncomfortable.

"The school is still in its early stages," he mumbled. "Twice a week I give a little biblical teaching. And of course there are the Sunday services. But the school is still hardly established, Mrs Bennett, hardly established."

"Then what am I supposed to do?" she asked, feeling confused and somehow disappointed.

Their faces grew animated.

"Our research papers on the tribes, Mrs Bennett! Many years of work and study and deciphering of the old scripts! Your husband tells me you are extremely proficient and capable—and have a clear concise mind. The acadamic part of the work no one can develop other than Bertram and myself—but the tidying and collation—ah . . ."

"And it would help," added Mr Bennett quickly, "if you could in time take over the two classes a week. And prepare for the doctor's surgery—he comes down from Quetta once a month and needs someone to organise on those two days."

"And the servants," said Mr Scavener, warming to his task. "I find the domestic side of the mission very tedious, very tedious indeed. It needs a woman's hand to run the kitchen and the boys and see that everything is in order. And they all speak English. They are mission trained. There will be no bother or interference."

"I see," said Sarah bleakly.

"But most important," added Mr Bennett excitedly, "is to keep the things in the study right—the thesis is most important."

Mr Scavener rose from his chair. "In fact, Mrs Bennett, if you feel well enough and have finished your breakfast, I will take you to the study and show you everything we have done." They both hurried towards the door, smiling, nodding and alive with enthusiasm.

Deflated, she followed them from the room. She was struck again, as she had been in Karachi, by the incongruity of the two of them together—Mr Scavener, tall, thin, sharp, with a forbidding face and skull-shaped head, and Bertram limping beside his friend, trying hard to keep up, and reach up.

The study was in the most appalling condition she had ever seen. A desk and three tables were piled with books, papers, old manuscripts, engravings and charts that formed a pyramid on each surface. The chaos was not confined to desk or tables. An avalanche of paper slid off the sides of the tables onto the floor to join the mounds of assorted books and folders already there. Dust, in various stages of thickness according to what Mr Scavener had worked on most recently, lay over everything. Several spiders and small insects scuttled over the litter and, in the far corner of the room, something crackled under a pile of paper and made the hair on the back of her neck rise.

"I can't bear snakes," she said quickly. "I can't touch any of this if there are snakes about."

They laughed jovially, and reassured her. A bookcase stood with the door open and books tumbling out on to the floor. She bent, picked one up, and a small stream of ants walked from the book, over her hand, and up her arm.

"You want me to sort all this out?" she asked quietly, waving an arm at the room in general.

"As you can see, my dear, dear Mrs Bennett, we are not very methodical." They laughed together again, two against one, two scholars against one ignorant little village schoolmistress who was nonetheless a good worker when it came to dreary, dull, unimportant tasks.

"It would be foolish to ask the house boys to tidy it up," replied Mr Scavener with continued amusement. "Foolish—and dangerous. They do not appreciate the value of the work. But you, in time, will understand what we are doing and what papers and books we need and where they must be put."

"You will like that, won't you, Sarah? You are so interested in other things—other peoples and different lands?"

"Yes."

"But of course, Bertram. We must not chain her to the tribes all the time. There will be other tasks, her wifely duties. I know you ladies like to spend time getting your households in order!" Mr Scavener beamed again, then added thoughtfully. "And if you could begin on the kitchens, my dear, it would be appreciated. The meals are not too desirable here . . . in fact not appetising at all. When the doctor was down from Quetta last month I felt quite ashamed of the table put before him."

Bertram patted her arm and stared fondly at her. He obviously had faith in her wonderful abilities—the abilities for which he had chosen her. "It's what you always wanted, isn't it, dear? To live and work in a foreign country, to learn and study and acquire new knowledge?"

A small, down-to-earth core of working-class resentment needled bitterly at the back of her mind. Mr Bennett had purchased a bargain. In return for her passage and her keep he and Mr Scavener had bought themselves a secretary, a housekeeper, a cook, a doctor's assistant, and when time allowed a mission teacher. They had really done very well for themselves and she had no one but herself to blame.

And there was the other thing too, the extra thing when Mr Bennett so desired, the thing that had happened only once before they left England, and which the divisions in the cabins of the ship had prevented since. Mr Scavener and Bertram were going to share all the privileges her coming would bring, but because Bertram was her husband he was entitled to something extra.

"And now," said Mr Scavener pulling a turnip watch from his pocket, "it is time for worship."

He led the way to the cloistered arches at the front and prepared to pray.

The mission—only at its beginning it had not been a mission—had been founded by Mr Scavener's father, a minor and rather unsuccessful official in the Indian Civil Service. Mr Scavener Senior, had been a romantic, a chaser of dreams, and such qualities in a land as barbaric and wild as Baluchistan are not tantamount to successful administration. Had he lived in Elizabethan times, he would have acquitted himself well under Raleigh or Drake, or in Stuart days he would have perished happily at the end of a Roundhead spear. As it was, he was born a Victorian and saw India as the new dream, the fulfilment of man's romantic and idealistic endeavour. His first years in India were spent very largely in listening and attempting to clarify the interminable and weary land disputes between various families and tribes. He had then been appointed A.D.C. to a pedantic and bullying senior administrator whose passion was the filing and documentation of all the papers relating to the district. Mr Scavener Senior, found his forays into the pagan land of India strictly limited. His time was wholly consumed in the District Office, controlling a team of Hindu and Christian clerks. And all the while his passionate soul burned to espouse a Cause.

Transferred to Baluchistan, he found one. His own part of the civil administration was to be just as tedious as it had been before, but at last he was allowed to glimpse what seemed to him a romantic and visionary life, that of the missionaries.

He heard, almost at once upon his arrival in Baluchistan, of the story of the founding of the mission at Quetta—of the two men, one who had journeyed by bullock-cart up through the Bolan Pass, the other who had travelled on foot. Two men braving the dangers of warring tribes, of exposure, of typhoid and dysentery. That one of the men had died shortly after the mission

at Quetta was founded only served to stress man's ultimate sacrifice—the offering of one's life for an inspired ideal. Time and again he listened to the news of
what the missionaries were doing, of the doctors' forays
out into primitive country, healing the sick amidst
danger and glory. This was work he could understand,
a purpose he could immerse himself in.

For him, it was too late to change. He was over forty
and although his dream still existed, the youthful energy
needed to change his mode of life, to take the necessary steps for acceptance by the Missionary Society, to
voluntarily forfeit the comfortable living he had acquired, the energy to do these things had gone. He
compromised by marrying the daughter of a missionary
and by supporting their cause whenever he could, hoping that perhaps one day a chance would be given him
to join their work of self-sacrifice without any effort on
his part.

The chance had come, but in the strangest and most
unpredictable way. Presiding over yet another long and
inevitable land dispute between a Brahui tribesman and
the people of a Sindi baniyah village, Scavener had
refused a bribe from the Sindi headman. The bribe
would really have made little difference had he accepted or not. The dispute had been in existence for at
least three generations and over the years eleven men
and two women had been either deliberately or accidentally killed when the feud grew to heated propor-
tions. Bribes, murders, the stealing of each other's cat-
tle and crops had, and would, continue for several years
to come. It was an integral part of tribal life.

The Brahui, however, hearing of Mr Scavener's re-
fusal to accept his opponent's bribe, had taken this to
be a sign of Scavener's support, and for some considerable time basked virtuously in the mistaken belief that
the government was on his side. He did not send Mr
Scavener a gift. His tribal pride forbore to do such a
thing. He left ingratiating actions of that nature to his
opponent whose rights to the land were based on false
premise. But when he died he gave instructions that the
honest and clear-minded Sahib Scavener should be given

the old stone temple that stood high on the side of one of the bleak hills, and that the people of his village should treat the Sahib as a tribal brother.

In fact the temple was not his to give as, in turn, it also was the subject of a tribal dispute, but as the rightful owner had thoughtfully died, and his sons had been murdered by the Brahui's sons, there was no one to prevent Mr Scavener from taking possession of his property.

Most of the Brahuis were nomadic; wild, shy, hereditary shepherds who tended to shun outside influences. But the Brahuis of Mr Scavener's bequest were comparatively wealthy and had been settled for some time on the land around the temple. They had no particular use for the stone building and they were well aware that the presence of an Indian Civil Servant near their village lent lustre to the community, and possibly authenticity to future claims. They waited to see what the coming of Sahib Scavener would bring.

With his wife, and their small band of servants—some of whom were Christians and others who were not but who were used to the Scaveners and their ways—he took up his abode in the stone temple upon his retirement from the I.C.S.

It was a very old temple and was falling into ruins in one or two places. No one, least of all the local tribesmen, could really remember what sort of temple it was or who had built it. It had just always been there, part of the hills, of the sun and wind and rock, immeasurably old and as mystical and harsh as the land on which it stood.

He did not consider becoming a missionary himself. He was too old and, bitterly, he had come to realise that he did not have the spiritual strength necessary for mission work in primitive countries. But at last his life had a purpose. He would make the mission ready for his son.

He repaired the building, he built extra chambers round the compound, he had new flat stones laid edge to edge beneath the cloistered arches, covering the chipped rock and broken earth that was already there.

He did his best to build up the goodwill of the passing tribes, and because he knew the country and the people, and epecially because he did not try to convert them (feeling himself unworthy) they came gradually to accept and use him. ,

In the spring when the tribes moved up from the plains to the grazing ground of the hills, they would use his temple as a stopping place, would water their camels at his *karez,* and would sometimes leave someone who was sick or drying in his care because they knew he could be trusted. Only once had the mission been in danger, when a group of Pathan horsemen had swept down from the hills intent on raiding and brigandry. Mr Scavener, whose spiritual dignity had become greater with the passing of the years and with the realisation of his own limitations, had met them at the front of the mission and had spoken to them in Pushto, in the firm and unmistakable tones of an Indian Civil Servant. His words left no doubt that he knew the law regarding their tribes, and the penalties they would be subject to if they broke that law. Twelve ferocious, hawk-faced Pathans towered over him, but behind the frail, short-sighted old man stood the power and vengeance of the British Empire—and the Empire did not forget when one of her sons had been murdered. The Pathans had contented themselves with driving off the mission sheep and goats, and frightening the servants. Then they had thundered off down the hillside leaving Mr Scavener, for the first time in his life, feeling he had taken part in a romantic adventure.

To the local tribesmen the Scaveners, first the father, then the son, became a useful village possession, there to be used when necessary, when advice or British partisanship was needed. The mission also purchased much of its food from the village, and provided work for those who so desired. They looked upon it as a benevolent institution solely for their private use.

Old Mr Scavener lived frugally, spending little on himself. His wife had died soon after their coming to the mission and now he saw little or no need to spend money on anything but the barest essentials of life. He

17

was saving every penny he could for the founding of
the mission when his son returned from Cambridge and
had entered the Missionary Service.

Alas for his dreams. While he was preparing for the
fulfilment of his lifelong vision, his son, in the company
of young Bertram Bennett, was becoming increasingly
absorbed, not in the prospects of mission work, but in
the study and research of ancient peoples. He did not
know how to tell his father, but he had no intention of
applying to the Mission Society for entry.

The old man had died before his dream could be
broken. His estate, which was considerable, was left
"for my son, Amos, to run the mission that I have
tried to prepare for him. Should he not be blessed by
entry into the Mission Society, I am content to know
that the funds I have provided will enable him to lay
the foundations for the future."

Amos was trapped, not merely by financial pressure,
but by the wishes of a dying man and the dictates of
his religious upbringing. He did not want to be a missionary, but since childhood he had been taught that
the spreading of the Lord's word was the only and most
worthwhile vocation for a man who was a Christian.

He came back to the temple, bringing his books and
research with him and taking over where his father had
left off—giving hospitality to the nomadic tribes in the
spring and autumn, taking household prayers every day,
keeping the mission in good order. The rest of the time
he spent in study, and gradually found that he was in
the centre of an area rich in research prospects. When
his friend, Bertram Bennett, was teaching in Ceylon,
Amos Scavener took a brief sabbatical and travelled
south to join his colleague for comparative study. He
wrote several papers which became standard works.
He conducted a lengthy and detailed correspondence
with the British Museum and various foundations all
over the world. He was invited on lecture tours (which
he occasionally accepted) and was given an honorary
doctorate for his work. Sometimes, but not often, his
conscience troubled him. He was not doing the work
his father had intended him to do, and—far worse—he

was not spending the money his father had left for the purpose of converting the heathen. Also, the small amount of mission work that was done—the daily services and the spasmodic needs of the nomadic Brahui tribes—he found irritating and onerous. He resented the time spent each month when the mission doctor came down from Quetta, and he found teaching tedious. The coming of Sarah was a godsend, for now his conscience would be eased. He had provided (albeit it was really dear Bertram who was providing) a Someone to project his father's work. Now he need not bother any more. And when Bertram wrote to him telling of Sarah's youth, of her energy and sense of responsibility, of her quick mind and love of books and study, and above all of her capacity for hard work, it seemed just what they were looking for. Someone to do the tedious, routine drudgery, help them with their research (at an elementary level of course) and possibly work up the mission side if she showed any talents in that direction. He envisaged a wonderful life from now on. His very dear friend, Bertram, his soulmate in academic exercise, working by his side, and Bertram's young, tactful, obedient wife to make their studies and their lives easier. He had no idea of the shock experienced by Sarah during her first few weeks at the mission.

Daily worship consisted of prayers, a hymn and short lesson in the presence of the household staff. She was reminded of her very first job—a parlourmaid at the Fawcetts'—when all the servants had been forced to file dutifully into the breakfast-room each morning to listen to the master pray. Here, the procedure was much the same, but the servants were noisier, dirtier, and far more numerous. Fat Lili, a devout convert Christian, joined robustly in the singing of the hymns (her favourite was "Onward Christian Soldiers") surrounded by her several offspring and some who were not her offspring. Some of the servants crouched on the stone floor, others leaned against the pillars and appeared to take no part in the proceedings. Children cried, and were comforted or slapped. Sometimes she counted as many as forty men, women and children, although there were only seven servants actually working at the mission. The rest were relatives, kinsmen, passersby—all living on the bounty of the Scavener Mission and counting their daily attendance at worship as fair payment for their keep. After prayers they all dispersed to the servants' quarters and the bulk of them were not seen again until the following morning.

The two weekly classes were of the same nature. Those children of the household who were of suitable age gathered in the courtyard and Mr Scavener (for the first two weeks, after which he delegated this duty to Sarah) read stories from the Bible and gave them rudimentary instructions in the reading and writing of English—which was the only tongue common to the group of converted Hindus, Punjabis, and hybrid tribesmen who made up the staff of the mission. Mr Scavener taught irritably and badly.

Sometimes a tribesman would come from the village or from the nearby hills and ask Sahib Scavener to prepare a letter for him to take to the authorities—or possibly he would want to know where to go and who to consult on some official tribal matter. Mr Scavener conducted this unofficial information centre with the same impatience that he showed when teaching, or conducting morning prayers. Mr Scavener's whole life was the research of the tribes and any time he had to spend away from that he bitterly resented.

On her third week at the mission she awoke one morning with a sense of something not right—something unusual in the pattern of normal waking and stirring at the mission. She lay for a few seconds, and then realised the noises were not right. The kitchen noises and the voices from the servants' quarters were the same, but the outside sounds, the high cries of birds and the wind, were blotted out by a bigger sound; the tinkling of camel bells, of donkeys braying, bleating lambs, of hooves on rough ground, children, men, the clatter of cooking utensils, of water being drawn from the *karez*.

When she peered through the window she saw, on

the side of the road and stretching down the hillside, a great sprawling mass of people, animals, fires, tents, and in the distance, on the hills rapidly turning from dark night-green to brown as the morning light came up, she could see small moving patches as more caravans came in.

The women, dark, beautiful, dirty, strode towards the mission, skin water buckets held on their shoulders, and with innumerable wild children clinging to their skirts. As they drew near she could see the gleam of bracelets on brown arms, and necklaces and headbands embroidered with beads and cowrie shells. It was still very early.

"Bertram!" She pulled on her wrapper and hurried out of her room. "Bertram!" She knocked, a brief, cursory tap, and hurried in. It was only the second time she had visited his room, apart from seeing to the cleaning, since they had been there. Bertram was curled into a tiny, frail bundle on one side of the bed. She pulled the mosquito net to one side and shook him.

"Bertram! Wake up! There are hundreds of tribesmen outside—and more coming—the whole hillside is covered with them!"

He was instantly awake. "Sarah?" he said quickly, and smiled. She was excited and a little nervous about the tribesmen gathering outside, but this trepidation was instantly replaced by a bigger and more immediate fear. Her husband sat up slowly on his bed and then reached out for her hand. "What is it, Sarah? Is there something wrong?"

"Tribesmen, Bertram! Outside the mission and spreading all over the hillside. I can't think where they've come from."

His eyes took in the smooth, lightly-tanned skin of her neck and throat, the loosely tied wrapper, and the great cloud of dark hair that swirled about her shoulders.

"How lovely you are with your hair down," he said softly.

"Come to the window, Bertram! Please! We are surrounded by people—camels, animals, everything. They are all pouring into the mission! Come and see."

"I expect they have come to wait for the doctor," he said slowly, beginning to stroke her hand.

"But he won't be here for two days!"

"They have to come a long way. Some have to travel two or three weeks, even more. They are prepared to wait two days if it is to see the Doctor Sahib."

She was always surprised at how strong he was. He was small and crippled but his grip was incredibly strong. She could not pull away without it becoming obvious that she did not wish him to hold her hand, without it turning into a trial of strength.

"Surely all those people cannot want to see him?" she asked, silently praying that his interest in the tribes would divert his attention from her, cursing the foolish impulse that had made her run into his room.

"No." He was staring again, reaching up with his other hand to wind it in her hair and pull her closer. "But when one of them is ill, the entire family will come. They never travel without each other."

He pulled hard on her hair, dragging her down to sit beside him.

"Sarah!"

The chord of sanity between them snapped. The pattern of gentle good manners they had built as a basis for living together, disintegrated. They were alone in a bedroom and he was forcing her down on the bed beside him.

*Perhaps this time it will be all right. Perhaps the last time, which was also the first time, was wrong because it was the first time and it will be different now. Perhaps I will be able to bear it without feeling sick.*

And then she felt his small, dry hands leave her hair and clutch suddenly at the neck of her wrapper. She saw his blue eyes—which were sometimes kind but mostly abstracted and absorbed—turn to the maniacal stare she remembered from before. Then she had seen them in candlelight and had wondered if the madness, the uncontrollable brilliance had been exaggerated by the light. Now, in daylight, she knew it was not so.

"Sarah!" he screamed. *Oh God, Oh God. No. Not*

*like that again!* The nightmare began to reform—
clutching hands, a contorted face, a growing sense of
terror in her own body that seemed to excite him all the
more.

She heard knocking, loud knocking. She heard Lili—
oh blessed, wonderful voice! She heard Lili pounding at
the door and calling ... calling ...

"Memsahib! Memsahib! You are there?"

The door opened, Lili came waddling in—fat, an-
gelic, normal—Lili—mother of twelve, all fathered in
normal, marital lust.

"Memsahib. The people have begun to come for the
doctor. Sahib Scavener, he ask that you rise as soon as
you can and begin to help for the coming of the Doctor Sahib."

"I am coming, Lili! I am coming now!" She dared,
finally, to look at the face of her husband. His eyes
were normal again, kindly, puzzled, a little afraid.

"There are so many people out there, Bertram. I
think perhaps it would be kind to Amos if we both
rose now and helped him."

"Yes ... yes ... of course, my dear. You are right.
We must help wherever we can." He held out his check
towards her, suppliant for a marital kiss, a signal of
affection that he was a normal husband, and she
touched his face briefly with her lips.

"I will see you shortly then, Bertram my dear," she
said reassuringly, and she rose and left quickly, knowing that now it would be all right again until something
touched the spring in him once more. For he did not
come to her of his own accord. Some incident, some
untoward beckoning attitude of hers, had to release his
madness.

And as the last time, he was especially tender to her
at breakfast, conciliatory to her wants, praising her
abilities to Mr Scavener, lauding his own good fortune
in winning her as his bride. Mr Scavener was not very
interested.

"We set aside a room for the doctor to see the
patients. You will see it is ready?"

"I'll do my best."

"He likes it made clean and scrubbed, and the

records of some of the patients must be taken from the
drawers. Lili will show you which ones. She knows the
doctor's ways."

"I will see her after breakfast."

"Now that they know a Memsahib is here, some of
the women will try to get ahead of their turn. It matters little to them that you can do nothing. However,
if with the help of Lili you can start collecting information about their complaints, it will assist him when he
arrives."

"Of course."

Mr Scavener put down his cup with ill-concealed
relief. "I shall be in the study. You can find me there if
you get into difficulty." He rose, and left the room.
Bertram rose too, kissed her again, and followed him.

Outside, the hills had turned to the khaki brown of
daylight. A slight haze hovered over them but as the sun
grew higher it began to disperse. As soon as she stepped
into the compound a fierce gaggle of Powindah women
surrounded her, pawing at her face and arms and
screeching each other down in their unintelligible
tongue. Lili slapped savagely at them and shouted and
the women quietened and giggled. Sarah hurried over
to the doctor's surgery and shut the door.

She enjoyed the next two days. It was confusing, and
occasionally frightening because the women were strong
and rough and overpowering. She understood little of
the language although once or twice a patient came
forward who was able to understand some of her simple Urdu. Under Lili's firm guidance she began to
learn what was expected of her, what questions,
through Lili, she must ask and write down. And what
women it would be advisable to keep apart. On one
occasion when Lili was not available she went to the
servants' quarters and told one of the Punjabi kitchen
women to bring water and tea to the surgery. The
Punjabi was intercepted just in time by Lili who
scolded Sarah as politely as she could.

"No, Memsahib. Not Punjabi. One woman waiting
out there is from Sind. The Punjabis, and the Sindhis . . . Aacch!"

"But she is a Christian, Lili!" protested Sarah. "Our Punjabi is a Christian."

"To the Sindhi, she is a Punjabi," said Lili impassively.

Lili knew, or was able to tell from a very brief word, who was feuding with who, and who must be kept apart in the mission compound. Lili, too, knew which women the doctor could not help.

"She is no good, that one," she said after Sarah had painstakingly written down a list of symptoms that Lili had translated. "She is ill like my *lumma* was ill. A bad pain, Memsahib. And my *lumma* died. That one cannot be helped."

"But the doctor must decide that, Lili."

"She will not see the doctor. He is a man."

It was true that the women Lili and Sarah saw were few compared with the men who had come for treatment. The doctor was a man and only a very few of the women would submit to his administration. The nurse accompanying him would attend to some of the minor ailments, but serious cases must travel up to Quetta to the women's hospital.

On the third day, towards the middle of the morning, a small dust cloud appeared on the hill road. The cloud materialised as a small, dilapidated car that bucked and jerked down the road towards the mission.

Sarah was faintly astonished to see a young Bengali with prematurely white hair alight from the car.

"Ah!" Mr Scavener leapt forward from the shade of the compound and clasped him by the hand.

"Doctor Sircar, this is Professor Bennett, my very dear friend from student days in Cambridge. And his wife."

The young Bengali bowed politely to Sarah and Bertram. He wore a crumpled linen suit (very much like the one Mr Scavener wore) and his hair was long and untidy.

"I'm afraid I have had to leave the nurse at an emergency case just outside Quetta. A Brahui child badly burned. I shall collect her on the way back but in the meantime we must manage without her."

Mr Scavener waved a vague hand towards Sarah. "Mrs Bennett will assist you as she can. With her, and the incomparable Lili, I hope your duties will not be too onerous."

"Thank you." He bowed politely again. "Now, with your permission, I should like to begin my surgery."

Sarah led him to the surgery, so-called, and then hurried away to fetch Lili. She was anxious to know how Lili, who knew the dangers of mixing Sindhis with Punjabis, would explain the presence of an educated Christian Bengali to the tribes. Lili, when confronted, shrugged her fat shoulders.

"He is the doctor," she said, and obviously saw no need to explain further.

He was quiet and controlled, thanking Sarah courteously for everything she did. She wrote notes where he wanted, did the simple cleansing and medical tasks that he asked of her, and in one or two cases with Lili as interpreter, she acted as liaison for a female patient who would not allow him to examine her but had to be diagnosed and treated from the next room. She saw him angry only once, when a man offered a foul-smelling wound on his leg that was festering under black and glutinous grease.

"Chaa!" he spat. "I come here every month! And still they prefer to go to the village *hakim*. Gangrenous! And he will expect me to perform magic!"

His voice had the accent of an English public school and at dinner that evening vague pleasantries were exchanged over the changing face of Cambridge between the time when Bertram and Mr Scavener were there, and Doctor Sircar's more recent sojourn.

She had hoped that, with the arrival of a working member of the Missionary Society, at least some little semblance of respect to that body would be observed, some slight pretence that Bertram and Amos were endeavouring to work towards the day when the mission would be teaching the tribes. But, after more trivial subjects had been attended to, after a cursory inquiry as to the progress of the work in Quetta, the conversation turned, as it always did, to the study of the Baluchi peoples, to the documentation of knowledge and the translation of tribal folk-lore. For the first time since arriving at the mission, Sarah began to feel angry and frustrated with them both.

They're dead! she thought. They're only interested in dead things because they themselves are dead. They don't use this knowledge, this expensive and painstaking knowledge they have gathered. It has been collected for no purpose. It is interesting . . . would be interesting if they were using it . . . using it to understand the people . . . or to teach someone else about it . . . but they have forgotten the point of learning . . . to pass on and interpret it, to use it for some purpose.

She looked from them to the young Bengali doctor, and their lives showed in their faces. Two dead, old faces, dried up like the parchment they worked on, useless faces, faces that were not being lived in. And the young Bengali whose work was harrowing, disgusting, exhausting . . . but alive. His face, carefully controlled and courteous as all educated Indians, tried to register nothing, but its very blankness, its rigid control suggested a welter of emotion and work and energetic conflict.

They have a chance to learn, she thought, raging with suppressed frustration. They have a chance to talk to him, to find out what he is doing and why! What he hopes to achieve. And they do nothing! They sit and talk about the dead, useless past.

The following morning the frustration welled and burst in her when Doctor Sircar asked politely, "And are you settling well at the mission, Mrs Bennett?"

"There is really no *mission* to settle at," she said bitterly. "I am just looking after two professors engaged in historical research. The only useful work I have done since I came is in the last three days."

Doctor Sircar looked quickly away from her and studied a paper on the desk in front of him.

"What did you expect?" he asked quietly.

"I thought I was coming to a teaching mission," she retorted. "I was trained as a teacher you know. I was prepared to work hard—at languages and local customs—and teach children out here. At it is, I am useless! I am contributing nothing! I should have stayed and continued to teach impoverished English children . . . there are enough of them. What I do here is nothing!"

It boiled out of her at last . . . the knowledge that she had made a mistake. It was not enough just to see the world, to travel to strange and exciting places. She had done this, and it was not enough. One must participate in those strange and exciting places. One must live with them, amongst them, experience with every sensation and emotion the lives those countries could offer. She must do this because otherwise she would begin to think, and that was something she couldn't do just yet. She would think about Charlie marrying May instead of her, and about Peter dying, and about not having Anna any more. And she would think about David Baron, and the hurt would well up again, bitter and corrosive because she couldn't help imagining how different life with David Baron would have been compared with what life was like with Bertram. David Baron was selfish, and violent, and wrong—but he was, like Doctor Sircar, vibrantly alive.

And she was living a dead life with two old men in an exciting, passionate country.

"But surely your husband acquainted you with the situation before you came?"

"He did not. He probably was not fully aware that I felt so strongly about it. He thought it enough that I was coming to India."

Doctor Sircar no longer looked down at his desk. His unfathomable black eyes studied her carefully.

"But you have your husband. Your duties are to him. It will be the same as though you had married but stayed in England. You will just be married, but living here. Looking after your husband and presently your children . . ."

"No!"

He caught the panic, the concealed fear and disgust in her voice, and said no more. He stood up and went to the window, pulling the slats of the blinds apart and staring out at the hills.

"It is such a waste!" she continued. "Such a dreadful waste! They are clever you know? Much more so than I. Mr. Scavener can speak nearly all the dialects, and Bertram is able to learn them incredibly quickly. And I—I am slower to learn the language, but I have more . . . more common sense than they. I understand about people you see . . . especially about poor people . . . poor people do not disgust me. The three of us, together, could be so useful."

"You want to be useful, Mrs Bennett?" he asked quietly. The colour flamed in her face. She wanted to be useful because she did not want to stop and think. If she stopped to think she would have to face her dreadful mistake.

"You obviously do not understand, Mrs Bennett, the position of the mission. Indeed, were it a mission in fact, instead of merely in name, the authorities would probably have to step in and take some kind of controlling action."

"I don't understand."

"You must have gathered, even in a few weeks, what a complicated and troubled land this is? Five, six, major languages. As many—more—differing tribes and peoples. The Pathans coming over the Frontier, and Bugti and Marri in the east, the Brahuis, the Punjabis, the Sindhis, Indian and Afghan, Hindu and Musulmen and Sikh. The country is held in peace only by rigid and clever administration."

"But the mission . . ."

"A mission—a private mission—working on its own without the watching eye and co-operation of the I.C.S. or the Missionary Society, could wreak havoc, could cause civil disturbance and outbreak amongst the tribes. Especially a teaching mission. A private medical mission—perhaps—people always need medicine and doctors and will take many outrages and affronts if they are receiving help. But a teaching mission . . . Have you heard of the Conscience Clause in the Government Code, Mrs Bennett?"

"Well . . . yes."

"In Shikarpur—some years ago—there was a highly competent and successful teaching mission—until one of the pupils expressed a wish to become a Christian. The school had to be closed, Mrs Bennett, and the en-

tire mission staff were forced to leave the city. This was
in a town, fairly sophisticated. Can you think what
would happen if your husband or Mr Scavener began
to convert the children of the local tribesmen? They
would do more than just take their children away. I
think it highly likely you would find yourselves at the
centre of civil disorder."

"Then why are we allowed to remain?" she asked
bitterly. "Why do the authorities let us come here in
the first place?"

He studied her face with impassive, dark eyes.

"You are useful, and you are harmless. The local
tribes trust the mission because of old Mr Scavener. It
is a place to stop and water the camels on the way
to Quetta. Some of the tribesmen from the village have
found work in your kitchens and those who do not
work," he raised one eyebrow humorously, "live very
well off their relatives who do. The mission is a ready-
built centre for me each month—it is easier for me to
come here than tour the surrounding countryside. The
tribes leave you alone because, amongst the local people, you are considered the property of the Brahui village. Also—you must have noticed—troops from the
Quetta garrison are constantly on manoeuvres near and
around the mission. It is a centre and, if necessary, the
authorities could use it as headquarters for whatever
purposes they required. And you are close enough to
Quetta not to be too much of a liability.

"Should any of these factors be changed, should the
mission suddenly become a mission and incur the
wrath of the tribes, you would be looted and destroyed
even before the civil authorities could step in and close
you."

"I see." The sum total of their uselessness was fully
exposed. Doctor Sircar stared at her bleak, ravaged
expression and he smiled politely.

"Perhaps I have been a little rude, Mrs Bennett.
And not altogether fair. Because it must also be admitted that Amos Scavener's reputation as a scholar—
your husband's too—is revered by several important
people in Quetta. As a scholar he is quite unsurpassed."

His toneless voice expressed exactly what he thought

of a man whose reputation as a scholar was unsurpassed.

"You have not been rude. Thank you very much,"
she answered, and her voice was as toneless as his.

"Shall we commence surgery?"

"We might as well," she retorted. "It appears that
assisting you is going to be the full extent of my worth
for the next several years."

Dirty children, fat and happy and dressed in rags
smelling of dumba grease; sores, cataracts, men with
stomach pains, Powindah women waiting inside the
compound, pushing and pawing at Sarah every time
she crossed the courtyard.

"And this is all," she thought. "This is all for the
rest of my life. Dead."

She was aware that he watched her for the remainder
of the day. Polite, inscrutable, he stared at her, measured her. When he came to leave he shook hands and
gave his measured bow.

"Mrs Bennett, I should wait a little. This is a difficult country. Give yourself time to settle down."

"It seems there will be all the time in the world to
settle down."

He paused, then continued, "If you feel you must
work to some purpose out here, I suggest that you talk
to the mission authorities in Quetta. I do not know
what can be done. But at least you can talk to them.
Mr Scavener comes up to Quetta about every two
months. If you join him on his next visit, I will introduce you to the head of the mission. Something may
come of such a meeting."

"Thank you."

"If you are sincere . . . if you mean what you say . . .
perhaps we can use you."

In a gurgle of dust and exhaust fumes the car began
to trundle up the hill road, lurching violently over the
broken surface. The hills were beginning to be touched
very faintly with red and she reflected that it would be
dark before Doctor Sircar got back to Quetta.

She would have given all she had to have been
travelling with him.

# *Fifteen*

WITH the departure of the doctor, routine at the mission settled very quickly into what it had been before. The tribal caravans vanished as mysteriously as they had come. There were morning prayers, the two lessons a week to the children of the household, the daily inspection of kitchen and servants, and the interminable hours spent in the dusty study. A couple of times troops came down the road on military manoeuvres and on several occasions she saw, on the distant hills, bands of horsemen moving across country. Camel trains passed from time to time on their way up to Quetta.

Every day she walked on the road a little, as far as she dared away from the mission (for Lili had warned her it was not wise to stride off into the hills on her own). The land began to take its grip on her, dry and arid, khaki and dun, but huge... huge and inviting with its sun-scorched landscape and soft sibilant wind humming through the passes and valleys. Sometimes, accompanied by Lili, she walked down into the village and would be invited into a hut to drink tea and eat sickly confections of dirty sweetmeats. The village—thanks to the mission—was prosperous and she was able to sense immediately that the tribesmen viewed the mission staff with tolerant affection. She frequently recognised a village face as one often seen in her own kitchens and she also recognised some of the mission blankets and household utensils in shameless, casual display around the huts. Remembering Doctor Sircar's words she did not interfere. Apparently it was all part of the mission's price for inviolability from tribal raids and looting.

It began to grow warmer, and a weary apathy descended on her that was nothing to do with the heat. For the first time in her life she had no purpose. For years she had worked and looked forward towards a goal of some kind, even though the goal was not always a pleasant one. There had been six years of drawnout study training to be a teacher, then being a teacher and hoping for something better (and waging a constant battle of survival against Miss Bennett). And then there had been the Alexanders, and Peter, and May being ill and young Anna needing a home, and always, always being short of money. And through it all, through the work and pain of losing people she loved, had been her own firm, unquenchable faith that fate had some great adventure in store for her ... some huge purpose for which she was being saved ... extravagant, wild, adventurous ... a missionary in Baluchistan!

And now she was here. For the rest of her life, or at least until Bertram died or decided to retire back home, she was trapped with two old men in a dusty study delving into the records of the past.

When Mr Scavener spoke of his next trip to Quetta she expressed her wish to go with him. Mr Scavener was plainly surprised.

"I ... er ... well, of course I had supposed that you would stay with Bertram and work on the next section of the Bugti papers."

"I would particularly like to go to Quetta, Mr Scavener. Doctor Sircar has suggested that it might be profitable if I spoke to some of the missionaries in Quetta."

Amos Scavener blinked. "They are splendid folk of course. Quite splendid! But of little use to us on this present phase of our research."

"I was thinking more in terms of the mission work we are supposed to be doing," she said gently. "I think perhaps it is time I tried to find out what is

needed here and what we may usefully be allowed to
do. At present I cannot feel I am of any great use
here."

"Nonsense!"

"My dear!"

They where vehement in their protests, and their
vehemence was in part an expression of alarm that
their painstaking assistant might be growing tired of
the dreariness of her work.

"We could not possibly manage without you!"

"Why! Since you and Bertram have joined me the
work has progressed at a quite incredible rate!"

"But I would like to go and see the missionaries . . .
the *real* missionaries," she said pointedly, and Mr
Scavener's face suddenly assumed the slightly guilty
expression it always wore when he was reminded of
his father's unfulfilled intentions for the mission.

"There are the prayers," he mumbled. "And the
classes you take."

"It is not mission work," she answered stubbornly.
"We all know that. We are just keeping a great house-
ful of servants who gratify our wishes by coming to
daily prayers and allowing their children to be taught
to read. We don't really do anything useful."

A shocked, strained silence fell over the breakfast
table. She had been so submissive, so quiet and humble
until now. Amos stared accusingly at his friend. How
had Bertram dared to bring such an abrasive element
into their home? But Mr Bennett was not aware of the
look. He had taken Sarah's hand in his and appeared
suddenly to have forgotten that Amos was there.

"I am sorry, Sarah," he said quietly. "I should have
thought about this more deeply. I believed I could
make you happy by bringing you here, but I forgot how
strong you are. You must have something to do—a
purpose. And it was wrong of me to suppose that my
purpose could also be yours."

His eyes were kind. The way they had been kind
when Peter was dying, and when she had met David
Baron in the street. His eyes looked as though for a
while he loved her and she felt guilty because she did
not—could not—love him.

"Perhaps it would be a good idea if Sarah did visit the mission people in Quetta," he said to Mr Scavener. "Perhaps, Amos, we are becoming too engrossed in our studies here. We must not forget that we also have a duty to propagate the Lord's word in a heathen land."

Mr Scavener's guilt broke out afresh on his face. "Yes," he muttered. "Yes, you are right. But we cannot all go to Quetta and I suggest, Bertram, that you and your wife go together on this occasion . . . stay for a week or so . . . and I will go up myself later in the month. You can stay in the house loaned to me by my schoolmaster friend. He has gone home on leave for six months and we can use his house whenever we wish. You will find it very comfortable . . . near the Post Office . . . most convenient."

"Thank you, Amos." Mr Bennett made no polite demur as he usually did when Amos nobly sacrificed himself. Sarah had the ridiculous feeling that she had somehow precipitated a major crisis in the lives of the two scholars, and that they were prepared to plan major reorganisation in order to cope with the emergency.

"I don't want to alter anyone's plans," she said weakly, and was instantly tutted to silence.

"It is decided," Amos announced. "We shall speak no more of it. You and Bertram will go to Quetta, and we shall see what transpires, what events will occur as a result of discussion and prayer." He rose and left the table. It was a magnificent exit and Bertram and Sarah followed—Sarah very humbly.

"I only wanted to talk to the missionaries," she whispered to Bertram. "That's all. Just talk to them!"

But Bertram had vanished into the study and the door had closed.

It was late afternoon when they arrived at Quetta, and the great peaks towering over the city plain were changing colour, slashed with red and orange and yellow. It was cold, much colder than it had been down at the mission, and it was also strange to be in a city again, a city that was very largely western in atmosphere.

It was predominantly a garrison town—the last bastion before the frontier of Afghanistan—and the streets abounded with military uniforms, British regiments, Gurkha, Sikh—officers and men from the newly-formed Indian Wing of the R.A.F. As the antiquated mission car slowed to the pace of the city traffic, she could hear, too, the strident tones of the English memsahibs, travelling in garris, car, and on foot, in and out of the city shops.

Over the city hung the three mountains of Murdar, Chiltran, and Rakatu, and although Quetta itself, with its English rose gardens and well-watered lawns was more sophisticated than Karachi, one could look up at the peaks and sense . . . know . . . that out there the desert and the brown, bleak hills were just as eerie as anywhere else in Baluchistan.

The bungalow loaned to them was pleasant, standing in a garden filled with sweet peas and irises, and with the front door shaded by a vine-covered portico. The bearer, who had been alerted by a message from the mission, greeted them at the door and shouted to the boys to bring in their luggage.

"Shall I bring tea now? Or would the Sahib and Memsahib wish to bathe after their journey?"

She hadn't realised there would be a bathroom. She had grown so used to the mission where Lili had to bring water in every morning and evening, that she had forgotten about things like bathrooms. And indeed it hadn't bothered her too much, not like it did Bertram. She had grown up, and lodged ever since her childhood, in houses where baths were taken in a zinc tub on the kitchen floor with water heated up in a copper. In London she had been more fortunate in that she was able to go to the public baths (towel carefully hidden in a leather bag so that the neighbours should not know where one was going). At the mission she had just gone back to jugs of hot water. But she knew that Bertram found these ablutions distressing.

"You go first, dear," she said. "I shall sit in the garden and have some tea. And I shall write to Doctor Sircar and tell him of our arrival."

She watched him bobbing off, a limp, a little jump, the odd movements he strung together that were not really a walk nor yet a run. Sometimes her pity became an affection so strong it was tantamount to love. She did not understand him, but a sudden glimpse of him walking, or the shy smile he gave her, made her forget the bad moments with him.

"Tea, Memsahib?"

"In the garden, please. And I would like paper, pen, and ink."

The garden was beautiful, peaceful and sweet-smelling, but in the cool air there was an electric stillness that made the flesh on the back of her neck prickle. She realised that no birds were singing although it was time for them to settle for the evening, and a slight sensation of foreboding descended on her. When the bearer brought the paper she took the pen in her hand and thought about what she should write. Doctor Sircar was an enigma to her. She did not know what he really thought of the mission, and she had the feeling his attitude to missionaries in general was not quite what it appeared to be. She put the address on the paper, hesitated, then wrote:

Dear Doctor Sircar,

I have done as you suggested and accompanied my husband to Quetta. We are here for one week. I was sincere in my wish to be useful. I must do something while I am in Baluchistan. I do not know how to be useless and I do it very badly. I would like to accept your offer and meet some of the people at your mission.

Sincerely
Sarah Bennett

She sealed the letter and gave it to the bearer. Before he went away he bowed and said, "The Memsahib's luggage has been taken to the Sahib's room. Shall I get one of the women to unpack it for you?"

"No!"

"Very good, Memsahib." He glided away before she could try and make him understand . . . before she could ask if there was another bedroom she could have on her own . . . before she could say that she would sleep anywhere, on the floor, in the garden, anywhere . . . rather than share a room with him. She ran into the house and flung open the doors between the rooms, a lounge, a dining-room, servants' quarters, bedroom, study—oh why was it a study! It was obviously intended as a second bedroom and the schoolmaster had turned it into a study. She walked back to the bedroom. Bertram's case was already unpacked. Her own rested on a stool by the side of the bed. There were not even two beds.

She was standing, staring sickly at the bed when Bertram came back.

"I feel quite hungry," he said chattily. "I shall be ready for my dinner. I hope Amos's friend has a passable cook in his employ."

He limped to the table and placed his brush and comb upon it.

"I think you had better unpack and prepare for dinner, my dear," he reprimanded. "It is a little later than one might suppose."

He was so ordinary again. So normal and so pedantic. He was like he usually was, kind, fussy, a little old-fashioned in manners and speech. Surely she had imagined the other times, the other two times. Against her own memories, her own panic, she undid her luggage and removed towel and wrapper.

"Most refreshing, the bathroom," he remarked jovially. "I do wish there was some way of having one installed at the mission."

She must have imagined the other times. This normal, fussy, pathetic little man could not be the one she remembered.

"I'll see you later. At dinner," she said quietly, and he nodded casually, as though he were not really listening.

It became colder after dinner, very cold. They sat on the verandah for a while and it was so cold she had to fetch a shawl to wrap round her shoulders. The drop in temperature did not seem to go with the oppressive atmosphere. The air was thick, unbreathable, as though the night were a humid one. She shivered, struck again by the sinister feeling that had impressed her earlier.

"How strange," said Mr Bennett suddenly.

"What?"

He leaned forward and peered through the gloom at the garden. "The birds—they are all flying away. It is nearly night and they should already be settling, but look—they are all flying away without making a sound. How very odd. I wonder why they are not settling in the trees?"

"I think I'll go inside, Bertram." She shivered again.

"Perhaps we should retire early. The day has not been a relaxing one. I think, yes, it would be a good idea to retire early."

The old fear, the thumping in her chest, returned. I'm being ridiculous, she thought, foolish and ridiculous. I am stronger and more able than he. Why am I behaving so foolishly?

"You go along, dear," she said, striving to speak normally. "I will come in a little later."

He rose, pecked at her cheek, stared once more at the birds and muttered, "Curious, very curious," and then he went inside and she drew the shawl tighter round her shoulders, fighting the double fear, of him, and of the oddness of the night.

Everything suddenly became distorted. The trees were bigger, the sky coming down closer over her. A dog barked in the distance, an eerie, melancholy sound. She could see things in the air, odd shimmering shapes that disappeared when she tried to look directly at them, and a pumping noise grew louder, louder, and louder, and then she realised it was her heart making the noise.

She sat tensed and strained in the cane chair, frightened to move, rigid with a growing terror that she did not understand. She wished she had not come to Quetta. There was something terribly wrong. She wished she had not come to Baluchistan.

She did not know if she slept. She did not think so because she was aware all the time of something evil about her, but certainly she lost consciousness of time because, when the fear abated a little, she looked at her watch and saw it was almost midnight. Bertram must be in bed and asleep. She rose stiffly from the chair and walked to the house. When she opened the bedroom door she paused and listened. His breathing was deep and regular and full of the little noises that sleeping people make. In the dark she undressed and pulled her nightdress over her head, then slid over to the bed and lay carefully on the edge of the mattress, as far away from him as she could.

In the morning she would be up and dressed before he awoke, but he would not think there was anything strange about it because she had, as a good wife should, shared his bed with him. And tomorrow, what could she do tomorrow? Plead illness and have a *charpoy* placed in the study. Yes, that would be the answer. She could have a recurrence of the fever that had struck her on her arrival in the country. He would accept that. That would do until the week was over.

Lying stiff, unmoving, daring scarcely to breathe, she drifted into a deep, uneasy sleep.

The nightmare woke her, the screaming horrible nightmare that was far worse than the other time. She couldn't see his face. She was spared that, so she didn't have to look at the insanity in his eyes or the cruel distortion of his face. But he was screaming like the other time—"Sarah! Sarah!"—and then his small, dry, scaly body was on hers, filled with superhuman strength, fingers biting like steel into her flesh, his knee grinding into her stomach, his teeth tearing at her throat and breast.

"No, Betram! No!"

"Be quiet, Amelia! You will do as I say! You hear! Amelia, you will do as I say!"

"It's Sarah, Bertram! It's Sarah. Your wife!"

He struck her violently across the face, then encircled her neck with his clawlike hands and pounded her head back and forth on the pillow.

"Quiet, Amelia!" he screamed. "Quiet, I say!"

She was bigger than he, and should have been stronger, but terror paralysed her, made her limbs un-

controllable and dead. She tried to think of something—anything—she could say that would calm him,
but she knew it was too late. He had gone past the
point of reclamation. He was immersed in his terrible,
mad, dream.

His fingers pounding her head back and forth grew
tighter and tighter. She thought this time he was really
going to strangle her but he stopped just as she was
about to lose consciousness, and then he began slapping her, poking and jabbing at her body to bring her
round again.

"Now you will do this!" he said obscenely.

Weakly, feebly, not understanding anything and no
longer able to think rationally, she began to cry.

"Amelia! Do what I say! Do this! And this!"

"Leave me alone, Bertram! Leave me alone"

"This! This!"

"Leave me!" she screamed. Hands encircled her
throat again, blows and kicks rained on her body. She
tried to fight him, to push him over, to hit his face or
his groin but he was possessed—his strength was fanatical and inhuman.

One hand twisted into her hair and jerked her head
round.

"Do this! Do as I say. You must do as I say!"

"Leave me!"

"I will kill you!"

He was clawing at her. The hand not holding her
head down was clawing at her body, violating it, hurting, sending shafts of excruciating pain through her.

"I hate you, Amelia! And unless you do as I say I
will kill you!"

The pain was unbearable. She felt as though she
were being savaged by a mad dog.

"Will you do this! Do this!"

"Yes," she sobbed. She would do anything to make
it end. Anything to have it over, have the nightmare
finished, the pain stopped, the horror ended. She did
everything he asked. She let her body be abused and
treated obscenely. She tried not to know what was
happening to her, she tried not to know what she in

turn was doing. She screamed when he hurt her too badly and she heard him scream also, but that was a sound born of ecstasy, of mad delight that had satisfied the terrible sick need in him. The point came when the desire and pleasure he experienced could ascend no more. His strength did not abate but he stopped torturing her and then she felt him striving for the final culmination of his manhood—the ultimate act between husband and wife that should be the seal of unity and instead was nothing more to her than disgusted relief because at least it did not hurt. He screamed one last time, called to Amelia again, and then fell limp over her body. She lay shuddering and sick, knowing that the worst part was over but recalling that, if it was to be the same as last time, he still had to play out the final act of her humiliation.

He rose suddenly and jerked her sore, bleeding body from the bed.

"Come, Sarah. Let us pray."

He pulled her down onto the floor and she knelt beside him. She was crying because her body hurt so much and she was tired, so very tired, but it was nearly over and after the rest she could play this part.

"Oh, Lord, we have sinned. We have transgressed as those first sinners in the Garden of Eden. We have profaned thy paradise, we have abused the gifts given to us. Forgive thy daughter, Sarah, who was tempted even as Eve was tempted and who fell as Eve fell. Forgive all thy daughters, Oh Lord, who are born with sin inherent in them. Who are born to tempt and corrupt thy male servants. Forgive thy daughter Sarah, lest she be constrained to the fires of everlasting hell for the abominations of her body. Amen."

"Amen."

"Ask for forgiveness, Sarah."

"Forgive me, Lord."

"Forgive her, Lord. Let not hellfire consume her lustful body. And on the dreadful day of judgement let her abominable transgression be judged mercifully. Amen."

"Amen."

"Prostrate yourself before the Lord, Sarah."

"Forgive me, Lord."

"You will be judged on the day of revelations, Sarah, when the earth opens and spews forth its dead—when Satan and hellfire burst forth from the bowels of the earth."

"I will be judged."

There was a roaring from beneath her prostrate body, a wild, violent thundering that seared up from the earth. The roaring of hellfire, the tearing open of the earth.

"I will be judged," she sobbed again, anxious to make Bertram stop because the roaring was becoming too real. It was beginning to make her body rock and tremble and it was making the bed shake too.

"Sarah!"

"I will be judged," she repeated desperately, but she could hardly hear herself because the roaring had come right into the bedroom, a huge, tumbling disgorging noise that drowned out everything she and Bertram were saying.

She opened her eyes and saw in the dim light the floor buckle into enormous waves, drop, rise, fall, twist sideways, rear up into terrifying heights that threatened to topple over on her.

"Hellfire!" Bertram screamed.

Sanity suddenly returned to her. She saw the walls swell inwards and break, heard the glass of the window crash and then the ceiling begin to thunder down on top of them.

"Under the bed!" she shouted, pushing him, thrusting, throwing herself under, feeling the floor and bed rise up again, rock, subside, thunder. And then a great crashing avalanche of weight descended, a choking, smothering, horrifying denseness of weight and pain that drowned out everything else.

"Hellfire and damnation . . ." someone whimpered into the crushing dust.

Sometimes it was almost peaceful and she dozed, or fainted, into a hazy dream, cushioned beneath tons of brick and concrete and roofing. She kept dreaming, or

perhaps she was not dreaming, perhaps it was real,
that she was held tight in a crowd of people standing
in the Old Kent Road. That was why she could not
move and every time there was a rumbling noise from
beneath her it turned into the growl of a crowd of
angry strikers. Then she stopped dreaming and began
to choke, her chest stifled, banded round with pain
and the terrifying sensation of not being able to
breathe. She began to panic. She was suffocating to
death . . . buried alive . . . torn down into constricting
terror. "Get me out!" she screamed. "Oh, God, get me
out. Quickly! Get me out! Out!"

Her frenzied limbs began to struggle, to beat frustrat-
ingly against the pain and nightmare all around her.
Dust fell and moved over her, clogging nostrils, mouth,
ears, eyes.

"What am I going to do!" she screamed. "Oh, God,
what am I going to do? Please help me, God. Please . . .
please . . . help me!"

Terror did not leave her and she cried and moaned,
weeping in fear and desperation, oblivious to everything else, struggling to move and begging God or
someone to help her . . . please . . . please . . . help
her . . .

Again she lost consciousness—she was playing Hide
and Seek with young Anna. Anna was counting up to
ten and she felt very proud because she was the one
who had taught Anna how to count. Only three years
old and she could count up to twenty. Anna shouted
"Coming" and Sarah burrowed deeper into the dark
cupboard. But there was something else in the cupboard . . . something horrible and moving . . . it was
Old Krelli . . . or Bertram . . . or . . .

She woke and gasped for air and space—anything to
stop her from choking to death. She managed to loosen
some rubble by her right hand. She worked hard at it,
gibbering to herself, meaningless, useless sounds that
were no more than an accompaniment to her scratch-
ing. When her hand was free she tried to move some
of the debris over her body, working slowly up towards her face, feeling that if only she could get her

face free the horror would subside a little. God ...
God ... God ...

At last she was able to brush her hand over her face
and the mere contact of one part of her body with
another restored a little of her sanity. She tried to wipe
dust from her mouth but her hand was filthy and only
made it worse.

I must breathe slowly ... must not panic again ...
breathe slowly ... recite, that's it ... say some lines ...
keep very calm and still ... don't let myself go mad ...
Jesus bids me shine ... oh, God! It's rumbling again!
Oh, God! Don't let it happen again!

The ground thundered and rocked, but subsided and
was still. Jesus bids me shine with a clear, pure light ...
I should have married Charlie ... but he didn't want
me ... if I'd married Charlie I'd be safe ... I wouldn't
be buried alive ... not moving! Choking to death! Oh,
God ... Jesus bids me shine with a clear, pure light!

She put her hand to her face again, and as she did
so she brushed against the iron spring of the bed. The
bed was over her head. It was broken and sloped right
down over her left shoulder, but just above her face it
formed a small tent, a shelter, an oasis that gave her a
few inches of breathing space. Almost immediately
she felt better because she was able to delude herself
that she was lying in a little cave with a roof over her
head.

I shall be all right. We'll see. I'm sure to be all right
now because the bed is protecting me. That's right. I
made us get under the bed when it started ... Bertram ... he was here ... "Bertram ... Bertram? ...
Bertram!"

She moved her hand in the small space that had become her home, her protective cave. She couldn't feel
anything that could possibly be Bertram lying anywhere near her. But he should be under the bed too.

"Bertram!"

Hours ... or was it moments? No, she must have
been here for several days now because she was
thirsty ... not just ordinarily thirsty ... but parched,
painfully thirsty. "Dogs go mad when they're thirsty!"

She thought of rain, and snow ... a field of snow in the moonlight and a fox running in front of her, and a letter being read by the light of a bicycle lamp. But she wasn't interested in the letter, not when there was all that snow about. She thought about the snow, scooping it up in her hands and swallowing it, rubbing it over her face, feeling it melt and run down her throat. "I'm thirsty," she whimpered. "Oh, God, I'm thirsty. Please help me, God ... Help me! ... Jesus bids me shine with a clear, pure light ..."

There was another long time of terror, of blackness and fear, an interminable forever when she dreamed and prayed and sang and called to God to help her.

Then she heard something moving ... down towards her feet ... something moving! Rats! They would be able to work their way through the rubble and get out! Horrible terrifying rats! She must move ... move her legs, get them away from the rats ...

"Help me! Will someone please help me!"

She heard a dim, muffled cry. That was all, no words, just a cry.

"Bertram?" The cry again. "Bertram?" Then the creaking noise towards her feet ... the rats ... the rats were eating Bertram ...

"Help me! Help me!"

The cry again, but louder. "Help!" she screamed. "Get me out!"

Then the noise of moving brick grew louder, so loud that it couldn't possibly be rats. It was an organised moving ... rhythmic ... big. It moved from her feet and then there was a groaning noise of timber and a shower of rubble came down from the bedstead above her. "Stop! You're making it worse!"

She could hear a voice. A wonderful voice. A wonderful, rough human voice. She could hear actual words now. "Lift ... Careful ... Noise."

"Here!" she cried. "I'm here. I'm under the bedspring. If you can clear by the bed-spring you can pull me out. Please! Get me out!"

Dust and cement fell down on her face again but she didn't mind. They were nearly there. They were right above her and she imagined them lifting the bricks and mortar, every action removing some of the terrible pressure from her body.

"Can you shout again, lass! So we know where you are. Don't worry. We'll soon have you out."

"Here! I'm here! Underneath the bed-spring!"

And then she felt two strong hands on her legs . . . another human being . . . contact with life . . . warm hands . . . strong and pulling her away from the darkness.

". . . Out . . . We'll try not to hurt, lass . . . Out you come."

In spite of the dust she opened her eyes and she saw a small glow of light above her that was blocked out by something. The something moved and the light grew bigger nearly blinding her. It was daylight, not a torch or lamp as she had at first supposed. The light was the bright light of morning.

The hands pulled hard on her legs and she felt herself sliding through the rubble. There was a moment when she was completely smothered and then she was through and other hands, other arms were lifting her up out of the hole into the daylight. A kind, weatherbeaten English face stared down at her, "You'll be fine now, lass. You'll be fine now you're out of there."

She recognised the accent, the way he spoke. "You're from Sussex," she said foolishly, and began to cry. "You're from my county, aren't you? I can tell from the way you talk . . . just like my pa . . . you talk . . ."

She started to tremble and someone put a blanket over her, just where she lay on the rubble. The soldier with the good, beautiful, blessed face, stroked some of the dirt from her mouth. "I'm from Dormansland," he said. "You know it?"

"Near my village . . . only a little way . . . my ma . . . pa . . . only a little way . . ."

"That's right, love. You'll be all right."

"My husband. He's still down there. He was with me under the bed but I couldn't hear him. And there are servants. At the back of the house there are servants."

The soldier picked her up very carefully and passed

her over to another who laid her on a clear patch of ground. She stared round her . . . at nothing. There was nothing to see . . . just miles and miles of rubble and brick . . . a vast devastated wilderness of grey and brown with here and there a few figures picking a path over the ruins. A leaden sky seemed to press down on the obliterated world.

"We'll get 'im out. Don't you worry. And in a minute we'll have you taken to hospital. Just lie quiet now."

Another soldier—dear English faces—unscrewed a canteen and held it to her lips. Water ran through the grime coating her mouth and settled in a small wet puddle at the back of her throat.

"What day is it?" she croaked.

"Friday."

"Only Friday?" She couldn't believe that she had only been buried for one night, that the panic-consumed lifetime had consisted only of hours, not days.

She stared about her again. There was nothing to stare at. Everything was the colour of dust. There were no roads or pavements, just miles of rubble and ruins, mounds of bricks, broken beams sticking drunkenly out of shapes that had once been houses. Small parties of soldiers were digging and moving rubble and from time to time one of them would descend into an abyss and pass up a blackened, broken body. She began to weep again. "All those people! Everyone is dead! They're all dead . . . or they're alive but buried!" Her own nightmare returned once more and she bit her lip between her teeth so as not to scream. Fifty feet away two soldiers sweated at moving a huge beam that was held down at one end by a mountain of broken concrete. Finally they got it raised in the air a little and she saw someone pulled out from underneath, someone who moved an arm and groaned. She couldn't tell if it was a man or a woman, Indian or British, it was just a black, formless shape.

She looked down at her own body, then raised the blanket and in doing so realised she had the use of both arms. Her nightdress was not recognisable as a gar-

ment. There were just a few shreds of grimy cloth
clinging to her body which was bruised and torn in
several places. Her legs were bloody and numb, but
when she reached down and began to rub them she
could feel life returning. Shakily she sat up. There was
a pain in her back and round her ribs but she was able
to move.

The soldiers were digging frantically at the hole over
the bed. They kept calling and then one of them looked
back and asked the name of her husband. When she
told him, they shouted his name down the hole several
times. She couldn't hear any reply.

She stood up, buckled to her knees, and stood again.
Blood began to run down her legs as lacerations re-
opened.

"I must do something," she said to the nearest
soldier. "I must help you dig."

He didn't turn round. "Stay where you are, love.
The lorry will be along in a minute."

"I know where he is ... my husband ... I can show
you where he is."

The soldier didn't answer. Perspiration streamed
down his face and cut the dust into grimy lines. He
was moving the rubble as quickly as he could.

She drew the blanket round her shoulders and
picked her way over the rubbish. The roof, practically
unbroken, sat drunkenly atop the rest of the house and
she lurched her way round to the back of it. There was
a pain in her stomach and she suddenly realised she
had no control over her bladder. Just out of sight of
the soldiers she began—painfully—to pass water.
When it stopped she curled her body into a tight ball
until the pain subsided.

There was more shouting from the front of where
the bungalow had been.

"This way! Move those bricks ... Gently! Don't
bring any more down. That's it."

"Bertram?"

When she limped back one of the soldiers was lifting
the body of a small child from the arms of someone
who was standing out of sight. The child was about

two and was alive. Automatically the soldier passed
the small form over to her and began digging again.
The child, a girl, stared with huge, unseeing eyes at
Sarah and made no sound, even when Sarah pulled
her into the blanket and wrapped it around both of
them. She tried to think of comforting words in Urdu
but none came and finally she sat down on a cement
block and just rocked to and fro, holding the child
against her own body, hoping it would comfort both of
them. The soldier with the canteen passed it over again
and she held it to the child's lips, trying to moisten the
cake of solid dirt over her mouth.

A lorry jolted towards them, twisting and turning in
order to find some kind of track. It stopped two or
three times and bodies were passed up and laid in the
back. The noise of wheels crunching over broken
masonry was incredibly loud.

The soldiers were shouting for Bertram again and
she listened with idle curiosity, wondering vaguely if
they would get him out but having to remind herself
forcibly that the man they were shouting for was her
husband, someone called Bertram Bennett who was
buried beneath the rubble.

"Here! Over here! I think we've found him!"

Her heart began to pound and the child in her arms
stirred restlessly.

"Move the bricks to the left. They're keeping the
bed-spring down and I can't move him."

Cut and bleeding hands tore at the bricks and something creaked beneath them. Another soldier lay face
down on the ruins and stretched his arms down into a
crater. She saw a head that she supposed was Bertram's appear out of the hole. The neck lolled to one
side and when they dragged him over the lip of the
opening his face fell down into the dust.

"Hold his head up!" she cried suddenly. "Don't let
his poor face drag in the dirt!"

They laid him on the ground and he had never
looked so pathetic. His frail body was blackened and
naked. His leg below the knee was mangled into a mass
of bone and dirt and dried blood. It was his good leg.
The other leg, the crippled one, was unharmed.

"Bertram?"

"He's still alive, Mrs."

She put the child down, took the blanket from her shoulders and draped it over the recumbent form. As much as anything it was to shield his poor body from view. The child clung to her legs and she picked her up again and sat down beside Bertram, crooning to them both, a low mournful sound that had no tune.

The lorry came nearer, bumping over the debris, and stopped. Two soldiers from a Sikh regiment lifted her husband into the back of the lorry and the soldier who was her friend, who came from Dormansland, who spoke with the broad vowels of the Surrey and Sussex hills, helped her and the child to climb up beside him. Then it trundled on over the shapeless land, stopping to collect the injured and leaving blankets to cover the dead. There were many dead. They were laid out in rows, indistinguishable as to sex and race. Indians, nearly naked or with their clothes torn to shreds, wandered bemused and stunned through the wreckage. A woman clawed at an impenetrable pile of rock and dust, then sat back on her heels and began to moan a long dirge of wailing grief. The dying embers of one or two bad fires glowed feebly in the dust and it was obvious from the charred wood and blackened stone that earlier, just after the earthquake, there had been several severe conflagrations.

On the plank next to Sarah and the child, a woman with a baby in her arms sighed gently and slid to the bottom of the truck. The baby began to cry and Sarah pulled the woman's shoulders back against her own knees, trying to stop her from rolling over again. The face stared up at her, the eyes wide open, a thin trickle of blood running from the mouth. When Sarah let go, the head lolled to one side and then the body slumped lifeless to the floor.

Sarah giggled. She'd been holding a dead woman and she hadn't known it. She looked at Bertram lying on the floor, and wondered if he was dead too and she just didn't know. The thought that they might be carrying Bertram to hospital when he was already dead made her giggle again, giggle and laugh. She put her hand over her mouth to try and stop the laughter but it insisted on forcing its way through her hands and finally she gave up and began to scream with laughter, rocking to and fro . . .

"Dead! All dead!" she gurgled happily. "Everyone dead! All the dead people going to hospital! Aahh!"

Her laughter became louder and louder and the little girl by her side began to whimper but she still couldn't stop laughing, only it didn't sound like laughter any more. And then she heard something else making the same noise and she saw that the baby, still held in the dead woman's arms, was screeching and screaming, and so she stopped laughing, and pulled the baby out of the woman's arms. As soon as she held it to her own tired body it stopped screaming. It sobbed slightly and then went to sleep. It had a small, grimy, inadequate cloth wrapped round its body and when she pulled the cloth aside she saw, without interest, that the baby was a boy, uncircumcised, and therefore probably a Hindu.

The lorry stopped. More bodies were passed inside, one an Englishman whose body was bent at a terrible and unnatural angle. He kept moaning and calling for Margaret. "Margaret? Come and help me, Margaret. Please come and help me." With the baby still in her arms she stumbled across the body of Bertram and an old Indian lying on the floor, and crouched by the injured man.

"I'm here," she said, laying her hand very gently against the man's cheek because that was the only part of his body she dared to touch. The rest was so broken and twisted she was afraid it would kill him if she even touched his hand.

"Maragret?"

"I'm here."

"Don't leave me, Margaret."

"I won't."

The lorry stopped again and she tensed herself, waiting for the extra terrible fresh burden of bloody bodies. But the two Sikhs began to lift them down, first the body of her husband, then the man who called for Margaret. When they lifted him down he screamed once, then died.

They left Bertram, an English woman, and the dead body of Margaret's husband, and then they drove away. The rest of the occupants of the lorry were Indian, therefore they would be taken to the Indian Military Hospital. She watched the lorry jolting away, and then realised that the dead woman whose child she was holding was being taken away with the lorry. She started to run but the little girl clung to her legs and so she stood still and watched the lorry trundle away into the distance.

All around her on the ground were stretchers, and bodies on the stretchers. Native orderlies, soldiers, one or two women, walked round with water and as quickly as possible, the injured were carried into tents. Everyone was dirty and wore torn and blood-stained clothing.

She sat apathetically on the ground beside Bertram, the baby in her arms, the small girl clinging leechlike to her side. When they lifted Bertram's stretcher and took him inside she stumbled behind, not knowing what else to do.

There was a table, and a doctor who looked ill and exhausted, and a room of chaos and screams and bad smells. Bertram was carried to the table. The doctor looked at his leg and said shortly, "Take the leg off," and just as quickly Bertram was removed from the table.

"No!"

The doctor blinked dully at her.

"You can't take his leg away! He won't be able to walk! The other leg is crippled. If you amputate that one he won't be able to walk!"

The doctor tried to look sympathetic, but he was tired, and he was beginning to feel like a butcher. He smiled, a baring of teeth in a strained, grey face.

"You're his wife?"

"Mrs Bennett. From the Scavener mission."

"Are you all right, Mrs Bennett? Have you any injuries?"

She shook her head.

"One of the ladies will give you some clothes. And look after you. If you feel well enough perhaps you could help them. We need help." He turned away and followed Bertram's body out of the tent. A woman pulled her by the arm and led her away from the table.

"I'll give you some clothes, my dear. And there's a bucket of clean water over there. You don't seem too badly hurt so you won't mind if the doctor doesn't see you until later. Just wash the blood off and put some clothes on." She looked at the baby and the small girl. "I'll see if we've got anything for them. Where did you find them?"

"In the earthquake . . ."

The woman nodded. "The military are putting up a refugee camp on the race course. You'd better take them over there once you've seen your husband is all right."

She handed Sarah a bundle of clothes, an outsize frock, some sandals, underclothes. When she'd washed and put them on she felt better. Her back hurt, but it wasn't too bad and although her legs were still bleeding none of the cuts was deep enough to be serious. The part of her body that hurt most was her throat . . . it was bruised, badly bruised, thumb and finger marks stood out very clearly once the dirt was washed away . . .

When she was clean she went back into the wards and began to help the kind lady—Mrs Beamish—washing, fetching bedpans, calling the orderlies to carry out those who had died. The small girl screamed when Sarah left her, but Sarah gave her the baby to hold and made her sit in a corner of the ward where she could still see Sarah. The child's dark eyes followed her wherever she moved.

It didn't seem any time at all before they brought Bertram back without his leg.

In a land of violence, the earthquake, which obliterated a city in half a minute, impressed and horrified even the most callous and fatalistic of the continent's inhabitants.

Quetta, the largest garrison town in India, stood as a seemingly permanent oasis of the British raj, a flower blooming in the cruel landscape of Baluchistan. There were soldiers, and schools, and civil administration, and balls and picnics and society. There was the Residency, and garden parties on the lawn, and the Quetta club and the races.

In the bazaar, the city itself, were all the races from east, south, west and north. Hindus, Moslems, Sikhs, Brahuis, Pathans, Punjabis all met, mingled, bargained, lived and died in a glorious mêlée of smells and colours and eastern civilisation. There were also the missionaries, the doctors and nurses who belonged to both worlds and who tried to teach and help a multilingual society which was determined not to help itself.

The plains and mountains and deserts around the city were filled with marauding tribesmen who were kept at bay by a huge garrison and the self-propagation of a civilised society.

And, in the space of a few seconds, the whole lot vanished, was swept into a pile of dust by a giant hand knocking over the bricks that had been a city. Over an area of seventy miles long and sixteen miles across, the earth tumbled and heaved and destroyed, and in Quetta thirty thousand died.

By some miracle the cantonment and twelve thousand soldiers were untouched, and this, nearly alone, saved the people who lay buried alive amidst the death throes of the city. The army dug, organised, instructed and dug again. Without them the whole thing would have degenerated into plague-ridden anarchy.

After a while the things she saw ceased to mean anything to her. At first the horrible, twisted, blackened bodies of the dead and dying made her feel sick, but the time came when she could look at them without really seeing them. Cartloads of bodies were taken to emergency burial sites and she became used to the smell, and to the sight of men trying to guess, for the purpose of disposal, the religion and race of an indistinguishable form.

On the second day looters, mostly Pathans, began to come into the city, human vultures and scavengers ready to seize their opportunities from the dead. The only emotion she felt in the days following the earth-

quake was anger, when she watched a looter wrenching
the jewel from the nose of a dead Hindu woman.
Later, as she watched the same looter being savagely
beaten by a police sergeant, apathy had descended on
her once more.

She stayed in the hospital for the first day, working
in the wards until, from sheer exhaustion, she fell into
a corner and slept for an hour before returning again
to work. She did what she could for Bertram, which
wasn't much. When he came round from the anaesthe-
tic he began to cry and nothing would make him stop,
not all her cajoling and pleading would make him stop.
He just lay with tears streaming down his cheeks and
once or twice he called for Amelia.

On the second day she took the children, the little
girl and the baby, down to the racecourse, intending to
pass them over to whoever was in charge. And on the
racecourse she found a chaos far worse than at the
hospital, a confusion of tents and stunned, bewildered
people and crying children and not enough food,
clothes, or blankets. Every so often the ground of the
racecourse would swell and buckle and rise and fall,
and the twenty-odd thousand refugees would scream
and disintegrate into terror again, although there were
no buildings to bury them this time. And so she stayed,
trying to help the small band of women and several
soldiers to organise some kind of discipline. The children stayed with her, and by the afternoon of the
second day she had acquired three more, two boys and
a girl, none of them older than six and all wandering
about lost and glazed and unable to remember what
they had been before the earthquake.

She went back to the hospital twice a day to see
Bertram, but there was nothing she could do, and the
rest of the time she stayed on the racecourse, trying to
make a little food go a long way, calming the hysterical, sorting families and religions and races into groups
which had disintegrated, some for ever. At night she
slept for as long as she could in a tent with a soldier
on guard outside. And every morning, when she came
out, there were a few more children who had been

dumped there because there was nowhere else for them to go and they were not old enough to be useful.

On Sunday, the third day, the smell from the rotting city impinged even on Sarah's tired apathy. It was not a smell. It was a foul, nauseous, disease that impregnated everything—clothes, hair, food, bodies, tents, blankets. Large bloated flies crawled in and out of the ruins, easing through foetid cracks in the rubble to where the soldiers could not reach. Sarah began to vomit, and went on vomiting on and off throughout the rest of the day. She was not alone and she wondered how the soldiers managed to keep on digging at the centre of the city where the smell was so thick it seemed to discolour the air.

That Sunday, early in the afternoon, the ground began to tremble again, badly this time, more than at any time since the night of devastation. The world began to rock and grind, people screamed and ran and trampled over each other, not knowing where to run but only intent on getting away from the recurring horror. And then, to the west, the top of the mountain bordering the plain blew into the air in a vast crescendo of rock and precipice. The gods had destroyed a city, now they severed a mountain in two.

And the baby died on that afternoon.

Every time she went to see Bertram in the hospital, the children trailed in a thin column behind her and very often, when she got back to the camp, she found she had collected a few more on the way. They were all young. The older children melted away, drawn to people of their own languages and clans, able to explain who they were and where they had relatives and property. The young ones were a liability. They could not explain who they were and no one wished to be responsible for them.

On the fourth day she saw Doctor Sircar. She was toiling across the hospital compound, her winding trail of children behind her, when she noticed him hurrying from the direction of the dispensary with a box of bandages and drugs. His face was grey and he was wearing pyjamas and a raincoat. She called but he didn't stop. She called again, then ran after him and tugged at the raincoat.

"Doctor Sircar!"

He turned, stared, nodded. "Good. They got you out then."

"We're both safe. My husband . . . Mr Bennett has had to have his leg amputated . . . but we're both alive . . ."

He nodded again. "I told the soldiers you were there. I didn't have time to come myself. Our hospital . . . you understand . . . But I told the soldiers there would be someone in the bungalow . . . that I had received a note and they must dig quickly."

A return of her old fear doubled up inside her, which was foolish because she was safe now, and she *had* been dug out, and she was free of the choking dust and the concrete grave in which she had thought she was going to die. It had not occurred to her that the note alone had saved her. That if she had not written it the soldiers would not have come so quickly, that if she had waited until the following morning before writing, she would probably have died.

"You're helping on the refugee camp?" he asked, looking at the stream of children who would not leave her. "These are some of the homeless?"

She nodded.

"As soon as your husband is well enough, you must get away. All the women are to be sent away as quickly as possible."

"What about the children? And the rest of the refugees?"

His face was cold and detached. She sensed he did not like her, and she could hardly blame him. All the English women were soon to be sent away, to be soothed and cossetted and helped to forget their dreadful experience. He, and those like him, had to stay and watch their own people salvage what was left.

"Provision will be made. We cannot expect you to do any more. You have all been very brave. Without you, all of you, many more of my people would have died."

He said the words, but the void between their two

races was there . . . resentment because her people had been braver than his, had been calmer and more unselfish and better organised than his, and could now go away and forget about it.

She heard someone else with her voice saying, "All these children—they won't leave me now. They're too afraid and they've grown used to me. I can only just manage to speak to them. One or two know a little English—I think they may be Anglo-Indians—some understand my Urdu—some I cannot talk to at all. But they will not leave me. They are frightened when I go. And I can make them do what I want, even without understanding me. I have taught them to wait in line for their food instead of pushing and fighting for it. And each of the older ones is responsible for caring for a little one."

"Yes," he answered stonily. "Of course, you told me you were a schoolteacher. You are used to controlling children."

"I think, if the authorities permit, I shall take them back to the mission. They will be safe there. They will have a home until something can be sorted out. Maybe one or two have families in other districts, but they can stay there until something has been worked out."

"How many children are there?" he asked slowly.

"Fifty or so. But there are more every day."

"Do you think you can care for fifty children at the mission?"

"No. But we cannot care for them here either. And if they stay . . . what will happen to them?"

He studied her intently, and then put his box on the ground and began to rub his arm.

"What about Scavener? And your husband?"

"The place is supposed to be a mission," she answered stubbornly. "I shall just take them, and ask afterwards."

"There'll be no trouble with the authorities," he said swiftly. "I'll talk to them. The army will lend you a lorry to get back and the sooner you can do so the better. I'll try and arrange something tomorrow. How many more children could you take?"

"I'm not sure," she said nervously. "You had better just send all those you find and we'll try and manage."

He smiled at her, the first time she had seen him smile naturally, a flash of white teeth in a brown-grey face. "Good. It will only be for a while until things are settled."

Guiltily she remembered Bertram. "What shall I do about Mr Bennett? I can't leave him, and Mr Scavener won't be able to manage on his own if he just gets a lorry load of children at the mission."

Doctor Sircar's smile vanished and he became, once more, the guarded expressionless doctor of the mission.

"The wounded are being evacuated as soon as they possibly can. Your husband will go to the hospital at Karachi, or Lahore. There is nothing you can do for him."

He was impatient and irritated with her. The loss of a man's leg was little compared with the overall disaster of the earthquake.

"In that case, as soon as he goes, I'll take the children to the mission. I must remain here until then. But I can look after the children while I wait."

"Very well."

He picked up the box again. "I'll speak to the authorities and get permission for the use of a lorry. As soon as your husband leaves I'll come and see the children loaded."

"Thank you."

As she left him and trailed into the hospital she heard him say bitterly, "After all, that was the whole point of your coming to Quetta. To get yourself a mission."

Mr Scavener's reaction to the arrival of Sarah (still in the outsize dress and sandals) and a lorry load of children, was to lock himself in the study.

A message had been sent down from Quetta two days previously assuring him of their safety, of Bertram's injury, of the arrival of some refugees. But the sight of nearly sixty—the number had grown—dirty, near-naked, lice-ridden children was too much for the ascetic scholar and, after one wild look, he fled.

Lili, who was standing at the front of the mission, was equally shocked but was brave enough to stand her ground and register disapproval.

"Ay . . . eee!" she cried, throwing the end of her robe over her face and rocking backwards and forwards several times.

"Don't be foolish, Lili," Sarah said tiredly. "Thousands of people have died. Quetta is in ruins, thousands more are homeless. These children have no parents, no homes, no relatives at all. The least we can do is take them into our mission."

"But, Memsahib! So many . . . and . . . ah . . . look at them! They are native children! Not Christians!" Her round, brown face under its mat of sheep-greased hair stared in appalled sincerity at Sarah.

"Well, we can turn them into Christians."

Lili sniffed. "So many? To eat and drink our food? Good-for-nothing natives!"

With difficulty Sarah restrained herself from mentioning the vast horde of relatives and friends who ate and drank and lived in the Scavener kitchens. She knew that if she was to carry her plan through she must have the support of Lili and the villagers.

"The older ones will be able to help you, Lili. And remember what our Lord said. 'Suffer little children to come unto me . . .'"

"Yes, Memsahib! But he meant *Christian* children!"

Behind Sarah the soldiers were lifting the occupants of the lorry down onto the sunbaked earth in front of the mission. The children did not move. They gathered into a large, smelly, cowed lump just behind her.

"Phaugh!" said Lili disparagingly. "They stink!"

Several of the little ones, the tiny ones, had not been able to control their bladders or bowels during the tiring journey from Quetta. Most of them in any case were still suffering from shock and fear. Sarah, whom they somehow associated with their past lives, had become their homing pigeon. They did not love her but she was the only familiar thing in a terrifying landscape.

"They will not smell when we have bathed them, Lili."

Outrage registered on Lili's face. "Give them baths? These dirty children!"

"If we bath them, they will not be dirty."

"I do not bath them! And where do they stay? Where do they sleep? In the mission? No! There is no room for them. They must go away."

Desperately Sarah sought for something that would enlist Lili's support. And after she had won Lili, she had to confront Mr Scavener.

"They can sleep in the compound until we have sorted things out. It is quite warm enough to sleep out of doors and they will come to no harm."

"There are no blankets," answered Lili sullenly.

"Then we must get some from the village. And some *charpoys* for them to lie on."

"From the village?" asked Lili slowly, and inspiration suddenly lit Sarah's mind . . . the bribe necessary to line Lili solidly up behind her in the coming battle with Mr Scavener.

"We must buy them from the people in the village, Lili," she said blandly. "And of course, those from whom we buy our food will need to be told that further supplies will be required. You can see to that, Lili. You can do the marketing as usual. And we shall need extra help for a while. One or two more servants . . . to be paid a wage . . ."

There was a moment's pause while Lili conducted private calculations, the profit to be made on middle-man deals, the bribes she would accept in the way of finding places for extra servants.

"Perhaps," she said slowly. "Perhaps the Memsahib will need an extra Christian girl to help with the teaching. My sister's child has been taught at the mission in Lahore . . . a good Christian girl with English and Bible and hymns. She would like to come as teacher."

"We'll talk about it later, Lili," answered Sarah, knowing she had won. Lili was firmly on her side and the children, after a few days, would become mission children and therefore Lili's children.

"Firstly we must help these little ones. They are hungry and tired, and they have come a long way."

Lili beamed. "Come unto me!" she said, holding out her arms towards the children. And then she repeated it, in Brahui, in Hindi, in Pushto, in Urdu, and Sarah was rewarded by the sight of a flicker of recognition in one or two faces that had previously not responded. She turned away satisfied, knowing that Lili would now protect and care for the children as her own. The bribe had been necessary for initial acceptance. But, like Ma Dance (who would not condone the miners for striking, but would have given anyone of them a meal and money had they presented themselves at her door) she would love and spoil the children once her own prejudice had been overcome.

Sarah led the children into the compound. They sat on the ground and then one of the boys brought jugs of water from the kitchen and Sarah and Lili passed down the line wiping faces and dispensing drinks. Within forty-five minutes tubs of water were brought out (by some new staff who had miraculously appeared after some frenzied whispering between Lili and her husband) and the children dumped in twos and threes into the wooden tubs, dried, and put into whatever garments could be found for them. Sarah waited until she saw the beginnings of a meal being carried out, and then she left the crowded compound and went to the door of the study. She knocked.

"Who is it?" Mr Scavener sounded nervous.

"Mrs Bennett."

The key turned in the lock and he stared dismayed through a narrow opening between door and frame. When he saw Sarah was alone he held it wider and beckoned imperiously.

"I had feared, Mrs Bennett, that some of that *rabble* might be with you."

"No. The rabble are in the compound being washed and fed."

"When are they leaving?"

Sarah drew a deep breath and braced herself.

"They are not."

He blinked, turned away, tinkered with some papers on a desk, picked up a pen and put it down again.

"They must be gone before Bertram returns to us. He must have perfect peace from now on, peace in which to recover and study."

"They will not be leaving us, Mr Scavener. They have nowhere to go. They are refugees, and they are part of the new Scavener mission."

A blotchy mauve stole up from beneath Mr Scavener's high starched collar.

"Are you forgetting yourself, Mrs Bennett? I know you have been under severe strain . . . the whole experience must have been quite distressing to you . . . and of course poor Bertram's tragedy has affected us all. But, even allowing for your nervous condition, I am surprised at your . . . pertness."

"Mr Scavener, I shall be blunt with you. I came to this mission prepared to work and give my life to helping the poor and ignorant and needy. I had no qualifications, no skills, no money. But if a willing heart and . . . enthusiasm counted for anything . . . I would have made a good mission teacher in time."

"You were told what your duties were to be," he said crossly.

"My duties consist of nothing that a good *babu* could not do."

"How dare you!" he spluttered.

"Mr Scavener. This place is not a mission, and you have been guilty of a grave dishonesty. Your father left his money in trust for the running of a mission, not for the benefit of your private studies. If you were not prepared to go about it yourself, you should have passed the money and the duties over to trained missionaries who were prepared to do so."

"Mrs Bennett! You exceed yourself!"

"I intend to exceed myself. Out there are sixty children who need homes. Most of them are too young to even remember what religion or race they are. You have a chance, Mr Scavener, to start your mission, just as your father wished. I suggest that once these children are settled in, we approach one of the established missionary groups and ask for their advice and blessing. Possibly, later, they will send us a trained missionary, someone who has dedicated his life to this kind of work."

Mr Scavener's disdain suddenly snapped. The mauve on his face turned to purple and he began to screech . . .

"This is *my* mission, and I shall do what I like with it! You have no right to tell me what to do with my father's money. You are no one! You are Bertram's little nobody of a wife! And you will do as you are told!"

His dignity had vanished—exploded out of him along with the saliva that sprayed over her when he shouted. She felt nothing but irritation.

"In that case, Mr Scavener, as I have no intention of doing as I am told, I think it better that we leave. When Bertram is well enough to travel I will go down to Karachi and collect him, and from there we can journey home."

His face mottled again. "Bertram will not leave. Not on any account. We have waited for years to do our study together, and nothing—certainly not you—will make him leave now."

"But he will have to," she said mildly. "He will be an invalid for the rest of his life. He will not be able to walk again, you know, not even on crutches. We have to get him a wheelchair, and from now on I must do everything for him. He will not want to be alone, Mr Scavener. And I would not leave him alone. We stay together, or we go together."

She thought he was going to strike her. Frustration, fury, violent resentment flooded across his skull-face.

"It is up to you to decide, Mr Scavener. You can have us both, and sixty children and a well-run mission, or nothing at all."

"How dare you," he growled. "How dare you wreck my life like this."

She began to laugh, hard, hysterical laughter that was akin to tears. "Mr Scavener! Thousands of people have just died, thousands more are homeless. Your best friend and colleague has lost his leg and will be a cripple for the rest of his life. In Quetta they have closed the city because of the flies and maggots and stench from the dead, and they are whipping lotters who have come in from the hills. The landscape has been torn in two. The top has blown off a mountain. And you talk of your life being wrecked!" She leaned against the wall and laughed so hard she thought she would never stop. Mr Scavener's fury turned to bewilderment, then unease.

"Mrs Bennett, please! I must ask you! Control yourself!"

"Oh . . ." she cried, bending forward to relieve the pain in her ribs. "Oh! How funny you are!"

Mr Scavener's uneasiness turned to fear.

"Mrs Bennett! Stop! We can talk about this again. We can come to some kind of solution. If it means this much to you, we can do something I am sure."

Her choking laughter subsided a little. "I have told you what we shall do, Mr Scavener. We shall stay, or go."

"I do not like children," he said distastefully.

"I shall try to see they do not bother you."

"I want no part of this. My work must go on! Nothing must interfere with the thesis!"

"Nothing shall," she said wearily. "I will continue to help you as much as possible. And perhaps, later, when the children are older, one of them can be trained to suit you as an assistant."

"I do not want to see the children. And the responsibility for what happens rests entirely with you."

She smiled sweetly at him. "You will not even know they are here. And they, even less, will know of your existence in the building. You shall live apart from the mission—like a hermit in a cave."

"You give me no option, Mrs Bennett," he said sullenly. "But I shall not forget this. And neither shall I forget your rudeness and impertinence. Bertram has made a grave mistake in his choice of a partner. I had my doubts when I met you at Karachi, but now I have seen you in truth. And you are an ignorant, vulgar upstart, Mrs Bennett! An ignorant, vulgar upstart!"

"Thank you," she said gently. "Thank you for my mission."

# Sixteen

THE sheer, physical labour of providing food, clothing, shelter, and some measure of discipline for sixty children was considerably more than Sarah had anticipated. The children had no one common language, they understood five or six tongues between them, and in any case most of them were still too shocked from the earthquake to make contact with them easy. In some cases the condition of shock lasted for several months and one, a boy of about eight whom they called George, remained dumb, through no medical cause, for his entire stay at the mission.

Mr Bennett did not return to the mission for six months. An infection set up in the stump of his amputated leg, and this was followed by pneumonia, and every time the hospital authorities at Karachi announced that he was nearly ready to return to the mission, he would suffer a mild relapse of one kind or another. Sarah, subduing faint feelings of guilt about him, was truthful enough to admit relief at his absence during this first period of confusion and trial. Once Bertram returned her duties were going to be doubly burdensome and she knew she would not have been able to cope with nursing him, and trying to organise the children at the same time.

Once a month she made the journey down to Karachi to see Mr Bennett. It meant almost a week away from the mission, allowing for the full day and night she spent in Karachi. And when she returned, invariably with the headache and fever that the train ride across

299

the desert of the Sind induced, she found, every time, that conditions and discipline at the mission had degenerated into chaos, the children running wild, dirty, the younger ones frightened and unfed, Lili sulking, Mr Scavener locked in his study in a state of near apoplexy, unlocking and opening the door only to take in a meal tray three times a day.

By the end of the summer they had arrived at some kind of order. The crumbling and disused rooms of the old temple had been cleaned and temporarily patched up. They were divided into boys' and girls' dormitories, *charpoys* were obtained for all the children and extra blankets for the coming cold winter nights of the mountains. At the beginning the children had worn anything Sarah could get hold of, and that meant mostly clothes bought from the village or borrowed from the servants' children. They had run around the mission compound, children of all shapes, colours and sizes, in a weird selection of native costume that gave the mission a bizarre theatrical appearance. But in July Doctor Sircar paid his first visit since before the earthquake, bringing with him four large crates of children's clothing, a donation from the relief fund. He also brought seven more children.

"I think it unlikely you will keep all these children here permanently," he said apologetically, as though trying to lessen the burden of the extra seven. "Some, I am sure, will be claimed by distant relatives in time. But for the present, if you can manage to care for a few more, it will help in the emergency."

"That's all right." Sarah was rummaging through the crates of clothes and was relieved to find that nearly everything had been thought of . . . undergarments, sandals, nightwear, and some extra blankets. Many of the children would be better clothed than they were before the earthquake.

"I hope," said the doctor nervously, "I hope you are not intending to teach religious subjects to these orphans—not until we have ascertained that they are orphans. We certainly do not wish to provoke any trouble with the hill tribes, and especially with your own Brahui villagers, by forcing conversion and Christianity on the children."

Sarah stopped rummaging and stared at him, a pair of boy's khaki shorts in her hand.

"You remember what I told you before," he said quietly. "We must be very careful about upsetting the tribesmen."

"I haven't even thought about teaching them."

"I see."

"Doctor Sircar," she said tiredly. "I can only just manage to feed, clothe, and keep these children in order. Most of them don't understand what I say and I am very worried about how Lili translates me. She appears to be the only one whom most of them understand and I am sure she doesn't tell them what I ask her to. If ever I get to the stage where I have finished caring for their physical needs, I shall then try to teach them English. And that will be as much as I can hope for."

"Good," he smiled.

"How strange you are," she said thoughtfully. "You are a mission doctor and yet you warn me against missionary work. It is as though you are not really certain yourself about the right thing to do."

The blank, impassive look closed down once more over his face, the look that shut her out from any of his private thoughts and forbade her to ask rude, personal questions.

"You are managing well?" he asked coldly.

"Well enough. I must get everything organised and running smoothly before Mr Bennett comes home. He is going to need a lot of my time."

"Do you need any help?"

"Not for him," she answered. "Not for Mr Bennett. But I wish there were someone—someone with authority—who could help with the children. Not servants, I have plenty of those, more than enough! Since the earthquake and the arrival of the children at the mission, everyone who works here has brought in at least three or four relatives, supposedly to help. I need

someone who can share the authority with me, who
can take charge when I go down to Karachi."

"Mr Scavener?"

"I am doing all this in open defiance of Mr Scavener," she answered. "He will be delighted if things go
wrong and the authorities step in and close the mission."

Doctor Sircar didn't answer. They stood in silence
for a moment in front of the mission. The boxes of
clothes were standing on the paved floor of the cloistered entrance to the compound and Sarah slowly let
the garment she was holding drop back into the crate.
Overhead in the hot, white sky, a kite circled and
wheeled. The distant brown hills shimmered in the
summer dust and the silence was broken only by the
thin, high-pitched wind over the scrub and rocks.

"The children are quiet today," she said softly.

"It is very peaceful here. Even with the children it
is more peaceful than Quetta."

"Yes."

"This is not my country . . . I am from Bengal you
know, from the east."

"I know."

The wind rose and fell, whined and sang, a wind
that brought no breeze of coolness, only sound. Doctor
Sircar shrugged his shoulders suddenly.

"There's nothing we can do about trained help for
you at the moment," he said. "All the missionary
groups are strained to breaking point—there is so much
rebuilding to do in the city. But later perhaps . . . I'll
see what can be done."

"Thank you."

"Commencing next month, I shall resume my usual
medical visits. And naturally I will care for the children here. Are they satisfactory at the present time?"

They were not. Two or three had bad sores, one a
severe case of dysentery. And there was George who
could not speak.

She led Doctor Sircar into the compound for a
makeshift surgery.

When the winter came that year, it was severe. The December rains turned the land into mud, and refugees from villages surrounding Quetta began to file past the mission down to the warmer plains. Most of them had lost home, family, and means of livelihood and with the advent of cold weather the ultimate misery of a damp, bitter winter became too much. They were pathetic, clothed in sodden rags and with only one or two camels and goats between an entire village.

Some of the survivors, although their villages were devastated, elected to stay behind, and the mission centres in Quetta tried to distribute blankets and warm clothing—a tiny compensation for the loss of everything they possessed.

As the Scavener mission was almost the first community going south that had not been touched by the earthquake, most of the caravans stopped there and Sarah tried to give warmth and shelter to as many as she could. There were so many that the most she could offer was a straw mat on the floor of a room with a few blankets shared by many. They left the mission in a dirty and foul condition, but their plight was so pitiful that Sarah bore Mr Scavener's hysterical protests in stubborn silence. It was the very least the mission could do and by the end of December most of the refugees had passed and, just after Christmas, she was able to go down to Karachi to fetch Bertram. The day she arrived in the city was actually the day of her first wedding anniversary but she tried not to think about it, and she hoped Bertram would have forgotten as well.

He was cheerful and ready for her, in possession of his new wheel-chair which in time, it was hoped, he would be able to manipulate himself.

At first, after the earthquake and his operation, he had been depressed and occasionally maudlin. He had cried a lot and once, in the hospital at Karachi, he had said to Sarah, "Amelia always said God would punish me. When I was a little boy she used to say that to me, 'Bertram, God will punish you if you don't do what I tell you' and God has punished me."

Now for the first time she felt a sense of deep, overwhelming pity for him. He had so many things that she did not have, wealth, a brilliant mind, education and the opportunities to exploit both the mind and the education. But he had spent his whole life crippled, not just his body, that was the least part, but his mind too.

"That's foolish, dear," she replied. "Do you think that God killed all those innocent people at Quetta just to punish you?"

He didn't seem to hear her, just turned his head restlessly on the pillow and stared at her with soft, puzzled eyes.

On her third visit to the hospital the doctor had asked to see her. He explained that Bertram would have to spend the rest of his life in a wheel-chair and that, because of the deformity of his spine, body movement of any kind would be difficult for him. He would need constant assistance.

"Fortunately I gather your husband's interests are scholarly and academic," the physician had said, "so the adjustment will not be so severe." Then he had paused, looked uncomfortable, and asked, "I cannot quite understand your husband's temperament, Mrs Bennett. Is he a man given to hysteria?"

Sarah had tensed, wondering what had happened, what had been said to make the doctor ask.

"No."

The doctor grunted. "I acquainted your husband with the nature of his future life, the limitations he must accept, and it was quite extraordinary. He seemed delighted, relieved . . . yes, he seemed relieved at the news."

When she went in to see Bertram she understood immediately what the doctor had meant. All the depression had vanished. He was smiling and he seemed animated and overjoyed to see her.

"Sarah, my dear! How pretty you look. And after that terrible journey down from the hills too!"

"How are you, Bertram?" She leaned forward and kissed him on the cheek.

"So well, my dear! I feel so very well! And I am

looking forward to coming and helping you with all the children! You must tell me about them. I wasn't really listening before but now I am most anxious to know what is happening. What a really splendid mission we are going to run, the three of us! Amos and I will continue with the research of course, but we must not neglect our duties to the poor orphans of the earthquake. We were spared, Sarah, so we must give all we can to those who have lost their loved ones!"

"Amos is not too happy with the idea," she said hesitantly. "He finds the presence of so many children disturbing, and he does not really wish anything to interfere with your work."

He had tutted in an amused and patronising fashion. "Poor Amos. He has buried himself so much in the past, he has forgotten the needs of the living. And besides . . ." He had suddenly taken her hand in his and smiled at her, a charming, gentle smile full of affection and warmth and . . . love. "I have known for some time, Sarah, that you did not feel settled at the mission. There was not enough for you to do. Two dry, dusty old professors cannot be very exciting for a young woman bursting with energy."

"Why, no . . . Bertram . . . that is . . ."

And then he had smiled again and gently raised her hand to his cheek "You're such a *shiny* person, Sarah! So bright and alive and . . . full of warmth. I want you to be happy. I like to see you happy."

She couldn't speak. Tears choked her throat and they were not just tears of pity. She didn't understand him, she never could, but there were times when his perception and genuine affection for her, made her wish she could love him, solve whatever sickness warped his mind.

"You're very good to me, Bertram," she managed to mumble finally.

"You are my wife."

She bent forward over the bed and kissed him, and it was the first time in their marriage she had kissed him with tenderness. His blue eyes lit and his funny little gnome's face was suffused with colour. She sat

holding his hand for the rest of the afternoon, talking
about the children, what they had to do, and whether
they should ask one of the missionary groups to take
over on orthodox lines. She had spoken, too, about
the progress of the thesis, but mostly it was about the
children.

And every time she had gone to see him after that,
it had been the same. He was ill again, with the infection, and pneumonia, but even in illness it was
obvious his mind was at peace, his life was set on a
pattern of tranquility.

The journey back to the mission was trying, the
native porters seemed adept at not being able to negoti-
ate the wheel-chair on and off the train. Several times
they jarred the chair badly and finally she got two of
them to carry Bertram onto the train, and then they
manhandled the chair on any way they liked. She had
brought one of the bearers down from the mission to
help, but washing, and clothing, and attending to his
personal needs on a long, tiring train journey put a
strain on both of them. Their arrival at the mission
brought a relief out of all proportion to what they
could expect to find when they got there.

Amos was waiting at the front of the compound and
could hardly contain his anxiety. Right up until the
last minute he hadn't been sure that Bertram would
actually return. He now hated Sarah so much he quite
expected her to whisk his friend onto a ship going back
to England, leaving him alone with nearly seventy undisciplined orphans.

"Bertram! You cannot know how gratified I am to
see you," he gasped relieved.

The two friends clasped hands, and Bertram turned
his head to look at a group of the refugees who were
standing beneath the stone arches staring at him.
"Amos, it is good to be back! And back to such splendid work! Sarah has told me of how you have opened
the mission to the earthquake refugees. At last, Amos!
The chance you have been waiting for! To fulfil your
father's dream of a Scavener mission!"

She felt almost sorry for Mr Scavener. He swallowed

hard, and then bared his teeth in a strained smile. "Ah, yes, well . . . your wife looks after all that. We shall conduct our work as usual, Bertram. Shall we not?"

And Bertram smiled blandly and raised one hand as though blessing not only the children, but also the mission and Amos. "The Lord will find time for us to do a little of everything, Amos. A little of everything . . ."

Mr Scavener had not even dared to dart her the look of malevolent venom she knew was dormant in him. He had just gulped and nodded at Bertram, and then followed feebly as Sarah pushed the wheel-chair through the compound.

The pattern of their future at the mission was established, and it was formed around the figure, the tiny, frail figure of the man in the wheel-chair. Mr Bennett, now totally incapacitated, showed a strength he had not possessed before and it became apparent that, of the two scholars, he was the more dominant. If necessary, Bertram could have done without the presence of his friend. Amos still became concerned and alarmed if there was any mention of Bertram leaving him to do his work alone.

Thus, when Bertram stated his intention of conducting a morning class with the children, helping Sarah to teach them English, Amos, after a weak protest, had given in and resentfully consented to be present at the classes. His assistance, bad-tempered though it was, did prove useful. His knowledge of the hotch-potch of languages spoken by the children was far in excess of Sarah and Bertram's. The afternoons and evenings were spent, as before, in the study.

In spite of the friction between Sarah and Mr Scavener, life at the mission became serene and orderly. It was busy, sometimes noisy, but there was a sense of purpose that brought peace. She was proud of her ability to change a group of confused, hysterical children into a well-disciplined class, each of whom she could address by name. She found that running a class of children in India, even of assorted races and languages, was not so very different from running a class in England. Keeping order, holding interest, knowing each one personally, was much the same. Sometimes, in the early evening, when she was helping Lili to ladle out the vegetable curry and chupatties to a jostling line of giggling children, she was reminded of milk duty at Miss Bennett's school.

During the first year, eleven of the children were reclaimed by distant relatives, including a little Punjabi girl of whom Sarah had become very fond. She had, during the first month of their presence, made a list with Lili's help, of what information she could gather from the children, what language they spoke, their names, the names of their families, what little they could remember. She'd hoped it would help when the time came for people to try and trace them. But after the first ones were found by their families, no one else was ever claimed and the mission inmates remained as they were.

In the second year, in 1937, Doctor Sircar augmented their affiliation to one of the missionary groups, and they were joined by Doctor Keynes. He was not a medical doctor. He was an experienced missionary and spoke three of the country's tongues fluently, and understood two of the other dialects. He was middle-aged, zealous, and delighted with the opportunity to form a Christian orphanage. Bertram and Mr Scavener relinquished their class duties and hurried back to the study for the entire day.

The pattern of the teaching changed slightly. Until now, with Doctor Sircar's advice in mind, Sarah had been careful that no suggestion of religious instruction should be given. But with the arrival of Doctor Keynes, the children began to attend morning prayers and the service on Sundays. There was still no religious pressure. Their main task, explained Doctor Keynes, was to house, educate, and prepare for adult life, the children orphaned at Quetta. Later, other children would be taken in (Doctor Sircar occasionally arrived on his monthly visit with a child he had collected somewhere) and later, perhaps, the local people themselves would wish to have their children taught there.

Doctor Keynes made her realise, in an abstract and detached way, what a curious and isolated place the mission was—an enigma in a land of enigmas. Outside the mission and the village, the country fermented in a rage of violence, resentment, tribal wars, and *J'Hai Hind*. The north-west frontier, that turbulent area of 40,000 square miles of which Baluchistan was only the southernmost tip, was at its most inflammatory period. A century of religious, tribal, family and internecine wars, had found fresh fuel in *J'Hai Hind,* Indian independence, a new war against the British, and a war that had the blessing of the Indian Congress Party. The wars, in fact, were the same wars they had always been—fakirs, mullahs, wazirs, preaching fervent hysteria against other tribes, other religions, and leading their hill soldiers into battle. But *J'Hai Hind* was a new, heady battle-cry that lent devoutness to the age-old cause of tribal bloodshed.

The mission, cocooned in a pocket of unreality had, for years, stood safe from the danger all around. But Doctor Keynes explained to Sarah how careful they must be with their teaching and efforts to convert. Even their own villagers who had a greedy and proprietary air towards the mission, could, if they felt conditions were changing too much, turn against them.

Sometimes, quite close, they could hear shooting in the hills and it was not always troop manoeuvres. Soldiers were ambushed and shot in minor skirmishes and some not so minor skirmishes. Sarah knew all this, and she knew that the mission was safe only as long as the local tribesmen allowed it, but the dreamlike quality of the hills wrapped about her and blunted her sense of personal danger.

She came to love the mission, the pattern, the busyness of a day composed of classes, of a small boy ringing a handbell in the compound at the appropriate hour, of wheeling Bertram from classroom to study, from study to bedroom, of getting to know children as she had in the old days. And it never seemed strange to her that she was happy doing this when before, in London, it had made her restless and dissatisfied ...

because here at the mission one could never forget that they were only a tiny part of a huge, barbaric country. In the spring and autumn the vast migration of the tribes covered the hills, coming up from the plains to Quetta, and returning for the winter. She would watch wild, alien peoples sweeping across the land and experience again the sense of space she had felt on her first morning at the mission. Often there were soldiers— easily seen in the middle distance, and occasionally— when going up to Quetta—they would pass a band of savage and handsome Pathans.

She had thought she could never bear to go up to Quetta again, but when at last, in the company of Doctor Sircar, she made her first visit, her fear of the earthquake was immersed in a fresh stimulation of energy at the sight of the city being rebuilt.

Without ever really knowing Doctor Sircar, she became a colleague, a companion to him. Two days a month they worked together and she learned to know his moods, his passions and his tolerances. The barrier of politeness between them remained, and turned to icy courtesy on his part if she trod too close to subjects he did not wish to speak of. He frequently mentioned Cambridge and his days as a student there, and he spoke at great length about Baluchistan—the people, the government, the tribes, the lack of education and hospitals, but he never mentioned his family or personal background, or why he worked as a missionary doctor. And in return he asked nothing about herself, except on just one occasion.

He had brought down her mail from home—it was another of the added excitements of his monthly visits—and in the evening, after dinner, she sat in her favourite place, in front of the stone arches looking out over the hills, and opened her letters, each one a contact and reminder of another life ... from her father, Aunt Betsy, May, one of her brothers, from poor old Miss Enderby, now retired and filling her penurious and wasted life with the borrowed glamour of a missionary friend; and from Gertie Alexander.

". . . Things is so much better now than they was before because of us all working—except for me and
dad of course. I keep on my morning jobs because I
like to have a bit of money to meself, but they all
like me to keep it running like when ma was alive.
It upsets me sometimes when I think of how we
never had nothing when ma was alive, she never had
nothing you know, nothing nice to eat or flowers or
anything except when she was going and David Baron
brought her all them things he nicked from the
market. And then she was too gone to enjoy them.
He was good to us, he was, and he's been good since.
Got jobs for George and Teddy. Only he's in trouble
now. He's got himself in trouble with the police again
and is Inside. Took part in one of them fights in the
east end—all them fachists or whatever they're called.
I don't really understand it except they want to do
away with lots of things like Jews and russians and
on account of him being both he went on the other
side and there was a big fight and he got arrested,
just like in the strike. He told my dad that it was up
to the British to do something about the nazis and
that is why he must go and fight at the meetings.
Which is funny, him thinking he must fight because
he is British and the fachists wanting to get rid of him
because he is russian. He got dad a bit excited again
and I thought he would go too, but then he went to
the Blue Eyed Maid like always. He wont never get
work now. It upsets me dreadful when he gets so
drunk but Sammy says it takes his mind off ma. I
don't see it myself as he always cries when he comes
home from the Blue Eyed Maid. He says why couldn't
the money have come in when she was alive . . . What
good is it now . . .'"

He hadn't changed. In all these years he hadn't
changed. Still spoiling for a fight, eager to espouse a
cause, to throw himself without restraint or caution into
something he believed.

"I hope your letter does not contain bad news, Mrs
Bennett."

She turned, and for a moment had to stop and think
who the young-faced, white-haired Indian was.

"No . . . well yes, in a way . . . a friend, someone I knew from the old days is in trouble."

Doctor Sircar bowed gravely. "Illness?" he asked.

"No. The law. He is a very . . . ardent believer . . . not in God or religion you understand. But in causes, the cause of man, or employment, things of that nature."

"He is in danger of prosecution? Of indictment by the law?"

She wanted to laugh a little. Doctor Sircar, in spite of his work and service, was still on the other side of the fence, the same side as Bertram and Mr Scavener, the side of education and money and the right and legal way of doing things. Trouble with the law, to them, meant a long and legal dispute dragged out with dignified arguments and minute elucidations. They didn't understand about poverty.

"He is in prison. He assaulted a policeman. I gather he became aroused during a Mosley march on the East End."

"Your friend is a fascist?"

"A Jew."

"I see."

She wondered if he did see. She could not imagine the icy Doctor Sircar understanding why someone should attack a policeman. And yet India was a land of violence where policemen and soldiers were constantly mobbed and attacked.

"If only he could control his passions," she said quietly to herself. "If only he could have learned to fight with discipline."

"Everyone fights the way they can. To believe in something strongly enough, to have a guiding passion for one's life, that is reason enough to fight any way one can . . . with secrecy, with painstaking endeavour, with lies and guile. Your friend can only fight with violence, but that is his way."

She turned to stare at him in the evening light, but his dark eyes were unfathomable and she was suddenly a little afraid of him.

"You must not grieve for your friend," he went on.

"For I perceive you do grieve. He is happy. He is doing what he wants to do."

"You don't really like us, do you?" she asked slowly.

"I envy you."

"But you don't like us."

"Do you like me?'

"I envy you."

They began to understand. He was Indian, but wealthy. She was British, but poor. They began to see how many divisions there can be between peoples, how many hatreds and resentments and barriers are formed for a multitude of reasons. And she sensed that he was stronger than she was, and therefore she was afraid.

"I think I'll go in now," she said abruptly. "Good night."

"Good night."

"I will be ready for you early tomorrow, as soon as you wish to begin surgery."

"Thank you."

"And perhaps you would be good enough to look at Bertram. He gets sore in his wheel-chair. He has one or two places on his back. I have rubbed them but I would be glad if you would look at him. And he still has the small blister where the amputation was. It must have rubbed against something."

"Of course." The simple medical conversation restored their usual equanimity. They were mission colleagues once more.

In bed that night she thought not so much about David Baron as about Doctor Sircar . . .

The sores on Bertram's back were bad. He was patient and he complained very little—she realised he must have grown used to pain and discomfort in his life—but she knew they caused him constant unease from the way he tried to move his body to a different angle. Doctor Sircar, however, gave the sores only the briefest of glances. He seemed more concerned with the tiny blister on the stump of the leg.

"This was here when I examined you last time, Mr Bennett."

Bertram smiled, then winced as Doctor Sircar pressed gently on the area round the blister.

"Does it hurt?"

"A little. But not in the ordinary way. Not until you pressed just then. My back hurts though. If you could give my wife something new to rub on my back it would help."

Doctor Sircar stood back from the bed for a moment and ran a professional eye over Mr Bennett's recumbent form.

"I have something. And, Mrs Bennett, perhaps you could make some rings for his back. You can devise something until I bring rubber ones down from the hospital."

He pressed the tiny blister again, very gently, watching Bertram's face to test the reaction. Then he replaced the covers over his leg and smiled reassuringly.

"The sores will go once you are propped on rings. And we must try to help you sit on one side if we can. And pad that blister, Mrs Bennett. In fact I will give you some dressings to put on it. Try not to let it rub against anything."

"I am so fortunate to have Sarah," said Mr Bennett. "She looks after me so well. And without neglecting any of her other duties. There are the children you know. She helps Doctor Keynes most ably, and still has a little time to spare for the work that Amos and I are currently engaged upon . . ."

Doctor Sircar began to pack his things away in his bag. He clasped it shut and then came back to look down at Bertram. "You should try to spend a little less time on your thesis, Professor. Sitting in one position, in one room, for all that length of time, does not help your back. Try to interrupt your day a little more . . . spend some time in the compound . . . perhaps get one of the boys to wheel you out a little way . . . not far but enough for you to see the landscape from a different angle. And rest . . . you should rest on your bed for a while every day . . ."

Over Bertram's face passed the fretful, impatient look he always wore when he was being persuaded to do something he did not want to do. He bore his disabilities, his ailments, his limitations with fortitude, but were he crossed in something he considered of importance, he could prove stubborn and unreasonable.

"I rest in the study," he said petulantly. "And really! My time is far too valuable to spend it as though I were an invalid. We are hoping to have this work ready for presentation in a few years you know! Several authorities, in varying parts of the world, are waiting with the utmost interest for the publication of our findings."

"Try to rest a little," said Doctor Sircar quietly, and then he followed Sarah from the room.

"Watch the blister, Mrs Bennett. It is in an awkward place and I do not want it to get worse." He hesitated.

"Is something wrong? Is there something wrong with him?"

"No. Nothing especially wrong. But he seems a little tireder, a little less strong. And he is losing weight. There's nothing especially wrong, Mrs Bennett. But just keep a careful eye on him. Change the dressings on the sores every day. Try to make him rest. Make sure he eats well. And make a point of noting anything different in his daily routine."

She was immediately worried, more than worried. The few years since the earthquake, since Bertram had returned to the mission, and since Doctor Keynes had joined them, had been so free of anxiety, so orderly and busy and tranquil, that she had allowed herself to be lulled into a sense of purposeful security. She had forgotten that life always had some unpleasant shock not very far away. Now she was forcibly reminded. Doctor Sircar apparently guessed her thoughts.

"Please do not worry. It is obvious a man in your husband's condition will not be in first-class health all the time. Like the rest of us he will have periods when his general health necessitates extra care. But this does not call for alarm. Just a little patience and some added nursing. And this, I am sure, you can manage."

"Oh, yes." She allowed herself to be soothed by the promise of extra work in looking after Bertram. This she did not mind. At first, nursing, washing, helping

him with the simplest needs of his body, had proved
embarrassing and undignified for both of them. Bertram
at one time had suggested a bearer and Lili's husband
had taken over some of the more intimate duties. But
it hadn't worked. Jamiat, or John as his baptised name
was, had proved willing but incapable of sensing the
frailty of a body that had been crippled even before
drastic surgery had taken place. Sarah, unable to stand
seeing how even being washed left Bertram exhausted
and hurt, had taken over the nursing again. She had a
boy whom she was training to help her, one of Lili's
numerous relatives, and who under her guidance was
learning to nurse gently and capably. But she could not
bear to let Bertram be clumsily manhandled again. And
it no longer embarrassed either of them. The relationship between them had changed. She had now almost
completely obliterated the memory of that other Bertram, the Bertram who was her husband. Now she
knew only the gentle, perceptive, suffering Bertram—
the man who had been kind to May when Peter was
dying, the man who understood some of the things she
felt, who had supported her against Mr Scavener, the
man who was a brilliant scholar and had a crippled
body. For this man she felt pity, admiration, and a
deep, abiding affection.

She tried to make him follow Doctor Sircar's advice,
to rest a little, to break his long routine of study. But
he was childishly sulky about any change to his established pattern and several times he snapped irritably at
her when she tried to make him sit in the compound
with her for a little while.

"I don't interfere with your day, Sarah. Please don't
interfere with mine!"

When Doctor Sircar returned on his next visit the
blister on Bertram's stump was bigger and it had begun
to weep a little.

"I'm not happy about this," he said to Sarah when
they were outside Bertram's room. "He has had the
blister for nearly three months. You have changed the
dressing regularly?"

"Every day."

"Even if it had not healed, it should not have grown bigger, nor infectious. And he has lost a little more weight. Does he eat properly? Or is he so engrossed in his study that he takes no time for food?"

"He eats well." Bertram always had enjoyed his food in an abstract and scholarly way. Considering his size he ate big meals, and was quick to complain if they were badly cooked or late in coming. "He eats well, and he drinks well. He has jugs of fresh lime juice at hand in the study all day."

Doctor Sircar said nothing. He left a new supply of dressings, and some medicine that was intended to put Bertram's general health back in good form.

Over the next two months she watched Bertram very carefully. The sore became bigger, very big, and the weeping changed to a thick and disagreeable discharge. And in spite of increased eating and drinking Bertram continued to lose weight. She did not notice it very much, for the loss was slight, but Sircar who only saw him once a month was able to gauge the change in him and she was neither surprised nor unprepared when he suggested that Bertram should be taken up to Quetta for examination at the hospital.

"I do not think there is anything severely wrong, Mrs Bennett, but I am just not satisfied. He does not faint, or collapse, or suffer pain, but he is not as he should be. I do not even think there is any immediacy about an examination at the hospital. Only I am shortly going on leave, and I think perhaps your husband would prefer to go while I am still with you."

She was surprised. "You? Going on leave?"

Doctor Sircar smiled but the smile was strained and slightly hostile. "You did not think I qualified for leave, Mrs Bennett?"

"Why . . . yes . . . I suppose I had just never thought about it. We have grown so used to you coming every month it seems difficult to imagine what it will be like without you."

He bowed politely. "There will be a replacement during my absence."

Curiosity struggled within her. She would dearly have

liked to ask where he went on his leaves, and what he
did when he got there. Did he have a family still in
Bengal? Was he perhaps ostracised by his orthodox
Hindu relatives because he had become a Christian and
worked on a mission? Did he go to a religious retreat,
or to a medical refresher course, or what? She wanted
to know but she dared not ask. Doctor Sircar's manner
forbade the asking of such intimate questions.

"I shall be returning to England for a year. To stay
for a while with my old tutor at Cambridge, and then
with college friends."

"You're going to England?" It was the one place
she hadn't thought of. She looked at him not even
bothering to try and conceal her astonishment.

"I have many friends in England, but little oppor-
tunity to see them. I shall stay, for much of the time in
Sussex. I believe you know that part of England, Mrs
Bennett? Perhaps you have heard of my friend's family,
the Holmden St Clairs. They live at a place called
Grantley Hall?"

"No, I haven't heard of them." She hadn't heard of
them, but she knew what they would be like, or rather
she knew what Grantley Hall would be like. It would
be like the Fawcetts' house where she had worked as
parlourmaid. The Holmden St Clairs would be served
and cared for by people like herself, and someone like
her pa would work in their gardens.

"I don't know them," she said. "But Sussex is a big
county. I only know the people round my own village."

"Ah, I see." He smiled again, not without malice,
and then she knew that he had mentioned his friends
deliberately, letting her know that he had a better right
to go to England than she did.

"But if you're going to Sussex anyway," she said
cheerfully, "do call in and see my pa. He'll make you
very welcome." And then she began to giggle, she
couldn't help it. Because the thought of Doctor Sircar
sitting in the front parlour making polite conversation,
staring at the illuminated text "Repent ye" with the R
of repent twined about with lilies and poppies, was too
incongruous to be taken seriously.

"Why are you laughing?" he asked stiffly.

"Just . . . my family, my people. I don't think you'd like them very much."

"I like courageous people," he answered inexplicably and then he gave another of his bows but this time the bow was intended as a compliment.

"So I think it a good idea if your husband came up to the hospital with me . . . on my next visit," he continued, as though the conversation about Bertram had not been interrupted at all.

"I'll see what he says. I will probably have to persuade him. He hates leaving his work here and . . . I don't want to frighten him into thinking he is ill."

"I think it would be wise if he went."

She hesitated a little, then said diffidently, "I know you only want him to go for an examination. But you must have some reason for suggesting it. If it was something fairly simple you would diagnose here, yourself, and either treat him or tell us why he must go to hospital. What is it you suspect? Why do you want him to go to Quetta?"

He moved restlessly. "I am just not satisfied. That is all I can say."

She gave up questioning, and began instead to prepare her arguments for persuading Bertram to go to Quetta.

"I'm all right here," he snapped testily. "I'm just a little tired and going up to Quetta will make me even more tired. I just want to stay here and get on with my work."

"You won't be absent long, Bertram. And they will be able to do something about the bad place on your leg, and the bedsores too. They can do things so much better at the hospital."

"They don't bother me that much. I'm not going to hospital just for a few bedsores."

He had never seen the suppurating place on his leg. It was at the back of the stump and he had no idea how bad it had become. It just felt very sore and bruised to him.

Surprisingly it was Mr Scavener who persuaded him

to go. Amos had been a little bothered by his friend's
health over the past few months. Once Sarah had
drawn his attention to Bertram's loss of weight he had
begun to noice other things as well; the number of
times Bertram had to stop his work during the day
because he wished to go to the lavatory, the continual
interruptions while he poured and drank lime juice (on
one occasion there had been a most disastrous experience when a glass of liquid had accidentally been over-
turned onto a valuable document), and even worse
there had been a few times lately when Bertram had
dozed off during the afternoon—in the middle of a
piece of research!

"I think, my dear friend, that on this occasion Mrs
Bennett is right. You should sojourn at the hospital for
a short while. And while you are there perhaps Mrs
Bennett can arrange for you to see one or two people
connected with our thesis. It could prove most useful
at this stage . . ."

Reluctantly, Bertram agreed. He would go up to
Quetta. She'd wondered if his disinclination was anything to do with his memory of the earthquake, but she
finally came to realise it was solely that he hated to
leave the sanctuary of the study.

They left with Doctor Sircar when he had completed
his March visit. The weather was cool and it was
Sarah's favourite time of the year. The Baluchistan
springs, although not like English springs, had a charm
that was sometimes destroyed by frosts and the *khojak*
winds. But on the morning they left it was bright and
fresh.

Doctor Sircar and Jamiat carried Bertram out to the
car and placed him carefully in the back seat, his
shoulders resting on Sarah's lap. He was propped and
padded in with pillows and wrapped well with blankets
because his limited movement made him more prone
to cold than the others. Doctor Sircar and the driver
sat in the front and the doctor told him to drive slowly,
as slowly as possible so that their patient should not
be jolted too much over the potholes and cracks in the
road.

Sarah had made the journey to Quetta several times and knew the route, where the track fell away to a steep escarpment, where the side of a mountain would rear up next to them, where the track would level onto a rolling plain with desert and scrub stretching away in all directions. And it was fortunately on such a comparatively flat stretch that the rear left tyre blew.

The driver was too close to the edge of the road and the sudden collapse of the tyre shot the car to the left, off the track, and careering down a gentle incline of dust and rocks. It came to a halt at the bottom of a slope.

"Good gracious!" Bertram said, looking out of the window at the road which was now several feet away from them. "What an extraordinary thing to happen!"

Doctor Sircar had jumped out almost before the car had stopped and was round at the door of the passenger seat. "Are you all right, Mr Bennett? Did you manage to stay on the seat without jarring?"

"I think so." Bertram looked a little frightened. Sarah had managed to hold him secure during the bumpy slide off the road but he was unused to violent movement of any kind. Doctor Sircar relaxed slightly. "I'm afraid we shall have to lift you out of the car while the driver changes the wheel. We'll make you comfortable with blankets and pillows."

He called the driver and Sarah pulled as many pillows out as she could from underneath Bertram. Doctor Sircar built a bed against an outcropping of rock. When it was finished it looked quite comfortable, a couch made of pillows with a padded rock to lean against. With difficulty they levered Bertram out of the back seat and onto the improvised bed. Sarah quickly covered him with blankets. His face had gone very pale and she guessed that shock had begun to register.

"I think we will drink our tea now," she said quickly. "It was nearly time for our stop anyway. We may as well have it now." She fetched the basket, without which no one ever went on a journey in Baluchistan, from the car and unscrewed the thermos. The tea was just as Bertram liked it, not very strong, but hot and with lots of sugar. He sipped it nervously and she noticed his hands were trembling.

"Will we be here long, Sarah?"

"No longer than it takes to change the wheel, dear. Doctor Sircar and the driver are doing it now."

From the back of the car Doctor Sircar was lifting down the wheel. The driver, using rocks, was propping up the car.

"He's not doing it very quickly, is he?"

She refilled his cup, and then squatted close beside him on the ground, trying to reassure him with the closeness of her body.

"Look how beautiful the mountains are, Bertram. You have so little time to stop and see them at the mission. Don't you think the colours are lovely?"

The misty blue of the early morning had vanished and the hills stood out sharply against the pale sky. They were clean and clearly marked with gullies and water courses. Bertram shivered.

"I hope they won't take too long."

"No longer than necessary, dear." She reached out and took his hand. He didn't always like her doing that. Sometimes, when she thought he needed the reassurance of her hand, he would pull it away irritably and snap, "Don't *fuss* me, Sarah." But this time his fingers curled round hers and he seemed to take comfort from her. They sat without speaking, watching the doctor and the driver sweating over the back wheel.

It took an incredibly long time and twice she had to interrupt and ask Doctor Sircar to help her move Bertram into a more comfortable position. She found it difficult to move him alone when he was on the ground. He drank the rest of the tea and nibbled some biscuits and dozed a little in between fidgeting about the delay.

By the time the wheel was changed it was well into the afternoon, and a light wind was beginning to whine down from the hills.

Doctor Sircar was hot and dirty. It had taken a long time to change the wheel because neither he nor the driver was very competent at that sort of thing and the doctor was aware, as the driver was not, that he had failed to be as efficient as he should have been.

"We will get the car back on the road first. Then we'll carry Mr Bennett to his seat. That way he won't be jolted."

She nodded. She was amused because, for the first time since knowing him, Doctor Sircar looked dishevelled and discomposed. The driver climbed into the car and drove it bumpily back onto the road. Then he came back and they began the performance all over again of getting Bertram into the back seat. Bertram tutted irritably while they were doing so.

"Really." "This is too bad." "It will be evening before we get to Quetta and it will be too late to contact the scholar I want to see."

Sarah soothed him as best she could, but he fidgeted all the way along the road grumbling at the three of them in general, but at Doctor Sircar in particular. And from where she was sitting she could see the back of the doctor's neck growing darker and darker, but whether from embarrassment or anger she could not tell.

Half an hour later, where the road passed through a narrow ravine, the second back tyre blew.

Doctor Sircar lost his temper and began to abuse the driver in a mixture of Urdu and English, blaming him for not having checked the tyres before they set out. The driver answered sullenly that it was not his fault if the doctor's car did not function properly and the afternoon threatened to disintegrate into a private exchange of insults between them. Finally the driver got out and stumbled to the back of the car to find the spare inner tube. When he came back he looked frightened. The tyre was in his hand, the three-inch tear in it visible to all of them. She thought the doctor was going to explode.

"What is it? What is it?" queried Bertram. "What does it mean? Can't we mend it?"

"No!" shouted the doctor. "We cannot mend it because he has brought nothing to mend it with. The first thing anyone learns with a car in this cursed country—

take everything with you—allow for anything to happen! And this . . . this incompetent has nothing to
mend a tyre with!"

The driver began to whine. "Not my fault, Doctor. I
was not on duty when we left . . . Joseph had the car
last. He has taken the . . ."

"Quiet!"

Although Sircar was talking to the driver they all
three immediately fell silent, even Bertram. The doctor
folded his lips tightly together, and then was controlled
and calm.

"We are not too far from Quetta. You must walk to
the first village, borrow a donkey or camel and then
go up to Quetta to fetch a car for us from the hospital.
And at the village you must send men back to collect
us."

"But, Doctor . . . Can we not wait until someone
comes along the road? Soldiers, or a camel train.
Someone will come."

"And if they do not we shall be here for the night,"
Doctor Sircar snapped.

"It is a long way. And my legs are not good." The
driver was in his thirties and appeared to be in excellent health. His carriage and face took on the pathetic
droop of a lazy man who is forced into action.

Doctor Sircar's face began to lose its control again,
and the driver hurriedly changed his mind. "I go. I go
now. To the next village and send men back."

"And then up to Quetta."

"Up to Quetta." The driver averted his face and
Sarah felt sure that once they were settled in the village for the night, they would wait in vain for the car
from Quetta. The driver would vanish into one of the
huts for the night and appear with some excuse on the
following morning.

He set up along the road, walking quickly and looking nervously up into the rocky hills on either side of
the track. Then he disappeared round the end of the
ravine. She climbed out of the car and made Bertram
as comfortable as she could along the length of the
back seat.

"Try to sleep a little, dear. It will be some time before they come back."

He grumbled and she stood at the door of the car until finally his grumbles died away and he dozed uneasily. She walked over to Doctor Sircar and sat beside him on a large rock. It was late afternoon and livid colour was beginning to touch the hills, orange, scarlet, pink. It was very quiet.

"It's strange . . . that we haven't seen anyone else on the road. There's usually someone . . . an army lorry, or a tribesman of some kind. But we haven't seen anyone today."

"No," he said tensely, staring up into the sides of the ravine.

"Is something worrying you?" she asked.

"Yes. I do not want to be here when it gets dark because we have no rifle, and I, like you, have noticed the absence of traffic on this road."

"What do you mean?"

"I think the absence of traffic indicates that something is happening that we cannot see. I shall be happier when we are in Quetta out of the reach of any night marauders in the area."

"But . . . there is no immediate unrest round here. We should have heard if there had been. We are always posted about the troubled parts of the country."

"All the country is troubled, Mrs Bennett," he said tiredly. "You know that."

The ravine was narrow, and the light was fading, and for the first time she was out in the hills at night. Facts that she had assimilated as no more than political and local news began to take on a more urgent meaning. Sixteen years ago there had been the Mollie Ellis affair, the abduction of a seventeen-year-old girl by Afridi tribesmen. And in the early thirties there had been the redshirts and a near revolt at Peshawar. And for the past two years the north had been rent by major battles with the Fakir of Ipi. This was the real India, not the mission.

"Do you think we are in danger?" she asked quietly.

Doctor Sircar stirred uneasily against the rock. "I

don't like the stillness, and the absence of any traffic at all. None of this would matter except that it will soon be dark. I hope that fool sends people back from the village as quickly as possible."

All the times she had travelled up to Quetta she had never once worried or been afraid. But always it had been daylight, just half a day's drive and the tribesmen all knowing that the precious person of the mission doctor was in the car.

"But you have always been so safe driving about the hills," she said. "They all know you, and they need you. None of the tribes would want to hurt you."

"Not those who know me," he answered slowly. "But if it is Pathans from the north . . . from different country, then we are no more to them than strangers and a motor-car in a ravine at night . . ."

She caught his tenseness. She listened, straining for a sound from the end of the ravine, the sound of men coming from the village with camels and a litter to carry Bertram. The ravine remained silent.

The distant hills, seen at each end of the ravine turned to dark crimson and purple. The sun suddenly moved behind the steep cliff facing them and they were in shadow. She shivered and pulled her coat up at the neck.

"Should we go back to the car?"

"Let us not disturb Mr Bennett. If we wake him he will begin to worry."

"I was thinking . . . perhaps we are a little exposed here?"

"If they intend to shoot us, Mrs Bennett. They will do it wherever we are."

The hills darkened still further, and the ravine became colder, blacker, and then she was suddenly overwhelmed by a familiar sensation of terror—the same uncanny fear that she had experienced on the evening before the earthquake, sitting in the garden of the bungalow with unreasoning fear growing round her.

"Let's get back to the car," she said, standing quickly.

She began to walk across the rocky ground. The last

light vanished from the ravine and it was dark; hills
and rocks turned into a hostile landscape and a prick-
ling sensation moved down her back and settled in a
patch of cold sweat at the base of her spine. She
heard Doctor Sircar stand up behind her, and then the
night was shattered by a blaze of shot, rifle-fire echoing
through the ravine, ricocheting against rock, flashes of
splintered light cutting through the darkness.

Sircar shouted "Get down!" but even before she
heard him she had instinctively thrown herself forward.

The barrage lasted for a few moments, then the
echoes died away and an oppressive silence fell over
the valley. She heard a rattle of stones behind her and
tensed.

"It's me, Mrs Bennett." He was sliding along the
ground just behind and her fingers unclenched from
the rock she was holding.

"Have they gone away?"

"No."

"We must try and get to the car! Bertram will be so
frightened!"

She felt his hand on her shoulder. "Wait here. Just
a few moments. Wait!"

"He's there on his own!"

"You must wait, Mrs Bennett."

She forced herself to lie still, fretting against the
pressure of his hand. She wanted to scream or shout to
Bertram, telling him it was all right, that she was
coming.

"Now?"

"Wait."

"But he's there alone! He'll be so afraid!"

"We are safer here."

"Why?"

She heard him swallow hard, then whisper, "They
are not shooting at us. They are shooting at the car."

"No!"

She wrenched away from his shoulder and scrambled,
half crawling, half running, to the car. There was
another wild burst of gunfire. A bullet spat by her leg

and she threw herself flat again, pressing her face and hands into the ground until the firing stopped.

There was an odd hissing noise, a curious whistling that she at last identified as air seeping from a bullet-hole in a tyre. Doctor Sircar scrambled up beside her.

"Don't do that again," he whispered fiercely. "They'll shoot at anything moving. At the moment their purpose seems to be to wreck the car. But if they see you moving they'll shoot."

"We must get Bertram out!"

This time he didn't protest. He moved forward with her until they came to the car. Then he reached his hand up and opened the door. She pushed past him and wriggled into the floor space in front of the back seat. Bertram was lying exactly where she left him.

"Bertram?"

She heard him move slightly, and felt relief that he was all right.

"Bertram, we have to get you out of the car."

She reached up her hand to take his, wanting again to reassure him. When she found his hand something warm and sticky was flowing down his wrist.

"Oh, God! He's bleeding. Come and help him. Please come and help him!"

She saw—felt—Sircar crawl into the space beside her. They were so crushed they could hardly move and she tried to stand up but he pulled her down again.

"Feel his hand! He's bleeding. It's running down his arm."

Doctor Sircar took the sticky hand in his and, released from the pressure of his arm she stood up again as best she could, crouching over Bertram's face that she could not see in the darkness.

"Bertram! It's all right. We're going to get you out. You'll be all right."

She heard him sigh and move a little.

"Bertram?"

He gave a small choking cry, and then he said loudly, "I hate you, Amelia. I hate you."

"Oh no! No, Bertram! Not that again. Please not that again."

"I hate you!" he screamed.

"No!"

Hands pulling her down again, forcing her to crouch in the bottom of the car and the air rent with more explosion—rifle fire flashing on the hills, making patterns of light and noise.

"He's dead, Mrs Bennett."

"Why did he say it again! I thought it was over! Why did he say it again!"

"He's dead." He placed the wet wrist back in hers and pressed her hand to where the pulse should be but even without feeling the pulse she knew Bertram was dead.

"He's dead," she repeated dully. "That's right. He's dead."

"Come, Mrs Bennett," he said gently. "We must get out of the car. It isn't safe here."

He opened the door and pulled her after him.

They tried to get back to the rocks but the rifle fire spattered all round them and finally they crawled under the car and remained there until the platoon of Gurkhas arrived. It seemed as though they were lying there all night but in fact it was no more than three hours. He said lying under the car would give them a little protection but after that final burst of firing it remained quiet. Once, about half an hour before the Gurkhas arrived, they heard firing to the north, but after that there was silence.

It was bitterly cold and without any conscious movement they huddled close to one another. She was shaking and her teeth were chattering but after a while the shaking stopped and she just became numb. It was like being back in the earthquake—lying crushed in a small space not knowing what was going to happen. Only this time she didn't have to wonder about Bertram. She knew he was dead.

Once the cold had penetrated her body, her thoughts calmed too. She spoke to Sircar only once.

"What was wrong with him? What did you suspect was wrong?"

"Diabetes."

"And the sore on his leg?"

"Gangrene."

After that they said no more, just grew colder and colder and when the soldiers pulled them out from under the car their legs were so paralysed they could not stand.

They learned later that the raid had been one of several in the area, the purpose of which appeared to be the wrecking of cars and military transport. With the exception of Bertram no one had been killed and, the kindly Gurkha officer told her, if they had carried him away from the car, he would never have been killed at all.

# Seventeen

SHE returned to the mission for no longer than it took to collect her things together and say good-bye to Doctor Keynes. He did not even try to make her stay. He knew how Amos Scavener hated her and now, with the guilt of Bertram's death lying fully at her door, all Amos wanted was to see her away from the mission as quickly as possible. Apart from one hysterical outburst when he hissed "murderess" at her as they passed in the compound, he did not speak to her at all. Meals he took, once more, in private in the study, telling Lili he would not eat in the dining-room until "that creature" had gone.

She felt nothing, not regret, nor anguish, nor resentment against her banishment. She packed her clothes, packed Bertram's clothes and private papers—not the thesis—said good-bye to Doctor Keynes, Lili, and the children, and left. Doctor Keynes was sorry to see her go.

"I know you cannot continue working here, my dear. The conditions and the ... temperament of Mr Scavener would make such an eventuality impossible. But we can never forget it was your initial efforts that brought the mission into being. And the mission society could use you in other centres."

"I don't know what I shall do yet."

"No. Well, remember for later that the mission field is now open to you. We have too few workers to release our good ones."

Impassively she had shaken his hand and left.

Doctor Sircar had managed to get her a berth on his ship but it was not due to sail for four weeks and she spent the month in Karachi, not speaking to anyone, writing interminable letters home telling everyone what had happened.

She boarded the ship. Ate at the right times, slept in a cabin with three other women, and spent a lot of time leaning on the rail staring at the wake of water streaming out from the boat. Sometimes Doctor Sircar stood with her but after one or two abortive attempts at conversation he responded to her silence with a silence of his own. At Aden and Port Said she did not go ashore. She stayed on board, aware of how pleasant it was with fewer passengers about.

She was not brooding, or grieving. She was just tired—and the water was so pleasing to watch, so green and cool and undemanding. When she looked at the water she did not have to think about anything.

At Naples she looked forward to a few hours of peace again—when the others all went ashore. But soon after they had left she was joined by Doctor Sircar who, on this occasion, refused to remain silent.

"I would like to know, Mrs Bennett, if you feel ill or in a state of tension."

"No."

"Your behaviour is certainly not normal, even allowing for the death of your husband. I am concerned for your health."

She turned and stared at him. "I'm not ill. I'm just tired."

"What are your plans for the future? Return to your profession of teaching? Missionary work? What?"

She looked at the water, bright blue, and at the sky, also bright blue, and then inland towards Naples which shimmered iridescently in the baking sunlight. And suddenly she knew what she was going to do.

"I shall go home," she said simply. "Home, to my village."

And she thought how good it would be to lie once more in the small back bedroom with the pear tree espaliered against the outside wall. And wake up at dawn when the rooster crowed, and listen to the birds outside. It was early summer and the fields would be blowing with long golden grasses, and buttercups and cuckoo-flower.

"I may be in time to see the hares boxing," she said dreamily. "It's rather late, but sometimes in our part of the country you can see them in May or June. You have to be out very early, or in the evening. Dusk you know, that's when all the hares come out. If you sit very still on a stile or on the ground they don't notice you at all. They hop all round you, and sometimes they sit up and stare back at you. And moles—that's something else you can see. If you get up just before dawn and keep very still you can see them trundling along a hedgerow, just like little old gentlemen . . ,"

A small frown settled between Doctor Sircar's eyes. "Of course . . . naturally you will go home first. But after that, after you have seen your family and settled your affairs, what will you do then?"

"I don't want to do anything," she said wearily. "I'll get a little job in the village, anything will do, and I'll stay at home with my people."

"You can't do that!" he said angrily. "You are needed!"

"No."

"You are tired, yes. And you have undergone a great deal. But you cannot . . . retire so soon. You and I, there are so many things that people like you and I must do!"

"No. You perhaps, you heal and stop pain and go where no other doctor ever goes. But I am not the same. Everything I have ever done has come to nothing."

There were the Alexanders. She had become involved with them, given part of herself to them, and had watched them disintegrate. There was David Baron, Charlie Dance, Peter and May, and then young Anna. She had loved young Anna and had thought of her as her own child. But she had lost Anna too, just like everything else she touched. Like the mission, and poor, poor, sad, unhappy Bertram.

"It does not matter if it comes to nothing!" he answered angrily. "Of course it will come to nothing, because you and I attempt the impossible! And we must go on doing this."

"I can't do it any more. I'm tired." She walked away from him because she did not want to talk about it any more. She wanted to think about the village. Already she could feel it acting as balm to her tired body and spirit. Every time she thought of hedgerows and weeds and wild flowers growing along the sides of the road, she felt better. I'm going to lie face down in a field, and listen to the crickets, and birds, and watch bees hovering between flowers. And then I will be at peace again.

The mere thought of the village made her feel so peaceful and calm that she couldn't even bother to go and collect her mail, brought in from Naples. She left it until the following morning, knowing it would be full of condolence and sympathy. There were all the letters she expected, the family, Gertie, Miss Enderby, the Dances, and one letter she did not expect, typewritten with a London postmark.

Dear Madam,

We have been notified that your husband, Bertram Cyrus Bennett, was killed in March of this year at the Scavener mission in Baluchistan. We further understand that you are in the process of returning to England at the present time.

Acting on behalf of your late husband we would respectfully inform you that as you are the sole legatee of your late husband's estate, we should be obliged if you would call upon us upon your return.

May we offer our condolences upon your bereavement.

Yours faithfully,
Charles Pacey
Pacey, Hopcraft, and Simpkins

She read it, but didn't really understand. She was going home to the village and didn't want to be bothered any more with Bertram's things. She didn't want to have to go through more papers, more sorting out, all the tedious, harrowing business that remained to be done when someone died. She had done it when Peter died. She had done it again now with Bertram. She wanted to forget about it. She pushed the letter under her pillow and tried not to think about it.

At three o'clock in the morning she woke up. Into her mind bore the realisation that Bertram had left her all his money. She couldn't sleep any more and as soon as it was possible she rose and went in search of Doctor Sircar. He was in the dining-room having breakfast.

"Look," she said, pushing the letter in front of him.

He read it. "But of course," he answered puzzled. "What did you expect?"

"I'm rich."

By her standard she was rich. Bertram had lived a comfortable if not extravagant life even before his legacy. Now it was hers. All of it.

"I would hardly say rich, Mrs Bennett. But certainly you are provided for."

He didn't understand either. Didn't understand the difference between poor, and being provided for. No one except the poor understood that.

"Will it make a difference to your plans?" he asked. "Your plans for returning to live in your village?"

"No. Yes. I'm not sure."

She thought of all the things she could do. Her pa wouldn't have to worry about money any more, nor about finding enough to pay for Harriet's keep in the home. Aunt Betsy should have some. Aunt Betsy was over sixty and still worked hard. She shouldn't have to work so hard. She should have some—and May, and young Anna, she could go to a different school, a good school. And there would be money to pay for her training, whatever she wanted to be, there would be money to pay for it.

I'm rich, she thought, and a joyful leap of excitement shot through her. She was ashamed and guilty about her excitement but nothing could stop it. And she felt a return of the tenderness and affection for Bertram

that the manner of his death had destroyed. Dear, dear,
Bertram, so kind and gentle and considerate. And she
pushed the other memories of him away. He had made
her rich.

She stopped watching the water quite so much for
the rest of the voyage. She talked to Doctor Sircar a lot,
discussed with him all the things her money could do.
And she told him about Bertram, about his perception
and his kindness, and his funny, irritable-ways. She
didn't tell him about the ... sickness, because that
must be forgotten.

She talked of running a mission of her own, of a
school in London, of travelling round the world, of
having her hair cut and permed, of buying some land
for her father, presents for Miss Enderby, French perfume, taking her Aunt Betsy to Scotland. Doctor Sircar
listened, and nodded, and grunted now and again. He
liked the mission idea, thought the school impossible
to accomplish, obviously disapproved of travelling
round the world, was not interested in her hair, or
French perfume, or Miss Enderby. When she spoke of
Aunt Betsy and her pa, he said surprisingly, "I would
like to meet your family, if it could be arranged."

Sarah waved her hand excitedly in the air and told
him she was sure one or other of her family would
probably come to meet her at Southampton.

They all came.

Her apathy now completely vanished, she stood
against the rail of the ship and watched the quayside
grow bigger, watched the black line turn into a crowd
and the crowd turn into individual people. And presently she was able to see them all. They were quite
close.

There was pa, beloved pa! And he was old. With
shock and fear she saw he was an old man, white-
haired, bent, and anguished. It hurt her to see him. He
won't always be here! she thought. Like the others he'll
die. Not my pa, my darling pa! I couldn't bear it if he
died! And quickly she let the thought of the money
assuage her fear. She was rich. Her pa wouldn't have
to work any more. He should have a holiday. She

would look after him. Make him happy, she wouldn't let him die yet.

Aunt Betsy was there, staring anxiously up at the boat, fatter, worried because she didn't often leave the village and the quayside was big and it reminded her of when Matthew was alive and she used to see him off on his tours abroad. Betsy looked just the same, a round, shabby little countrywoman in a plain felt hat pulled well down over her ears.

May was there, slimmer and . . . more elegant. May was a Londoner now. And beside her was Charlie, huger, redder, and with an enormous bouquet of flowers leaning against his shoulder. Behind him she could see a solid phalanx of Dances—Maisie, Ruby, Maxie, Bertha, Cyril, all of them with bright, rubicund faces, obviously enjoying the outing which Sarah's arrival had given them reason to plan. A chara, she thought. I bet they hired a chara and they've been stopping for refreshments all the way down from London!

Anna was gripping tightly to May's hand, quiet, unsmiling, but with desperate concentration in every line of her body. She was afraid it would turn out to be a mistake and Sarah would not be on the boat. She saw Gertie Alexander (a spare seat in the Dance chara) and two of her brothers, and one of May's brothers too. Her ma was not there but she hadn't really expected her to be.

And then, standing right at the back of the crowd, well away from everyone, hands hunched in pockets and face scowling, she saw him . . . David . . . like he used to be, thin, fierce, erratic, fighting lost causes again, believing in things, behaving selfishly, irrationally, but always fighting . . .

"There's my family," she said to Doctor Sircar who was standing beside her. "They've all come to meet me."

"Mrs Bennett," he said earnestly. "I hope the end of our work together, and the end of this voyage does not mean we shall not meet again."

"I hope so too," she said politely, waving down at

Anna whose face suddenly lit with relief when she saw
Sarah.

"I would very much like to see you while I am in
England," he said hurriedly. "If you would give me
your address I could write to you."

"I'll do that." All the Dances had seen her now and
were shouting and waving things at her, hankies, empty
stout bottles, and right at the back someone had
brought a pineapple and was holding it aloft.

"This is my address in Cambridge," he said, thrusting a piece of paper into her hand. "I would very
much like you to come and stay at Cambridge while
I am there. I know my old tutor and his wife would
be delighted to have you, and I think you should enjoy it."

"I'm sure I should." Pa had lifted Anna into the air,
but she was really too heavy for him and finally one of
her brothers took her and perched her on a shoulder.

"Please, Mrs Bennett. You will come won't you? I
do not want to lose touch with you. You will write to
me, and you will come to Cambridge?"

She turned to look at him and was surprised because
he was no longer detached. He was anxious, and uncertain. She smiled warmly and held out her hand. "Of
course I'll come. It is very kind of you to invite me."

"You will not forget to give me your address?"

"There's plenty of time before we go ashore." David
had seen her. He was still scowling, but he had seen
her.

"I'll go to my cabin and write the address now," she
said. She waved again at the people on the quay and
held up a finger to indicate that she wouldn't be gone
long. Then she hurried back to her cabin to try and
find a piece of paper. She was gone a long time because she kept bumping into people who wanted to say
good-bye, people to whom she had hardly spoken on
the voyage but who now received a warm and radiant
farewell from her. She felt excited and impatient. She
wanted to go ashore, see them all, talk to them, decide
what she was going to do.

She scribbled her address on a piece of paper. When

she arrived back on deck the gangways had been run out and the passengers were beginning to go ashore.

"I wondered where you were," worried Doctor Sircar. His skin seemed much darker in the pale air of England. He looked quite interesting.

"There it is." She pushed the piece of paper at him, then held out her hand to say good-bye.

"You won't forget you promised to come to Cambridge. I shall write as soon as I arrive."

"Lovely," she waved, hurrying towards the gangway. "Lovely."

And then she was walking towards them with the old familiar lift of anticipation and hope that she always felt at the beginning of something new. Nothing had really worked out right until now, but that didn't mean it wouldn't the next time. She was rich now. That made a difference. And she was still young, only thirty-five. All kinds of things lay ahead of her, new people, and places, and different experiences.

She remembered Doctor Sircar and she turned and smiled at him, a brilliant bright smile that made him catch his breath. Then she looked back at her family, forgetting all about him.

Life was good. It was eventful and unknown, a big adventure. It was 1939. Lots of things were going to happen.

# Bibliography

Elizabeth Balneaves, *The Waterless Moon*
*The History of the T.U.C. 1868–1968*
Sir Henry Holland, *Frontier Doctor*
Robert Jackson, *Thirty Seconds at Quetta*
*Leslie Bailey's Scrapbook 1918–1939*
Sylvia A. Matheson, *The Tigers of Baluchistan*
J. M. Morris, *A Nursing Sister in Baluchistan*
H. V. Morton, *The Pageant of the Century*
E. Gertrude Stuart M.B., *An Austin XII on the Frontier*
Arthur Swinson, *North West Frontier*
Julian Symons, *The General Strike*
R. J. Unstead, *Britain in the Twentieth Century*

*Author's Note*

The Scavener mission in Baluchistan is entirely
imaginary and is in no way intended to represent
the work of the missionaries in India before the
Second World War. To those wishing to learn of
mission life and work during this period, I can only
recommend Sir Henry Holland's magnificent book,
*Frontier Doctor*.

## ABOUT THE AUTHOR

DIANE PEARSON was born in London, and spent a large part of her childhood with grandparents who lived in the countryside of *The Marigold Field,* and their reminiscences provided her with a good deal of background for the book. An editor for an English publishing company, she lives in Croydon and has recently published her second novel, *SARAH.*

## CSARDAS by DIANE PEARSON

'Only half a century separates today's totalitarian state of Hungary from the glittering world of coming-out balls and feudal estates, elegance and culture, of which the Ferenc sisters – the enchanting Ferenc sisters – are the pampered darlings in the opening chapters of Diane Pearson's dramatic epic.

Their world has now gone with the wind as surely as that of Scarlett O'Hara (which it much resembled): handsome, over-bred young men danced attendance on lovely frivolous belles, and life was one long dream of parties and picnics, until the shot that killed Franz Ferdinand in 1914 burst the beautiful bubble.

The dashing gallants galloped off to war and, as they returned, maimed and broken in spirit, the new Hungary began to emerge like an ugly grub from its chrysalis. Poverty, hardship, and growing anti-semitism threatened and scattered the half-Jewish Ferenc family as Nazi influence gripped the country from one side and Communism spread underground from the other like the tentacles of ground-elder.

Only the shattered remnants of a once-powerful family lived through the 1939 45 holocaust, but with phoenix-like vitality the new generation began to adapt and bend, don camouflage and survive . . . '

Phyllida Hart-Davis *Sunday Telegraph*

'Long, fat, romantic, historical . . . a huge canvas . . . I defy anyone to remain unaffected.' *Evening Standard*

0 552 10375 6   £1.25

# A SELECTED LIST OF FINE BOOKS
# PUBLISHED BY CORGI BOOKS

| ☐ 09475 7 | A RAGING CALM | Stan Barstow 60p |
| ☐ 10446 9 | A KIND OF LOVING | Stan Barstow 75p |
| ☐ 09597 4 | DEBORAH | Colette Davenat 75p |
| ☐ 10012 9 | DEBORAH: THE MANY FACES OF LOVE | Colette Davenat 85p |
| ☐ 09897 3 | THE LION OF ENGLAND | Margaret Butler 60p |
| ☐ 10152 4 | HOUSE OF THE TWELVE CAESARS | Phyllis Hastings 60p |
| ☐ 09926 0 | BARTHOLOMEW FAIR | Phyllis Hastings 40p |
| ☐ 09923 6 | THE MASTER OF LIVERSEDGE | Alice Chetwynd Ley 40p |
| ☐ 09922 8 | LETTERS FOR A SPY | Alice Chetwynd Ley 40p |
| ☐ 09791 8 | THE HOUSE AT OLD VINE | Norah Lofts 75p |
| ☐ 09792 6 | THE HOUSE AT SUNSET | Norah Lofts 75p |
| ☐ 09889 2 | WALK INTO MY PARLOUR | Norah Lofts 50p |
| ☐ 09316 5 | THE GLASS BARRIER | Joy Packer 40p |
| ☐ 09306 8 | THE HIGH ROOF | Joy Packer 40p |
| ☐ 10271 7 | THE MARIGOLD FIELD | Diane Pearson 85p |
| ☐ 10414 0 | SARAH WHITMAN | Diane Pearson 85p |
| ☐ 09891 4 | CHIA, THE WILDCAT | Joyce Stranger 45p |
| ☐ 09892 2 | ZARA | Joyce Stranger 60p |
| ☐ 09893 0 | BREED OF GIANTS | Joyce Stranger 60p |
| ☐ 09399 8 | A DOG CALLED GELERT | Joyce Stranger 60p |
| ☐ 09462 5 | LAKELAND VET | Joyce Stranger 45p |
| ☐ 10004 8 | FORTUNE'S WHIRLWIND | John Jakes 65p |
| ☐ 10005 6 | TO AN UNKNOWN SHORE | John Jakes 65p |

*All these books are available at your bookshop or newsagent, or can be ordered direct from the publisher. Just tick the titles you want and fill in the form below.*

CORGI BOOKS, Cash Sales Department, P.O. Box 11, Falmouth, Cornwall.

Please send cheque or postal order, no currency.

U.K. send 19p for first book plus 9p per copy for each additional book ordered to a maximum charge of 73p to cover the cost of postage and packing.

B.F.P.O. and Eire allow 19p for first book plus 9p per copy for the next 6 books, thereafter 3p per book.

Overseas Customers. Please allow 20p for the first book and 10p per copy for each additional book.

NAME (block letters) ...................................................................................................

ADDRESS ...................................................................................................................

(MAY 77) ...................................................................................................................

While every effort is made to keep prices low, it is sometimes necessary to increase prices at short notice. Corgi Books reserve the right to show new retail prices on covers which may differ from those previously advertised in the text or elsewhere.